WAITING

Somewhere out there, she knew, was a man who was part of her. She didn't know what he was doing; he might be sitting in the saddle, huddled in a bedroll, squatting before a chuck wagon—or in some other woman's bed. But he was out there somewhere. And so she was waiting for him, whether he liked it or not. Tandy would continue to come out to this spot every day for the rest of her life; she was stubborn, and that's what she had made up her mind to do.

THE WILD AND THE WAYWARD

Georgia Granger

A Dell/Bryans Book

Published by
Dell Publishing Co., Inc.
1 Dag Hammarskjold Plaza
New York, New York 10017

ISBN: 0-440-09674-X

Printed in the United States of America

First printing—November 1979
Second printing—June 1980
Third printing—July 1980

THE WILD AND THE WAYWARD

1

It was past noon of a mid-April day. The sun baked the harsh Oklahoma prairie, heating it, in spots, as hot as an oven. Deep inside one of the prairie's numerous jackrabbit holes, a buck hare had just curled himself into a restless ball of fur. The hare wanted to nap after a lively morning in which a small owl hawk had almost caught him. Not that the hare was too worried. He had outwitted the sky creature every morning since the spring thaw had awakened it a few months back. Granted, his having to watch the sky constantly kept him from sniffing out the edible grasses and seeds his cousins enjoyed; he had a leaner body and his tiny ribs showed. But at least he was alive. For that, he felt thankful.

Yet he was having a difficult time relaxing in his tiny burrow. Perhaps some of the blackened grass he'd eaten had disagreed with his digestion. But no, it was more than that. His whiskers flicked back and forth uncontrollably. Something was definitely wrong.

He burrowed his nose deep into his stomach, a position he found most comforting when alarmed. His right hind leg offered a resting place for his chin and once again he closed his eyelids and waited for numbness.

And then he felt it. A slight quiver of the ground beneath him. It came repeatedly, as if some large animal were running nearby. The quiver grew in intensity. And now, the jack's delicate nose could smell the rustling of air being pushed above, some of it trailing down into his lair.

Instinctively, he was up, nose twitching, trying to identify the vibration's source. Slowly, step by step, he stretched his long body up the hole, nose stuck out ahead, sniffing at the movement of air that should have been still this noon time. He hesitated, eyeing the exit with distrust. The ground was beginning to shake. Still in his hole, he searched the bright yellow sky but saw nothing that might be causing it. Little by little he inched upward until he could push his nose over the rim. Still nothing. Then he stuck his head up and swung his gaze around the prairie, ducking back inside occasionally to avoid any possible sudden attack. What he saw perplexed him. Surface air from the northeast was definitely being pushed his way. He could smell the direction it was coming from rather than see it, for the fine tufts of grass nearby remained erect and stiff, giving no clues to the eye. But the hare's nose never lied.

Totally absorbed now, the hare scanned the horizon. His vision, unlike the hawk's, was not meant for long distances, but it did seem to him that the northeast horizon was a bit dustier than usual.

A dust storm? Not likely; with no breeze stirred where he was. But the ground's rumblings grew and grew; his whole body seemed to absorb them. His eyes fixed then on tumbleweeds rolling towards him. They were coming in bundles, bouncing up and down from the far ravine. The hare had seen tumbleweeds before. These got larger and larger, until, when they loomed gigantically near his head, he ducked down in his hole and waited for their passing.

The ground kept shaking.

The hare thought.

Whatever was approaching was far more terrible than a tumbleweed-blowing rainstorm. It was worse than a prairie fire or a buffalo stampede, both of which he has seen more than once and would recognize.

He was hypnotized by the sounds. He stuck his head up out of the hole again. The prairie to the northeast was now a dust cloud. The hare gaped. Amidst this swirl of dust were horses, humans, wagons, carts—he had never seen such a conglomeration of living things and lumbersome objects! It was pandemonium. It was all coming towards him, in a rush so unexpected and terrifying that for several moments the hare stood transfixed.

It was civilization coming. It was a catastrophe.

The hare's frail lean body huddled into a frightened ball of fur that barely had time to duck into the hole before the first wagonwheel rolled prairie mud into it.

My God, would he survive? Would anything?

Almost a year and a half later, Tandy Lee Woodrowe Girondin sat not too far from that hare's burrow, looked out over the prairie and wondered the same thing.

As she often did, once the summer heat subsided, Tandy came to this spot in the early evenings, and stared westward; sitting atop the sod roof of an abandoned dugout. Such dugouts were easily found. They were like scars on the land. They called to mind the hapless victims of the Oklahoma land rush, mid-April, 1889, one and a half years before. They were the deserted testaments of the shattered dreams and futile endeavors of the pioneer. Tandy had had those dreams and hopes herself, and so she felt for those gone, as she felt for all mankind right now.

She sat gazing westward, huddled in a ball with her knees tucked under her chin, like a rabbit. She was sixteen, and she was lonely. She watched the sun's deepening colors as it sank towards, then touched the horizon. Moments like these—so still and beautiful—gave her mind a rest. She could live without thoughts, ideas, wishes—yes, even without hope.

Somewhere out there, she knew, was a man who was part of her. She didn't know what he was doing;

he might be sitting in a saddle, huddled in a bedroll, squatting before a chuck wagon—or, far worse, be in some other woman's bed. But he was out there—somewhere. And so she was waiting for him, in no hope that he would return and whether he liked it or not. She would continue to come out to this spot every day for the rest of her life; she was stubborn, and that's what she had made up her mind to do.

Mrs. George Newcomb! She often thought of herself that way. She smiled in tender remembrance. He himself didn't like the name George. When she'd asked him what then should she call him, he'd given her one of his infectious smiles and said, "Give Bitter Creek a try." Bitter Creek Newcomb! Come to think of it, that sounded much better than George to her ears.

She smiled again, indulging her reverie as she often did as long as a tip of the sun remained up to warm her. Why did she love the man so? Well, she just did, that's all. And everyone knew she loved him—she was proud of it. Mrs. Bitter Creek Newcomb! She was determined that one day she'd have that name for real. She wasn't a child any more. In the five months since he had been gone she'd become a woman. Surely he would notice!

Tandy rubbed her breasts against her knees for reassurance. They had developed surprisingly quickly. She was proud of them. People could now tell she was a girl even with her hair piled under her hat. Not that it mattered what other people thought

—only B.C. Damn! Why wouldn't he come home and find her? She turned her head around and stared to the northeast.

They had come from that way, two hours after the reveille bugle had sounded and people had started trampling over each other to get here first. In a way she was glad she and B.C. had been part of the rush, despite the dust, despite the people glaring angrily at them in fear that they'd try stealing their claims. They had found their own claim, driven in a stake and sat down beside it, all smiles, hugging each other that they were now landowners.

"Oh, B.C., we did it! We did it!" Tandy could recall her words. She had literally jumped on top of him to hug him in ecstasy.

He had laughed. "Slow down, tyke," he'd said gently putting her on her feet. "We just got our stake in. Now we got to protect and keep it. That's the hard part."

"But it's ours, isn't it?" she'd asked. They'd claimed a small plot in a box canyon, one that had been generally overlooked in the rush. They had been told about it by Tandy's Cherokee friends, who had raised her. There were many such hidden pieces of land—shallow plots eaten into the canyon by winds and the prehistoric wanderings of the Cimarron River. It was good enough for a start at least. It was theirs!

There was another incident Tandy recalled. It went back further still, to Arkansas.

"You're a tag-along." B.C. had smiled as he always did when he wanted to remind her of how young she was. "You're just here to keep my feet and vitals warm."

She'd hugged him. "I want to keep you warm all my life!"

And she'd meant it—with all her heart and soul. She knew from the start he didn't take her seriously. But she loved him. She'd made that plain the very first day she'd met him. He wasn't a terribly tall man—in fact, he was only slightly taller than she was—but his body was compact, hard as a burl. Once, while he washed the caked mud off his muscular torso, she had watched. A hunk of mahogany, she'd thought, knotted with burls, wet and glistening in its strength. He had as handsome a face as she had ever seen, with steady blue eyes that just about bore through hers to probe her insides. Yet his mouth was soft and full of smiles. How her young heart had fluttered!

"I want to go with you," she had uttered without hesitation. They had taken a walk together. That is, he had started off on his own, a habit of his, and she had tagged after him. They had talked, loose and easy, about everything and nothing. He was going west, he said, to take part in the big land rush everyone was talking about. He was going to make a start for himself. "I want to go with you," she'd begged.

"A tyke like you?" He'd lifted an eyebrow.

"I'm over fifteen—plenty old enough to have a man." Girls in Arkansas were being wed at thirteen.

Her Cherokee girlfriends were considered old maids at her age.

"Yeah," Bitter Creek had answered with a soft smile. "But where I come from it ain't proper. Hell, you're like my kid sister. I can't figure you as a woman."

"But I will be one of these days," she'd promised eagerly. "In the meantime I'll scrub your clothes, I'll feed you, I'll take care of you."

"It ain't in the cards, Tandy. I'm not ready to be saddled down yet."

She was desperate. "I won't stand in your way—promise. I just want to be near you when I become a woman. And I want to be there when you are ready to take a woman."

He gazed down at her and she'd nearly melted. She didn't dare to breathe. Finally he'd scratched his head. "I don't even have my sights set on where and what I'll be doing," he answered. "There's a lot you don't know about me. There's a lot I don't know about myself."

"I don't care. I know you can do anything you set your mind to and that's good enough for me. I got the confidence in you, B.C."

"I'm obliged that someone has," he confided. "It's good to hear once in a while. And I got to admit you're good company to have around." He gave her another one of his melting smiles. "You're a comfort, Tandy m'girl. We'll give it a try."

Tandy could recall that incident as if it had happened yesterday. She could recall almost every time after that when she had touched him. In the

Oklahoma evenings, both bundled up in the same blanket, their bodies separated by the clothes they wore—even then, she could feel his body. She knew he could feel hers, bones and flat chest maybe, but female just the same. And still a virgin!

It was not that she hadn't tried, Lord knows. But B.C. was firm in his conviction that one did not bed down with one's sister—or, at best, anyone who was still wet behind the ears. She *would* have to fall in love with a man with principles! Yet, she respected him for his principles. He made her feel special in a way. Or maybe it was her own idea that he valued her too much to take advantage of her innocence. She had to admit she'd been afraid of sex, backward about it, even though she had seen enough cattle and dogs and such in her time to be pretty well informed. Also, her Indian friends had been quite open and frank; the way a man and woman went together was something deeply embedded in her mind at an early age. But when she was with B.C., nothing she'd learned seemed to count. Her sense of innocence combined with great surges of desire from her body had bewildered her. But she was ready for him now. She would spread her body in front of a stampede if B.C. wanted it so.

Tandy sighed. Her eyes surveyed the horizon hunting for a movement. Oh, B.C., where are you?

"I'm going off for a spell," he had said one late afternoon five months before. Her heart had dropped; she had instinctively stopped her preparations for supper. "Where're we going?" she asked, knowing what the answer would be.

He was shaking his head, his back to her as he stared out the curtained door. "Ain't going to be *us* this time, Tandy girl." He was trying to be as kind to her as possible. He had turned, his face very serious, with a hurt look to it. "This is something I've got to do by myself, y'understand? Working on the ranch here has been good. I really enjoyed it. And you've been good too. But it's like the farm we tried, Tandy. Just as there was too much against me keeping that land, there's too much against me staying here."

"But you're doing good at the Turkey Track. I heard 'em say you're doing good. And," she added eagerly, "if you don't like it here, I know Mr. Halsell wants you over at the HX Bar. He likes you, B.C., I know."

"It ain't that, girl. It ain't that at all. It's just I'm not made to be hogtied by someone else's rope. It ain't in me to follow someone else's orders. Y'know I ain't got it in me to be bossed around—by no one! And that's the way I feel right now. I feel everything's closing in around me. I can't be my own man. I can't do what I want to do, go where I want to go and be what I want to be. I just don't aim to be hogtied that way."

"And so what are you going to do?" she asked tentatively.

B.C. shrugged hesitantly. "There's some of us, we got a hankering to go west of here into Indian territory and become deputy marshals. There's talk the country is looking for deputies to keep watch over the land. It's a large area and we'd be more or less on our own. The pay ain't bad either."

"How long you going to be gone? What about me?" she'd asked, wide-eyed now and swallowing at the lump in her throat.

"I already spoke to Halsell. Said you could move into one of the dugouts on his ranch. You could cook and help him there 'til I get back after the snow."

"I know you got to do what's in your heart, B.C. And you know I'd never try to stop you. But I got to admit it hurts something awful to hear you talk so. And you know how it's going to eat inside me to have you gone."

"I know, gal, and you know I'd do almost anything to make it right for you. The last thing I want to do is hurt you." He frowned. "Maybe it would be more comforting if I took you back to your ma."

"No!" Tandy's answer came out so fast it even shocked her. She hadn't realized she had felt that strongly. "I ain't ready to go back there. Not this way I ain't."

"I understand," B.C. said and came to her and placed an arm about her shoulders. For a long time she had held him and he her and that was another memory that had helped her survive the months.

"You know I'll be waiting for you, B.C.," she had said that night as they cuddled under the blankets in front of the fire. How she had wanted him to take her then. It would have been so romantic. But she also knew not to press too hard. She didn't want to force him to move to the other side of the room as he was apt to do when she had her urges. "I ain't the pope, girl," he'd remarked drily once. "You should have a mind to behave your age."

So she had been content to be held, to lay with her head on his arm, just below his shoulder so that her nose lay against his chest. She could look up into his face, run her fingers along the line of his square chin or lips until he would gently push her hand away. She'd squeeze tightly against him until he yelled out for freedom and fresh air.

"I'll be waiting for you, B.C., you can count on that!"

He had smiled and nodded his head. "I'm not likely to forget you, gal, that's for sure."

She'd lain there silently, enjoying their last moments together. Already her thoughts were with him in his travels. "Who'd you say you're going with?" she'd asked curiously.

Half asleep, he'd sighed his answer.

"Oh, y'know the bunch over at Halsells. Bob, Grat, Emmett. Y'know I've talked 'bout them before—them Dalton brothers. They're one of a kind, them Daltons!"

"Oh," she'd said.

2

Tandy Woodrows Girondin was a survivor. She'd inherited the trait from her mother, the beautiful and mysterious Miranda Woodrowe, who hadn't married Tony Girondin until long after Tandy had become thoroughly confused as to who her real father was. Could she ever forgive her mother for her lies and deceptions? For a long spell, she'd thought her father was Grande Woodrowe—poor, talented, gentle Grand Woodrowe. But it was Tony who had been her real father. She'd been fathered out of wedlock by a man who for years had been a distant stranger to her, and the shock of the discovery had been almost too much for her to handle. Maybe Tony Girondin was her legal as well as her real father now—but it was as if she'd lived her early life in a dream world now blown to smithereens.

But she would make it! It was in her blood to survive. She'd been birthed by an Indian midwife; she had grown up with Indian friends. Miranda herself was supposed to have Indian blood in her. Tandy reckoned that was how she'd inherited her dark hair and eyes. She didn't have her mother's fervor for the Indians' welfare, but she was grateful she knew their ways. Knowing them was helping her through the loneliness and hardships of the wilderness. Even though Mr. Halsell treated her nicely, she had insisted living alone in the dugout, waiting her time for when Bitter Creek would return.

As Tandy sat in Oklahoma looking westward, she had no way of knowing that Bitter Creek Newcomb was actually facing her. Perhaps, if the arc of the horizon had been lots flatter, their lines of vision might even have met. However, the thought of home and Tandy was far from B.C.'s mind at the moment.

In hiding at the crest of a knoll, B.C. was studying a small group of men seated around a bramble-bush fire in the hollow below him. B.C. was uncomfortable. The evening breeze had a bite to it, as it often did in these New Mexico hills. He'd been waiting over an hour and anticipated it would be at least another hour before he would catch these men with the goods in their hands. Still, he was in no hurry. Selling alcohol to Indians was illegal in the territory; that was plain fact. And there was good reason for it to be illegal, as far as B.C. was concerned. The firewater the Indians bought drove them crazy enough to destroy local ranches. That put the ranchers' backs up and brought about a hell of a mess, with skirmishes between whites and red-men every which way you turned. Indians burning out ranches, white posses burning out Indian camps

—whew! Pretty soon, the Washington people would pressure the marshal into "prompt" action of some vague sort, which would result in still another confrontation between whites and reds. Bitter Creek shook his head. It was getting to be too much lately. It was far better to catch the scalawags dealing in whisky, kick their feet out from under a rope and save a hell of a lot of red tape.

The trouble, Bitter Creek ruminated as he kept one eye on the encampment below, was that the damn territory was too big. There weren't enough deputy marshals to cover it. He kind of liked being allowed to ride wherever his nose pointed, but way offsetting this was the loneliness and monotony of his routine and the fact there was hardly any money in it—even when he could collect his back pay!

He got two dollars for each arrest. He could make more if there was a reward out for the culprit, but such were few and far between. The ten-cents-per mile expenses he got could take care of his equipment and horse, but then the prisoner's food and keep would have to come out of his pay. All in all, Bitter Creek had learned early either to stay close to home or make sure his prisoner wasn't a heavy eater.

He sighed and rested his chin on his arm. There were times his mind wandered back to Oklahoma, to the Turkey Track and HX Bar ranches, to his attempt to start a place himself, and to Tandy. He smiled to himself, for it felt good to think that someone was waiting back there for him. Even though she was just a child!

Bitter Creek squirmed around in the dirt to get a pebble out from under his chest that was beginning to dig into bones. He counted the bodies below to make sure none had slipped away in the dark. No, all seven were still there in the firelight—two white men laughing with five young bucks as they passed bottles around.

He himself had sat around many such campfires; not with Indians maybe but with white youngsters just as cockeyed wild as these buckaroos. That was a long time ago, he mused. Young Grand Woodrowe had been such a youngster, kind of testing his oats at a time when Bitter Creek had stumbled on his camp. A likeable lad, young Grand—he'd struck up a friendship with him, maybe because they were both so adept with animals and ropes. Or maybe because they both liked a good laugh. Anyways, Bitter Creek had accepted Grand's invitation to his parents' small ranch and had there met and been impressed with his father. Doggone, he'd spent an entire afternoon watching Grand senior paint a mural in a leanto he used for a studio! Bitter Creek hadn't thought he had that much appreciation for art in him—but the painting had been pretty damn lifelike, fascinating to look at.

Grand's mother had also fascinated him. Miranda, her name. Never had he seen so beautiful a woman, except maybe in the *Gazette* illustrations. She had a black mane of hair that reminded B.C. of a newborn colt's, glistening and sleek. Now, there truly was a woman! And there was, of course, Tandy. Tandy Lee Woodrowe. A replica of her mother if there ever was one, just smaller and with a bit more salt in her blood. Bitter Creek smiled. He'd been teased about Tandy, plenty. Certainly, it would have been a feather in his cap to have someone like Tandy always at his side. He could see the elder Woodrowe was twice the man for having the likes of Miranda at his. But it remained difficult to think of Tandy as other than the sister of a friend, or the gorgeous Miranda's very young daughter.

Bitter Creek sighed deeply. For one barely in his twenties, he'd seen his share of life. He'd once, in a store that had many mirrors, seen his many reflections staring back at him. So many many faces. It was as if each face represented a part of him that had experienced something different from all the other parts, but that all the parts had mixed together somehow to become one human being. He didn't know how. Wondering about it sure as hell frazzled his mind sometimes.

Bitter Creek, seeing a flash of movement below, quit. He counted quickly. One Indian was missing. It was dark now and he had to squint to see where he'd gone. Then he chuckled. There he was—out near the horses, beyond the campfire, relieving himself. Bitter Creek relaxed. He studied the rest of the Indians, noting their movements had become sluggish. They were obviously pretty well soused. Not so the whites. He knew the whisky-sellers only pretended to drink and would remain alert so that they could steal from the Indians once they were helpless.

Eyes narrowed, B.C. decided to wait a bit longer. He didn't want a ruckus with the savages. Let them pass out dead drunk—they seemed well on their way. He'd wait until the white men had gotten what they wanted and then go down and take it from them. The so-called spoils of war, Bitter Creek thought. It was a way to get compensated for the back pay due him.

Slowly, Bitter Creek edged from the lip of the embankment and slipped down to where he had tied his horse. Gently patting the animal, he put on its feedbag and dropped in a couple handfuls of oats. "I'll be back afore you finish eating," he said softly. "With this bag over your big head, you ain't in no way going to let on we're here, are you?" He didn't wait for a reply. He patted the sleek neck again, then went to his saddle and got the 12-gauge sawed-off Remington shotgun he used for close-range work. John Slaughter had taught him this gun back at Bitter Creek, the town B.C. had taken his nickname from. Nobody with a touch of brains would try bucking a 12-gauge at close quarters. He'd forced many a desperado to give up just by pointing the gun at him. Because it was one thing to dodge one relatively small lead bullet and quite another to stand up against a hail of buckshot that could cut you in half.

Slipping down the embankment, B.C. stayed in the dark and circled around behind the whisky dealers' campfire. All that took was time and patience, which he excelled in. Now he could pick up guttural sounds from the camp. He inched forward on his belly until he was on the fringe of the light.

There, he leaped to his feet, ground his boots in firmly and raised the shotgun to his stomach.

"There's a buckshot aimed at your middles," he said in a loud voice. "I'm the law. You do one thing foolish, it'll be your last."

He waited, eyes darting from figure to figure.

The Indians probably hadn't heard him; they lay on their backs, bottles of rotgut clutched to their chests, writhing like rattlers with their heads cut off. Two bearded white men, who'd had their backs to B.C., slowly turned. They saw his face and they saw his gun. Shrugging, they lifted their hands high. But their eyes continued to dart about, so Bitter Creek gave them time to consider and reject their various options before he moved more into the light.

"Okay," he said then. "You with the hat, just you. Put your hands on your head tight-like, so it won't fall off if I have to pull this trigger. Now walk towards me, slow."

B.C. waited, eyes darting from one man to the other. The man with the hat came up and B.C. let him see the star on his vest. The man's face burned with hatred. Bitter Creek backed off just a bit.

"Okay—now you. Same thing. Hands on head and come this way." He waited. When he had them both within ten-foot range, he relaxed. "I'm a deputy marshal," he said. "The name's Newcomb. That's in case you want to come looking for me. If you ever get out of prison that is." He smiled.

"I'll keep you in mind, Newcomb," the man with the hat growled.

B.C. nodded. Then he stepped to one side, giving them some room. "Now, you and your friend spread out on the ground here so I can find what little treasures you've got for me."

"You goddam sonofabitch," the man with the hat muttered. But the two, in unison, got to their knees, then lay on their stomachs, their eyes never leaving the snout of the shotgun pointed at their faces.

Bitter Creek made quick work out of emptying their pockets and holsters. They had money and watches, among other things. "Okay, now on your backs." He was more careful with them this time, keeping far away from their legs. Satisfied he had their guns and everything else that was loose, he edged over to a rock and sat down to reckon up his loot. Their guns, he figured, he could trade for supplies. There was $150 in cash, in two leather pouches, which made him smile. He hefted a gold-plated pocket watch. He had never owned a watch and didn't want one since time wasn't important to him. But he figured he could sell this one for maybe $25. The other things were Indian trinkets, beads and baubles and such. They were—well, pretty. He pocketed them.

He spoke easily, "Okay, we can do this the right way or the unpleasant way. The unpleasant way is for you to take your boots off and walk all the way back to town alone. The right way is I let you ride your horses and I ride behind you."

It was a thirty-mile walk back to town on a night

that would freeze a man's butt off if he didn't get killed by the Indians he'd cheated first.

The two men glowered at B.C., indicating they had made their choice. B.C. nodded. "Mount up," he said. Once they were astride their horses, he put a noose around each man's neck and wrapped the other end of the rope securely around the horse's middle. It was a good way to keep them from galloping off, since if they tried it and he shot the horses out from under them, they'd strangle.

"Now we'll just go get my horse and be off in a jiffy," B.C. said.

The processing and filling out of papers was simple work for B.C. by now. The marshal was on some kind of an errand so he treated himself to a tub of water and a shave at the small shack behind the saloon.

He was in much better spirits as he came out of the alley and stopped to stretch his frame. He had heard that his friends were in town and he glanced up the street to see if he could spot their horses tied to the rails. More than likely they'd arrived at the marshal's office and were waiting for their pay, the same as he should be doing. Always waiting for their pay!

The little office was crowded as Bitter Creek stepped in. Instantly he became aware of tension in the room. The marshal was behind the desk, face flushed from the verbal attack he was receiving from the three men B.C. thought of as his closest buddies.

"What's going on?" B.C. asked, glancing from one to the other. Although they had not seen each other in over a month he didn't bother greeting them or they him. Greetings weren't expected. All three were good looking and resembled one another slightly. Their blue eyes were sharp and serious. Although they were as young as Bitter Creek, their handlebars accentuated their scowls and added years to their appearances.

"We ain't getting paid again," Bob Dalton announced. Handsome Bob swung back to stare at the marshal. "Four months back pay and he still hasn't received it!"

"Or he ain't giving it to us, one or the other," Grat Dalton added.

The marshal was a tall, elderly man tired of his deputies' complaints about money. Who needed them on top of all the other things he was responsible for? He looked around and shrugged for Bitter Creek's benefit. "Washington still hasn't sent the money. You know Washington."

"How the hell do them politicians expect a man to live?" Emmett Dalton exploded. "We're working our balls off while they're way off in some marble building deciding whether we deserve it or not?"

"You boys know it's not my doing," the marshal answered. It wasn't that he didn't sympathize with these boys. They were good workers and did well in the brush. It wasn't as if he was holding their money back from them.

"Y'mean mine hasn't come in either?" Bitter

Creek asked hesitantly. When the marshal shrugged his shoulders, B.C. looked to the others. "Jesus Christ, they want us to do this free, I bet."

Grat, the eldest of the Daltons, came up to the desk. "Marshal, can't you send them another telegram to sort of poke them into doing something fast?"

"I've done everything I can do," the marshal said. What he didn't tell them was that the cost of a telegram would have had to come out of his own pocket. The marshal set a limit as to what he was capable of doing.

Bob kicked the side of the marshal's desk and went over to a wall to lean against it. Emmett, the youngest Dalton, walked over and joined him. "What'll we do now?"

Bob swore. "Damned if I'm going to continue being shot at for no cause." He turned to the lawman. "The pay itself stinks, marshal, but we ain't complaining on that score. It's just that if we never get it—well, hell, we're just spitting into the wind. There's gotta be a better way of making a living than this."

"Damned if I know what it is," the marshal said flatly. "I've been doing it for forty years and I haven't got a better way straight in my head yet. Let me know if you come up with something. I'd appreciate it."

Grat shook his head. "C'mon Bob," he said, tugging at his brother's sleeve. "Let's talk it over by ourselves."

"Whyn't you boys go over to the saloon and have a few drinks to cool down a bit. Y'all been on the trail a mite—cool your tails off." The marshal, having had his say, gave them a kind smile. In a few days, he figured, they would be back asking for another assignment. Now was a bad time, though. He was much relieved when they walked out.

B.C. and the Daltons had their fill, and it was more than just whisky that heated their innards. They sat at the small round table in the Cactus Saloon, moodily staring at the wet rings that Emmett was designing on it with his glass.

"What are we going to do now?" Grat mumbled. He had asked that question often in the last two hours. As usual, there was no answer. Bitter Creek was lost in his own angry thoughts, boiling inwardly from a sense of overall injustice. The federal government's holding back his pay was just one more black mark against it in his book. He'd had a long series of wounds at government hands, dating back to childhood. The railroad people had come with federal marshals to his parent's ranch in Kansas. They had literally dumped him and what possessions his parents had saved into a wagon, telling the Newcombs never to return; their land was now the railroad's and that was that. So it had begun and so it was continuing. Would the government's perfidy never end?

"We could go back to punching cows," Emmett suggested.

Bob screwed his face up and waved his hand dejectedly. "What's worse? Pay is even less."

"But at least we got paid," Emmett insisted.

Bitter Creek, his mind soaked in whiskey, sluggishly recalled Oklahoma. Life there hadn't been that bad—not really. He'd made a safe living, far safer than what he was into now. He wondered whether his claim was being used. They'd taken it from him, damn them! They had come one late morning, them ranch owners and the man with the star, Bill Tilghman. Bill was a good ol' boy with a reputation for fairness in the territory. Once, right after the rush, he'd been fair enough to B.C. A "sooner," some tramp who had snuck into the territory before it was legal to homestead there, had tried to force him and Tandy off their claim. Tilghman had stepped right up and told the man he was a liar, that he had hidden in the brush to stake a claim and had not taken part in the rush. Ol' Tilghman knew plenty about those sooners and wanted no part of 'em. But then Tilghman had come back again, this time with that rancher. And this time, it was B.C. he was against.

"Sorry, son," Tilghman had said. He'd tried to explain the rancher's claim included B.C.'s little hollow of ground. End of dream—and another grievance to be added on to the rest.

"What about you, Kid?" Bob was asking, bringing Bitter Creek back to the present.

"Dunno," he answered thickly. "I'm with you 'bout this marshaling business. Ain't worth a boar's tit if we aren't going to be paid for it. I'm all for starting something else."

It was quiet again until Grat shook himself. "We could go hunt up ol' Bill in California. Hear there's all sorts of things to do out there."

They all thought it over. "I dunno." Bitter Creek hesitated. "I'd rather set a course back to the HX Bar."

"What's Oklahoma got calling for you?"

What indeed, Bitter Creek thought. It was part home—Oklahoma and Kansas, the Cherokee strip, the HX Bar Ranch. He felt more comfortable in country he knew. He was tired of running from one place to another. And, too, Tandy was there, a persistent vision. Was she still waiting for him?

"I think I'll be heading back," he said finally.

They all three gazed at him in a stupor that made ideas come slow. "You're not meant to brand cows," Bob teased.

Bitter Creek nodded his head in agreement. "But then, I don't know what the hell else I'm meant to do." He smiled crookedly. He was having a difficult time focusing on his friends.

"Hell," Bob answered, "neither do we. Tha's why we gotta go looking. We'll find something." He glanced heavily at his brothers. "Then again who knows? Maybe we'll all go back." He belched and grinned sheepishly.

Bitter Creek nodded and rose unsteadily to his feet. "If you do, look me up. I'll be around."

They waved loose hands at him. "Be seeing you, Kid," Bob said. "We'll mosey out to California and see what brother Bill's got to offer. Maybe we'll bump into you again one of these days."

"Maybe," Bitter Creek answered, trying to get his bearings. Already his mind was on the trail back.

3

They didn't have what Tandy could call a very romantic reunion. All summer long she had dreamed of that hour, that minute when Bitter Creek would come into her arms. She pictured herself atop the dugout in her best dress, with a gentle breeze blowing against her long black hair. Suddenly, he would appear riding from out of the sunset, looking down at her, their two figures set against a backdrop of blazing colors.

Or it would be an evening, after dinner when there was still the faint aroma of yeast about, perfumed with the sweet cinnamon smell of watered apple slices. The fire would give off a ruby glow to the cabin's inside, putting their less desirable possessions in shadows accentuating Tandy's most precious ones. A large gold-leafed china cup she had proudly given to B.C. on their first Christmas together sat on a shelf covered with a white scarf she no longer wore. Below the shelf, the warped old clothes cabinet they'd found discarded on a wagon trail was hidden by purple satin curtains, something she had sewn from an old dress during the lonely evenings. Over on the far side, near the small stove, their pallet displayed a light paisley quilt, neatly spread to cover the ugly dark blankets. She was prouder of the quilt than anything else, for it had been her first attempt at a large sewing project. She would have loved to be daring enough to be lying on it as Bitter Creek entered the room. Maybe in an off-the-shoulder nightie which she would have to start making soon.

That morning she had decided to wash her clothes, having saved enough water for it in the rain barrel. She went outside in loose dungarees, wearing one of B.C.'s shirts with the sleeves rolled up, and started scrubbing the knees of her spare pants with lye. Bent over the barrel, cursing the stubbornness of the mud stains, a result of her having spent a week on her hands and knees filling up rat holes along the cabin's walls, she was too absorbed to notice the approach of a horseman from the west.

She stopped, her wet arms resting on the brim of the barrel, when she felt his presence. A prickly sensation came up her spine, as if all her pores were suddenly erupting. The feeling edged up rib by rib to her shoulders.

"Oh hell, no," was her first thought. She was not ready for him, not this way! But she turned around anyhow and her heart jumped into her throat as she stared into his handsome, glowing face.

"B.C.!" she murmured. She wiped back the strand of hair that hung over her eyes with a wet wrist, her eyes searching his.

He had come upon her as quietly as he could, having dismounted some distance from the cabin, when he'd first taken sight of her. His approach had given him time to examine her as she bent over the barrel. A mite bigger, filling out, he noted. A smile came to his face as he recognized the familiar voice and movements of the girl. It was good to see her.

"I come back," he said. He made it sound like an apology.

"So I see," she answered, and then, not being able to contain herself any longer, she rushed at him and threw her arms about his neck. "Damn you, B.C.," she said in a tiny voice as she hung onto him. "Damn you anyhow."

Bitter Creek put his arms about her waist and held her. She seemed to have grown; her head now came up to his shoulders and there were more soft places on her than he remembered. "That's a fine greeting, I must say," he laughed and stroked her hair. "Is that all I get being gone this long? Just a damn you?"

She was silent a moment, absorbing his warmth, adjusting herself to his frame, branding that impression into her mind so that she would never lose it. "You know I'm glad to see you," she finally said. "It's just—you caught me unaware."

"Well, it's me—and I'm back. I told you I'd be back."

She made a small fist with her left hand and beat

it against his chest lightly. "You said you'd be gone a short while," she sniffed, and it was then that Bitter Creek realized she had been silently weeping.

He bent back and picked up her chin with a finger. "Hey now, little one," he said softly, looking into her dark eyes for the first time. "I'm back—here—now. That's all that's important, ain't it?" He smiled and kissed the top of her brow.

"Oh B.C.," Tandy whispered. "I missed you something awful!"

"Well, sure enough I missed you too, girl."

She smiled as she bent back and looked up at him. "You did? Really?" she asked hesitantly. "Did you really miss me, B.C., or are you just saying it to be kind?"

"Kind?" He frowned. "You think I'd say something like that to you outta kindness? I sure did miss you. Ain't had no one to mend my socks, or cook a decent meal, or scratch my back—"

"Oh B.C., be serious," she smiled.

He studied her face and what he saw sobered him. The little girl he remembered was growing up, getting to be a beauty. A young filly, free, proud, full of life and enthusiasm. Yep, his little Tandy had grown up a mite since he'd been away. It bore some thinking and a careful step.

"You been making out okay?" he asked. "I mean, you been taken care of proper?"

She loosened her hold on him and stepped back, suddenly conscious of what a sight she must appear. Embarrassed, she quickly arranged strands of hair that had escaped the long tresses she had tied in back of her head. "I must look a sore," she said, and seemed to shrink from his study of her.

"You didn't answer my question," he reminded her.

"You didn't answer mine," she countered and stared back at him boldly. "Did you miss me—or are you just giving me soft soap?"

Suddenly he smiled, recognizing a more familiar Tandy. "Answer mine first," he coaxed. He made himself comfortable on the small wooden bench at the side of the dugout.

She took a deep breath and shrugged. "I been okay. Mr. Halsell's been more than kind to me. Sometimes he sends a wagon out for me. He'll be glad to see you back."

"Everyone else been okay to you?" he asked suspiciously.

Her eyes twinkled. "Would you be jealous if I told you I had myself another man? It would serve you right, you know!"

"Ain't no man going to have you, Tandy Lee Woodrowe Girondin," he answered with a grin. "Ain't no one born yet who's good enough for you."

His words pleased her and she wrinkled her nose and came closer to him. "You're good enough for me, B.C., and you know it. I waited all this time for you—should prove something, don't it?"

"No way for you to talk, girl," he answered her, taking his hat off to wipe his brow. He'd been gone too long. Things were going to be more difficult than he thought.

"I'm not ashamed of what I said and how I feel,"

she answered him, her voice rising in anger. "And I'm no girl—or haven't you noticed." She proudly pulled the shirt tight over her chest, amused as well as scared when his face reddened in obvious discomfort.

"You're still young enough to take over my knee, girl," he answered sternly. "Nothing's changed between you and me. You'd better get that straight in your thinking or it'll be me off again."

"But why?" she asked wonderingly.

" 'Cause that's the way it is," he said. "You and me—well, it's hard to explain." He looked up at her and saw the hurt. "Give me time, Tandy," he said.

"You needn't run away from me, B.C.," she said, frightened that maybe she had pushed too far again. "I've waited this long and I'll wait more if that be the case. But you might as well get it into your thick skull I aim to be your woman one of these days and there's no pulling me away from that fact."

Bitter Creek shook his head and smiled. He looked around him, at the entrance to the dugout with its heavy worn canvas covering, at the swept area in front, the water barrel and her heap of wrung-dry clothes still waiting to be hung on a line she had tied to an upright pole not far away. "You've done a woman's job, Tandy, m'girl. I admire you for stickin' it through. I couldn't think of anyone finer to be tied to. But," and he shook his head, "you're just a filly still trying its legs. You got plenty of growing up to do without thinking of taking on a man—'specially someone like me."

"Why not?" she asked quickly. "I do all them

things now, don't I? I do everything a wife can do except making love to you, B.C. That's a fact you can't deny."

"And that's another thing," B.C. answered. "You're too young to be having a family."

"There's plenty much younger than me having babies, Bitter Creek Newcomb," Tandy shot back loudly. "I'm as ripe to have babies as any woman—and I could raise them twice as good!"

"Not with me, y'can't," he shot back as hot. "I'm no way near ready to have kids to worry about. And no way am I going to let you raise 'em alone."

Tandy glared at him, legs spread wide in defiance. Finally she nodded. "All right then, we don't have to have a family right away. That don't mean we can't make love together!"

"Now you hush up, girl," he said angrily. "You're too young to be thinking of such things. When two people make love, their lives change. Everything changes. There's things each one is beholding the other to. You may have growed some in body, but it's a responsibility you know nothing about."

She knew he was angry and it frightened her. She waited nervously before replying in a soft voice. "I don't aim to push you, B.C. I just wanted you to know how I feel. But I don't aim to push. If that's the way it's got to be now, then I will live by that." She looked at him, tears welling in the corners of her eyes.

Bitter Creek studied the crown of his hat as he twirled it in his hands. Slowly he rose and went to her, head downcast. He put an arm around her shoulders shyly and tucked her under him. "We'll take things a day at a time, okay? Meanwhile, we got a heap of stories to swap and you got a heap of back-scratching to catch up on."

4

Winters in the Oklahoma Cherokee strip were apt to unnerve a person, make him forget whatever promises he'd made or dreams he'd had for the future. A lot hightailed it to somewhere better when the cold winds came. Not so Tandy. Her spirits stayed high. Although some mornings she shook beneath the sewn pelts of her makeshift parka before the small black stove heated up, her innards were nearly bursting with warmth and happiness. Even during the times when Bitter Creek had to ride line for Mr. Halsell and was gone for days, she could battle the worst that nature gave.

The last days of March in 1891 brought a promise of the end of the cold. New things took root and blossomed outside, and Tandy was in a good mood sorting out the small packets of seed B. C. had brought home. She was determined to grow lots of vegetables this year. Bitter Creek had promised a good supply of water from a distant waterhole in return for her promise of fresh beans and spinach and things. Things were going well. She hummed, envisioning how she would get her garden patch started.

Bitter Creek had been good to her, sharing what small wages he made at the HX ranch and at various evening jobs in nearby Guthrie. "What do I need it for?" he would smile when she showed hesitancy at taking the money. He was, in fact, over-generous. He seemed to take great delight in bringing her all kinds of things from town whenever he had a chance. These treasures she kept in open display around the dugout, constant reminders of him and of those evenings of delight when he'd brought them.

One morning, while she was uprooting the hard earth with the iron hoe Bitter Creek had borrowed from the Halsell ranch house, she spied a horseman in the distance. She knew instantly it wasn't B.C. and didn't stop her work. However, she moved to one side so she could keep an eye on the rider. When it became obvious he was headed for her, Tandy stopped work and edged to the dugout. She had learned long ago to be wary of strangers, and Bitter Creek had spent considerable time instructing her on the use of the shotgun that leaned against the wall within her easy reach.

"Howdy, m'am." The rider bowed slightly and touched the brim of his black stetson. He was a big man with a kindly face, yet Tandy drew away in spite of herself. The man sat his horse with the habit of command; his eyes alone drew instant respect. A greying, drooping mustache hid a straight mouth that had not smiled in a long, long time. He was dressed in a dark suit, dusty from travel, with a vest that was tight over years of good care and experience. He watched Tandy's inspection of himself, waiting patiently for her curiosity to subside. He was used to such inspections.

"I'm told you're George Newcomb's woman. That so?"

Tandy's head came up sharply in pride. "I am—and this land is his," she answered calmly, waving her arm about her. "I've seen you before, a couple of years back."

He studied her more closely, trying to recall her. "That's about the first time I met Newcomb."

Tandy nodded. "I know. I was there." How could she ever forget this man? A legend in Oklahoma as he had been a legend back in Dodge City. He'd seen it all, so they said, and had done it all along with the best of them. This was Bill Tilghman—the law.

"And what do you want with B.C.?"

"B.C.?"

"Bitter Creek," she explained and watched him digest it with a slight nod of his head.

"Want to ask him a few questions. You expecting him soon?"

"He's riding line. You might catch him over to Mr. Halsell's place." She started to point the direction but he interrupted her.

"I been there. They sent me here. He's headed back soon enough." He looked about, noted the shed in the back was empty, eyed the wind-flapped curtain entry to the dugout, then relaxed.

"You mind if I wait him out?" It was a courteous inquiry Tandy knew was not to be denied.

"You may put your horse in the shed if you want. There's water here." She waited until he had dismounted. "I'll set you a place for dinner." She turned without waiting for an answer and ducked into the dwelling.

The small stove was well heated, the coffee pot brewing forth a strong aroma by the time Tilghman slipped into the room. With his head uncovered, he was smaller than Tandy had first thought; for an instant, in the darkness, he reminded her of what she felt a grandfather should look like. She noted immediately that his hands were clean from a good scrubbing and that he had slicked back his thinning hair with water.

"You may sit there." Tandy pointed to her best straight-back chair, the one that didn't wobble, and continued slicing chunks of meat into a simmering pot.

"Much obliged," the lawman muttered. It was obvious he was less at ease indoors than he had been outside; he was stiff in bearing and quite aware of Tandy. His eyes darted quickly about the neat room, taking in all her things, resting just a moment on the shotgun. "You take good care, m'am."

"Thank you kindly," she answered, glad that he noticed. "We're doing just fine here." Her mind went back to their first dugout, half as small. What little time they had had there. She glanced over to Tilghman and saw that he was studying her, registering his recognition.

"You were that tyke with him couple years ago." He had a habit of stating things rather than inquiring.

Tandy nodded. "It was our first claim." She could laugh about it now. "In fact, it was our only claim."

He stared down at his large hands clasped together on his lap. "I'm sorry things turned bad for you."

Tandy shrugged. "You had to do what you did," she answered. "As you see, we survived."

He nodded and again glanced about him. "I can see that. And you stuck with him. He's a lucky cowpoke."

She was almost beginning to like Tilghman. She was still in awe of him though. After all, here was a man who was reputed to have killed over a handful of the most notorious badmen in the territory.

"You got a wife, marshal?" she asked, handing him a cup of coffee so that his hands would have something to do.

He watched her carefully to see whether she was going to join him. She sat on the cot, hands locked together over her knees and stared back at him, waiting.

"Yes'um," he answered, taking a sip of the brew. "A fine woman. Just got her moved to Guthrie." He was stiff. She couldn't decide whether it was because of her or because it was his way. Then his face seemed to soften. When he looked at her now, his eyes seemed brighter and yet gentle. She listened to his stories about Dodge City, Bat Masterson, Indians, his wife. Her curiosity and enthusiasm encouraged him on through the late afternoon and into the early evening until he suddenly stopped.

"He's here," he said softly. He glanced at the door, then at her.

Tandy jumped, only then conscious of the soft hoofbeats. She got up quickly and instinctively looked around the room to make sure everything was in its place.

"You better go out and tell him I'm here," Tilghman advised. He had witnessed too many rash incidents resulting from men returning and finding strangers in their homes.

Bitter Creek had stopped on his way to the shed, having noticed Tilghman's horse. He was turning around to come back when Tandy ran up to him. "Who's here?" he asked suspiciously.

"Bill Tilghman," she answered and hugged him, unaware that he wasn't returning her embrace. "He's been waiting to talk to you."

"Now what's happened?" B.C. asked with an edge of bitterness in his voice. He started for the dugout but Tandy pushed him to a stop.

"It's all right," she answered. "You go take care of your horse first. He's waited this long, he can wait a bit more."

Bitter Creek took one more look at the dim light emitting from the dugout door, then looked down at her. It was past dusk and there was barely enough light in the sky to read her face. "You all right? He tell you what he's here for?"

"Don't worry," she said. She took the reins from his hands and led the horse to the shed. "We've been having a decent talk waiting for you. Did you know he was once captured by Indians?"

As they rubbed the animal down and fed it, Tandy told some of the tales the lawman had related. "Bill's an all-right lawman," Bitter Creek acknowledged. "I have nothing against him. He's fair and that's about all a man can ask for when dealing with him."

"Howdy, kid!" Tilghman's voice came from behind them.

They both spun around in surprise, Tandy grabbing hold of Bitter Creek's arm. It was only too obvious, once they got their breath back, that the lawman had stolen up on them on purpose.

"You don't have to sneak up on us like that," Bitter Creek answered angrily and turned to finish caring for the horse.

"Just thought I'd come out for a breather," came the soft response. It was directed more towards Tandy, who had not yet recovered completely.

"You thought he'd try to do something," she accused him.

Tilghman's eyes narrowed. He tucked a thumb under his belt to show he meant no harm. "In my profession, you can never be too cautious." Then he turned to Bitter Creek. "I wasn't sure how you'd receive me."

B.C. stopped his work for a moment and stared quizzically at the lawman. "Just what kind of a reception you think I'd give you?"

Tilghman's gaze was steady. "As I said, Kid, I can't afford to take too many chances."

"It ain't Kid any more," Bitter Creek answered, his voice still tight. "I go by Bitter Creek now." He glanced at Tandy and gave her a smile meant only for her. Then, finished with the horse, he turned full figure to Tilghman. "I don't have no reason to try anything 'gainst you."

The lawman studied him with hard grey eyes trained to measure a man. He'd come against the worst and the best, the typical and the most untypical. This youth had plenty of claw and could go either way. "I had to be sure, Bitter Creek," Tilghman finally answered and backed away to lead the group back to the dugout.

Usually, the first thing on a man's mind after riding the range for several days was to feed a stomach that had been growling for warm substance and flavor. Tandy and Tilghman knew Bitter Creek's need and allowed his silence. Tandy put a makeshift table top on the flour barrel close to the cot where B.C. was to sit after he finished washing his hands and face. He did his washing up quietly and then he spent some time scraping dirt from under his fingernails with his knife.

Although Tandy was dying to tell B.C. about her plans for the garden and to question him about his own travels, she did neither—just served up the food while maintaining an unnatural decorum. Tilghman seemed self-conscious too. Their restraint from usual habits just made the occasion all the more awkward for all three.

After the meal, the two men slowly pushed back in the chairs and stretched, happily released from the burden of closeness.

"You must come again, marshal, when there are tomatoes. The stew is much better with tomatoes and rosemary." Tandy fussed over the clearing of dishes. She had decided she would clean them in the morning. She was dying to get to their talking.

"The eats was better than most I can remember, m'am," Tilghman answered politely. "But that don't mean I won't take you up on your offer, thank you kindly." He took out a long-pointed stick from his shirt pocket and began methodically to pick at his teeth, glancing from one of his hosts to the other. "You've got yourself a fine woman, Kid—excuse me, I mean Bitter Creek."

"Thank you, Bill," B.C. answered and then winked. "She's a mite scraggly here and there, but come a good rain, she'll sprout out in just the right places."

Tandy blushed, pleased that they were talking about her. She chided, "That's no way of talking in front of a guest, B.C." She tried to be serious. "Mr. Tilghman was being mighty polite and there's no call for spoiling his words."

This brought a slight smile to the weathered face of the lawman. "M'am, you already are a beauty. There's no unkind word that has the strength to hide that truth. You're also a funning gal to have around and that's a pure delight to these old bones."

Tandy glanced quickly at B.C. to make sure he was taking all this in. "Now, marshal, I do appreciate all your gallant words, but I am sure you did not come out all the way from Guthrie just to compliment me."

Her words brought a sober mood instantly to the room.

Tilghman nodded. "You're right in that," he said quietly. He turned his attention to B.C. "I'll get right to what I have to say. I heard tell you were with the Dalton brothers a short while back."

Bitter Creek grinned. "I sure was. We rode together when I was working at the Turkey Track and they was working here at the HX."

"I mean after that."

"Sure. We all went over to New Mexico territory—took on jobs as deputy marshals hunting whisky runners, drunk Indians, stuff like that. They're good ol' boys. Why you askin' 'bout them?"

Tilghman frowned and stared at the floor before answering. Then he said, "How long you been back?"

Bitter Creek shrugged and turned to Tandy.

"He came toward the end of the hot spell and been here ever since," Tandy said defensively. She didn't like the line of questions the lawman was asking and was worried.

Tilghman looked at both for a long moment, deliberately taking his time, testing, measuring. Finally, he took a small paper pad from his inside jacket pocket and thumbed through notes he'd made. "Before you came back here, did they give you any idea where they might have been headed for?"

The question was an easy one and Bitter Creek grinned and relaxed. "Sure. They was going out to California to hunt up their brother Bill. He's a big-time lawyer out there wanting to be governor or something like that."

Tilghman studied B.C., then turned back to his notes. "You seen them since then?" he asked.

"If I had, they'd sure as shootin' be eating right here alongside us." B.C. was now more than curious. He was uncertain. He didn't like the way Tilghman would look at Tandy after each of his answers, as if needing her assurance that what he was saying was the truth. "What's all the questioning about Bill? Why are you so interested in my friends?"

The lawman took his time placing the pad of paper back into his jacket pocket. "I got word the other day that a train was robbed in California. The culprits were identified as the Dalton brothers."

"Aw hell, marshal." B.C. snorted his disbelief. "There's got to be a mistake."

Tilghman shook his head. " 'fraid not. Got a positive identification on all three—Grat, Emmett and Bob."

Bitter Creek shook his head. "Naw, they wouldn't do a thing like that. They're on your side of the law."

The older man leaned back in the chair. "A badge don't necessarily guarantee a man's honest, Bitter Creek. I've hunted many a person who once wore a badge. I don't know why and probably never will, but sometimes it's harder to stay a lawman than to go against the law.

"I knew them boys. Talked to Halsell. Everyone says the same thing 'bout 'em. The Daltons are good fellers. But you also got to remember them brothers were blood relatives to the Youngers and to the James boys. They all got some bad blood in 'em. Maybe we all do for that matter. But the ugly fact is, the Daltons robbed a train and whatever good they done in the past is behind them now."

"I'll be doggone," Bitter Creek said slowly. "The Daltons robbing a train—wow. There's gotta be some mistake."

Tilghman sighed. "There was, but it was their mistake, no one else's."

Tandy was leaning against the dirt wall, absorbed in what she was hearing. "My God," she murmured, "you could have been one of them."

Her words brought both men around to face her. She stared wide-eyed at B.C. "It could have been you that Marshal Tilghman come for."

Bitter Creek turned to the lawman, eyes narrowed with sudden realization. "That's why you sneaked up on us tonight. You thought I might have been part of that robbery."

Tilghman shook his head. "No. I'd checked up on you and knew you was here at the time of the robbery. What I didn't know is where your loyalties lay."

"Loyalties lay?" Bitter Creek said hotly. "Jesus Christ, marshal, they're my best friends. They will always be my friends. What they do is their business, doesn't change whether you're friends or not."

Tilghman nodded slowly. "That choice is yours,

of course. I just wanted to know the lay of the land."

"Well, now you got it—and that's the way it's going to be."

"I can sympathize with you, Bitter Creek, on that issue. A good friend is hard to come by. But I'll tell you this: the Daltons are wanted by the law and if they come into my territory, I'm going to put them behind bars." He waited to let his statement sink in. "And," he emphasized, "anyone getting in my way, they'll stand for the consequences!"

Bitter Creek stuck his chin out belligerently. "I'm obliged for your warning, Bill. I just hope the time never comes when I have to make a decision in which you are involved."

"You already have a decision to make," Tilghman said flatly. "You might as well start facing up to it now. The Daltons are reported headed back for this area. They'll be needing friends to help 'em hide. What I want to know, is just how much help you're planning on giving 'em."

Bitter Creek glanced over at Tandy nervously, then looked back at the lawman. "To be honest with you, I dunno," he answered. "And I'm not quite sure I'd be telling you anyhow. But 'cause you been fair to me, I can say I don't rightly know at this time. I'm not going to shut my door in their faces if that's what you're asking."

"Will you let me know when you see 'em?" It was a blunt question.

"No—hell no, I won't."

"Then I'll be telling you this. Step lightly. I'm

going to be keeping an eye on you and I'll make your life very difficult if I find you helping 'em."

Bitter Creek flared up. He didn't like being threatened, never had. "You might as well get it into your head that I'll be helping them, Bill." He tried to keep his voice level. "You nor anyone else is going to tell me who my friends are or who I can't see."

"And I'm telling you as both lawman and friend —you keep on this side of the law. Break it and you'll come bucking right up against me. And you'll lose, Kid, you'll lose."

The two men glared at each other across the small confines of the room. It was Bitter Creek who wavered first. Pounding his fist on his knee, he got up, swept past Tandy and walked outside.

An uncomfortable silence was left in the room. Tilghman stared at the doorway, lips pursed as he went into deep thought. Tandy had a difficult time interpreting him. The change in him scared her. Gone was the grandfather image, the wise teller of heroic tales of a few hours ago. He was a menace now, threatening them, and she was scared.

Tilghman turned slowly and caught her terror. "His friends will be his undoing," he said huskily. He hesitated as though wanting to say more. "I wish you the best, m'am." With that, he got up and took his hat from the peg on the wall. He fingered it, watching the brim pass through his fingers. When he looked up at her, his face was hard, hiding whatever emotions he might be feeling inside. "I haven't seen it proven yet that going against the law is healthy. And, believe me, I seen all sorts try to prove otherwise. I can't say I enjoy doing what I have to do sometimes—but I do believe in it and that's good enough for me for the time being." He hesitated. "You and him, you're both young. I hate seeing anyone going to waste, and I see him right now sort of balancing on a fence. It would do you both good to talk it over 'fore he jumps down on the wrong side." He turned to the doorway and then hesitated again. He turned his head and the look he gave her had hurt and sadness in it. "If he sides in with the Daltons, you can bet I'll be back."

He was gone. Tandy slowly released the breath she had been holding. She felt numb. She waited, hardly moving, listening until the hoofbeats of Tilghman's horse could be heard no more. She felt like crying, was hard put to hold back tears. She walked to the front-door curtain and peered out. Soon, her eyes adjusting to the darkness, she spotted B.C. at the side of the dugout, arm outstretched to the roof's edge, staring out into the prairie where Tilghman had disappeared.

She went to him and hesitantly put her arms about his middle, drawing herself up close to his back, her head resting lightly between his shoulder blades. "He scares me," she murmured and held on tightly.

"That's what he meant to do," Bitter Creek answered, his hand resting lightly on hers at his waist. "He's trying to push us into helping him."

"But I am scared, B.C.," she said. "Really scared, y'know what I mean?"

He nodded and gripped her hands tightly. "Yeah, I know. But we come out of things worse than this. We'll do it again."

"But what if they do come here?"

He sighed heavily. "Most likely they will. Bob, Grat, Emmett—they're my friends. We've shared too many campfires together."

"I know you can't turn your back on them," she answered. "And I don't think it's right that Tilghman expects you to."

"No way can he do that. But I don't think we got too much to worry about. We're not the only ones the Daltons can turn to. Their folks live near, and they've got lots of other friends all over this country. There's too much for Tilghman to cover. All he can do right now is try to put a little scare into us."

She laughed, beginning to feel more at ease. "Every time he comes to visit us, it hasn't been much fun, has it?"

Bitter Creek laughed, turned in her arms and held her lightly. "Ol' Bill? He's just doing his job, that's all. I reckon if I was in his boots, I'd try the same thing too. But you have nothing to fret about. All them Daltons know this country like the back of their hands. Ain't no way Tilghman is going to catch 'em."

"It's not them I worry about," Tandy answered.

"It's you. I don't want you to get into any trouble." She looked up at him with an impish smile. "After all, I haven't had a chance to prove to you what a good woman I am."

"You mean going to be," Bitter Creek corrected her and returned her smile. "You're right. Can't do nothing foolish till I see what you turn out to be. 'Course, there's always the chance you'll put on too much fat here and there." He pinched her in a couple of ticklish spots. "Then you'll be too ugly to care about."

"You won't give a woman half a chance, will you?"

She laughed. It was all right. She was used to his teasing. She felt confident in her future with him; in her heart she knew that one day she would have her way. She was working on it, and she had patience. In fact, the anticipation excited her and there were moments every once in a while, deep dark moments she kept only to herself, when she sometimes wondered whether she'd just as soon have the victory never come.

"Oh, B.C., what am I going to do with you?" she asked dreamily.

"Well, first and foremost," he answered, pushing her away, "you're going to let me eat another cookie I saw you making. Then, it's some good sleeping."

She hugged his arm as they retreated back into the dugout. "And I've got to tell you about the garden we're going to have and all the good things we're going to eat."

Bitter Creek grinned at her pleasures. "Little girl," he answered gravely, "I'm going to make sure we'll both have all the good things we'll ever want. You wait and see!"

5

"Tandy, I'd like you to meet Bob, Emmett, and that there's Grat Dalton."

The three riders doffed their hats and bowed slightly, their eyes traveling over Tandy appreciatively as they dismounted with Bitter Creek.

One must have about the same feeling when being introduced to the president of the United States, Tandy thought. She inspected the three newcomers with wide-eyed awe. For the last two months, it seemed that Bitter Creek had done nothing but regale her with the past exploits of the Dalton brothers and the other riders from the Halsell ranch. She had never tired hearing of their hell-raising, their prowess not only with ranch work but the handling of the rope, rifle and handgun.

"We've been sort of expecting you," Tandy said shyly. She knew instantly that she liked all three. Their smiles were genuine as each returned hers. And there was an obvious comradeship between the brothers and Bitter Creek. That alone was enough to win her over.

"Well," Bob Dalton drawled lazily, "if we'd known such a beauty was in the neighborhood, we would have moseyed over sooner." He turned to Bitter Creek and nudged him in the ribs playfully. "How'd such an ugly puss as you get ahold of a beauty such as her?"

B.C. grinned. "Oh, I dunno. She rolled in with the last windstorm we had, I think." He reached over and tugged at Tandy's hair.

That evening, over a hot meal, they all exchanged tales. Soon after Bitter Creek had left New Mexico, the three brothers had tried a career of horse trading which was quickly discouraged by pressure from the law. "Well, y'see," Bob explained, "one of the difficulties was the owners of the horses we was selling didn't quite appreciate us selling them."

"Didn't the law get to you?" Tandy asked excitedly.

"Well," Bob continued, "that was another problem. Y'see, we was still the law. We was still deputies. 'Course that didn't stand too well with the law either."

"Y'know?" Emmett spoke up. "Maybe that's why they invited us to leave the territory?"

The three brothers and Bitter Creek all laughed.

Their travels had led them to California finally, where they had found their brother Bill. " 'magine, a Dalton being such a big wheel in politics," Grat, the oldest, boasted.

"He sure got you outta trouble a couple of times," Bob grinned.

Bitter Creek shook his head. "Can't you boys ever stay out of trouble?"

"Some of it's not exactly our fault, y'know," Bob answered. "I mean, it's not as if we didn't try. But soon as some clown starts ordering us around to do this or do that, it sort of rubs us the wrong way."

Bitter Creek grinned. "You boys just don't like to work, that's all."

"Hey, we don't mind it once in a while," Grat said. "It's just that we found something easier and a heck more exciting than roping cattle."

"Y'mean robbing trains?" Tandy asked excitedly.

The brothers exchanged glances with B.C. "You heard about that too, huh?"

"Tilghman was here a couple of months ago," she started to explain.

"Yeah, Bitter Creek told us," Bob stated soberly. "I guess things are more serious than we thought."

Tandy looked at B.C., confused.

"Someone got shot during the holdup," he explained.

"Oh, my God!" Tandy gasped, then looked at each of the brothers as if seeing strangers. All she could see in her mind was a dead body for which these three were responsible.

Bob lowered his gaze as she turned to him. "It wasn't something we wanted," he explained in a soft voice. "Just happened."

"He tried to shoot us," Emmett volunteered. "It was him or us."

Tandy jerked her head to clear her numbness. She told herself that as long as men carried guns, there would be killings. In fact, Bitter Creek had said he had killed a man but had refused to talk about it. He also had told her Bob Dalton had killed a man over a girl years ago. She hadn't thought too much about such things. She supposed almost every man in the territory had at one time or another killed someone. Only now did the fact of murder strike home to her.

"It's not as though you killed him on purpose," Bitter Creek was agreeing.

"But it's still a killing," Bob answered moodily. "The law calls it murder. They tried to pin it on Grat here—in fact, they had him going to prison."

Tandy's interest was renewed. She looked at the tall lanky Dalton. "You went to prison?"

Grat smiled self-consciously. "They tried to send me," he answered modestly. "But I managed to escape from the train before we got there."

"They're still talking about it in California," Emmett boasted. "Ain't been an escape like that until Grat here showed them how."

"Does that mean you all are outlaws?" Tandy asked.

"At least in California we are," Bob answered.

"Bill Tilghman is near to busting his tether waiting for you all to come back," Bitter Creek said. "He's not going to rest easy 'til he catches up with you."

Bob Dalton grinned. He sucked some meat and gravy from his thumb. "Just goes to show how good we are. We've been back some time, George. We been trading horses until lately. Found people don't take too kindly to horse thieves so thought we'd better stop 'fore we get 'em too mad."

"You coming back to Halsell's?"

"You always was a joker," Bob answered. "You think we come all this distance to go back to punching cows or settling down?"

"What's wrong with settling down?"

Bob was disappointed. "Are you kidding? You see what them sodbusters are doing around you? Haven't you noticed nothing?" There was bitterness in his voice. "When we first come back here, we couldn't believe our eyes. Why, we no sooner got outta one town than, bang, you head blame into another one. There's towns sprouting up all over. Haven't you noticed? Ain't no stretch of land left, pard. And that's a damn shame. A man can't ride in peace no more. It's a wonder ol' Halsell still has a ranch left with all them dirt farmers tearing up everything and stringing wire as if they was tying up a Christmas package. You realize there will be a time soon when a cowboy won't be able to ride a day in a straight line no more? Remember when the only thing you had to watch out for was rabbit holes? Now it's fences, and towns, and people." He shook his head. "No, ranching is finished around here."

"Well," Bitter Creek scratched the top of his head. "I gotta admit it is getting a bit crowded."

"Crowded?" Bob was still irate. "We ain't even

seen the beginning. People are coming in all the time to this territory. There's say they're going to open up more of the strip. Damn government is going to let more people come in here, can you imagine that? And you want to know why? It's them railroad people. They're the ones bringing in them people. They're laying tracks all over the place, buying land for more railroads so they can bring more people in so they can buy more land to build more trains to bring in more people." He threw up his hands in disgust. "And them politicians, they don't give a damn about us. All they care about is how much money they will get out of all this. It's them railroad people who's paying 'em off to open up this land."

"I know all about them railroads," Bitter Creek answered tightly.

"That's right," Bob nodded. "They drove your folks out. Your folks would probably still be living if it weren't for them damn politicians. We's all been pushed by them. The Daltons, the Youngers, the Jameses, we all got our butts kicked. But at least they kicked back."

"Is that what you're planning to do?"

Bob grinned. "And why not? Ain't one person I know who'd shed a tear to have them railroads kicked where it hurts."

"And look where it got your cousins," Bitter Creek reminded them.

Bob shrugged. "They fought for something and they died for what they believed in. That's saying more for them than anything I know. I'd rather die for something I believe in than in bed of old age having been pushed around all my life."

"Aren't you afraid of getting shot?" Tandy asked curiously.

Bob shrugged. "I figure we all face some kind of death every day. Could come from a stampede, a rattler, Indian, gun going off by mistake, some kind of disease, lightning from the sky—who knows? Wouldn't matter to me whether it was one of those or a bullet. Wouldn't want to suffer or anything like that. I'd want it quick but other than that, no, I wouldn't care."

"But you're talking of going against the law," Tandy persisted.

"What law? You mean the law them railroad people and politicians make so they can have their way? We all done fine until them railroads come and set up towns and brought in the law to protect their property and their banks. Oh, there might have been a few wild ones gone astray, but they were usually taken care of. You see, Tandy," Bob continued in a serious vein, "I take the law as being set up by people who don't care a cat's ass about us poor guys. Now I ain't blaming 'em for doing such things 'cause if I was them I'd want to protect my things too. But going against the railroads and going against the law is the same thing as I see it. And it don't bother me none to fight both of 'em."

Bitter Creek sighed and shook his head slowly. "I dunno, Bob. I ain't got no love for railroads or, for that matter, banks. But riding as outlaws don't exactly feel comfortable neither."

Emmett, who along with his brother Grat had been content to let Bob do the talking, leaned over and grabbed B.C.'s arm. "You call this comfortable? I mean, you enjoy working for someone else, doing all the hard work while he sits at home counting his money?"

"It's a living and we're doing all right," B.C. answered. He looked at Tandy for confirmation.

"Yeah, but you got to admit, it ain't the same any more. I mean, you can't let loose in town no more without the law asking you to quiet down. Y'remember how we all used to raise hell every once in a while? We'd shake the territory something awful, didn't we? But can you do that any more?" He nudged B.C. until he got a shake of the head.

"And I heard the cattle can't come up from Texas no more 'cause of the fences and towns. The Chisholm hasn't been used in years now."

"I'll tell you something that scrapes at my backbone," Grat volunteered. "It's them banks. I heard that all the money they got in them banks ain't even theirs. Belongs to the little people. Can y'magine that? I mean, they squeeze the little people to put their money into the banks, and then the railroad bigwigs come along and use that money to buy land so they can kick them same little people outta the way. Now that's what I call unfair!"

"So unfair," Bob said, "that we decided we'd do something 'bout it. We're going to take that money them banks have, and give it back to the little people. Going to do the same thing to them railroads too."

"You're going to rob trains *and* banks?" Tandy asked incredulously, her heart beating faster.

"It's a living like anything else," Bob answered. "And we got the majority of people on our side. We're going to be sort of heroes. I mean, who cares what happens to other people's money, 'specially if it belongs to the railroads?"

"Tilghman cares."

"It's a hell of a large area for him to cover. We been here over a month and seen no sign of him. You gotta remember we was born and raised here. We know this land inside and out."

"But he'll get help."

"So will we. In fact, we're collecting us a band now. We got Charley Bryant, Dick Broadwell and ol' Bill Powers so far. Y'know any of 'em?" When B.C. shook his head, Bob looked at his brothers. "Oh yeah—ol' Bill Doolin is joining us. Y'remember ol' Bill, don't you?"

Bitter Creek grinned. "Sure, we used to ride line together once in a while. Is he really going to join up with you?" B.C. shook his head. "Hard to believe. But maybe not. He didn't like ranching that much if I recall. But one of the best with a gun. He's a good man to have around all right."

"They're all good. And we're looking for more. What do you say?"

Tandy's hand instinctively reached for her throat. "No," she whispered but it had carried to the men.

They turned to her, but all she could do was shake her head.

"Aw c'mon, Tandy," Bob coaxed. "Wouldn't you like a few of them gold coins to spend? Think what you and B.C. could do with a sackful of money. It ain't a bad life, y'know? Not like the stories you hear. We got us a good place to live no one's ever going to find and you won't be alone. There's women there to keep you company. We can always use another, 'specially someone like you."

"I'm not worried about myself," Tandy answered. "My worry is for B.C." Immediately she wished she hadn't mentioned her feelings. She didn't want to embarrass Bitter Creek in front of his friends. But the Daltons seemed to understand.

"Worry is our middle name," Bob smiled reassuringly. "Keeps us on our toes. But we're getting together men we know we can trust and who can take care of themselves. And it's not that we're going to do anytihng bad. You listen to them lawmen and you'll only hear their side of the story. They're getting paid by them politicians, bankers and railroad magnets to make us look bad. But we'll have the people on our side."

"I don't care whose side anyone is on," Tandy said hotly. "All I know is I don't want Bitter Creek getting killed."

There was an awkward silence until Bitter Creek got to his feet. "I think what Tandy is trying to say is we like where we are. It's not that I don't appreciate your offer, Bob. Maybe under other circumstances, I might have accepted. But for now, I can't."

Bob studied his friend for a long while, then shrugged and got to his feet. "So be it. I'm not one to change a set mind. But you'll always be welcomed, y'know that. Anytime. We appreciate you hearing us out and feeding us. Take care."

They were gone just as suddenly and unexpectedly as they had appeared. Tandy knew there had been hurt and disappointment and she eyed Bitter Creek carefully. "Well, I'm glad that's over with." She knew he was thinking about them. "I like them, B.C., but they scare me at the same time."

Her words seemed to have awakened him, for he gave a start and stared over at her. "You don't ever have to be afraid of them," he responded. "You won't find any better friends than them."

His sadness disturbed her. She knelt in front of him. "They're welcome here anytime, you know that. It's just I get scared when they begin talking of you joining up with them."

Bitter Creek ran his fingers through the top of her head, lifting the dark strands in his fingers and absently staring at them. "They're just talking. But it was good to have them visit, I admit that."

There were more visits from the Daltons in the following months. Each time they came, both Bitter Creek and Tandy listened in rapture to their tales: of the first Dalton gang train-holdup near Wharton; of small skirmishes between the gang and the law; of a small bank they robbed in a Kansas town, and, finally, of a clash with a posse. The winter months came, which meant a dispersal of the gang members. It was difficult enough to battle the elements without adding on the chore of robbing banks and being chased by posses.

It was not until early June of the next year that they heard of the Daltons again.

Tandy was outside, kneeling in the middle of her garden, counting each small tip of green that protruded above the broken surface.

"This time we're going to have a good crop of lettuce," she called out over her shoulder to Bitter Creek. "This time I'm smashing every little insect I find."

When she didn't get a response, she turned and saw B.C. concentrating on an approaching horseman. She looked too and her heart fell.

It was Bill Tilghman.

The lawman rode up to them. "M'am!" He touched the brim of his hat to Tandy but gazed straight at Bitter Creek. He made no effort to dismount, certainly no effort to smile or display any recognition of their last meeting. "I'll come right to the point," Tilghman said evenly. "The Daltons are at it again—this time a train at Red Rock."

"Not my doing, marshal," Bitter Creek answered, squinting up to the big man.

"Didn't say it was," came the answer. "But my people are clamping down on them. Hard! We managed to get Charley Bryant and soon we'll catch up to the rest."

"Charley was a good boy, I hear."

"He had a mean streak. Killed a couple of people before he got his. There wasn't much good in him at all."

B.C. shrugged and tucked his thumbs in his belt. "What's all this got to do with us?"

"I know you've been seeing them Daltons. I know for a fact they've been here at least a couple of times." He didn't wait for any objections or denial knowing he wouldn't get any. "I want to get those boys, and I want you to help me."

"No way, Bill." Bitter Creek shook his head. "They're my friends."

"That wasn't an asking," Tilghman stated, his voice hard and even. "It was a telling. You been helping them outlaws and that's agin' the law. You help me out and I'll see to it you don't go to jail."

"Jail?" Tandy gasped. Bitter Creek reached out to stop her.

"You can't lock me up for helping friends, Bill," he said.

"I can and I will. I tried to warn you last time, tried to warn both of you. But now you're in deep trouble and the only way you're going to get out of it is to help me get them boys."

"Damn you, Tilghman," Bitter Creek cried out. "Damned if I'm going to let you bulldog me into setting a trap for my friends."

Tilghman leaned forward, arms over the pommel, and stared down at him. "That's your choice. But it'll mean I'll arrest you."

"No!" Tandy grabbed B.C.'s arm tightly, looked up at the rider, then turned to B.C. with begging eyes. "You can't let him take you to jail, B.C.!"

Bitter Creek stared at her. Slowly he turned back

to Tilghman. "You wouldn't dare take me now," he said softly.

A slow reluctant smile cracked the lawman's face. "You don't know me very well, do you?" he answered.

Tandy shook Bitter Creek. "Please—"

He was torn, hurt and confused. He glared at Tilghman and knew the man was not bluffing. "What do you want me to do?" he asked.

Tilghman straightened in the saddle. "Not that much, really. You just let me know the next time you expect the Daltons to be here, that's all. I'll take care of the rest." He hesitated, glancing from one to the other. "Either one of you can send word to me. I'll make sure they never find out."

"Get the hell out of here, Bill," Bitter Creek said. He was having a difficult time controlling himself.

"Just mark my words,'" Tilghman said as he gathered the reins in his hands. "It's you or them. I'll be waiting." He swung the horse around and left them.

The two stood motionless, spellbound over the incident, absorbed with the slow shrinkage of the rider disappearing into the horizon. Tandy clung to Bitter Creek's arm and after a moment pressed her head into his shoulder.

She murmured. "What are we going to do?"

B.C. shrugged and tried to turn away from her. She held on tightly. "I dunno," he answered sharply. "I just dunno what the hell we're going to do."

"Damn him! Damn him anyhow! Every time he comes to us, he ruins something!"

"That's the law for you," Bitter Creek mumbled absently. "A man's got to do things their way or no way at all. It ain't fair, Tandy. T'ain't fair one bit. I don't like being tied down that way. I don't like people telling me what I can or can't do."

"But what'll we do?"

He shrugged, feeling low and defeated. "I dunno. I can't go against my friends. And damned if I'm going to jail. I just dunno."

Tandy suddenly gripped his arm. "I know. We can head for Texas. I know my brother would welcome us, B.C. And you said you liked him. He's got a big ranch there and we could help him and we'd be away from all of this."

B.C. sighed and looked around. "One thing is for sure," he muttered. "We can't stay here. Ain't safe for either us nor the Daltons."

Tandy looked about her and was saddened. "Oh, my poor poor garden," she whispered. "Just when we got it to grow."

"Shhh, gal," B.C. comforted her. "I'll make it up to you, I promise. I'll make sure you get another garden—a home, a ranch. You'll get everything you always wanted. Tilghman or no Tilghman, we're going to have those things."

"I just want you, B.C.," she answered. "You know that. Can we go to Texas?"

"I dunno. Not yet," he answered as he led her back into the dugout. "Right now I don't know where we'll end up. We gotta get packed and out of here soon as we can. That's our first worry."

Tandy hesitated, her heart thumping in anguish

at the prospect of their leaving. She watched B.C. move about the room, trying to decide what to take and what could be left. She knew she couldn't press him. She knew Texas would be the right direction for them to take. Yet, underneath all her hopes, she knew he wasn't the kind to leave without seeing his friends one more time.

She sighed. Maybe, just maybe, there was still hope. There was always hope, she told herself. Besides, how much more excitement could a girl ask for than to be led into the hideout of the most celebrated outlaw gang the territory had ever known?

6

The part of the Cherokee strip that Bitter Creek took her to was unfamiliar to Tandy. The area was rugged and thick-wooded, cut ages ago by the Cimarron River snaking its way across the landscape. There was a maze of gullies and crevices, small canyons and deep cuts which would have confused most riders.

"We used to come here after a roundup," Bitter Creek explained as he followed some unmarked trail only he knew. "It's a good place to let loose and relax."

The trail was quiet and restful, with many trees along it offering a welcome shade from the hot sun. Here and there, thick underbrush camouflaged hidden caves and niches. Outlaws could hole up in those caves, Tandy thought; they seemed ideal places for refuge, since no lawman in his right mind would dare to venture into this wilderness.

A sharp turn into what seemed a high embankment suddenly disclosed still another opening in the high walls. The avenue was narrow, with barely enough room for horse and rider. Once in it, Tandy saw clearly where horses had beaten down the undergrowth and pushed aside bushes. The signs indicated they were near their destination.

The trail suddenly opened up into a glen, an almost breathtaking amphitheater of rock and trees. A large fan-shaped rock archway to one side, Tandy saw, led into a natural cave, wide and deep. The smell of horses and smoke hit her. She looked around at B.C., slightly dazed at the unexpected magnificence of this clearing.

Bitter Creek twisted in the saddle and grinned. "We're here!"

From trees all around, men suddenly came running, whooping and hollering at the sight of Bitter Creek. Some were strangers to her, but Tandy instantly recognized all three Daltons, which put her mind at ease.

As the men gathered about, seemingly oblivious to her, she inspected them, unconsciously smiling along with everyone else. It was like a homecoming; she felt very good about Bitter Creek's obvious popularity among the men. Most had exchanged the usual cowboy garb of levis and leather vest for button-collar shirts and dark grey suit pants. They were all young, Bitter Creek's age, and a few just as handsome.

"Y'finally came to your senses, huh?" Bob Dalton pounded Bitter Creek on the back and grinned widely. "You're a mite late for the celebration, but we're happy you made it this far."

Tandy noted one particular cowboy in a black suit and white stetson who kept hanging onto B.C.'s arm and slapping him on the back. "You ol' hot dog," the man kept repeating happily, "Bob done tol' me you was around, but I swear I never 'spected seeing ya this soon." He was a handsome one, slimmer and taller than B.C., and his eyes were bright with pleasure. "By God, you sure enough missed a big one."

Tandy was amused and waited patiently on her mount. It wasn't too much of a wait, however. Pretty soon, B.C. pulled himself away and turned to her. "Hey girl, get down and meet some good ol' boys."

They all backed away, bashful now, like little boys at their first hoedown. Tandy dismounted and came forward. A bit nervous among these strangers, she was quickly put to ease by their friendly smiles.

"Want you to meet the best rail-splitter in these parts," Bitter Creek said. He was obviously hinting at some inside joke since most of the men laughed. "This here is Bill Doolin." With that, B.C. pulled forward the white-hatted cowboy who had been hanging onto his sleeve. "This here is my girl, Tandy."

Doolin made a fast appraisal of her, then suddenly stuck out his hand. "Any friend of my ol' buddy here is indeed a friend of mine. And being the prettiest friend ol' George ever had, I hope to be the best friend you will ever have."

Tandy hoped her face wasn't too red. It took her a while to disengage her hand from his clasp. "Your words are mighty bewitching, Mr. Doolin, I'm sure. But I do have a question to ask of you."

"Ask away, little lady," the outlaw answered genially. He seemed pleased she was taking an interest in him so soon.

"Why did B.C. say you were a rail-splitter?"

Though this brought even louder gaffaws from the surrounding men, Doolin's smile never cracked. "Well, you see, when Bitter Creek and me worked for ol' man Halsell, he needed someone with a steady hand and a good eye. He naturally picked me over them other cross-eyed varmints. I could split a rail straighter than the railroad can lay a track. 'Course I can do them other things but rail-splittin' is the thing they's most jealous of."

All laughed and Bitter Creek jabbed a playful fist into Doolin's shoulders. "When he came out here, 'bout the only thing he could do worth writing home about was chopping wood. Everything else he had to learn from us."

Doolin shrugged and winked at Tandy. "So if you see any flaws in my performances, you'll know who to blame."

Bob Dalton stepped forward and said seriously, "It's good to see both of you here, Tandy." He stepped back to introduce the others. "This little runt is Dick Broadwell. I think he's even younger than you and Lord knows he's gotta lot of learning to do. The big one behind you is Bill Powers." Powers held himself back from the others; he alone acknowledged her presence with a mere nod.

Doolin came up and grabbed her hand again.

"C'mon, little lady, I want you to meet my woman." Reluctantly, Tandy let him pull her up a small slope to the ledge entrance of the big cave. Halfway there, she stopped in her tracks. Standing on the ledge, hands on hips, was a woman who looked more than anything else like a weathered version of her mother. In fact, from her theatrical posture, Tandy thought at first it *was* Miranda, which made her gasp in disbelief. Then she saw the tougher, deeply tanned skin on this woman's face—as if she'd lived all her life outdoors—and Tandy's illusion faded.

But, Tandy mused as she approached the ledge, the woman was beautiful like Miranda; that was for sure. She had long black hair, keen dark eyes and high cheekbones that hinted at a trace of upper-plains Indian blood. Even in her full riding skirt and loose-fitting blouse, the grace of her mature figure was apparent.

Tandy knew she was being closely inspected in return and was uncomfortable. A feeling of competitiveness and jealousy arose in her, which she had difficulty coping with.

"I'm Tandy Girondin," she introduced herself and stuck out her hand, perhaps too eagerly.

The woman glanced down with an amused smile, put out her hand and allowed Tandy to shake it.

"This here is Rose," Doolin said after it became obvious the woman was not ready to speak.

"Just Rose?"

The woman shrugged. "Rose will do." Her voice was low and husky, and Tandy knew instantly she would have to try and copy it. It sounded exciting and very desirous. She wondered whether B.C. would be so affected.

"Have you been here long?" Tandy was curious and wanted desperately to find some avenue of approach.

"You mean this cave?" Rose looked around her with a strange smile on her lips. "Yeah, I been here a long time." She looked at Doolin for confirmation.

"Yeah," he answered and squinted to recall. "I come with Bob and Emmett early part of ninety-one. And you and Bob broke up—" He stopped and glanced nervously at Rose, then at Tandy. His voice dropped. "Yeah—'bout a year I guess." He turned and went back down the path to join the men now lounging on the grass.

Rose chuckled as she watched him go. "Bill's still touchy about Bob and me. He's hard to figure at times." She glanced at Tandy and saw the questioning look. "Bob's the one who brought me here," she explained with a sigh. "He's a good man but the problem with him is he's too hot in the pants, know what I mean?" Rose took another look and smiled at Tandy's wide-eyed expression. She felt she had to explain further. "He's hungry for women, gal. You better watch it when your man is gone. Ol' Bob will try getting under your skirts for sure. He likes young ones." There was a slight edge of bitterness in her voice.

Tandy shook her head. "I don't want anyone else." This woman made her feel so immature she didn't know whether she felt shame or anger.

Rose laughed and came forward to put an arm

around Tandy's shoulder. "Don't take me too seriously. I guess you and me better get along 'cause we're outnumbered by them men."

Reluctantly, Tandy allowed herself to be drawn back into the cave. "I'm not sure how long we're going to stay here," she said timidly.

"I thought Bitter Creek came to join up with us," Rose said. She sounded surprised.

Tandy shrugged her shoulders. "I dunno. Marshal Tilghman gave us no choice."

Rose chuckled. "Welcome to the club. The law has pushed us all together. You two are better off here than anywhere else I know."

"I have a brother in Texas we thought we'd go to."

"Texas? You going to let someone run you out of the territory?" She looked over with a frown of disapproval. "What are you going to think of your man if he runs away with his tail between his legs? You ever think of that? I mean, I don't know much about Bitter Creek, but he doesn't strike me as the kind that takes kindly to running away from anything. None of these cowpokes are. They're fighters—fight for what they believe in, fight for the fun of it too."

"They don't look violent."

Rose shook her head. "Not that kind of fighting, although you can bet your bloomers they can take care of themselves. I'm talking 'bout standing up to those who push and bully their way into this territory."

Tandy understood. "You mean the railroads and politicians."

"And banks, and anyone else who thinks they're better than us. The law too!"

"Then you like this way of life?"

"Like it?" Rose laughed. "I love it! You will too. Where else can you do as you please whenever you please? And where else can you tell them dudes to go shove it? I go out there with them boys and I shout out I'm Rose of Cimarron and you all better watch your step or I'm likely to squash you under my foot. Do you realize what a good feeling that is?"

Tandy breathed heavily and shook her head. It was fascinating, what she'd just heard, and her heart beat fast. She was envious of Rose.

"Well, c'mon," Rose said. "We'll see what we can fix up for you and your man."

The cave was broad and deep with crevices in the rock walls deep enough to make for small sleeping quarters. Rose showed Tandy around, pointing out a curtained crevice as her and Doolin's and suggesting another Tandy might pick for herself and B.C. The rest of the cave was shared by the single men, who took turns sleeping on the outside ledge so as to keep close watch on the trail and the horses. All the horses were tethered in sheds at the far side of the glen, near a natural spring they could drink from. Also at that side of the glen, Tandy noted, was an open-pitted privy with a beaten path from the cave leading to it.

After a while, coaxed by Rose, the men started

bringing up the sacks of provisions and household things Bitter Creek and Tandy had brought. Under Doolin's supervision and with considerable horseplay, they put a makeshift curtain up to block off their bedroom and left.

For a moment Tandy found herself alone with her things. A straw-filled mat would serve just fine for their bed, she figured. She sat down on it and surveyed her new quarters, trying to appraise what else would be needed to make the place into a home. But it was too soon for that; the initial sights and sounds of this fresh adventure were still with her. She smelled Rose's cooking outside. Hastily she got up, took time to place their things in neat piles, then went out to see if she could help.

Rose smiled when she saw her. "You'll be a relief," she said. "I don't mind cooking, but I can sure use someone to take over once in a while."

"I don't mind cooking either," Tandy said timidly.

Rose nodded and pointed out where she kept utensils and supplies.

"Don't hesitate to ask the men to cut firewood when you need it," she said. "That's the least they can do to help us out. Can you write?" When Tandy nodded, Rose eyed her critically. "Lucky for you. Tell you what. I'll let you keep track of things we run out of. When the list gets big enough, we give it to one of the guys and he goes over to Ingalls and gets whatever we need."

"Who pays for it?"

Rose smiled. "Bob sets aside so much money for

supplies after each job. It's up to us to make sure he knows how much we need."

Tandy nodded with every word, hoping she would remember everything told to her. "Do you ever go with them? On a job, I mean?"

"Go with them? They damn well better not try to leave without me," Rose answered. "I wouldn't miss that kind of excitement for all the sex in the world—know what I mean? And now that you're with us, maybe I'll get to do more than just hold the horses."

"You mean handle a gun?"

"Hell," Rose said with a thin smile. "I've used guns lots."

"Against someone?"

"Nearly killed a man once. He had it coming." Rose kept busy preparing the evening meal. "Don't you worry, after the first few times, you'll get used to it."

"I doubt it."

"Why not?" Rose stepped back, wiped her chin with a wet elbow and looked at Tandy curiously.

Tandy breathed deeply. "I think I'd be too scared."

"Nothing to be scared about," Rose answered, shrugging. "Bob plans it all out and he's a genius. I tell you, he could figure a way for us to steal Tilghman's teeth in broad daylight if he set his mind to it."

Oh my gosh, Tandy thought. What had she gotten herself into? She glanced towards the men sitting bunched together nearby; every once in a while they laughed out loud at some story being told. She wondered if maybe Bitter Creek hadn't already been persuaded to join the band.

Her face felt hot and she fanned herself. What would her mother think of her if she knew she was camped with the notorious Dalton gang? And what would she think if she actually participated in one of their robberies? Tandy couldn't bear thinking about it.

The dinner turned out to be one of the most enjoyable Tandy had ever had. She found herself liking everybody, except maybe Bill Powers. As when she'd first met Powers he sat moodily apart from the others, speaking very little, certainly not enjoying himself. Tandy decided to ignore him, much like the others were doing.

Halfway into the meal, Bill Doolin prompted Bob Dalton. "Go ahead and tell ole Bitter Creek 'bout our next job, Bob."

Dalton rarely needed coaxing to go center stage. He shifted forward on his knees and told of his plans as if he were about to lead a gang of boys in a game of hide-and seek. "There's a train comes through Adair regular. From what we hear, she carries a pile of money on her. The station is at the end of town close to trees, about the best cover we could ask for. We've been laying low for over a month now, and the way I figure it, they's getting tired of waiting for us. Which means it's a good time for us to show up and catch them by surprise."

Bitter Creek shook his head. "I been hearing

them trains are loaded with guards hoping to get you."

"Whoeee!" Doolin slapped his side. "We may get a little action yet!"

Bob reached over to shake B.C. out of his worried mood.

"There's nothing to be fretting 'bout. Them trains are hiring Indian police, and we know they can't hit nothing if they stuck a muzzle in your stomach." Bob grinned.

"The question is," Bill Powers spoke up sullenly and they all turned to him in surprise, "does the train have enough money on it to make it worth our while to take them chances?"

"Geez, Bill," Grat declared, "ain't no way in hell knowing such things for sure. We just know what we hear. It's the chance we have to take once in a while. Bob ain't led us wrong yet, has he?"

Powers grumbled, more to himself than out loud. "I just don't aim to be facing bullets for no empty safe."

"Everybody knows that railroad takes plenty of money between the east and Texas. We ain't never hit them so chances are they're carrying a goodly amount. We've done pretty good so far, haven't we? And we ain't got hurt, have we?"

"What about Charlie Bryant?" Powers asked bitterly.

Bob scowled. "Charlie wasn't with us when he got caught. You know damn well none of us are responsible once someone leaves camp."

Rose broke the silence that followed. "You haven't failed us yet, Bob. My bones tell me the plan is a good one."

"Heck, yes," Doolin insisted. "We're the best there is and we can do anything we set out to." He grinned over at Bitter Creek. "And now with B.C. here, we got us an army better even than the Jameses or Youngers."

Some cheers went up and Tandy's breath caught.

Bob said quietly, barely containing his excitement, "How 'bout it, B.C.? You here to join us, ain't you?"

Bitter Creek licked his lips and glanced about at them. "I know you're the best there is, as well as the best friends I could hope for. We came here 'cause you're all friends. Its just, I don't know whether I should go that road."

Again, it was Rose who spoke up. "Why not give it a try? Bob can set you up where you won't have to do much. Just sort of watch and see if you like it. In fact," and she put an arm around Tandy and smiled, "you both could probably help out. You two are a team, aren't you?"

Tandy was won over instantly. She felt she'd steal the suspenders off Tilghman's pants if Rose asked her to the way she just did. She turned to Bitter Creek and nodded hesitantly. It was half a question and half a statement.

Bitter Creek seemed relieved and his mouth broadened into a wide smile. "Maybe we could do that—sort of see how things go."

"That'a boy." Doolin leaned over and gripped

B.C.'s arm. "We'll put iron into your back and make you six feet tall, you ole rascal! You wait and see—ain't nothing like you've ever experienced before!"

Bob Dalton didn't say anything. He just grinned.

7

Tandy could scarcely believe she was doing it. Atop a buckboard, she had driven from the cave to the outskirts of this little town. With the gang riding behind her, she felt like a mother hen with chicks under her wings. It was dusk and Bob had planned their arrival well. Before them, barely discernible, were the outbuildings of the small village, smoke curling from the chimneys of the bigger homes, dull lights fanning out every once in a while. All was silent and serene.

"This is where we part," Bob said at her side. His voice was low and serious, no more laughing and joking. He pointed the direction for Tandy. "Keep on this fork and you'll find a crossing to get you over the tracks. Then circle around. Keep far enough away so you're as much in the dark as possible but close enough so you can see us. Shouldn't be any trouble spotting the station."

He glanced about him, then leaned over his saddle to her. "Train ain't due for an hour, so don't fret none, even if you hear some noises. The train will come from there." He pointed. "Right behind the engine there's usually just one express car—looks like a box with only a few windows and big doors. There could be two or more even, I dunno. But you watch them doors. As soon as one swings open on your side, that'll be your signal to bring the wagon in. When you do, make sure the horses are headed toward the engine, get it? And stay away from the passenger cars." He tried to study her face in the dark. "Okay?"

All Tandy could do was nod her head, biting her lips in nervous excitement. It was like some dream. She knew she was there, yet felt as if she were floating on air.

Bob nodded his head and tried for an assuring smile. "We'll tell you when to get. All you have to do is come back the way you went. We'll catch up to you soon enough. That's all there is to it."

"Will there be shooting?" she asked timidly.

This time he smiled. "Apt to be, I reckon. But none to worry you 'bout. The shooting will be at us on the other side of the train. 'Sides, you keep that bonnet on and no one will ever shoot at you!"

The riders watched her disappear into the darkness, listened for the buckboard sound to ebb away, then turned to concentrate on the village before them. Having gone over their instructions on the way to Adair, there was little need for talk. Rose and Bitter Creek slowly edged their horses to Bob's side and watched with him.

"No one's ever seen your faces so you should be

able to ride through with no trouble," Bob said in a low tone. "Take your time riding through and keep your eyes open. If there seems to be extra people around, 'specially at the station, turn around and come back."

"You think they might be waiting for us?" Bitter Creek asked.

"Never can tell. I doubt it though. Once you get there, try to keep the station agent busy 'til we get there. We'll be behind you shortly."

Rose and Bitter Creek went first, followed five minutes later by the six other riders. If the citizens of Adair gave much note to the new arrivals, they spoke of them passingly and only among themselves. It was a warm evening and the older people were out on their porches, smoking, talking in subdued voices or just rocking in their chairs, content to rest and watch the night come on.

The three Daltons rode side by side down the one small street that divided all of Adair's few stores and homes. The only place open for business was the saloon, which spewed yellow light onto the dusty road and cast the brothers' large elongated shadows on it as they rode by. Behind the Daltons rode Bill Doolin, Broadwell and Powers, matching slow-footed gaits. They wore their hats low over their foreheads even though chances were slim that people could identify them in the night. No onlooker bothered trying. It wasn't that unusual for travelers to come into town just before the train was scheduled to arrive.

The station, with its boarding platform, was dimly lit from the agent's office. It was the agent's last call of the day, the 9:45 "Katy." He had already eaten his supper and had returned a good hour and a half before the train's arrival to check out the cartons and crates that would be placed aboard the express. He wasn't surprised that no one had come to buy a passenger ticket, just a little downhearted since he could have used the extra commission on his earnings. His face quickly lit up as he lifted his head and saw the couple who'd begun to tap on his window.

"Evenin!" The agent left his cartons, went over and sat down at his stool, instinctively lifting the window and reaching for a pad of tickets.

Bitter Creek grinned and leaned forward. "Train on time tonight?" he asked casually.

The agent glanced behind him at the clock and sighed. Almost everyone asked the same question. How should he know? It came when it came. "No trouble down the line," he said pleasantly. "Should be on time." He turned back to B.C. and waited patiently.

Bitter Creek smiled back and hesitated, "Uh, me and my woman," he turned slightly so the agent could see the figure of Rose in the shadows behind him, "was wondering how much it'll cost to get us to Guthrie."

An easy question. Now that Guthrie was the territorial capital, many wanted to stop off there. Even though he knew the answer, the agent, by habit, made some notations on a pad. "You want a return trip?" He was conscious of the back door opening but gave it little mind as he did his calculations.

Bitter Creek smiled. "Uh, just make that one return. That's one one-way and one round-trip."

The agent nodded and redid his figures. He had found people were less likely to balk at the cost if they thought he was doing good arithmetic. He squirmed on the stool and then suddenly realized that something was sticking into his back. He froze and slowly looked up at Bitter Creek, who was still grinning at him through the window.

"Just take it easy and you'll be able to go home tonight no less for wear." Grat Dalton whispered into the agent's ear and brought his handgun into view over his shoulder. He twisted the man around on the stool so that he could get a better view of the others in the office. The agent found six Winchesters pointed at him.

"Jesus Christ!" was all he could manage.

Grat chuckled. "T'ain't none of us him. You'll have to guess again." Before the man could answer, Grat lifted him to his feet and pushed him to a corner bench. Two of the other men came forward with ropes; before long, the agent was hogtied and gagged.

"How much more time?" Bob asked as he began opening drawers.

Bitter Creek and Rose had come into the room. They all began methodically to dig into the packages and boxes. "Got 'bout half an hour according to the clock," Bitter Creek said.

Emmett had found a burlap sack which he placed in the middle of the floor. As the boxes were inspected, things that were wanted were placed into the sack, the rest thrown into a corner far from the agent. Rose was estatic over a porcelain chamber pot she unwrapped. Bob, inspecting it, gave it back to her. "We don't need that," he said flatly.

"But it will look pretty," Rose protested. She wrapped it up again and placed it in the sack.

"Christ!" Bob snorted. "We're going to have enough to do without fretting whether we'll break that dumb thing or not."

"Aw, c'mon," Doolin said. "If she wants it, why not take it? Free, ain't it?" Frowning, he began inspecting a set of Charles Dickens books he found. "What's a cooperfield?" he said. "No, wait. Copperfield."

The agent thought they were all crazy.

Ten minutes later, his office was in shambles. The Daltons had left nothing untouched. The sack was full, as was a small wooden crate and a separate box Rose had found for her porcelain commode and a set of dishes that had come from the Sears mail-order company. For a few moments after she packed the dishes, Rose stood and studied an advertisement from Sears that had come with them. It was for sewing needles and it began, "An Astonishing Offer." Finally Rose shrugged and slipped the advertisement into her bodice.

Satisfied they had taken everything of value, Bob said, "Okay, let's go out and wait."

There was a gentle breeze from the north as they

came out of the station building. Glancing towards both ends of the track, they could see the silver lines snake off into the night. The sack and boxes were placed on the platform close to the rail. Then, slowly, one by one, they drifted apart and took up positions in chairs and benches along the building's side.

Bitter Creek, heels of his boots hooked over the bottom rung of his chair, leaned back with his Winchester across his lap. Squinting out into the dark, he wondered whether Tandy was somewhere out there watching them. He twisted his head and stared at his comrades in silence.

"You still with us, George?" Bob Dalton's voice cut into the night from the bench nearest him.

"Still with you, Bob," B.C. answered. He was surprised that everything had gone so smoothly and at how calm he felt.

"Soon as the train comes, you go out over the other side. When it stops, you get the engineer. Broadwell, you come up on this side to help out. Rose, you stay back here until we get the express door open. Let us know if any of the passengers decide to get out." Bob's voice was urgent but confident; they could have been talking about rounding up Halsell's cattle for all their danger seemed to matter to him.

Broadwell and Powers took out cigars and lit them, eyeing the stars, their minds on other things. It was peaceful and quiet and the minutes passed by ever so slowly. Time was of no consequence to them. It felt good to sit and relax, not to worry, not to think.

Bitter Creek was the only who jumped at the far-off sound of the train whistle. The others glanced his way and he felt ashamed that he had displayed his nervousness. He leaned back against the building.

The whistle echoed again. To their right, a faint glow began to expand as the train made its approach. At Bob's nod, Bitter Creek stood up, moved casually across the platform and jumped down across the tracks to disappear into the darkness on the other side. The others hardly moved. Broadwell and Powers, puffing on their cigars, watched all the way as the engine roared into the station. For a moment only its headlight spotlighted them. Then, as if concentrating on something beyond them, it steamed past, then slowed and finally came to a halt.

The two rose in unison, Broadwell stepping quickly toward the cab. The rest spread out, waiting for some movement.

As soon as the engine came to a halt, Bitter Creek grabbed the cab's metal railing, swung himself up to the step and lifted his Winchester into the startled faces of the fireman and engineer. At the same moment, Broadwell swung up behind their backs and pushed them silently against the controls. He patted their middles, then looked elsewhere for weapons. A handgun was strapped to the side of the window. Broadwell untied it and threw it into the darkness over B.C.'s head.

"You okay?" he asked with a boyish grin.

Bitter Creek nodded, not daring to take his eyes from the two trainmen. He motioned for the two to sit down, then sided over next to Broadwell and took a glance back down the platform to see what was happening.

Two men carrying lanterns were approaching. One was obviously a conductor. The other was a dark-skinned porter. Behind them walked Grat, with a gun.

"I better go help the other boys out," Broadwell whispered to B.C. He watched for a moment until he saw that Grat had the two new trainmen neatly prone at the side of the building. Then he jumped from the cab and trotted towards the express car.

Bob butted his rifle stock against the express car's wide door. "Hey, in there, open up," he barked.

There was a scuffling inside and someone called out, "Is that you, Frank?"

"No, this ain't Frank," Bob answered sharply. "It's a hold-up man. Now open up this goddamn door."

There was a moment of silence. "I can't do that," came the nervous answer.

"Jesus Christ!" Bob fumed. "Emmett, go get us some lamps." Then to the door: "Listen in there! We don't want no harm to come to anyone. But we aim to get into this car one way or t'other. Now, open up and you won't get hurt." Again there was silence.

Emmett returned with three kerosene lanterns and Bob ordereed them lit. As soon as they were, he grabbed one and held it close to his rifle. "Take a look, in there! We mean business out here. You can open that door and live to tell about it, or keep it closed and we'll dynamite it open. 'Course, there's no telling what condition you'll be in after the explosion. What's it to be?"

He waited, then sighed. "All right then, we do it the hard way. Ain't going to be our fault if you lose a leg or arm." He motioned to Doolin and Broadwell who slipped under the express car and began to tap their rifle butts gently on the metal strutting.

"Y'hear that, brave one?" Bob called out. "We're ready to light the fuse. Sure you won't change your mind?" He waited again, frowning. "You want us to know where we can ship your parts to?"

Again there was silence, then a shuffling as the door rattled. "No, wait!" a shaking voice called out. The door slid open.

The man had no sooner stuck his head out than Powers grabbed him and pulled him roughly out onto the platform.

"Y'all come over here now and join some folks," Grat drawled, sticking his head out from the side of the building. He beckoned with his gun and the man, getting an encouraging tap on his shoulder from Powers, steadily walked Grat's way.

Instantly, Bob and Emmett were inside the dimly lit express car. Rose came forward quickly and Doolin helped boost her in too.

"Whoeee," Bob exclaimed as he opened the metal cash box. "We done struck a gold mine." The others immediately began rummaging through the boxes and sacks that were stacked in the back of the car.

"Hurry up," Powers shouted from the platform. Nervously, he eyed the end passenger cars, fearing that the train's spending too much time at this small-town station would result in somebody back there getting suspicious. Sure enough, the next to last car's lights turned brighter. Suddenly, a man put his head out the window and looked their way.

"We been spotted," Powers yelled and raised his rifle. His shot shattered the window just above the man, who instantly ducked for cover. Then, abruptly, all the windows in the car were lifted and the glint of rifle barrels danced in the night.

"Christ! We got a fuckin' army back there!" Powers shouted. He dove under the wheels of the express car as a fusillade of bullets sprayed the platform.

Bitter Creek, up front in the engine cab, gave his two captives a look warning them to behave, then rested his carbine on the tender and returned the fire. From his viewpoint, it seemed every window held at least two rifles. Smoke and noise blasted the countryside. Everybody, Daltons and their surprise attackers, was shooting at the same time.

Bitter Creek ducked down to reload and shot a glance down the street. Several Adair people were trotting up to see what was happening, oldsters among them. Bitter Creek swore. The next volley from the passenger cars kicked up dust pockets in the street, and a couple of the Adair people cried out in pain and fell. Frantically, Bitter Creek waved for the rest to get out of the line of fire. Then he returned to concentrate on helping his comrades.

"How much more time you need?" Doolin yelled into the express car. He kept trading shots as he spoke.

"We just found another strong box," Bob yelled back gleefully. "We've hit a bonanza here!"

"Well, you don't have time to count it, damn it," Doolin swore. "These folks are bad shots, but sooner or later one of us is going to get hurt."

"Keep them back there and there ain't nothing to fret 'bout," came Bob's cheery answer.

"There's some coming from the other side!" Broadwell warned. He skipped between two cars to the train's rail side and began firing at some figures who were running up in a low crouch. A few well-aimed warning bullets sent them scurrying back towards the end of the train.

All along Grat, some distance off with his three trainmen captives, had been impatient to get in the action. Broadwell's last few shots made up his mind for him. "You all promise not to take part in this and you can go inside and get safe," he yelled at the three. Without answering, they got to their feet and scampered into the station. Glowering, Grat watched them go, then came running to join his brothers.

"Okay," Bob yelled down. "We're going to bring Tandy in." Jumping to the express car's far side, he, Emmett and Rose slid open its heavy wide door and let a pan of light spread over the countryside.

Meanwhile, Doolin edged over next to Broadwell and kept up a volley of shots designed to drive their attackers back into the passenger car. Penned up behind windows, unable to shoot rifles without exposing their entire arms, shoulders and faces, the attackers took to using handguns, which at the distance created more noise and bother than danger. Only the gang's patience was needed to quell such a nuisance.

Tandy's wagon appeared out of the darkness and rolled up close to the express car on the far embankment. Both horses and driver were scared; Tandy, her hands full with the reins, was at the same time cowering from the fusillade of pistol shots coming in her general direction. Then, when she saw how well Broadwell and Doolin were handling the situation, she stopped trembling and got ready for the business at hand.

Emmett jumped down and ran to the wagon. Things were thrown to him from the express car.

"What about my commode?" Rose yelled. "I'll be damned if I'll throw that."

"Oh geez," Emmett muttered and ran back to be handed the box it was in.

"Careful, don't break it," Rose screamed. Emmett gave her a hard look. "You sure there's nothing else you want?" he asked. "Damn it, woman, carry the thing yourself—just get out of here quick with it!"

Rose nodded, took the box and ran off to join

Tandy in the wagon. On a brief nod from her, Tandy flicked the whip, and the two women sped away.

Meanwhile, Emmett jumped back into the car with Bob, soon to be joined by the rest of the gang with the exception of Bitter Creek. Bob looked them over. "Anyone get hit?" he asked.

"Are you kidding?" Doolin grinned. "You were right. Them Injun police can spit straighter than they can shoot."

"Thank your stars for that," Bob smiled.

"Where's Rose?"

"She went with Tandy," Bob reported. "We'll give 'em a few minutes, then get out ourselves." They went on light duty, taking turns at keeping the guards in the passenger cars pinned down with well-aimed rifle shots from the siding. After a while the return fire diminished, then just about ceased. Several more minutes passed before Bob rolled over on his stomach and smiled. "Appears they've run out of ammunition," he said. "Let's go count the money."

Without waiting for an answer, he jumped from the car and made his way swiftly to the front end of the station where the horses were tied. The others quickly followed, firing backwards as they ran. Once mounted, they reloaded their guns under the protection of the building, then galloped to the engine, bringing B.C.'s mount with them.

"Mighty obliged you letting us use your train for a while," Bitter Creek grinned down at the two captives. "Maybe next time we can have a longer chat." He winked at the two, then leaped from the cab onto his saddle.

"Yaihiii," he yelled at the top of his lungs. The others shouted in like manner, shooting their guns into the air as the horses pranced around in the confusion. Then off they rode, following the tracks until they reached a dirt crossroad. A mile to the left on that road, Tandy and Rose were waiting in the darkness. Veering that way, they galloped in a close bunch, still whooping and congratulating themselves.

Bitter Creek was yelling the loudest. He was still releasing tension he hadn't realized he'd been under throughout the robbery. It felt good to let it out. He was thankful it was dark. He hoped his friends would think he was shouting just out of his joy at their getting away with so much money.

But the robbery had meant more than money to him. This was the first time he had dished out the sort of medicine the railroads had forced him to swallow. Let them start their own score against him! Who cared? It was his turn now, by God. It felt good getting in his licks, damn good!

8

As was his habit after raids, Bob Dalton temporarily disbanded the gang once the Adair holdup money had been divided up. Broadwell and Powers went back to the Halsell ranch and hired out as line riders. The Dalton boys themselves chanced a visit to their folks' homestead not too far away. Bill Doolin's folks lived a couple days ride into Kansas but Bill had no inclination to visit them. " 'Sides, I got my Rose here," he said. So the four of them—Tandy, B.C., Doolin and Rose—found themselves left together to pass the next few months in the cave alone.

They were all in fine spirits. Each had a full share of the $17,000 that had been taken at Adair. Bitter Creek and Tandy figured they were in a good position to save theirs, having no appreciable expenses at the moment. They talked it over privately one night on their pallet.

"We'll have enough soon so's we can go to Texas maybe and buy us a spread. No more claiming or anything like that," B.C. whispered. "We'll get us money to buy us proper things, enough so we won't have to borrow from no bank nor be under no obligation to no one."

As for Rose's and Doolin's plans, Bill had no compunctions about announcing them publicly. "Maybe we'll save enough to go to Chicago—or maybe even all the way to New York," he said while they were eating supper one night. "I'd like to see all them places you see in the *Gazette*. Or maybe we'll have enough to take us on a boat trip to all them places in Europe."

He said it wistfully and there was silence as he chewed. Tandy recognized the statement for what it was—Bill's wishful thinking. She looked at Rose and said quietly. "Where do you want to go if you have the chance?"

The older woman shrugged. "I'm where I want to be. I don't think I'd like all them crowds of people around me."

"You don't want to see all those tall buildings and shops and stage shows?"

"I've seen all I care to see. There's plenty of excitement right here; I don't need to go no place else. I figure Bill and me—well, no matter what he says, we have plenty of good times right here, especially after we come back from a job. That not so, Bill?" She nudged him and winked, and Doolin grinned sheepishly.

Tandy felt herself blushing. She knew perfectly well what Rose meant. She had heard their carryings on only a few feet away. Her one regret was that Doolin and Rose weren't hearing hers and B.C.'s. Oh, she knew Bitter Creek got excited at times. She could feel his heart pound and sense him squirming around when Rose and Doolin started up. But when she tried to press close to him, he would threaten to move away.

Tandy studied Rose, wondering if she could help her. Surely Rose would know how she could arouse B.C. But dare she confide in her? It would be embarrassing, but what she was losing in time alone—goodness, it was *precious*.

She sighed. She'd just have to get up the nerve to ask Rose for help. But it turned out to be even more difficult than she'd thought. Few were the times when the two women were left alone long enough, for a heart-to-heart talk. Bitter Creek and Doolin, with little to do while they holed up from the law, hung around the cave most of the time, talking, whittling, cleaning their weapons, generally just making nuisances of themselves as far as Rose was concerned.

Tandy's opportunity didn't come until late August, on a booming hot day that began by driving them all deeper into the cave for its coolness. By mid-day, however, even the cave had heated unbearably, and Rose had had enough.

She stood up and, arms akimbo, stared down at the two lounging men. "Okay, you two. Us women need some privacy. I for one am going to take a standin' bath, so I don't want either of you hanging around. Scat out of here. Go take a swim in the river or something—just give Tandy and me some breathing room."

Doolin looked at B.C. and B.C. looked at Doolin. Wordlessly, they shrugged and stood. "River suit you?" Doolin said. "Hell, yes, it's wet," B.C. said grudgingly.

"And don't come back 'til dusk, y'hear?" Rose called after them as they left. She shook her head and grinned as she turned to Tandy. "Hope you don't mind, honey, but I even get edgy undressing in front of ol' Bill."

Tandy's smile wavered a bit. She drew in a deep breath and told herself to be firm and get it done with. The moment had come!

But not yet. She couldn't find the words. Out of the corner of her eye she watched Rose drag out two large flat metal basins from her room and set them side by side in the middle of the cave.

"This is going to feel mighty good," Rose said agreeably. "Here now, you take these buckets and fill them from the water barrel. They're heavy and you're young, so better you than me."

Tandy filled the buckets and returned with them. She watched Rose pour in the water for their baths.

"Don't you ever bath or swim in the river?" she asked timidly. "I've never seen you do that."

Rose stopped and smiled at her. "I don't put much of a limit on what I do, honey, but I do draw the line showing myself off naked to any man happening to be riding by. It's bad enough with what men got in them. You don't want to make things worse by flaunting yourself, you know," she chuckled. "I'm strictly a one-man-at-a-time woman, not like them whores you hear about."

"But you've known many men."

There was an amused smile on Rose's lips as she stood back after filling the basins. "I see they been talking about me." She sighed. "I've known my share," she admitted.

Tandy hesitated. "Do you mind my asking you something personal?"

Rose shrugged.

"Bittter Creek says your ma was Calamity Jane." It came out more as a blunt statement than a question but Tandy still waited for an answer.

Rose almost burst out laughing. "Honey, you don't really care about that, do you?"

"I do, Rose."

Rose shrugged. Only for an instant did her eyes dim as she tried to recall her past. "It's what I was told," she then answered matter of factly. She sat on a stool, feet far apart, lifted her skirts above her knees and fanned herself. "I was raised by people in Kansas," she said. "They told me Calamity dropped me off at their house one day—couldn't be strapped down by no child, she told 'em." Rose stared at her hands lying loosely on her lap.

Tandy saw she was more deeply affected than she pretended to be. "Gosh, Calamity Jane is a legend," said slowly. Then she was sorry she'd said even that, and tried to make amends. "I bet you've seen and met all sorts of interesting people," she added brightly.

Rose laughed, amused at Tandy's curiosity. "I've been on my own lots longer than you been," she said. "And I guess you're right—I've met my fair share of interesting epople. I remember once when Hickok and me—"

Tandy let out a gasp. "You knew Wild Bill Hickok?" she exclaimed.

Rose looked surprised that she'd been doubted. "We hooked up a bit when he was down at Dodge City. I was pretty young then but we hit it off pretty good for a couple of weeks."

"Why, I can't believe it. I never knew anyone who had even seen Wild Bill."

"Hell, honey, I knew 'em all and probably more. I didn't keep track of names back then." She laughed at Tandy's look of amazement. "Hell, I even had a fling with ol' Jesse James himself. Can you believe that?"

"Oh my God!" Tandy uttered and clapped both her hands to her mouth. She gazed at Rose with renewed appreciation. "No wonder you fit in so easily. You got their wild blood in you. What were they like? I mean, was it thrilling knowing them?"

Again Rose laughed. "I wasn't exactly measuring a man by how he handled a six-gun." And then she giggled to herself. "On second thought, maybe I was. . . ." She laughed out loud and winked at Tandy.

The young girl blushed and dropped her eyes. "Oh Rose, I don't see how you could have done it."

Rose's face puckered. "What is that supposed to

mean? All men are alike really. Don't you find that true?"

Tandy's face was glowing an even darker red. "I have no way of knowing that," she answered shyly.

"Oh my God. Y'mean, Bitter Creek there is your only one?"

Tandy hesitated. Here it was, at last. "Bitter Creek isn't even my first," she managed to stammer out.

Rose pondered for a moment, then said flatly, "Now that doesn't make sense. He's either been your first or we ain't talking 'bout the same thing, honey."

Tandy twisted her fingers together. "What I mean is—is that B.C. and me—we haven't—we haven't done nothing yet." It was out!

Rose stared at Tandy open-mouthed. "My God, y'mean you're still a virgin?"

Tandy nodded. Mortified, she heard Rose howl with laughter. "Honey, that's the damndest thing I ever did hear. I mean, either that Bitter Creek has had his thing cut off by some Injun or he just ain't a man." Rose stood up and came to her. She raised Tandy's arms and spread them wide. "Geez, look at you—you need a bit more meat on you here and there, but there's got to be something wrong with a man who can't get it up with what you got, sugar."

"There's nothing wrong with Bitter Creek!" Tandy defended him stubbornly.

Rose dropped Tandy's arms and shook her head. "How you know? Ever seen him naked? Ever seen him big and hard, wanting you?" Rose turned away, grumbling. "I mean, who would ever have believed it? I seen you two snuggle up to each other something fierce like and I woulda swore you been hitting it on." She swung around once more to face Tandy. "I mean, who woulda figured B.C. can't get it up?"

"He's too much of a gentleman," Tandy replied.

"Gentleman?" Rose snorted. "We're talking about just being human, girl. I mean, you got good looks, you got tits bigger than some gals I've known, you got all the rest of the equipment a man likes. So it's gotta be ol' Bitter Creek."

"It's me, not B.C.," Tandy cried out. Sudden tears flooded her eyes. How she had waited to tell someone that! Now it was gushing forth uncontrollably. "It's me, Rose. He thinks I'm too young to carry on like that."

The news sobered Rose. "He must be right plumb out of his head if he thinks that."

"Well, it's true! It's what he thinks!"

"Doesn't he know age has nothing to do with it? Geez, I lost my virginity at twelve. Gals are carrying on now 'fore they know how to cook."

"I know that, and I told him," Tandy explained. "But he says he's been raised differently. Besides, he and my brother were best of friends and he says he can think of me only as a sister. Says he won't or can't have nothing to do with me until he thinks I'm a woman."

Rose swore. "What else you got that puts him off—a nose that reminds him of his favorite bunny? What a bunch of nonsense."

"I tried, Rose. I've really tried," Tandy said.

"How much? I mean, you ever snuggle against him with all your clothes off?"

"Oh Rose," Tandy blushed. "I couldn't do that! Not with him wearing his long johns and all."

Rose shook her head. "Hell girl, that there is your problem. How's a man ever going to get worked up if you don't whet his appetite?"

"But he knows I want him," Tandy pouted. "I want him to want me too."

"Honey," Rose said. She came forward and placed her hands gently on Tandy's shoulders. "If what you tell me is the truth, you're going to be an old lady 'fore he gets the nerve to see what's underneath them clothes of yours. If you want a man, you sort of have to encourage him to want you. Then, once you got him, he thinks he's got you. The rest is easy."

"I know that," Tandy said vehemently. "It's the getting to it that bothers me."

Rose closed her eyes. "God give me strength," she muttered. Then she cast Tandy a long, hard but tolerant look. "We got to work on that, don't we? We women got to stick together, right? Can't have no man not appreciate us when we want to be appreciated, that's for sure. Now, tell me. How *do* you go about exciting B.C.?"

Tandy's heart fluttered. "What do you mean?"

Rose went on doggedly. "I know you two know how to hug each other. But I mean, you know where a man likes to be touched to get him hot?"

"Hot?"

Rose drew in a deep breath. "Yeah, hot. And hard. That's what you want, isn't it? How the hell else is B.C. going to want you if he doesn't get hot and hard?"

"Of course it's what I want," Tandy began. "But—" Again, tears welled in her eyes. She didn't know what she was supposed to do or say. She let Rose take her in her arms.

"That's okay baby," Rose said gently. "We're going to work this out, you wait and see. Tell me this. You ever try to touch B.C.? He ever try to touch you?"

Tandy wiped her cheeks and shook her head. "We hold each other in bed," she volunteered. "He lets me put my arm and hand on his chest. I touch his face," she added eagerly, wanting to please.

Rose frowned. "Honey, you got a long ways down to go. Can you tell if you do anything that you know for sure he likes?"

Tandy thought a moment, then sadly shook her head. "He doesn't want me to do too much. There are times I try to wiggle right close to him. But each time I do, he says he's going to move off. I'd rather lie quietly next to him than have him sleep somewhere else."

Rose smiled triumphantly. "But that's good. I'm guessing you start to get his blood going. Means he's not made of stone after all. But we got to do something really good so he won't want you to stop. That's the problem!"

Tandy looked at her questioningly.

Rose thought a moment. "Let me put it this way.

You have places on you that feel good when he touches you—or even when you touch yourself?"

Tandy bit her lip. She knew the answer immediately and nodded her head, hoping Rose wouldn't ask her too much about those spots.

"Well," Rose continued in a soothing voice. "A man's the same way. I mean, they like to feel a woman's body and they also like a woman to feel them. Gets them all excited and everything. Once you got a man in that condition, ain't no way in the world he's going to want to move to the other side of the room."

"Y'mean, that's all I got to do?" Tandy asked incredulously. It seemed too easy.

Rose nodded. "We're just talking about the first time. Once he gives in, he'll be hanging on to you like a dog in heat."

"Oh my," Tandy gasped. "I'm getting all hot and sweatin' just thinking 'bout it."

Rose laughed and pulled away. "C'mon, we'll both cool off."

Rose went to the basins and began to disrobe. Tandy hesitated, watching as she slipped the shirt over her shoulders, exposing her full breasts and strong, slim back. With a shrug, Tandy got her own shirt off. She didn't feel too good about undressing. It wasn't that she was embarrassed by nudity; she had undressed in front of her Indian maid many times without thinking of it one way or the other. But she found herself self-conscious in Rose's presence. Though it came as no great surprise to her that Rose had a good body, her waist was even smaller than she had imagined, her hips smoother, her breasts more enviably round and beautiful. Compulsively, Tandy glanced down at her own small breasts.

"You have a nice figure!" Rose's voice startled her and she jumped. "No, you shouldn't be ashamed of it," Rose went on softly. "I wish I looked as slim when I was your age."

"But you're slim now," Tandy blurted. "You have so much—you're so much more beautiful."

Rose laughed and stepped into one of the basins. "Oh, I know what I look like. A bit too much here." She slapped at her buttocks, "But I'm not ashamed of what I have."

"I don't know," Tandy said hesitantly as she stepped into the basin near her. "Most women I know don't like to talk about their bodies and such things."

Rose shrugged and squatted so that she could scoop the cool water over her shoulders. "Why not, I say? I'll tell you more. I don't go for corsets nor halters and such. I like to feel free. I like my breasts and I like my belly and thighs. I like to run my hands over all of me. See, here, I'm doing it. I don't see what's wrong with liking your body jus' as I don't see nothing wrong with you and me talking 'bout it."

Tandy gulped. It was more than the water trickling down her skin that caused her goose pimples. "I never had anyone I could talk to. I surely do appreciate all you've said."

Rose gave her a puzzled look and shook her head.

"I'm not done with you, little gal," she answered. "We got us a heap of learning to do if we're going to convince Bitter Creek his woman is indeed a woman."

"Oh, do you think I can do it?" Tandy asked excitedly.

"I'll show you a few tricks. We'll get your confidence up, along with everything else." They both giggled.

They splashed each other for a while, simply enjoying the water. Then, "Here," Rose said, "let me scrub your back." She stepped out of her basin, got a short bar of white soap, then came back to step in with Tandy. "Turn around," she commanded, and began to lather Tandy's back.

"Mmm," Tandy murmured. She lifted her hair up so that it would not get in Rose's way. "That feels good."

"Sure it does," Rose answered. Her hands came around Tandy's middle, sleek and slippery with suds, then slowly slid up until they cupped both of her breasts. "This feel good too?"

Oh my God! thought Tandy, I'm going to die, it feels so good.

"You see," continued Rose, "when someone touches you, it stirs up your insides, don't it? Same with a man. Touch him just right, like I'm doing to you, and he'll get the same feelings."

"I can't stand it," Tandy exclaimed. She grabbed for Rose's hands, pulling them down to her waist. "I'm ready to bust!"

Rose chuckled. "That's good. Now you know

what it's like. 'Course, some men aren't gentle and some aren't patient. And there's some who don't even care how you feel—they just want to get on, stick it in, let loose; 'fore you know it, they're buttoning up their pants and running off to have another drink, all 'fore you can even start to feeling right."

"What'll I do if that happens?" Tandy asked curiously.

Rose shrugged. "Sometimes nothing can be done. A lot depends on you and what you want from your man. Most of it is teaching him, just as I'm doing to you. Let him know what you like. Believe it or not, that'll stir him up too—usually." She hesitated, absorbed in her own past, then sighed. "There's some men who think they was only put on earth to bang away at a woman and that women don't have such feelings." She sighed again and her fingers absently rubbed over Tandy's middle and legs. "Guess that's why I took up with Bob and Doolin. They like to do it same as me. They're gentle and exciting and that's half the battle." She glanced hurriedly at Tandy. "But I don't think you have much to fret about with Bitter Creek. I'd say he was one of the gentle kind, and that's good. Is that how you feel about him?"

Tandy nodded. "I truly do love him," she answered.

Rose smiled. "I reckon you probably do. The first boy I had I loved too." She sighed and went back to scrubbing Tandy's knees. "I hope you hang onto them feelings," she murmured softly. She shook her head to clear her mind of whatever she was thinking. "Here now," she smiled. "You scrub me down."

Tandy hesitantly picked the bar from her hand and waited. When Rose had squirmed around and put her back to her, she placed the bar on it, careful that her palm didn't touch the skin.

"Go ahead," Rose said. "I won't bite you."

Very slowly, Tandy circled the soap bar, blinking repeatedly. She felt nervous. She did not know for sure how to interpret her emotions.

Rose glanced over her shoulder and sighed. "You do need some learning," she said, smiling. She reached around her, got Tandy's hands, pulled her close up against her back. Then she circled Tandy's arms about her torso and placing her hands on her breasts. "Now," Rose said stoutly. "You do what I did to you."

Very slowly, Tandy slid her soapy hands over the full breasts, cupping them, feeling their giving sway, kneading gently, exploring until her touching became a grasping. She could feel the hardness of Rose's nipples as they pressed solidly into her palms. Suddenly, Rose's legs began to shake. Tandy sighed and pressed her face into her wet back.

"That feels good, don't it?" Rose asked huskily after a moment. "It sure feels good to me." They were silent as Tandy's hands pressed and slid up and down Rose's body. "That's what B.C. will be feeling too," Rose finally murmured. "Believe me, he'll be doing that to you one of these nights and you'll be feeling like I feel now. Y'see how it works?" She waited, slightly leaning back into Tandy. "Tell me what you feel?" she asked softly. "Tell me how you feel deep inside."

Tandy was breathing hard. She closed her eyes to concentrate. It didn't take much. "I can hardly stand up I'm so weak." She answered as if in a dream. "I feel—I feel as if someone knocked the breath out of me, only it doesn't hurt." She concentrated once more. "I feel as if—as if—" She couldn't say it.

"You feel something down there?" Rose asked. Her hand reached behind her and slid between Tandy's legs.

"Oh God," Tandy moaned and jumped back, almost tripping out of the basin. Rose quickly turned around to catch her. They held onto each other breathlessly for a moment until Rose bent back to stare down at Tandy, a small smile across her lips.

"You shouldn't be afraid to be touched down there," she said softly. "That's even better than up here." She touched Tandy's hardened nipple gently. "You should want B.C. to touch you down there," she said. As they hugged each other, Rose's hand again slipped down between their dampened bodies and her fingers slid gently between Tandy's legs, pressing upward into the dark pubic triangle. "Now," Rose whispered softly, "doesn't that feel good?"

Tandy hardly dared to breathe. She was caught somewhere between somewhere and nowhere, hanging in suspension, at a dizzy height with swirling pools of wetness surrounding her. She could hardly stand it and finally caught hold of Rose's arm for support. "Oh yes," she murmured.

"You'll have to let B.C. know," Rose said. "He will want to touch you there and with him, it will be even better."

"Oh yes," Tandy whispered, eyes closed in a dream.

"And you'll want to touch him too," Rose continued. "Touch me so you'll know how he will feel."

Ever so slowly, Tandy's hand slid down between their bellies, hesitating at the feel of the hard coarse hair, then sliding forward between Rose's legs. She gasped as her fingers probed.

"See how it feels both ways," Rose said with a slight catch to her breathing. "You'll know how to touch him. You'll know and he'll like it as much as you like it."

Tandy thought she was going to faint for sure. It was too much. She slowly shook her head back and forth. Tenderly, Rose pushed her back and they stared at each other, flushed, gasping, not daring to break the silence for a while.

Rose reached out then and stroked Tandy's cheek. "Remember these things, sweet little girl," she said softly. "The first time should be the best time. And, since you love him, it *will* be the best. Make the most of that moment as you can."

Tandy was touched. They stood facing each other, not a word said, oblivious to their nakedness. "Thank you, Rose," she finally stammered. "Thank you from the bottom of my heart."

The older woman smiled hesitantly. "I guess we won't be calling you our little girl much longer."

Tandy smiled and her face heated up a bit. "I'm going to try," she answered.

9

Dusk came. Both women hummed quietly to themselves as they prepared biscuits and stew for supper. Content with their private thoughts, they did not speak.

Tandy still felt flushed, though not from the day's heat. The evening actually brought a chill; fall was in the air. She had put on a light denim jacket and felt far more comfortable after she'd buttoned it.

She felt no quilt. She was, if anything, overexcited. She knew how it felt to touch and be touched, and the knowledge gave her a strange new sensation of power. She never realized she could feel so powerful. She had waited a long long time for this feeling. She no longer felt like an innocent bride cheated out of her wedding night. In fact, she felt more like the man, the groom—that sure of herself!

"Here they come back," Rose's low voice startled her out of her daydreaming. Tandy closed her eyes. Oh please, heart, calm down! I can't seduce him right here and now!

She would have rushed out to greet Bitter Creek had Rose not cautioned her against it. From their table the two women could hear the men unsaddling and putting their horses to feed. Their laughs drifted into the cave every once in a while, and each time she could distinguish B.C.'s voice, Tandy's heart seemed to skip a beat.

"I presume it's safe for us menfolk to come back now?" Bill Doolin grumbled as they came in. But he was grumbling for grumbling's sake. They both looked refreshed, hair matted down from a good wetting in the river.

"Yes," Rose answered. "And I must say, you two smell a heap better."

Tandy went to Bitter Creek's side and caught his hand tightly in hers. He looked down at her just a mite absently. Then it seemed to dawn on him that she too had spent a few hours bathing.

"You look mighty scrubbed down," he said with a wide grin. "How's it feel to get clean—good as me?"

"I feel much better," Tandy said softly.

Rose placed the plates around the table. "We had a mighty fine time, thank you," she answered in a firm voice betraying nothing.

Tandy had been studying B.C.'s face. Something was wrong. She could tell by the shy smile on his lips and the way he looked at her and then at Doolin.

"What is it?" she asked in a low guarded voice.

"What d'ya mean what is it?" he asked with an innocent look on his face. He looked over at Doolin and they winked at each other. "What makes you think something's up?"

Tandy dug a finger into his side. "I can always tell when you got something up your sleeve."

Bitter Creek pulled away and looked up both his sleeves. "I don't see nothing. You see anything, Bill?"

Doolin came over and took a close look up both sleeves. "Naw, I don't see nothing, 'cept maybe a couple of them bugs." He picked off an imaginary bug between two fingers and let it drop to the floor.

"C'mon, you two," Tandy said.

Bitter Creek and Doolin exchanged glances and shrugged. "We was going to tell you after supper," B.C. explained, then grinned. "Guess who we met coming home?"

Tandy suddenly felt a lump in her throat. She tried to hold in her fears. "They're back!" She closed her eyes, hoping against hopes that she was wrong. Not now, not when things were about to go her way —the Daltons couldn't be back!

Bitter Creek nodded happily. "Bob and Grat were riding in jus' as we come up from the river," he said. "They was coming to get us. And you should hear what them boys is planning on doing. You won't believe your ears."

Tandy, shaking her head morosely, allowed Bitter Creek to pull her over to where Rose was sitting. Both men stood before them, excited and grinning.

"Go ahead, Bill, tell 'em," Bitter Creek prompted.

"Ol' Bob's gone and really done it this time," Doolin said, open admiration in his voice. "He's going to make a name for himself that'll make ol' Jesse James toss and turn in his grave with envy. We're going to be better known around here than the president of the United States, that's for sure."

Rose shook her head and sighed. "Bill Doolin, Tandy and me are going to get stiff in the joints if you don't start telling us."

Doolin nudged his partner. "Ol' Bob got it planned we're going to take two banks at the same time." He let that sink in, nodding his head to encourage both women to get as excited as he was. "Two banks at the same time!" he repeated, thinking they might not have heard. "No one has ever done that before."

Staring from one blank face to the other, he frowned, obviously disappointed that neither appreciated his information.

"That's plumb crazy," Rose finally said flatly.

"No, it ain't," Doolin explained. "Bob told us how it can be done and you know anything Bob says will work."

"What town is going to let us get away with robbing *two* banks?" Rose asked. "You got to be talking about a big town, big enough to have two banks. And that means lots of people."

Bitter Creek held up a hand. "But Bob knows of just the right place. He grew up near it, knows the town like he knows the back of his hand. And the Daltons have friends there too, people who'll help us out if need be. He says we'll be able to ride in and out 'fore anyone knows the better."

"Where is this place?" Rose asked.

"Just above the Kansas line—place called Coffeyville," Doolin answered. "They've already headed that way and we're to pick 'em up on the trail."

"No," Tandy said faintly. "I mean, can't we stay out of this one?"

Rose glanced at her sympathetically, knowing what was on Tandy's mind. "When do we have to leave?"

" 'Fore sunup," Doolin answered. "We got some travelin' to do to catch up to 'em."

Bitter Creek came to sit down beside Tandy. "Aw, honey," he said gently. "Bob knows what he's doing. He's got it all laid out and tells you not to fret. He don't even want you and Rose in town—it's going to be that easy and quick."

"What do you mean he doesn't want us there?" Rose demanded. "Since when don't we take part? I thought that's what we agreed on—we all take part in everything."

Bitter Creek shook his head. "This time its different. Bob has it all planned. He wants you two to be hiding out with fresh horses. We'll be making a fast break outta Coffeyville and chances are we'll probably pick up a posse after us. Now, you two will be off somewhere where we can change onto fresh mounts. That way, we'll be outta the territory way ahead of anyone."

Rose thought it over before reluctantly agreeing it was a good plan. "But only this one time," she warned. "Next time, I want to take part myself."

Bitter Creek turned to Tandy and brushed the hair gently away from her face. "Aw, c'mon honey," he said softly. "Ain't nothing going to go wrong with this plan." He was misinterpreting her silence. "And once it's over, we'll have another long spell together."

Tandy gritted her teeth. "Oh, you men!" she said vehemently. She shook her head and got up. "You —you don't know nothing!" She swirled around and stormed back to their curtained room.

Bitter Creek stared after her in astonishment. "What's biting her tailbone?" he asked.

Rose got up and looked to the back of the cave. "You wouldn't know," she answered tightly and frowned. "The timing is bad, that's all."

Bitter Creek hesitated. Then another light seemed to dawn on him and he relaxed. "Oh, one of them things," he muttered.

Rose swung around, hands on hips. "You men!" she sneered and whipped away to busy herself at the stove.

The two men glanced at each other and shrugged. "Don't try to figure them out," Doolin warned B.C.'s questioning look. "Best leave 'em be for now. Let's start packing."

Later, the four ate in silence. Tandy had finally returned and kept her distance from Bitter Creek. And he, with sidelong glances at the two women, carefully stayed away from her, watching carefully and wondering over her strange mood. With little interruptions, the meal was eaten hurriedly.

"Well." Doolin sighed and pushed back from the table rubbing his stomach in appreciation of the good food. He glanced from one solemn face to the next. "Well!"

Since no one volunteered to accept his invitation to a conversation, he shrugged and stretched his arms over his head. "Might as well finish packing," he muttered. Wordlessly, the two men got up and went over to a corner where they had piled rifles and provisions next to the saddles.

The two women glanced at each other and sighed. Silently, they put away the food and dishes. Rose had already collected a few things they could take on the ride and these were neatly arranged to one side for the early morning getaway.

When they were finished, Tandy sighed in obvious disappointment and dejection. Rose touched her arm gently and beckoned for her to retire. When the girl had disappeared behind the curtain, Rose turned and inspected the two men who were dealing out cards near the open fire.

"If we're to get an early start, I guess it's time to get to sleep." She feigned a yawn and glanced at the two and waited.

"Be there shortly," Doolin answered without looking up from his playing.

Rose frowned. She knew it would be useless to push too much. "It's getting cold," she tried one more time. "A girl could freeze to death without someone to keep her warm."

Doolin and Bitter Creek smirked and exchanged jabs in their ribs. "That's what I love 'bout October nights," Bill answered but still made no attempt to follow her. "We'll be in shortly, soon as we finish a game."

Rose shook her head in disgust. "That's what Hickok said—and look what it got him." She gave up. At least she had tried to help. Men!

It was much later when Bitter Creek brushed aside the curtain and slipped into their small niche. The fire had died down to embers and thus the cave was swallowed up in almost complete blackness. And, with the heat gone, the frosty night was all the more biting.

Tandy shivered under the blankets and huddled in a small ball waiting for B.C. to discard his shirt and pants. She could hear him begin to shiver and as he stepped over the pallet and pulled back the blankets, she shoved over to admit him.

"Jesus Christ," he murmured, "it's colder than a chicken plucked of its feathers." He squirmed close to her. "Geez!" His hands came in contact with her bare skin and he jumped back.

Tandy grabbed hold of him and drew him back to her. "I need to get warm," she said huskily.

"Well, I darn well should hope so. You're stark naked!" He pulled the blanket tight to himself as if he were the unclothed one.

"I been waiting for you," Tandy answered in what she hoped was her sexiest sounding voice, like Rose's.

"Jeezus, Tandy," Bitter Creek whispered. "You mustn't do things like this."

"Why not?" she asked, moving her body against

him. She tried not to think about his wearing long johns but that the coarse cloth was his skin. "Don't I feel good to you?" She managed to find his hand and draw it to her side.

He quickly withdrew it as though it had been cast into a branding fire. "Doggone it girl," he said tightly. "It ain't right, you and me. I'm only human, you see, and—"

Tandy tried to lean into him. "And I say it's about time you and me got together." How bold—how exciting!

Bitter Creek squirmed away and shook his head. "Tandy, you can't do this to me. It ain't the right time."

"Why not?" she asked quickly.

He shook his head trying to think correctly. "It's—it's just I still feel wrong about it."

"Why not?" she asked, seeing him slip away from her. "Time's good as any other. Please, B.C.—"

But he had swung his legs out from under the blankets. He hesitated and turned to her and took her hand. "Tandy girl, I wouldn't be worth a tinkers dam if you and me started something like this. Not now." There was a genuine misery in his voice. "For one thing, I got to set my thinking straight about a couple of things. You've got to help me set them straight. Also, we got to ride early in the morning. It wouldn't be good—nor right—to start something knowing what we got to do tomorrow. I don't want that kind of thing. Do you?" He waited, searching out her eyes in the darkness until she reluctantly shook her head.

"When you and me get together," he continued in a soft whisper, "I want it to be right. I don't want to be worrying 'bout other things or the next day." His hand reached out for hers. "Do you understand?"

Tandy nodded her head. Tenderly, he lifted her chin with his finger. "Now, you either get something on you—or I'm going to freeze outside these blankets."

Angry and hurt, Tandy rose onto her knees and fumbled in the nearby basket for a nightgown. She slipped it on, not caring a bit whether B.C. was looking or not. Finished, she dug back under the covers, crossed her arms over her chest and stared up into the blackness.

Bitter Creek hesitated, then grudgingly slipped back under the blankets, stiff and nervous. They lay there side by side, unmoving and quiet until Bitter Creek sighed and slipped an arm under her stiff shoulders and tugged her into him.

"It isn't I don't want you, Tandy m'girl," he said gently. "You've become as tempting as tempting can get and I guess I didn't realize just how much until now. One of these days—" He sighed. "One of these days I guess it's inevitable that you and me will—" His words wandered off with another sigh.

Tandy's anger melted and she moved close into him. "Oh B.C.," she answered with a smile. She had him! Maybe not tonight, maybe not the next few nights, but she had him! He was hers and they were finally going to get together and be one, soon.

She knew instinctively that the next time, whenever that time came, he would not resist her.

Thank you, Rose, Tandy thought happily. Thank you so much! And her dreams that night were some of her happiest.

10

They caught up with the Daltons three days later just over the Kansas line. It was late in the afternoon. Riding with the three brothers were Broadwell and Powers. They were all waiting at the prearranged spot with a string of horses.

The welcomes were strained and right away Tandy felt that things were different. They were too serious, too tense. She missed the jokes, the laughter, the light easy mannerisms. The gloom was caught up quickly by both Doolin and Bitter Creek and she didn't like the change.

"We're camping down by the stream," Bob Dalton said. "We'll be leaving you two gals here with the horses in the morning."

"When do you expect to be back?" Rose asked.

"By full sun. Have everything packed and ready to go. We'll probably have only time to change saddles."

The two women kept to themselves that night, having foond conversation and light talk was not wanted. "They seem so moody," Tandy sighed, glancing over at the circle of men gathered around the fire. They were staring into the colors.

Rose glanced their way, then continued with wiping the plates. "They're probably just tired."

Tandy shook her head. "Maybe they're trying to do too much."

"What? Y'mean taking on two banks?" Rose shrugged. "Hey, gal, you're talking about the Dalton gang, remember? We're invincible!" She looked over at the group again and studied their profiles. "Maybe it's good they're sober. They'll take things more cautious. But Bob hasn't failed us yet and he won't this time, y'wait and see!"

"I don't know," Tandy said slowly with a worried frown. "I just got a bad feeling 'bout this."

Rose sighed. "Now, don't you start showing your worries. They don't need that added to their troubles. We're here to support 'em, give them a little boost. C'mon Tandy, don't let 'em see you act like this."

Tandy tried. She busied herself repacking the supplies and preparing things for the early morning breakfast. But when all these things were finished she had nothing left to do, so she sat down on one of the large boulders that protruded among the trees and watched Bitter Creek and the others out in the clearing.

There were a few jokes being told, for every once in a while someone's laughter would drift across to her. They spent some time cleaning their hand guns and rifles. Then they concentrated on laying out their long riding coats, brushing them as if they were all going to a Sunday prayer meeting.

Later, when they were all wrapped in their blankets in a tight circle around the fire, Tandy was compelled to grip B.C. tightly. He smiled and reached out to hug her back.

"Don't you worry none," he whispered low enough just for her ears. "Bob says the law in Coffeyville ain't nothing to worry 'bout. He's got fake beards for us so we won't be recognized. He's thought of everything."

"I can't help myself," she confided, close to tears. "I just got this feeling that something awful is going to happen."

"To us?" Bitter Creek stared over at her, then grinned. "Shucks, there isn't an army of marshals big enough to take us on."

"But one of these days, them railroad people and bankers and the law, they're going to get together to try and stop you."

He smiled. "That's going to be a long time away. Nothing to get worked up about now. By that time, you and me, we'll be in Texas tripping over a bundle of kids." He always knew that kind of talk made her content and happy. But tonight, for some reason, it didn't.

She awoke much later and looked around. All was quiet. She squirmed around so she could see those behind her. Emmett was leaning against his saddle stirring the fire, which still crackled with a small blaze. Tandy watched him unnoticed for several minutes.

She'd had a horrible dream and her body was wet. There had been a body and it swirled in red and blue circles, lots of circles. There were flailing arms and legs, and a face torn apart, shredded like some jackrabbit in the claws of an eagle. It had been B.C.'s face and she had screamed but no sound had come. And then she had awakened.

She knew she somehow had to try and stop her man. This Coffeyville robbery, this plan, was wrong. Something terrible was going to happen.

She'd had a few other dramatic premonitions similar to this in her life. The last had been the one she'd had of Grand Woodrowe's death. And it had come true. However, this time she was going to do something about it!

She looked around, wondering just what she could do. Her mind whirled with thoughts and ideas: holding a gun on him until they left; giving him some potion so he wouldn't wake up; chasing the horses away so they couldn't ride. Horses!

She glanced at the tether line. The row of horses stood patiently, half asleep, like open-eyed statues. She would never be able to get away with it. Her glance wavered and rested on the saddles lined up on the ground, readied for the morning ride. An idea struck her, from some tale of long ago.

Quietly, she edged out of the blanket and rose to her feet. Trying to appear casual, she went over to the food and supply sacks, squatted before them and began searching among them until she found the knife she wanted. She looked up and in that instant saw Emmett lifting a small branch into the fire. She slid the knife into her sleeve and stood up.

"Can't sleep?" Emmett asked softly when she approached.

Tandy spread her hands before the warmth and shook her head. "Have to go to the privy," she explained hoarsely. She waited a proper moment to warm herself, then sauntered casually out of sight into the darkness.

She had estimated correctly. The saddles were fairly close by and luckily Emmett had his back turned. She waited, watching his back, then, slowly lifting the hem of her nightshirt, stepped towards them. She frowned. She thought she could identify Bitter Creek's saddle easily, but without his bed-roll on it, his saddle looked just like another one lying there. She tried to recall. Doolin! Oh, damn! She realized that Bitter Creek and Bill Doolin had identical saddles. She glanced again at Emmett, realizing that her absence would be noted soon. Oh well! Quickly she squatted and searched for the girths. She didn't want to make it too obvious. The knife sliced across the leather tie but not quite through it. She frowned and wondered how much weight it would take to tear it apart. She tugged. A man's weight, that's all it needed. She cut a bit deeper into the leather, then slapped the stirrup skirt down to hide her work.

The other saddle she did the same thing to, again arranging the skirt to hide the cut. So she would save both men, one for her and one for Rose. A repayment for Rose!

Satisfied, she stole back into the darkness, waited

a moment, then walked back into the lit circle. "Goodnight," she whispered to Emmett and slid back into her blankets with a sigh of relief. She wondered whether she would be able to fall back to sleep.

Morning came with a violent jerk of her body. She was sure she had been awake, but she obviously hadn't been, for the camp was already busy with preparations and moving people. She was the last to arise and she quickly fumbled into her pants and shirt.

"I'm sorry," Tandy murmured as she came up to Rose, who was busy frying hash over the renewed campfire.

Rose shrugged her shoulders for an answer. The men were down by the stream, gathered around a basin of soapy water and shaving with their long-bladed razors. Tandy watched absently as their hands brushed over their chins. They had changed into suits and their best white shirts, unbuttoned at the neck, no collars. There was a bit of teasing about Emmett's attempt to grow a mustache. Powers brushed at his large handlebars proudly. The rest were clean-shaven and for a moment Tandy felt proud of them.

They ate sparingly and took their time sipping the dark strong coffee, hunched close to the warmth of the fire, absorbed with staring at the flames. The eastern sky was beginning to grey and the outlines of the surrounding trees were becoming more visible.

Bob Dalton stood up and stretched. "Better saddle up," he said calmly. Wordlessly, they put down their mugs and rose. Guns were strapped on, inspected one more time. Then they took their rifle scabbards to their saddles, picked the saddles up with the other hand and dragged them to the horses.

Tandy watched breathlessly. She winced as the girths were tightened under the horses' bellies.

"Damn it!" Bitter Creek lifted the broken strap in his hand disgustedly. The others were mounting.

"Thought you checked your things," Bob said, leaning down to watch.

"I did," Bitter Creek answered angrily.

"We'll ride on. You catch us on the road." He turned and signaled to the others to follow. The riders, without a glance toward the women, rode out of the encampment and down to the stream, which they crossed with a flurry of splashes. Finally, they scrambled up the other embankment and disappeared from view.

B.C. watched. As soon as they were out of sight, he swore and threw the strap down in disgust. He glanced at the two women, then swung the saddle off onto the ground.

"We got any leather?" he asked, bending to inspect his problem.

Both women came over to watch. "Can't you use that piece?" Rose asked.

B.C. shook his head. "Too short." He glanced to where the riders had disappeared, obviously anxious. "I can make do with a piece of rein." He took out his pocket knife and began to cut a length from one of his reins, muttering under his breath.

Tandy stood back, silently staring at his work, praying for some miracle that would make him stay in camp forever. She was already trying to figure out what to do to delay him further.

Suddenly, they were interrupted by a figure appearing above the far rise, on foot and leading his horse down the embankment.

"It's Bill," Rose said, concerned.

Doolin waded his horse across the stream, saddle slung over his back. Even from that distance, they could see the anger in his face. He came directly up to them and threw the saddle at their feet. "Someone cut the damn leather!" he said. "Someone cut it clear through." He spied the lost end of B.C.'s girth and retrieved it. After a close inspection, he threw it on the ground too. "Someone cut yours too," he stated. He turned to the women.

"Don't you look at me like that, Bill Doolin," Rose warned. She stared him down. Then, slowly, all eyes turned to Tandy standing with head down off to one side.

"Jeeesus Christ!" Bitter Creek murmured. "You do this thing, Tandy?"

She toyed with her fingers nervously and nodded. "I didn't want you to go," she said weakly.

Doolin spun around to kick out at his saddle. "God damn it, girl," he shouted. "You just don't do that! They're depending on us being there with 'em."

She had never seen Doolin angry and she was frightened. She began to doubt her actions and now was all the more confused.

Doolin turned and stared at her. "I just don't believe you done it." He looked down at Bitter Creek for an explanation.

B.C. was as dumbfounded. He swallowed and stood up. Tandy looked up at him with watery eyes. "I had a dream you were killed," she sobbed. "I had to do something!"

Bitter Creek stared at her as if he didn't believe what he was hearing. "But I told you nothing was going to happen to us. You had no right to do this to us."

"I would have done anything to keep you here," she answered him. She no longer tried to control her tears. Her body racked with the grief she was feeling. Having no more strength, she turned and ran behind the nearest tree where she could hide and cry more.

The three watched helplessly. Finally, the two men turned to Rose. "I dunno," she said, throwing up her hands. "I guess she thought she was doing the right thing. I dunno."

Doolin stared at her a moment, then looked over to Tandy. He turned and kicked the saddle again. "I don't believe this!"

Bitter Creek kept looking Tandy's way. What little anger he had felt had dissolved into a mass of confused feelings. He felt sad, and sorry for her. "Aw, c'mon Bill," he said finally. "I'll work this out when we get back."

The two men worked together, fashioning the leather making do with what they had. Minutes passed before they finally resaddled and were satisfied the girths would hold. Mounted, Bitter Creek nudged his horse over to Tandy and leaned down.

"I know you think you did right," he said softly. "In a way, I appreciate your caring for me. But all it done was take twenty, thirty minutes away. Hardly worth it, don't you think?" He tried to grin but she wouldn't turn her head away from her arms. "Don't you worry none. We'll be back." And then they were gone.

It was quiet in the clearing but Tandy still held onto the tree trunk. She had stopped crying and her head hurt and she was feverish. She jumped as Rose's hand gently touched her shoulder. "Rose," Tandy moaned. "I tried, I really tried."

Rose sighed and leaned her back against the tree and stared up into the breaking morn. "Honey, you're not going to get me to say you did right. I'll give you credit for nerve though."

"But I really felt something bad was going to happen!"

Rose shook her head. "When you've been with this bunch as long as I have, you'll find out there's something special about 'em. You'll find out them Daltons can do just 'bout anything. There's just no need of thinking bad 'cause it's never going to happen."

"Then you think I was foolish."

"And young. Believe me, I know what I'm saying."

Tandy had plenty of time to think about it. The morning was spent clearing the fire and packing the supplies, getting everything ready for the return of the gang from Coffeyville. It was still too early for them to ready the horses and so the rest of the hours they walked around, threw stones into the small stream that gurgled nearby, and waited, wondering.

"Did you ever do anything like that?" Tandy asked. "Y'know, something crazy like I did?"

Rose leaned back against a fallen log near the water's edge and closed her eyes. "I've done all sorts of crazy things most my life," she finally answered. "As long as you're not tampering with someone else, you can be as crazy as you want."

"You still think I done wrong." Tandy was still hoping someone would understand her actions.

Rose sighed. "It's over and done with. Luckily, no one got hurt. But there's no telling how the Daltons will take to it. I mean, Bob could take it you didn't have trust in him or his ideas."

"Do you always believe he's right?"

Rose frowned. "Sure, why not? I mean, Bob's got a way 'bout him. Sort of, he can't do no wrong. You haven't lived nor been around people I used to know. They were losers—nothing to their grit, doing day to day stuff, content to go home to their cabins week in and week out. Out here, we're free—can't you feel it? I mean, we do as we please, live as we please. Where else can you do that?"

"But you can't do that forever," Tandy claimed.

"Why not? What's to stop us?"

"Look what happpened to Jesse James, and to the Youngers."

Rose shrugged. "Jesse let his guard down. And

the Youngers? Well, they didn't have the brains that we have. As long as we learn from their mistakes, we can make it. Y'gotta stop living in that dream world of yours, Tandy."

They sat alongside the water for a while, silently absorbed in watching the swirls and movement. Finally, Rose looked up at the sun and sighed. "C'mon, it's 'bout time we get things ready for their return."

Time went by painfully slow. The horses were ready, bridled, their own two mounts saddled and packed. Tandy sat against a tree lazily glancing up at the blue sky, humming a song from long ago. Rose was getting impatient and kept wandering down to the creek to stare across to the far embankment. She would stare for several minutes, then kick her skirts around and trudge back, a frown on her face. She had done this several times when finally there was a crashing of brush from the other side.

Doolin and Bitter Creek charged down the embankment and spattered across the creek in a flurry.

"What's the matter?" Rose cried out, looking past them, expecting the others. "Where's the rest?"

"Never mind!" Doolin's voice was sharp and crisp. "We ain't got time to explain."

Rose glanced back towards the far embankment, still expecting the other riders. "Are they coming soon?"

Doolin stopped and grabbed her arm. "They ain't coming!" His eyes bore into hers, and he savagely pushed her arm away. "Just mount up. We'll tell you on the way." His voice had a ring to it that was not to be denied.

Tandy had felt the tension. She'd turned from Bitter Creek and quickly tightened the loose girth of her mount. As she lifted herself onto the saddle, he came over to her, his face grim and a bit white. "Stay close to me," he said hoarsely, and swung his saddle onto a fresh horse.

Few words were spoken. The two women, knowing they'd have to restrain their curiosity, helped collect and divide up the spare horses. Finished, they spurred out of the encampment, leading the spares, up the far side and back onto the trail to Oklahoma.

They rode at less than all-out speed, preserving the horses for whatever might occur. It was obvious the men expected trouble. They continually glanced over their shoulders until the women found themselves doing the same. It wasn't until several hours later, when they were well past the Kansas border and into the Cherokee strip, that they came to a halt atop a small knoll.

They pulled into a tight circle and dismounted. Doolin, still peering at the horizon for signs of pursuit, took off his hat and wiped his brow.

"All right," Rose said calmly. "What happened? And what do you mean, the rest aren't coming back?"

Doolin glanced at Bitter Creek, then spat the dust from his mouth. "They're dead—all of 'em!"

"Oh, my God!" Tandy gasped.

"All of them?" Rose asked increduously.

Doolin nodded his head and bit his lip. "All of 'em. They was dead before we had a chance to get to them. It was so quick—like lightnin'." He looked up into the sky, his eyes blinking rapidly. "Gawd, can you believe it? Bob, Grat, Emmett, Broadwell and Powers! All dead quicker'n you can say their names?"

Rose quivered. "How'd it happen?"

Doolin shrugged his shoulders. "Don't know exactly. B.C. and me, we was on the high road jus' 'bout coming into Coffeyville lookin' for the gang. This dude friend of Bob's come ridin' out like his tail was afire and told us what happened. He could hardly get it all out, he was that het up. Seems like Bob decided not to wait for us. They went in by themselves and took on the two banks." He shook his head. "Gawd damn him—he thought he could do it all alone!" There was a hesitation and he twisted away.

The women turned to Bitter Creek. B.C. tried to explain further. "From what we could get outta this dude, the people knew the Daltons were coming. They had set up an ambush—they just shot them to hell."

Rose shook her head. "I can't believe it. They was with us just this morning. Bob had it all planned out. He said there were friends there. What kind of friends would set up an ambush?"

"And you would have been part of it," Tandy gasped, the whole incident slowly registering in her mind. "Both of you would have been killed too."

Bitter Creek turned to her, his face somber. "That's right," he said. "We woulda been."

"But maybe if you two had been there, you might have been able to fight your way out," Rose stated.

Doolin cut her short with a wave of his hand. "No, it was a setup—no way out even if we had been there." Doolin stared again toward the horizon and spat in that direction. "That's the sorriest mistake they made," he growled. "If they think they've ended this thing by killing off the Daltons, they got another think coming."

"Y'mean, we're going to carry on?" Bitter Creek asked.

"Why not?" Doolin turned to them. "You and me, pard, we'll start a new gang. If them people think the Daltons were something to watch out for, they ain't heard of what fear is."

"You think you can do it?" Rose asked.

"Damn right I can," Doolin answered vehemently. He didn't wait but plunged spurs into the horse's flank and raced down the slope, headed back toward their cave. The others watched him for a moment.

"Y'know," Rose said slowly, "I just do believe that man means it. C'mon."

They followed Rose in pursuit of Doolin. Tandy kept close to Bitter Creek, every once in a while glancing his way, studying his set jaw and stern look ahead. The shock of Coffeyville still numbed her but underneath that was the greater realization that her instincts had been correct, that if she hadn't acted on them, Bitter Creek would not be riding beside her now.

She felt good about that. She had accomplished something important, and it gave her a sense of power. Her feelings hinted at how these men must feel after their deeds.

But they were human. They weren't as invincible as Rose had claimed they were. They could make mistakes and that realization frightened her. She could make mistakes too. This was one business where mistakes could be fatal!

11

All four were exhausted by the time they arrived back at the cave. By now, they knew, every lawman on the territory would be aware of the Coffeyville incident and a hard search would begin for them too. Bitter Creek, in particular knew this; if he were still a deputy marshal, he realized, he'd be in on the chase.

As she walked into the cave, Tandy had a terrible feeling of loneliness. Her eyes caught various reminders of the dead Daltons. All she could do was sit on a bench and stare about her.

Rose strode in, took one look about, and undid her bonnet. "This place needs a good cleaning," she remarked to no one in particular. But it was obvious her heart too was elsewhere for she went back to her curtained room and disappeared.

Bitter Creek came in, followed by Doolin. They dropped their saddles in one corner and came to sit by Tandy's side. "It's not going to be the same without 'em," B.C. remarked solemnly.

"They were good friends," Doolin agreed, blinking his eyes rapidly. "We won't forget 'em."

"What are you going to do?" Tandy asked timidly, almost afraid to ask.

"What are we going to do?" Doolin said tightly. "I tell you what *I'm* going to do. I'm going to round up some new men and make sure this country gets to know the name Doolin just like it did the Daltons, only more so. Them bank people and railroads ain't even begun to know what they're up against!"

"Oh Bill," Tandy sighed. "Aren't you afraid the same thing will happen to you as happened to Bob and the others?"

He thought about it. "I don't rightly know how that happened. I know I ain't going to take too much for granted. I'm not going to trust towns no more, no matter who I grew up with. I'm not going to tackle things unless I know we can pull it off. And I know I'm going to get together the biggest and best band of outlaws this country ever see. Ain't no railroad law ever going to be able to touch us like they did the Daltons."

"But you said it was the townspeople who set the ambush."

Doolin shrugged. "But you can bet your boots it was them railroad people and bankers that prodded them into doing it. I mean, we haven't done nothing to ordinary folks. Why would they want to ambush us like that?"

"Maybe times are changing," Bitter Creek volunteered.

"And so will we," Doolin persisted. "That's all

the more reason why we should strike back. Them rich dudes have put the fear into the people. They control them with all their money and all their threats. Well, I say it's time someone put the fear back where it belongs. Right into the laps of them bigwigs. I'm not scared of them—neither are you, B.C.!"

"I'm not scared of them," Bitter Creek confirmed. "And you know I'm with you on whatever you decide."

Tandy's heart sank. Whatever hopes she had begun to build for the two of them leaving for Texas were crumbling. "Shouldn't we lay low for a while?" she asked hopefully.

Doolin agreed. "We won't be doing anything for a while, you can bet on that. Also, we need time to get everyone together."

"You want us all to go out?" B.C. asked curiously.

"Just us. The girls will stay here."

"Why do we have to stay here?" Rose asked, having come up to them silently from behind.

" 'Cause we might be needing you here," Doolin answered. "No chance of the law finding this spot, so you'll be safe here."

"I'm not complaining about being safe," Rose said. "Though maybe now that you're in charge, you'd let me do something."

Doolin released a smile. "You'll have plenty to do, don't worry. Right now, B.C. and me can do things better by ourselves. We know who to look for."

"Where are you going to start?" B.C. asked quickly to stop an argument.

"I'll be sashaying over to Ingalls. There's some good boys over there I thought I'd ask to join up."

"Ha!" Rose exclaimed. "You're going over to that Edith woman!"

Doolin twisted around to face her. "What's tugging at you, Rose? You been on my tail all day."

Rose returned his stare, then dropped her eyes and sighed. "I don't know," she answered grudgingly. "Maybe it's just their ghosts." She shrugged her shoulders. "Maybe I just have to get something outta my system."

Her mood sobered all of them. Finally, Doolin sighed and straightened his back. "Well," he announced. "T'ain't going to do any of us any good moping around feeling sorry for ourselves. We'll all have a chance to do something, Rose, I promise. But right now, we got to get a band together."

"Who'd you have in mind?" Bitter Creek asked.

Doolin drew in a breath. "Thought I'd ask ol' Red Buck Waightman—and Charlie Pierce—"

"Waightman's got a mean streak in him," B.C. stated.

Doolin nodded. "Red Buck's a hard man, but right now he's the kind we need. And I can handle him. Then I was thinking of Tulsa Jack Blake, Crescent Sam and Dynamite Dan Clifton."

"Clifton would be good to have."

"Yeah, ol' Clifton can pick his teeth with a stick a' dynamite." Doolin grinned, slowly easing back into his old style. "You think of any more?"

Bitter Creek nodded. "There's a few still riding at Halsells' last I knew about. I was thinking of Bill Raidler. And Arkansas Tom's a good kid."

"Yeah—and what's his name—ol' Little Dick West! Be sure to bring him along. He was the fastest gun on the ranch, I remember. You head over that way and see who else you can round up. Damn it, we're going to be the highest flying daringest doingest bunch o' outlaws ever rode together. Ain't that right, Rosie?"

Rose sided over to him, placed her arms about his neck and looked down at the top of his head. "I always knew you had it in you," she said in a husky voice. "I know once you set your mind on something, you're going to do it."

Doolin leaned his head back against her stomach and grinned at them. "We're all going to do it. You, me, B.C.—and Tandy here. We're all going to do it."

Tandy, enveloped in the moment, felt her whole body magnetized towards B.C. She looked around timidly and rose to her feet. Without a word, she slipped past them to the back of the cave and their curtained room.

Rose watched her, then turned back to Doolin with a secret smile. "C'mon, Bill," she said.

Doolin lifted his face and watched her retire to the rear. When she had disappeared behind the curtain, he turned back to Bitter Creek with a lazy smile. "I do believe duty calls," he grinned. "It's going to be a long night."

Bitter Creek smiled and nodded. "See you in the morning," he called out. He checked the fire, then walked casually to their room.

Tandy raised her head tearfully. She was sitting on her knees in the middle of the bed, shoulders stooped forward in complete misery. She couldn't have gotten her period at a worse time. She had felt discomfort on the ride in but had hoped it was due to the strenuousness of the trip. Only when she had inspected her drawers and seen the dark stain had she known otherwise.

"What's wrong, Tandy girl?" Bitter Creek asked, quickly kneeling beside her.

She burst out crying and lodged her head under his neck. "It's my monthlies," she sobbed.

Bitter Creek sighed and smiled. "Hey, that's all right, girl," he murmured in her ear. "I'm sorry for you, but it'll go away, won't it? It always does."

She shook her head and banged her fist lightly against his chest. Men! They don't know a thing about a woman! "But you're leaving, and I wanted —I wanted—"

"Shhh," he said and gently rocked her. "Maybe it's a way of saying it's just not the right time." He was trying to find the right things to say.

"You been saying that for years now," she sniffed.

"But we both know the day's coming—real soon now. Don't we?" He tried to lift her face up to look into it.

"But I wanted it to be tonight, before you leave."

"I'll be back right soon enough."

"Ohhh B.C.!" Her voice quivered. "Will it ever happen? Will we ever be together long enough?" Her voice was small and gasping between sobs.

"Sure we will," he answered.

She clung to him. "Why can't you and me just ride out tomorrow—together?" She felt his head start to shake and she hugged him. "We can go to Texas to Grand's ranch. Please, B.C. We did what you wanted. And your friends aren't here any more—"

"I still got Bill, and there's Rose, and there's going to be new friends soon. And I'm alive, ain't I? And we got each other, ain't we?"

"Yes but—" Tandy could not think of anything more. "Then you want to stay?"

Bitter Creek cocked his head to one side and thought. "Maybe it's just I'm not ready to settle down, I dunno." He thought about it some more. "I don't even know whether it's 'cause of them railroad people any more. I think it is. I mean, it's still satisfying to rob 'em and know they're squirming in their overstuffed chairs. It's good to know I'm doing something agin' 'em and they can't stop us. I mean, with all their money, all their power and threats and people, they can't stop us. And that does me good—sort of makes up for a lot of things, y'know what I mean?"

He held her tightly. "I don't aim to do this forever. It's just that I got to give 'em more what's due 'em. Somehow, settling down to ranching wouldn't suit me right now."

"Oh, I dunno either, B.C.," Tandy murmured,

suddenly very tired. "I just want to be with you, that's all. Let's go to sleep."

Before she knew it, she and B.C. were riding a pair of white stallions over the rolling plains, laughing and holding hands. And all around them were strangers watching them, and applauding and smiling.

A month passed before she saw Bitter Creek again. The nights got colder. For many desperate moments, she felt sick over the thought he might stay away the entire winter or, worse, that something terrible had happened to him.

One day three horsemen broke into view: Doolin, Bitter Creek and a stranger a couple years older than them who sat his horse stern and straight. They waved joyfully as they made their way to the corral.

The two women came to the lip of the cave and watched, inspecting the new rider closely. He looked vaguely familiar, though they'd never seen him before. He had a broad face with stubbly chin whiskers. There was a familiar fierceness about his deliberate movements, the way he jabbed his knees at his horse, for instance.

"You'll never guess who this is," Doolin said, smiling as he came up and gave Rose an embrace. "This here is the last of the Daltons—ol' Bill himself."

"Bill Dalton?" Rose questioned. "Why, I thought you was in California."

Dalton smiled and shuffled on his feet uncomfortably. "Lately, the name Dalton isn't looked upon with too much favor, 'specially when you're trying to break into politics."

"Left it all behind," Doolin commented, stretching himself out on the floor of the cave and scratching his back against the hard surface.

"Kicked out is more correct." Dalton tried to smile his experience off. "But that's all right with me too. If they want me to be an outlaw, then outlawing it'll be."

"And a damn good one he is," Bitter Creek added, sitting alongside Tandy. He reached over to his saddlebag and turned it upside down, spreading out the flood of coins and paper money that fell out.

"Oh my goodness," Tandy exclaimed. "Where in the world did you get all of that?"

"All that?" B.C. grinned and winked at his companions. "Hell, that's only our share, honey. We got us a haul this time."

Rose turned to Doolin. "What in hell did you all do?" She was half angry and half flabbergasted.

Doolin leaned on an elbow and kicked his saddlebag over to her. "Sort of a spur of the moment idea," he said casually, although he could not help display a wide grin of satisfaction. "Ol' Bill here met up with us at Halsell's so we sort of figured we'd see how he would fit in." He winked over at Bill Dalton.

"Wanted to see how I'd do under gunfire," Dalton explained to the girls. He had been through all sorts of tests throughout his career and nothing fazed him by now. "Y'gotta admit, I did all right. Can't say the same for Crescent Sam though."

Doolin smiled. "Aw, don't you worry none 'bout Sam. He can ride circles 'round them tin star men. He'll sashay in one of these days."

Later, after they had eaten and were sitting around the fire absorbing the comfort of the heat, Rose jabbed Doolin in the ribs. Bill Dalton had made an excuse to wander the glen to think things out and Rose interrupted Doolin's own thoughts. "Okay, Bill," she inquired. "Y'might be able to fool everyone else but not me. You been testing Dalton ever since he come here. If your eyes could speak, you'd have run out of words a long time ago the way you keep staring at him. Something bothering you?"

Doolin shrugged and turned away, not caring to answer. Rose looked over at Bitter Creek, who also shrugged, deciding to keep out of it. Rose persisted. "You got something agin Dalton? Is that's what's eatin' you?"

Doolin turned to her. "I don't know about him," he finally answered.

"You don't think we can trust him?"

He didn't answer.

Rose stared at him, trying to guess at the answers. "What's the matter? You afraid he might try to take over?"

Doolin straightened and she knew she had found it. "You're afraid he's come to take over, aren't you?"

Bill squirmed. Bitter Creek watched, then spoke up. "If he is, he's got himself a bobcat by the tail. I sure as hell am not going to choose him over you, pard."

"None of us are, Bill," Rose added. "If he wants to have a gang, let him start his own. You're a born leader—and like B.C. says, there's no way he's going to take over from you here."

"He doesn't appear to me to want to lead," Tandy voiced her opinion. "I don't think you have any worry, Bill."

"That's why I took him up to Spearville. Wanted to see just how far he'd go with me," Doolin said.

"And he proved himself out," Bitter Creek added.

Doolin's spirits improved. Whatever doubts he might have harbored seemed to have vanished and his grin reappeared. "Sure as hell I don't mind a Dalton being part of the gang," he admitted. "But it's going to be the Doolin gang. That's the way it is."

"That's the way, pard." Bitter Creek matched his grin. "We're all behind you."

Tandy glanced up at B.C. She was happy for him and enjoyed his friendship with Doolin. She was conscious of Bitter Creek's closeness to her too. She'd spent over a month without him, plenty of time to dream of him, to contemplate their future together, their togetherness. She sighed.

Gone such a long time and they were still absorbed in talking. She touched his leg and felt his heart beat against the side of her face. She glanced around as they talked and tried to estimate how tired they all might be, how soon she could feign a yawn and retire.

Nestled by the fire, Tandy's body felt prickly. It was almost the same feeling she had when frightened that someone or something was stalking her. Her back itched and she squirmed with restlessness. She tried to lie still.

It was later. She must have dozed off, for Dalton had returned and they were all talking in soft tones so as not to disturb her. She jumped in her awakening and grabbed hold of B.C.

"What's the matter honey?" he asked.

She blinked around to get her bearings, then smiled at him lazily. "I think I'll go to bed now," she murmured and abruptly stood up.

"We all better get some sleep," Doolin said. "I got ideas that need talking over tomorrow. We got to have clear heads." As he watched Tandy, a slow grin spread over his face. He understood why she wanted to go off with B.C. and he was pleased about it. They all said their goodnights and retired to their rooms.

Tandy had placed her porcelain cup in a different location on the shelf that Bitter Creek had built for her. She couldn't make up her mind where she liked it most, next to the small blue dish that she kept her soap in or next to the glass kerosene lamp that flickered its light against the cap's gold design.

She was conscious of B.C. undressing, placing his pants across the box of supplies still unpacked from their sodhouse. She heard the pressing of the straw mattress as he sat down, then his labored breathing as each boot was slipped off his feet.

She returned the cup to its former position near the lamp and waited, back to him, barely able to breathe. Then she turned off the lamp.

There was a rustling and then stillness and she knew he was settled beneath the blankets, waiting. She still pretended to be busy, lifting things up, placing them back again. As she bent over, she cast a quick glance in his direction. He was on his back, hands under his head staring up into the blackness of the cave's cold ceiling.

"You been away a long time, B.C.," she said softly.

There was a shuffling movement. "It wasn't exactly my choice, honey," he answered, matching her muted whisper. "And I sure missed you a heap too."

"You do anything exciting?"

Silence. She knew she would never hear all the truth. But then, she didn't particularly want to know about his ventures into town, of visits to bordellos or to other women. Those times, with those women, were merely to release tensions, those things men were supposed to have and needed to release. But that was all right, as long as she was his woman and he came back to her. That is, she would tolerate his womanizing until she could satisfy him. After that, she hoped there would never be need of his going elsewhere.

She reached up in the dark to take a small bottle

from the shelf. Perfume! She had saved it for how long? Who knew and who cared? She quickly dabbed herself, neck, shoulders, ears and stomach. Quickly, she returned the bottle and bent to slip under the blankets.

Bitter Creek half turned to her, pushing himself back against the stone wall to give her room, not touching but trying to peer through the darkness. "Hmmm," he said cautiously. "You smell good!"

"I been saving it," she answered. She lay on her back, eyes transfixed to a spot above her, unable to move. She was suddenly afraid. Oh God, she thought, after all these years, am I going to panic? I can't do it!

Suddenly she felt his finger tips touch her side by accident, stay there a moment, then quickly withdraw.

"You're naked—again!" His voice was lower and a bit shaky, she thought.

"No," she answered, still without moving. "I got on my perfume!"

She waited, painfully aware of time, how slowly it had moved that evening. She knew the room was quiet, yet there seemed to be a roaring in her head. She lay there sensing a nearly unbearable build-up of pressure within her.

Her anxieties ceased with sudden abruptness as Bitter Creek's hand inched forward, slowly, up her side and onto her flat stomach. He had done this many times before, but this time it was different. This time there was no cotton flannel between her skin and his hand. This time there was nothing to dull his touch. His hand was so gentle. It came to her middle, then stopped and rested there. Slowly, with tears building up in her eyes, Tandy turned on her side to him. Carefully she wound her arms around his neck, drawing him in close to her.

"Oh B.C.," she murmured. They kissed. It was new. It was different. Not like the other times, except for maybe their very first kiss a long time ago. This time, there was fullfillment in the kiss, as if all the pieces had finally come into place. The kiss slowly grew in intensity, into a desperate feeling of not being able to get enough. It was as if she had been hanging over a waterfall and had let go, tumbling downward. But the water was warm, the feeling was warm, and there was nothing to be afraid of except to taste the deliciousness of that moment and abandon all else.

"Ohhh B.C.," she murmured in his ear, and they held each other as if doing that too for the first time.

Tenderly, he released her and cupped her chin. She could see only the outline of his face, but sensed his eyes boring into hers. Slowly, he pulled away from her and sat up. For a moment, she panicked, then realized he was unbuttoning his long johns and slipping them off.

A new sensation rippled through her body and she pressed her legs together instinctively. Lord, would she be able to breathe? At last, the time had come! Would she be prepared for it? Would she disappoint him?

His body was lean. She remembered running her hand over the fetlock of an Appaloose pony her brother once rode to their ranch. It felt so firm and rippled with hidden muscles beneath the cool skin. So did Bitter Creek's shoulder as her hands timidly sought him.

Her fingers spread out through the hairs on his chest, coarse, curly and strong underneath. His hands were following hers and she froze as they found her breasts. She paused, taking in the deliciousness of his touch. Rose! Again, she pressed her legs together. She was getting damp and ready for him.

She let her fingers slide to his waist, so narrow without a hint or ripple of fat. She was pleased—no, she was proud! He was a magnificent animal. She waited for him, but he seemed more than content just fondling her breasts, cupping them, gently massaging, then pressing his fingers over her hard nipples. Oh God, she thought, it was more heavenly than she dared imagine. She couldn't stand it any longer. Her stomach was beginning to feel cramped, empty.

She took a deep breath and let her fingers run down his hip to his thigh. She spread out her fingers, feeling the hair on his legs beneath her palm, coarse, electrifying. Slowly, she edged downward, the hair becoming coarser and thicker, until her fingers closed around his hardness.

So this was what it was all about, she thought, but felt more than thought. She drew herself to him, not letting his hardness go but pressing its tip into her belly, then sliding it downward, slowly, carefully, gently into her own wetness.

"Ohh, B.C.," she mumbled, and rolled over onto her back, pulling him with her. She was not conscious of his weight, only the delicious meeting of their bodies, his pressing into hers.

They waited a moment, tasting each other. Then he pushed himself up from her. As if it had been a lifetime habit, she took hold of him and guided him to her. She was wet and sensitive and all her nerve endings seemed to be concentrated in that one area. Gently, very gently, he eased into her, then stopped.

"It's okay," she whispered and locked her hands behind his back. "Don't stop now. Oh God, don't stop now!" It hurt only for a second, hurt less than she had feared. But then, she had been preparing herself for this moment. "Oh my God," she gasped and she pressed him to her. "Don't move!" She couldn't stand it any more. "Don't move," she whispered and kissed him, his mouth, his cheek, his neck and ears.

"Tandy," he whispered.

"Shhh," she mumbled. "I been waiting too long for this moment, B.C. I don't want no words—not yet. I just want you."

She knew he was grinning. "Well, sweet girl," he breathed. "You sure enough got me!"

Tandy squirmed under him. "Hmmm," she answered dreamily. She hooked her ankles behind his legs and wondered how long she could keep him inside her.

She had waited so long for this moment that she cried silently to herself. Now—now, they were one! She felt complete, fulfilled. She was no longer a young girl, but a woman! A woman who could compete with the best—Rose, her mother, anyone!

She rolled her body around under him, wanting to wrap him as a blanket with her own body. "I love you, B.C.," she sobbed, unable to contain the rush of her feelings. "I love you, I love you, I love you!"

12

They were told to expect a crowd for the evening meal. The two women had made a list of supplies needed which the three men would purchase at Ingalls on their way home.

Winter was definitely in the air and canvas was spread across the entrance to the cave, stretched by ropes and braces. The makeshift curtain would suffice for those who would stick out the winter in the glen. It was unusual for the gang to gather this late. In previous years, the Daltons had disbanded long before now to winter elsewhere in more comfortable quarters. However, Doolin was persistent that the year end with a jolt to the railroad people. "I want them saying my name all winter long. Want to haunt them in their dreams, not knowing when we'll strike next!"

Tandy was looking forward to winter. That would be the time when she and Bitter Creek could be together without too many interruptions or distractions. Even this one last plan Doolin was cooking up couldn't douse her spirits, though she tried to keep from bubbling over too much. Once, she had caught Rose staring at her with a whimsical smile on her lips and knew the older woman guessed the source of her happiness. She didn't really care. In fact, Tandy delighted in the fact that one of these days Rose would press her into divulging her secret. But it would be different. It would be woman-talk then.

"Have you met any of these men?" Tandy asked Rose as they waited in the glen, absorbing the noon sun filtering through the trees.

Rose shook her head. "No, but I sure have heard enough 'bout them. That's all Doolin's been talking about for days. B.C. too?"

Tandy felt her face redden. "No, we've been talking about other things." Apparently Rose chose not to pursue the matter and she was relieved. "Why do you think they all joined up with us?" Tandy asked shortly.

"Why not? I suppose the same reason we all did."

Tandy giggled. "I joined 'cause Bitter Creek did."

Rose hesitated. "You're the exception. You're always the exception!"

"What do you mean by that?" Tandy asked frowning.

"Oh, don't mind me," Rose said.

"No," Tandy persisted. "What did you mean I was the exception?"

Rose sighed and took her time answering. "I sometimes think you don't belong here. I mean, you admit you're only here 'cause of Bitter Creek."

"What's wrong with that?"

"The rest of us are here 'cause it's a way of life for us. We're fighting for what we believe in. We're doing what we want—we're free—" She threw up her hands. "There's a million reasons, but not out of love for someone."

Tandy had detected the bitterness in Rose's voice and it hurt. It hurt all the more because she had been in such a good mood. "I see no difference," she said defensively. "I'm here with Bitter Creek, but whatever reasons he has are my reasons also."

Rose let out a short sarcastic laugh. "Hell, honey, you wouldn't be here if it weren't for him. You don't go along with our ideas and ways."

Tandy thought about it. "Well, I don't like the shooting and the killing," she admitted.

"I had a boyfriend killed by a buckboard," Rose said. "Your life can end anywhere, no matter what you do. And you know as well as I do, none of the boys want to hurt anyone. It ain't us that start shooting first. As Doolin says, we only shoot to discourage people from doing something stupid, like trying to kill us. When a man starts aiming a gun to kill any one of us, there's no two ways about it. You got to shoot back."

"Well, I know that," Tandy admitted reluctantly. "It's just, ranching is more peaceful."

"Not any more," Rose answered. "Why do you think these cowboys are joining us? Ranching ain't the way it used to be. Them cowboys can't do what they're used to. Why, I remember when the Chisholm trail was open—I mean, if you ever wanted to see what hell-raising was all about, you shoulda seen them Texas cowpokes. But no more. The law and the towns told 'em no more. So you don't see trail drives no more. Pretty soon you won't even see ranches, because there'll be no more cowboys." Rose sighed and looked over at Tandy. "I tell you girl, this is the last of the good old days, right here. You should feel privileged you're taking part in them."

"Well, I do," Tandy admitted. "I mean, I really like Bill and the rest. And, lately, I do sort of feel like I belong, regardless of what you might think."

Rose studied Tandy. "I don't exepct you to feel the same as me," she finally answered thoughtfully. "Maybe its 'cause you feel more like a woman than me, I dunno."

"But you are woman, and you got feelings."

"That's not what I mean. You're more concerned with your man—having a ranch, being with him. Me, I just want to be part of whatever's going on. I'm not for that ol' wifey bit of staying home and having babies. Not me! Just 'cause I wear skirts don't make me entirely different from the rest of them males. I can do almost anything they can do!"

"But don't you ever wish for something else? I mean, haven't you ever wanted a home—a real home—and a family?" Tandy looked over at the older woman's profile. She knew Rose was irritated, knew somehow that she'd cut her to the quick, though she hadn't meant to.

"I had a baby once," Rose finally said in a low voice.

"You?" Tandy became curious. "What happened?"

Rose shrugged and turned her head away from Tandy to stare into the trees. "It's somewhere—I guess. It was a boy. Had it in the back room of a saloon in Dodge City." Her sigh was audible. "I nursed it for a while 'til I could get back on my feet, then gave the kid to this woman. She couldn't have any, apparently, and wanted it badly. Also, she could take better care of it. 'Sides, what in hell would I have done with a kid? That's the last time I ever got myself into trouble like that."

There was silence. Tandy stared at Rose with new interest. The story, though it had come as no great surprise, made her feel sad. "I'm sorry," was all she could manage.

Rose turned and smiled. "What for? I done the kid a favor probably—and certainly myself. Can you imagine me with a kid? I'd probably be behind some hash house, washing dishes and doing laundry. And that, honey, ain't my cup of tea. So don't you go being sorry for me. All I can say to you is think it over before you start having kids. You won't be able to keep this kind of life, believe me. I mean, do you want to raise a kid in this place?" She waved her hand about her. "And, if B.C. got you a house, can you imagine what it would be like? He'd be off and every once in a while, if you're lucky, he might be able to sneak in for an hour or so to see you. You call that kind of life something worth dreaming about? Not to me, it isn't!"

"But I don't want that either," Tandy explained.

"If we ever have a baby, I'd want B.C. and me to move down to Texas. I have a brother there who would give us land. We could set us up a ranch all our own and start a real life."

"Well, maybe that might happen, honey," Rose said softly. "But you know how these cowpokes are. You can't be pushin' 'em into something they don't like. B.C.'s just the same. You'll lose him for sure if you try. You'll just have to give him time."

There was another long silence. "It's good that you got a family to go to," Rose said then.

"Only a brother," Tandy said quickly, then thought about it. "I mean, I got a mother—not too far away, for that matter. But I don't know whether I want to see her again."

"Your dad?"

Tandy closed her eyes and tried to bring back those things she had long buried in some closet of her mind. She told Rose of her mother, Miranda, the elusive awesome woman who was always leaving her and her father to fend for themselves. Her father! That still hurt. Her devotion for a man thought to be her father, poor Grand Woodrowe. And then, a stranger, her mother's lover, who turned out to be her real father! Tandy sighed and looked up into the sky with blurry eyes. "I dunno—I'm all mixed up, I guess."

She could feel Rose watching her. "Don't try to figure out the past," the older woman said. "I stopped trying a long time ago. I been passed around between families so many times I lost track. The Smiths, the Jacks—" Rose sighed. "Hell, it don't matter none really. I'm me and that's all I have to worry about."

"You got Bill," Tandy spoke up.

Rose let out a small laugh. "Yeah, I got him right now. Who knows who the next one will be."

"You think there will be someone else?"

Rose laughed. "With Bill's roaming eye? Honey, Bill's more than one woman can handle. He's never one to be strapped down for too long a period. But I knew that when I took up with him."

"Then, why did you?"

"Why not? He was the best man around, and still is in my opinion. So I enjoy him while I can. I don't worry about tomorrow, can't you tell?"

Tandy shook her head. She took a deep breath to clear her lungs with the fresh sweet cool air. It felt good.

"You're a romantic, Tandy," Rose commented. "In a way, that's a charming thing to see in this wilderness. But it's going to do you no good in the end. This isn't romantic country, nor is what we do romantic stuff. Can't mix the two together no matter how hard you try."

Tandy didn't want to listen. "We'll find us a place," she said stoutly.

"I wish you luck, girl," Rose said, shrugging. "I truly mean that."

Tandy stared over at Rose, then squinted off into the sun's bright light, her brow furrowed. She didn't like Rose's tone; she doubted the sincerity of her good wishes.

They were mostly silent for the rest of the afternoon. The riders appeared towards dusk. The two women rose and watched them come galloping in on the trail from the west, shadowed darkly by the setting sun. There were five new ones with Doolin, Bitter Creek and Dalton. Tandy waved at B.C. vigorously, then at the others, happy to have them all come in and end the brooding time she'd been spending with Rose. She kept watching them until they dismounted, turning her back on Rose.

Bitter Creek and Doolin advanced, waving the five newcomers to follow. They lined up before the women respectfully, hats doffed. Only two stared back boldly and these were the first to be introduced.

Doolin did the honors. Grinning, he said, "This sawed off shotgun goes by the name of Little Dick West, for a reason you needn't be concerned 'bout." Tandy blushed. The short cowboy gave Doolin a tolerant smile, then turned a steely blue-eyed gaze on Tandy that made her blink from its intensity.

"Little Dick suits me fine, ma'am," he said pleasantly. "Hope you'll get to like it."

Tandy, slightly flustered by his even tone, smiled but didn't reply.

"Now, it is said," Doolin continued, regarding West with open respect, "that Little Dick can get his gun out of that holster faster than a jackrabbit can mate. I dunno whether that's true or not, but I seen him put holes in six cans 'fore I could bend my trigger finger."

The others laughed and jostled Little Dick's side good-naturedly. "Shucks, ain't no way any human being is faster than a jack rabbit," Little Dick said modestly, still looking at Tandy.

"Next to him is Red Buck Waightman." Doolin's introduction to this man came with a forced casualness, as if he were reluctant to imply anything about him, even in jest, that might be taken as derogatory. Tandy could guess why. Waightman was a huge man with a beet-red alcoholic complexion creased with a perpetual scowl; he also had slab-like arms and fists that looked like they could throttle or crunch a man with equal ease.

"Red Buck, meet Tandy and Rose," Doolin said cheerily.

"Pleased to meet you," Tandy said.

"Yeah," Waightman said.

Rose just nodded at him.

"The runt over at the end," Doolin went on, "is my friend, Arkansas Tom, sometimes known as Roy Daugherty."

Tandy managed to avert her eyes from the glowering Red Buck to the cowboy mentioned. He was a beanpole of a young lad, possibly her own age, with a pock-marked, scabby face that made her palms itch. Roy Daugherty, or Arkansas Tom, smiled awkwardly, turned to Doolin for approval, got it, then grinned, showing yellow teeth. A mangy pup, Tandy thought. She turned her attention to the man next to him.

"Next is Dan Clifton. He was born with a stick of dynamite in each hand—knows it better'n his own stick. We call him Dynamite Dan."

Tandy smiled hesitantly. Clifton was balding, which made him appear older than the rest, but he had a smooth face with hardly a trace of beard. He wore his cowboy hat far back on his head, as if proud of his hairless temples, and there was something dandyish about him, from his glistening white smile to his jet-black pants to the silver buckle at his slim waist.

"And the last one is ol' Charlie Pierce," Doolin said with a sigh. "Ol' Charlie and me go back quite a ways. Why I don't know, 'cept he don't know no better." He turned to Rose and Tandy. "Well, what do you say? What do you think of the Doolin gang now?"

Rose cleared her throat. "If nothing better, we sure got ourselves some handsome faces," she commented. "It's going to be good company for a girl to keep."

Doolin turned to his friends and winked. "One of the prerequisites for joining up is they keep their hands off our women. Not that any woman in their right mind would have anything to do with 'em."

"Don't forget the other two," Bitter Creek added from the back.

"Oh yeah," Doolin added. "There will be two more. Tulsa Jack and Little Bill—you'll be meeting them later. Right now, they're setting things up for me."

"Setting what up?"

Doolin grinned. "Rosie, I told you I wanted to do something big 'fore winter sets in. Actually, we come back here for you. I tol' you I'd give you something important to do the next job."

"It's about time." Rose came forward eagerly. "What's on your mind?"

"First things first," Doolin answered with a smile. "First we get some grub into us. After that, we'll go over the plans."

As the men were finding niches in the caves for themselves and their belongings, Tandy edged over to Bitter Creek. "Do you know what Bill is planning?" she asked timidly.

B.C. smiled and put an arm about her waist. "Don't you go worrying, honey," he said. "Bill's got us a plan that'll keep them money-belted bigwigs fumin' and fussin' all winter long. It's sort of like a little Christmas present he's givin' 'em."

"Quit joking, B.C.," Tandy protested lightly. "I want to know how dangerous it's going to be."

"Tandy, you gotta understand everything we do we consider serious. Jus' 'cause we kid some don't mean we don't keep our eyes open to what's about. So, don't you go fretting your heart none; we got ourselves a—"

"A sure fire plan," Tandy finished for him bitterly. "That's what you used to say about the Daltons."

Bitter Creek looked at her sharply but said nothing.

"Will Rose be in any danger?"

B.C. shook his head. "You don't give up, do you?" He gave her a squeeze. "Rose is going to be our ace in the hole, and that's all I'm going to tell you for now."

Tandy smiled and leaned against him. "I'll always fret for you—until we get to Texas."

Bitter Creek gave her a hard look. "You're going to hang onto that idea like a bee smelling a rose, ain't you?"

"I'm going to hang onto that idea and hope until you give in to me, Mr. George Bitter Creek Newcomb!" Tandy laughed and put her arms around his neck and kissed him on the cheek.

There was good-natured bantering around the enlarged campfire later as they all devoured the meal. Most of the talk was of incidents experienced by those who worked the Halsell ranch together. Bill Dalton regaled them with his descriptions of California and exchanged stories with Doolin and Bitter Creek about his brothers and their exploits.

Tandy watched and listened. She found herself liking Little Dick who, come to find out, had a dry sense of humor, especially directed toward Doolin, who often laughed the loudest. Arkansas Tom, being the youngest and most vulnerable, took the most ribbing. The big man, Red Buck, paid little attention to the talk; he was fully absorbed in trying to fill his stomach. As his plate emptied, he found all he had to do was lift it out in the general direction of Tandy, who promptly took it to the stove to refill. Rose deliberately stayed away from the man and his ill manners.

"You all right, Rose?" Tandy asked as the two women bent over the pots.

Rose wiped the sweat from her forehead and gave her a wan smile. "Must have been something I ate. A bit weak but I'll be okay."

Later, with the bowls and plates put out on a plank to dry, they all spread out before the fire, feet nearest the heat, most on their elbows or sides staring into the flames. Talk had died and there seemed to be a brief interlude of contented silence.

Tandy had time to study each of the new men again. None was as handsome as either B.C. or Doolin, but they all shared the same sort of wildness and innocence that drew her closer to them. She felt protective towards them. That is towards all except Red Buck. Towards him she felt cautious.

"We're going to rob a train," Bill said suddenly, "but this time, it's not going to be around no station or town." Tandy was startled. Doolin looked around at the men's quizzical expressions. "We're going to mix up them railroad people bad. Something like the James boys did once in a while. Here's how." He drew a diagram on the dusty floor while they all crowded around. "We'll stop the train right here, close to where the tracks cross the Cimarron. That's wide-open country and there'll be nobody around to bother us. We can drag fallen timber from the riverbank to lay out in front of the engine. Soon as it stops, we jump 'em." He turned to them and grinned.

"Whoeee," Dynamite Dan whispered.

"What 'bout the guards on the train?" Red Buck asked. "You make it sound simple and it ain't."

Doolin nodded. "Right, Red Buck. That's where Rose and Little Bill come in. Little Bill's already headed for Adair with Tulsa Jack. He'll board the train there. Rose, you'll board the train at the next station—here. It'll be up to them two to find out if there are any guards and how many. If there's too many, Little Bill will stand outside on the platform, and that'll be a sign we won't do anything. But if Rose appears, that means we go." He looked around triumphantly.

"I like it," said Dynamite Dan, nodding.

"Why we need both of 'em?" Red Buck persisted.

Doolin explained patiently. "I'm going to make sure we don't run into an ambush. With two on that train, 'specially one being a woman, we make doubly certain nothing goes wrong."

Red Buck stirred on his rump and growled. "Aw, why not stop 'em anyway—no matter who the hell is there?" He looked around to see if an idea of his had any impact. "A couple of sticks of dynamite in them passenger cars and there'd be no worry 'bout guards noway." He attempted a grin but it faded when the others looked away.

"We do things my way," Bill answered, a sharpness in his voice that surprised Tandy. "We're not looking to kill anyone. Let's get that straight. Don't want no gunplay either, if we can help it." He looked Red Buck squarely in the eye. The big man held the stare, then shrugged and leaned back.

Bill looked at each man carefully, then nodded in satisfaction. "Good," he said with a sigh. "We all get some rest and be up early to take Rose."

Without question, the men rose and shuffled out to their bedrolls spread out under the stars.

"I'm going to bed," Rose said and got up unsteadily.

"You okay?" Bill asked. He frowned as he watched her stumble back to their quarters.

"She said she wasn't feeling good," Tandy explained. She arose herself, tugging onto B.C.'s hand for him to follow. "Good night, Bill."

"Yeah," Doolin called out, his eyes still studying the fabric Rose had retired behind. There was no doubt that he was concerned.

13

"Honey—wake up!"

Tandy awoke from a scary dream in a daze. She clutched at Bitter Creek's arm as he gently jostled her into consciousness.

"C'mon honey. Bill wants to talk to you!"

She fumbled around in her basket of clothing until she found a pair of pants, then quickly slid them on, shivering. She wondered what was happening that Doolin wanted her. She glanced about trying to guess the time but the cave was black. A faint fire glow came through the curtain, along with the crackling sound of new logs burning. There was a faint aroma of last night's coffee being warmed up.

The cave was quiet otherwise, and she guessed it was too early for the others to wake up. Then she thought of Rose. Something must be wrong with Rose. She tucked her heavy cotton nightshirt into her pants and hurried to the fire. Doolin and

B.C. were crouched together there, Bill looking even more worried than he had the night before.

She'd guessed right about Rose.

Bill nodded at her briefly and said, "Rose has been up most of the night. She's sick. Her face is hotter than a branding iron."

"You want me to go to her?" Tandy started to move but Bill shook his head and held her back. She looked down at him curiously.

"I need you, Tandy," Doolin said softly. "We need you." He hesitated, glancing at B.C. "Rose will be okay but she can't make this trip. That leaves me with a couple of choices. I can send one of the boys in her place. But that would mean one less to hit the express car." He looked at her seriously to see if she was understanding what was being said.

Tandy stared at him. She didn't quite see what this all had to do with her. But, as Doolin stared hard at her, it suddenly occurred to her that he was about to ask her to take Rose's place. She turned to Bitter Creek wide-eyed, then back to Doolin. There was a sickening sensation in her stomach.

Doolin went on. "I could let Little Bill handle it all by himself. But then, if something happened to him, we'd be set up for a trap." Doolin let it all sink into her mind. He continued slowly. "But if you went in Rose's place then we'd all be safe again. No chance of any slip-ups, y'know what I mean?" He waited for an answer but when none came he glanced over to Bitter Creek for help.

"Hon?" B.C. placed his hand over hers gently

and shook it slightly to arouse her. "You don't have to do it if you don't feel right." He looked at Doolin for confirmation, then back to her. "We don't want you to do nothing you don't feel good about. Bill thought, though, since you did a bang-up job the last time, you got the spunk to be able to do this thing."

Doolin smiled widely. "I know you can do it, Tandy girl. There's really nothing to it. We put you on the train. You go up and down the aisle for whatever reasons you see fit and check out everyone. If you think anything's suspicious—anything at all not right—such as there's too many men on the train with guns—you know—then when that train stops all you have to do is just stay in your seat. Ol' Raidler will get up and get out, sort of out of curiosity to see what's happening. That's our sign there's trouble about. But—now listen carefully, honey." He edged close to Tandy to make sure she was listening. "If you think things are normal—then, when we stop that train, you step outside the end car. That's so you're out of the way. Raidler will handle the passengers and we'll take care of the express. When we're done, we'll pick you both up with the horses and we'll ride home."

Tandy breathed out; it seemed her first breath in quite a while. "Just like that?" she asked.

Both men grinned. "Jus' like that. We'll have set them railroad people on their ears and they'll be so darn mad it'll be a warm winter here in Oklahoma territory."

They waited. Tandy blinked her eyes uncertainly. "And if I don't go?"

Doolin sighed and leaned back. He carefully placed his hands on his knees and inspected them as he hunted for words, allowing time to quell the anger she had ignited in him.

"We do the best we can," he explained. "With you, the chances are real good that nothing will happen." He waited a moment. "Without you, we could run into problems." He deliberately looked over at Bitter Creek with a troubled expression on his face.

Bitter Creek realized what Doolin was up to and was a bit irritated at his friend. He turned to Tandy. "Aw, honey, I'll be okay. You do what you feel right in doing."

Doolin quickly added his ideas. "Of course. I agree. Ol' Bitter Creek can handle himself good. We all can. But as long as I lead this outfit, I want to do everything in my power to make sure there's no mistakes, no way no one can trap us or sneak up on us or overpower us. We're good, Tandy girl, and we'll probably make it without a scratch. So will Bitter Creek here. It's just, you'd be our assurance nothing will go wrong—sort of take some of the worry off our shoulders." He smiled good-naturedly.

Tandy frowned. "You don't give a girl much of a choice, do you?"

"Me?" Doolin smiled. "Did I say you had to do this? Did I?" He turned to B.C. wide-eyed with innocence. Then he turned back to Tandy. "But I knew you'd do it 'cause of B.C. here—and because you got spunk. Why, I declare, its like having two more with you and Rose here. I'm mighty proud of you. Wait and see, this is going to be one of the best things you ever done."

Tandy thought about it. She thought about it for the rest of the early dawn as she and B.C. rode silently toward the small railroad junction. She had dressed in her finest, a purple tight-waisted gown with folds that draped close to the ground. It had a corsetted top that pushed her breasts high over the bodice, which was half hidden under the grey shawl that she held tightly around her shoulders.

She had twirled her hair on top in a bun, making her look more austere and older than her years. She had decided not to wear the veiled hat only because she had a long horseback ride to the station.

"You'll have a wait before the train comes in," Bitter Creek said as they approached the small town. "It'll give me time to cut through to where we'll stop it."

"How will I know Raidler?" she asked suddenly, trying to recall the instructions given by Doolin.

B.C. grinned. "He'll probably think you're Rose but that's okay. He knows a woman will be getting on here. Hopefully it'll be just you. But in case there's another woman, you're to carry a handkerchief or something white in your hand. You got something?"

Tandy nodded. "How will I know him?"

"He'll get to you," B.C. smiled. "Little Bill's one

of the best. Me and him been friends longer than most. Wait 'til you hear the stories he's got. Been to college and all that."

Tandy had much to think about, seated on the bench by the tracks, the wall of the small station against her back. The shivers that passed through her body were not from anticipation from the job she was about to do but from the cool bite of the morning. She found that she had to rise and walk back and forth a couple of times to slap away the cold.

She was surprised at how calm she was. She couldn't believe it. She was actually going to take part in a train robbery—at least as an accessory which was practically the same thing. It was something she used to read about. Certainly the women she had pictured were in no way like herself.

It was exciting! She wondered what her mother would say. It was strange that she thought of Miranda at such times; this one wasn't the first. She wondered whether Miranda had ever done anything as daring as robbing a train! She doubted it, and giggled to herself. It was strange how one thing led to the next. Here she was, almost an outlaw!

The sound of the train's whistle startled her. Nervously, Tandy took out the small hanky from her bag and twisted it in her fingers. She glanced at the few small houses and storefronts squatting like ghosts down the dirt road. A dog barked from somewhere behind one house. Then there was a sound of a door being slammed and pretty soon a man bustled across the road toward the station, his arms flailing into a jacket. Bald-headed, stooped, he was too busy with this chore to notice Tandy until he had unlocked the side door. He twisted around the corner and looked her over quizzically, probably wondering how she had gotten there and why.

"You needing a ticket?" he asked in a raspy voice.

Tandy nodded and rose to come toward him.

"Where to?"

The question startled her. No one had told her where to. She mumbled something, desperately trying to think of a place she knew the train passed through.

"Y'say Guthrie?" the man asked.

Tandy nodded, relieved. Things were going better than she'd expected. Slowly, she regained her confidence. "One way, please," she added and dug into her purse for the money, pleased with herself that her voice did not shake.

She waited patiently as the train stopped, hissing off steam to each side, hiding the locomotive almost entirely. The two express cars seemed forbidding, the two small windows giving little hint as to what was inside. A side door opened in the second car and a man leaned out, looking up and down the train. He was shirtsleeved, with handlebars that gave him a sinister look. Tandy could not estimate whether he was a guard or mail-sorter. He stood waiting there, glancing at the open station door, with only an occasional look at her.

She thought she saw movement in the first express

car but it could have been a shadow that was dancing about along the sides of the cars from the steam. A lean, dark-suited conductor trudged up from the rear passenger cars, slapping the side of his trousers at each step with a wrapped signal flag. When he was in front of Tandy, he hesitated and looked her over from head to foot. "You takin' this train?" he asked gruffly. She nodded. Without a word, he cocked his head toward the back and went on into the station building.

Slowly, Tandy sauntered down the dirt track to the first passenger car where a small stepping box had been placed. She was conscious of exchanging glances with a few faces in the windows above her. Well, she thought, this is it! At least no one else was getting aboard; Bitter Creek's friend should be able to spot her. She wondered which of the faces peering down at her was Little Bill Raidler's.

At the entry, Tandy paused, once more to glance down the length of the train to see if anyone else was boarding, then stepped into the coach. She was pleased. Though her heart was beating fast, she knew she was in control of herself. She only hoped her face showed her calm. Quickly, she glanced down the length of the car. There were only six passengers, all men, a few giving her a casual glance. Two wore bowler hats, obviously drummers of some sort with their big black suitcases within reach. She gave them no heed.

Another man, with hat pulled low over his face, was a cowpoke; his saddle was thrown over the seat in front of him and he was scrunched back against the window with his feet propped up. The other three men she could not guess at. They were older, garbed in grey suits with white shirts and vests. As she walked slowly by, she noted each carried a holstered gun. But no rifles were in sight. It was difficult to judge whether they were guards or merely passengers. She thought three would not be too many to worry about.

Carefully, she made her way between the cars and pushed herself against the far door. There were more people in the end car—over a dozen with a good handful of them women. The passengers gave her a sleepy inspection, then went back either to rest or look out the windows at the small town. Tandy slowly made her way down the aisle, spotting an empty seat in back. The couples she barely glanced at. The men returned her stare, some with inviting grins as they moved over to make room for her. She smiled back and continued on her way, noting those who carried guns. In this car, there were a few who carried rifles and these would bear watching.

One, in particular, drew her interest. A square-faced cowboy with a lazy soft smile watched her all the way down the car until she sat across the aisle from him. His eyelids were half closed, yet she knew he was studying her. When she turned to study him, he bowed slightly and touched the brim of his hat in a salute. Quickly, she turned away and stared out the window.

"May I sit here?"

Tandy jumped at the closeness of the voice. She had been absorbed in the passing landscape as the engine took up speed. She looked up and saw the square-faced cowboy. She brushed her skirt closer to her and inched to the window.

"Thank you." His voice had a gentle touch to it that made her want to smile. "I bet your name is Rose," he said as an introduction.

Tandy grinned and shook her head. "No," she answered. "But only because Rose couldn't make it."

He frowned at her for a moment as he contemplated his next move, not sure he liked this development. Suddenly, he seemed to make up his mind, or at least, remember his manners. "S'cuse me. Name is Raidler, William Raidler." Again, he touched the brim of his hat.

Nice manners! Tandy nodded her head. "I'm Tandy Girondin," she said, and looked around to see if anyone could hear. "Rose got sick last night so I'm taking her place."

"Tandy? Tandy—" Raidler looked at her, then slowly grinned. "You're the Kid's girl!"

Tandy's eyes snapped. "I'm Bitter Creek's woman," she answered firmly.

"Bitter Creek," he corrected himself. Then he allowed his eyes to travel over her body. It wasn't an insolent stare, but one of appraisal and open admiration that he took no pains to hide. "And you're right on that—a woman. But from the way ol' Bitter Creek talked of you, I had a portrait of a younger girl." He smiled again. "Not that you aren't young. We are all young at heart. How about a young woman? Would that suffice?"

Tandy grinned. "Your words sound pretty, Mr. Raidler, thank you kindly."

"No need of thanks when honest observations are being made. Bitter Creek—you see how easily I can call him that now—he didn't go into much detail on how pretty you are. And, to tell you the truth, I was prepared for someone a mite older than you."

Tandy laughed. She felt very much at ease with this man. It felt good that he was one of B.C.'s close friends.

"You wouldn't have been disappointed if Rose had been able to come," Tandy declared. "She's a very beautiful woman."

"Ah," Raidler smiled. "Then fate willed in either event that a beautiful maiden would be at my side for this adventure."

Tandy's smile faltered as she suddenly remembered their purpose. She looked out the window to collect her thoughts, then turned back to the cowboy. "When will the train be stopped?"

"About an hour from now," came the answer. "If you want to get some rest, I'll keep an eye out for you."

Tandy shook her head. "I don't think I could sleep even if I wanted to."

"Is this the first time you've done anything like this?"

She nodded. "I helped out a couple of times, but

only holding the horses or driving a buggy. Nothing this close!"

Raidler grinned. "Nothing to it, really. But then, this is my first time also." He turned to her, then beamed a smile.

14

Time was something rarely measured in the territory. It was true that one of the treasures men seemed to value was a large circular golden pocket watch to be worn in the vest. But it was for show, not necessarily for the time of day. There was no need of timetables. Things happened usually by force of habit, whim of mind, or nature taking its course. An hour's train ride was a goodly number of minutes, a span in which one could take a quick snooze or engage in a good conversation over past experiences. An hour's time was something that could be waited out before the edge of patience dictated doing something else.

An hour's time on the train to Guthrie was a too brief a moment when it came to being with Little Bill Raidler. At least in Tandy's mind it was. It seemed he had hardly begun to describe college life in the east when there was a tooting of the train's whistle and a steady slowing. Their conversation stopped and both looked out the window.

On the right, the Cimarron, muddy and lazy, cut its way through the prairie, its side lined with scrub brush and a few poplars, dull yellow in the mid-morning sunlight. Tandy tried to squeeze her face tight against the cold glass to catch what was ahead but the straightness of the track afforded no view of the front. She thought she could see the bulwark of a bridge but wasn't sure.

"This must be it," Raidler said in a low voice and looked about to see how much commotion the slowing of the train was causing.

A few curious passengers began to open the windows to lean out but so far, no one had unholstered a gun or taken up a rifle.

"What do you say, girl?" Raidler murmured, his voice no longer having an urge towards laughter in it.

Tandy shrugged. "There don't seem to be any guards waiting for us, unless they are in the express cars."

Raidler nodded. "A couple of these dudes here might be law but I agree with you. I don't think there's nothing we can't put a handle on. You better get up and wander to the platform. Make it appear you're just curious or you want to stretch." He held her arm down for a moment as the train slowed. Then, satisfied that it was coming to a halt, he nodded his head and helped her up. "Just keep your head low if things start popping off."

Tandy nodded and glanced about the car, noting a few were staring at her. She tugged at her clothes, trying to appear nonchalant, feigning a small yawn and stretching her arms. She took a step forward, then appeared to make another decision. She turned and opened the door to the end platform and stepped out.

She didn't know what to expect. It was quiet except for the screeching of the iron wheels grinding to a final stop. The morning was beautiful and brisk, with a bite to it suggesting a light frost. It felt good to take a deep breath. She followed with her eyes the two brown ribbons of rail that drew closer together as the distance enveloped them at the horizon.

Her trance was suddenly jolted as shots broke the stillness about her. Instinctively, she pressed her hand to her heart and flattened against the side of the car. She was conscious of a shout from inside the coach as Bill Raidler rose from his seat, gun in hand, and ordered all to keep their seats. There were more shots and yelling from outside. Hesitantly, Tandy edged outward and peered around.

Up front, beside the express cars, she spotted Doolin, Waightman, Dan Clifton and Arkansas Tom bringing their horses closer, firing their guns into the air and shouting to the people inside. Quickly, Tandy slid to the other side and peered. Bitter Creek, Dick West, Charley Pierce and another rider whom she guessed to be Tulsa Jack were doing the same thing on their side. Already the engineer and fireman stood alongside the engine, hands held high, watching and not daring to move.

The shooting suddenly stopped as the gang realized there was no resistance. The riders were gesturing to those in the cars to open the doors. Quickly, Tandy dodged to the other side of the train.

Sure enough, Doolin had motioned to Dynamite Dan to dismount and the bald man was bending low under the first express car. Tandy wondered whether he actually had any dynamite or whether this was another one of Doolin's scare tactics. It must have worked, for soon the door slid open and three men quickly jumped out, hands held high, and scampered away.

As the outlaws jumped into the express car, Tandy leaned back to wait. She wondered what it might have been like had she and Raidler not been on board the train—if the cars had been loaded with marshals. It was too horrible to think about! Somewhere, in the back of her mind, she felt good. She had contributed her part. Perhaps, just perhaps, she was partially responsible for the robbery having gone off so smoothly.

It was quiet, so much different from the one shoot-out she had participated in. It seemed so out of place to be robbing a train in the middle of a still, peaceful prairie. It was like a dream, too unreal, too unlikely. Everything was in slow motion.

She jumped with the war-whoop and gunshots as the riders charged down the length of the train to the rear. Tandy peered out and waved.

"Let's get to the passengers," Waightman shouted but Doolin waved him back.

"We got enough without getting passengers mad at us," he answered. Arkansas Tom drew in close with the empty mounts. Tandy reached out and swung onto her pony and backed away. A whistle brought Raidler backing out of the car. With some final words to those inside, he holstered his gun and swung down onto his mount.

"Let's go!"

They all shouted and, in a cloud of dust, left the stranded train to itself. Tandy bent into the wind, felt her hair loosen and fly out in black streamers. She didn't care. There was a smile on her face as she shared the excitement with the others.

Bitter Creek nudged his mount closer to hers. "You okay?" he shouted out and reached out with a gloved hand to touch hers.

She nodded. She felt glorious and wished she and B.C. were alone. They could ride off together somewhere, stop and lie down. All she wanted was to feel his arms about her. She quivered with the thought. It was too glorious for words. She let go the reins and held onto the pommel, content to sway with the animal, to shut her eyes, knowing they'd be together.

The group stopped mid-noon on a rise that overlooked a broken landscape in a panoramic dish below them. Satisfied that no one was following, they dismounted, loosened the girths and roped the horses together so they wouldn't stray off.

Wordlessly, they squatted on their haunches, at first not saying much, just looking around, some grinning, others rolling their smokes.

"That was as easy as scratching my hind side," Little Dick stated to no one in particular.

"Easy?" Bill Dalton wiped at his nose. "That train coulda been robbed singlehanded."

"They weren't expecting us this late in winter," Raidler commented dryly. "But 'tis far better to be late than not show up at all."

"Jeez!" Little Dick shook his head. "You always got a word for everything?" It was said in good spirit.

Raidler grinned. "I guess there's been words written for just about every occasion."

"Well," Arkansas Tom declared, "I bet nothing's been wrote 'bout the Doolin gang!"

"Written," Raidler corrected. "If there hasn't, I imagine after today's episode, plenty will be said."

"Whooeee." Doolin shook his head. "Them railroad people ain't going to sleep a wink. They's going to have one big misery wondering whether they should guard their trains all winter from now on."

"They've been having it too easy winters," Bitter Creek added. "No reason why we should be the only ones to worry 'bout surviving over the cold."

They laughed. It was small talk that always cropped up during breaks. Again, there was plenty of time—always plenty of time. For one thing, the horses needed a breather. For another thing, people need a rest or a smoke once in a while. And there were times when it was good to stop for words to be said.

"I appreciate you all coming and taking part," Doolin spoke up. "We done what we set out to do and I couldn't ask for more. You're a good bunch. You wait and see—the Doolin gang is something that's going to be reckoned with. Today's thing was just a warning!"

"When do you want us back?" Tulsa Jack asked. A tall, lanky nondescript cowboy with a long face accentuated by long handlebars, he reminded Tandy of an illustration of a scarecrow.

She stood by her horse, watching the tight circle of men, content to stay in the background, yet feeling very much a part of them. In a way, she was going to miss their not being around.

"We'll get together right after spring roundup. How's that?" Doolin looked around at the nod of heads.

"I'm going down Dallas way so might be a bit late," Tulsa Jack murmured apologetically.

"That's okay," Doolin answered. "Jus' stay outta harm's way if you can. All of you."

"Where you two heading?" Raidler nudged Bitter Creek's side, glancing at him and Tandy.

B.C. smiled and shrugged. "I reckon we'll stick it out at the cave this time around. We're saving our money to go and visit a place like Chicago or New York. Or maybe we'll just save up to buy us a ranch someplace when we're through."

Raidler nodded his head. "We'll miss you at the HX but understand. Your—ah—woman, is something else." He winked at Tandy and then turned to Doolin. "How about splitting our shares so we can get at it?"

An agreed sum was given to Tandy to give to Rose to pay for the food and supplies used in the cave. The rest of the money was split evenly among the nine men.

Parting was something felt more than said. Separation from friends was such a frequent happening that goodbyes were needless exertions of energy. A few nods, perhaps a sheepish grin or nudge in the ribs, sufficed. Loneliness could not be expressed in words.

Before Tandy quite realized it, they had all departed except for her, B.C. and Doolin. Bill watched the last of the riders fade into the distance, fumbling the reins of his horse between his fingers. Finally, he turned to them and, with a shy grin, shuffled his feet.

"I—ah—got things I gotta do," he mumbled like a youngster before a teacher. "You two go ahead."

"What about Rose?" Tandy asked. "Won't she be expecting you back?"

Bill shrugged and refused to meet her eyes. "Tell her I hope she'll get to feelin' better. But I gotta go over to Ingalls. I'll be back in a while."

Tandy stared at him, then at Bitter Creek, whose frown warned her not to press on. For some reason, she was not looking forward to passing on the news to Rose. "Well, I hope you won't be gone too long," she said, a bite in her voice she hoped Doolin would chew on.

Bill took a deep breath and shook his head. "Well, I'll be seeing you two. Take it easy."

"Be seeing you," Bitter Creek called out. Bill, mounted, turned away. B.C. came over and put his arm around Tandy as they both watched the rider disappear into the brush. He turned and smiled down at her. "Guess that leaves just the two of us!"

She leaned against him and sighed. "I wish we could stay here for a while."

He looked at her quizzically and smiled. "Right here in the middle of nowhere?"

Tandy jabbed him, her mind still half on Doolin. "I—I just want to be with you, that's all. It feels good just to be by ourselves."

"We're going to have that all winter," he said.

She nestled in his arms, both gazing off to the horizon. She closed her eyes and was content.

"I gotta say," Bitter Creek whispered to her, "you done a good job. I mean it. I am real proud of you."

"Are you?" she asked happily. "You know how I feel, B.C.? Ever since you and me have—been together—you know, since we made love—I feel we really belong together. I feel we're one, y'know what I mean? On the train, I was scared—and nervous—but there was also a part of me that was calm. I think it was because I knew you were around, near by. And that we were working together." She tried to find something that described how she felt. "I feel like I done something real bad—not horrible—just sort of naughty. I mean, I didn't feel robbing that train was hurting many people—just those who deserve to be hurt. And knowing that, made it all sort of exciting—and scary, but exciting. Y'know what I mean?"

He nodded. "I think I do. I got them same feelings. I don't think it's bad what we do, not really. It's not like stepping all over the little people—or hurting the common folks. Sort of like stepping on people who step on others, robbing those who rob others."

"But they say it's against the law."

Bitter Creek shrugged. "Most of the law was made up to protect them big people. The law is hired out by them Washington bigwigs. When you look at it, most of the law is to protect them and it's the little people who gets tossed into jail."

"Or pushed into being outlaws," Tandy reminded him.

"Yeah," he sighed. "Or being pushed into what we're doing."

Tandy hugged him and they kissed, a long-suffering kiss that brought their bodies closer together. "C'mon," she coaxed, "let's hurry back. I want you!"

It was dusk when they broke through the narrow cut in the rocks into the glen. A bitter cold, whipping across the plains, had begun to numb their bones and they both were relieved they had arrived home.

Bitter Creek lifted Tandy down to the ground and took the reins from her hand. "You go get warm. I'll be in shortly, soon as I take care of the horses."

Tandy nodded and rushed up the incline of rock to the canvas curtain. Ducking her head, she brushed past it and stepped into the cave.

"Jeesus Christ!" Rose cried out. "You scared the hell out of me!" She was seated in front of the small fire, a blanket bunched over her thin shoulders, sipping on the warmth of a cup of coffee. Her eyes were swollen and half closed and she looked horrible in the dim light.

"I'm sorry," Tandy said, and came quickly to the fire. "How do you feel?"

"How the hell do you think I feel?" Rose answered sharply, pulling the blanket tightly around her. "About as bad as I look!"

"Well, you do look pretty awful," Tandy admitted. She stared at Rose, concerned about her appearance.

"I don't feel good—so leave me alone."

"But maybe I can help you."

Rose shrugged and hunched further over the cup in her hand. "Not a thing you can do. Not a thing no one can do."

"You need another blanket?" Tandy asked, feeling helpless. "You can have one of ours."

"I said I don't need nothing," Rose shot back weakly. "Who's asking for your help anyway?"

Tandy stared at the bent back. She felt an anger beginning to boil within her and she clenched her fists. "If you don't feel well, perhaps you should get back into bed and get some more rest," she said tightly.

"I been in bed all day," came the answer. "And I don't need you to tell me what to do."

"You don't have to get mad at me," Tandy replied. She turned to go to the back of the cave.

"Where is everybody?" Rose asked, sniffling.

"B.C. is taking care of the horses. The rest left for the winter." She waited for the inevitable question.

"Didn't Bill come back with you?"

Tandy sighed and picked at some of the dirty dishes. "He said he'd be back shortly. Went to Ingalls, I think."

"Jeez," Rose muttered. "A lot he cares about me."

"He does," Tandy said, feeling sorry for the woman and trying to comfort her. "He just had some things to do."

"I know. It's that Edith woman he's been seeing!"

"You're imagining things, Rose," Tandy answered. "C'mon to bed. You'll feel better in the morning."

Rose snapped her head around and glared at Tandy. "Things are going pretty well for you, aren't they?"

Tandy stared at the woman guardedly. There was a heaviness in her tone that she didn't like. "What does that mean?"

"I mean, look how easy it's been for you stepping into my shoes, Little Miss Rose of Cimarron," she said. "I suppose that's what you'll be wanting us to call you soon."

"I'm not trying to take your place."

Rose sneered and for that effort had a fit of coughing. "You took my place on the train," she accused Tandy. "And now that Doolin's dumping me, I suppose you want him too!"

Tandy was shocked. She could hardly believe what she was hearing. "You haven't got cause to say such things. I thought we were friends."

Rose glared at her. "No friend would try to take

over," she blurted and turned back to stare into the fire.

"I have no intention of taking over anything," Tandy objected, and came around to stand in front of Rose. "And just what would I take over in the first place? I thought we were all in this together."

"But you liked taking part, didn't you? I could see it in your face the minute you came in. You loved it, didn't you, honey?" Her words were cold and biting. "And now I guess I'm suppose to be the one holding the horses while you get the action."

"You're sick, Rose, you really are," Tandy answered angrily. "I have no intention of taking anything away from you—or taking your place—or whatever!"

"But you enjoyed what you did, didn't you?"

Tandy was caught off guard. She had to have time to think about it. Yet she knew the answer right away. She just didn't know whether she was ready to admit it.

"Yes," she raised her head defiantly. "I did enjoy it—in a way. I thought I had begun to understand how you must have felt too. But that doesn't mean I want to take anything away from you!"

Rose looked at her. "In no way baby, will I let you!"

Tandy looked at the woman. She had difficulty recognizing this form shadowed in the firelight. With her stooped shoulders, the blanket still drawn over her head for warmth, Rose looked like some drone she had read about who lived in deep dark forests and ate weird things and did terrible things.

"What's going on?" Bitter Creek's soft inquiry startled her and she whirled around.

"Nothing!" Tandy said and quickly averted her face. "Rose isn't feeling well, that's all." Even with her back to him, she knew B.C. was searching her for the truth, knowing something was wrong between the two women. Finally, he shrugged and threw the two saddles into a far corner.

"Well, whatever it is, better get over it." He reached over and pulled her over to him with a hug and a smile. "We got us a long winter together and we can't keep our backs to each other." Women! He'd never understand them if he lived to be a hundred!

15

Tandy walked listlessly through the small clump of trees that spotted the hidden ravine. The late spring weather offered a freshness that gently swayed the new leaves from the low wind that swept from the north. The string of horses, eleven of them, including her own, waited patiently along the tether rope, every once in a while taking a swipe at some nuisance crawling along their legs or back.

She had been left alone since very early morning, the gang having left in the dark. She tried to maintain a calmness before they had left, but once they had disappeared, and when it had become altogether too quiet, she had almost succumbed to a lonely cry. It was going to be a long day for they wouldn't be back until late afternoon.

It was Doolin's intention to expand their activities not only throughout Oklahoma, but also in Kansas. Since most of the cowboys had either been raised or worked in that state, it was felt all knew the area well enough to find escape routes and hiding places if necessary. The three major rail lines, the Santa Fe, the Southern Pacific and the Kansas, Missouri and Texas line, known as the Katy Railroad, would be their immediate targets. "A little something for everyone," Doolin had grinned.

His first planned objective was the Santa Fe line at a junction just above Dodge City, near Cimarron, Kansas. At first Tandy had been excited about participating. After a long winter of inactivity, they were all restless. Life in the cave had gotten on everyone's nerves.

Bill Doolin had found it more and more convenient to be away. This left Rose by herself and morose, a feeling which turned to bitterness. The sight of Tandy and Bitter Creek together only added fuel to her behavior. At first Tandy had felt sorry for her. But after a while, even she understood why Doolin stayed away.

Slowly, as the weeks passed, she and Rose drew further apart, which all the more aggravated conditions. Then the gradual return of the gang members broke the icy silence that had prevailed. As each man came into camp, the evenings and days were spent recalling the winter months, with stories repeated and embellished as each new person appeared.

On one hand Tandy was delighted to see these men, glad for their company and for the satisfying chores they provided her with. However, their presence took Bitter Creek away from her, and, except for the evenings, she saw little of him.

His renewed high spirits were of some consolation

to her. They used to lie close together under the blankets, their bodies brushing against each other while he would recount some of the stories told that day. At times, he was almost too absorbed in these tales and Tandy found it a challenge to get him to concentrate on her just a bit.

"I love you, B.C.," she whispered one night, pressing both his shoulders into her and wrapping a leg over his.

"I thought you wanted to hear about Charlie Pierce's brush with the law," he asked innocently.

"I don't want to hear anything more from you," she pouted, then pressed her lips under his chin. Sometimes his whiskers hurt her but she really didn't mind. Her hand slid between their bellies and found him. "Aw, B.C." she complained. "I don't arouse you any more."

He laughed quietly and tightened his grip around her. "Geez, a man just can't change in midstream girl. First, you want to hear all about what happened, and then—bingo—you want me stiff as a board."

"Ummmm," she murmured, her hands massaging him gently. "I'm all ready. I can't see why you can't be."

"Ain't possible just like that."

She smiled. "You was ready the first time."

"I wasn't telling no stories to you either."

"Well, concentrate."

"I'm trying to."

"Hush!"

* * *

Tandy sighed as she looked around the ravine recollecting those winter months. She wished B.C. and she were together, right then. There had been many times she wished they were the only two in the territory. She sighed again. There was that feeling between her legs again and she pressed them tightly together. Damn! What a time and place to want him!

She busied herself as best she could under the circumstances. Late in the afternoon, she ventured to a small knoll a half mile away, the Winchester slung over her shoulder. At the top, she looked around, squinting northward where the men had trekked but saw no telltale signs of dust. Disappointed, she dropped to her knees on the grass and sighed, wishing there was someone around to talk to. Even Rose would have been welcomed. But the wound had been cut deeper when Doolin had suggested Tandy take a more active part in this holdup. Rose's protests had been hurtful and only further widened the gap between the two of them.

Tandy felt like lying down on the coarse grass but the sun was hot and she knew better than to risk falling asleep under it. Besides, her responsibilities were with the horses. Begrudgingly, she turned and made her way back to the clump of trees in the ravine. There she resigned herself to a long wait.

They charged over the horizon an hour before dusk, widely scattered. Tandy could not judge whether their speed was caused by pursuit or by their jubilation. Quickly, she threw the saddle on her mount just in case there was need of a quick getaway.

They were noisy and excited as they came across the dry gulch and into the trees. Tandy knew then that things had gone well. Bitter Creek, smiling, slid off the saddle and encircled her, swinging her around. "You shoulda been there, gal. Not a shot fired—clean as a whistle and we got us a bundle!"

"They didn't know what hit 'em!" someone shouted out.

"There's no stopping us!"

The others dismounted, all except Doolin and Rose. "We better keep moving," Rose suggested.

"Aw, c'mon Bill," Little Dick grinned. "We didn't spot anyone following—we're clear!"

Doolin looked around, uncertain. "We're too close to be taking it easy," he managed.

"I agree. We shouldn't stop now," Rose stated. "At least not 'til we're closer to home."

"Ain't no one chasing us," Dynamite Dan boasted. "No one's dared to follow us now or ever. Them sheriffs are too busy elsewhere to go chasing us all the way to Oklahoma. We know it and they know it!"

They all looked up at Doolin, waiting for his answer.

"Can't we at least count how much we got?" Arkansas Tom asked, eyeing the bags tied to Bitter Creek's saddle horn.

Doolin shrugged and looked toward Rose. "Guess it won't hurt to rest a spell." He too was eager to see what those canvas bags contained.

"We got plenty of time later for that," Rose persisted.

"Aw, Rose," Doolin said, dismounting. "Y'worry too much. Who's going to want to chase us way down here?"

"Marshals have jurisdiction," Raidler answered in his quiet, unruffled voice. "They have the right to go anywhere they want, unlike a sheriff."

"Okay," Doolin answered. "But there was no marshal nowhere near to us."

Raidler refused to give up. "I've heard tell the government has been pressured into appointing more marshals in this territory just so they can handle the very likes of us."

The group sobered a bit and turned their attention to Little Bill. He looked around at them unperturbed at the sudden attention he was receiving. He shrugged and grinned slightly. "Well, it was bound to happen, y'know. We've been allowed to do pretty much as we please. You didn't think that would last long, did you."

Doolin screwed up his face. "Yeah, but it's still a hell of a big territory no matter how many marshals they sic on us."

Raidler nodded his head. "True, but then you've got to take into account they've hired just about the three most knowledgeable to go against us. We should take that into consideration."

"Who?"

"I bet Bill Tilghman is one," Bitter Creek volunteered. "I bet they put him on as a marshal."

Raidler nodded. "There's Chris Madsen, Tilghman, and Heck Thomas. People are calling them the three guardsmen. I think it's very appropriate myself."

There were a few shakes of heads in the group. "Wow, hate to meet up with all three at once," Tulsa Jack commented.

"Well, you see," Rose said, still atop her horse. "We shouldn't stay around here any longer than we can help it."

"Aw, c'mon Bill," West coaxed. "Don't let Raidler's talk scare you. A quick count, that's all. Something to whet our appetites 'til we get home."

Doolin shrugged and nodded to Bitter Creek, who went to the saddles and unstrung the bags which he tossed on the ground at Doolin's feet. The men squatted around in a circle wordlessly as Doolin took out his knife and cut the rawhide bindings.

Tandy stared at the men, at first fascinated by their findings and their talk. As the money was counted out and placed neatly into stacks, she glanced up at Rose. The woman was looking down at the huddle, her face an icy mask. Tandy knew that expression, knew the boiling anger it hid. With a shake of her head, Rose slowly dismounted. She hesitated, as though she planned to interfere with the counting. Then she turned and slowly patted the long neck of her horse, staring away.

Tandy felt a tug at her heart and, raising her skirts, walked over to Rose. "Do you really think there is any danger of our being here?" she asked, not really believing it herself but wanting to begin a conversation.

Rose turned and stared at her quizzically, as if questioning her reason for approaching. "Any time we're away from the cave we're in danger," she finally answered. "But it's even worse to take too much for granted so close to the place we robbed. It's just bad practice."

"Bill seems to think we're okay."

Rose glanced over to the men with a scowl. "Sometimes Bill has a habit of getting carried away by things."

"Don't you trust him?" Tandy realized it was a loaded question but hadn't meant it to be.

Rose inspected her closely. "As an outlaw and as a leader of outlaws, Bill could be one of the best with just half his mind put to it. It's when he doesn't put his mind to it that I begin to wonder. And I don't care if you tell him that or not."

"What makes you think I would tell him?" Tandy asked, suddenly aroused. "I still value our friendship, Rose, and I value what you think. So you have no reason to say such things."

Rose looked her over, then shrugged. A subtle smile appeared on her lips. It was difficult to determine what was on her mind at that moment. "Whatever you say, honey."

The comment only infuriated Tandy more. "Why are you so against me, Rose?"

The older woman studied her. "Let's just say it's the timing," she answered. "It's just a bad time, okay?" Her gaze took in Tandy's troubled face and she shook her head. "It's not only you—it's everyone. I mean, look at 'em." She pointed to the men. "A couple of miles away we rob a train. The railroad's probably contacted every law officer west of the Mississippi River by now and probably every trooper. And what do they do? They gotta make sure they got enough!"

Tandy was plagued with worries herself. She glanced about the horizon as if expecting the three guardsmen themselves to suddenly pop from behind the trees with guns blazing.

"Do you think they're out there?"

"Sure," Rose answered. "It was only a matter of time before them bankers and railroad people got organized. Who do you think puts the pressure on the government to hire them marshals? The railroads!"

"Are they that powerful?"

"The country is run by them! And you can bet your corset they're going to do everything they can to get us. That's what happened to the James, the Youngers, the Daltons—and will happen to us probably."

Tandy was scared. All she could think about was Coffeyville and how the Daltons came to their end. Would the same happen to the Doolin gang?

Suddenly, her vision caught something on the high knoll she had visited early in the afternoon. She hesitated, and shielded her eyes against the dipping sun. Was it her imagination? Or was it real?

"Rose—" Tandy squinted, holding her breath.

She was positive she had seen something. "Rose?"

It probably was the tone of her voice that drew the older woman's attention. "What's the matter?" she asked, suddenly at Tandy's side, staring in the same general direction.

"I saw something—at the top of that rise." Tandy pointed.

It was quiet for a moment. "Someone up there?" Rose asked, studying the horizon.

"No," Tandy answered. "I mean—there were two—looked like two figures. They were staring down here and then suddenly they both dropped to the ground. I can't see them any more."

Rose stared, both of them silent and motionless now. "Wait!" Rose's arm reached out and grabbed Tandy's arm. "I think I see 'em. Right on top—I think someone moved his head." Without moving, she called over her shoulder. "Bill! Come here!"

There was a pause in the conversation among the men. Then Doolin sighed, rose and sauntered over to their side. "What?"

"We think there's someone up on that hill."

Doolin shielded his eyes and stared. "I don't see nothing. Where?"

Tandy started to raise her arm but Rose struck it down. "Don't point. They're watching us."

Doolin snickered. "If they're watching us, then they know you two see 'em." He paused and looked for a while. "You sure you saw someone? Sure it wasn't just a tumbleweed or some animal?"

"We both saw something, Bill," Rose answered.

"There are two men up there. I can still see a head or something."

"What's up?" Bitter Creek had joined them at Tandy's side. She quickly explained.

"What'll we do, Bill?" Bitter Creek asked.

Doolin hesitated. "Better not take any chances. Get the money sacked and saddle."

"Should we use the fresh string of horses?"

"Not yet," Doolin answered, still not turned away from his vigilance. "Each one leads his spare. If this turns out to be a run for it, we'll need fresh hoof soon enough. Right now, we'll mount up and ride out slow and easy like nothing is wrong. If there is a posse up there and they make a show of it, we ride like hell."

Bitter Creek went back to the others to relay the message. The money was quickly shoved into the sacks which were tied and tossed to Bitter Creek to sling over the saddle horn. Girths were tightened quickly and each man grabbed for a lead rope from the extra horses. It was done quickly and efficiently with few words being spoken.

Tandy left first, quickly followed by Rose with a spare mount in tow. The others followed by twos at a brisk lope. It had been agreed that the ones in the rear would be responsible for keeping an eye out and warning the others if there was pursuit.

They had climbed back onto the dirt road and ridden about half a mile when Tulsa Jack, in the rear, let out a yell. They all turned in unison.

Behind them, slightly to the west of the rise,

almost directly in line with the red disk of the fading sun, a column of cavalry appeared out of the shadows. The dust that trailed behind them indicated they were coming at a full gallop. From the top of the rise, three riders went galloping down to intercept the troopers. Even from the distance, it was obvious that two were bare-chested Indian scouts, the other a tall, white-hatted, grey-suited lawman.

"Jesus Christ—that fella looks like ol' Madsen!" Bill Dalton cried out. "Let's get outta here!"

The front four had already kicked their mounts forward; the others spread out behind them rode hell-for-leather to catch up. The plains were flat. Dalton began looking ahead for a protective clump of brush or a ravine, but nothing was in sight except for the pale blue flat arc of the horizon.

The gang rode hard, fast and relentlessly. After fifteen minutes, the white lather under their saddle blankets began to fleck off and they could feel their horses laboring. Doolin, in the lead, stopped and beckoned his companions past him, yelling out as each passed by, "We change mounts in about ten minutes. Everyone on his own!"

"What 'bout them troopers?" Arkansas Tom inquired.

"Y'better unsaddle fast or you'll be asking 'em yourself," Doolin shouted and grinned. It was going to be a good show. As cowpokes, all had had to make quick exchanges of mounts. This time their lives hung in the balance; the troopers, a good distance behind, would quickly fill the gap at the rate they were traveling.

It was a gamble. A good guess would be that the troops had been on horseback for quite a time, probably all the way from Fort Supply. Another good guess was that the front rider with the big white hat, Chris Madsen, a man who knew this territory better'n his own hand, had been the one who'd found their escape route.

Doolin had to smile and shake his head. That lawman was sure hard to beat at times. Now, the only way to get out of this trap was to outride the troopers, keep enough distance ahead of them so that with night coming on, the gang might perform a disappearing act. Doolin smiled. It sure was worth a try becoming to his reputation. Put that in your hat and smoke it, all you big-wheeling moneymen!

Tandy felt a tug at her sleeve and Bitter Creek edged up close to her mount. "Stick close to me," he yelled out, "but keep an eye on them troopers. If they get too close, you skedaddle—I'll catch up to you later!"

"No!" she yelled back. "I'm staying with you no matter what!" She knew he was muttering some oath at her so she grinned and looked ahead, not really caring what he thought or was saying at the moment. Her heart was palpitating strongly and she was having a difficult time keeping her body in the saddle. It took all her concentration.

Bitter Creek looked behind him and waited for Doolin's wave. When it came, they all pulled back on the reins. There was a madness of dust. Squealing horses jostled each other as they crowded together in confusion. The riders were off them before they came to a complete halt. The men had lead ropes to the fresh horses tied to their waists, belts or arms. In a couple of deft motions, saddles were unfastened, lifted off and thrown onto the new horses. Tandy watched, fascinated at first. Then, as she twisted and looked behind, she was jarred into an awareness of their present predicament. The troopers seemed almost upon them; they appeared to have doubled their speed. She saw more clearly their blue uniforms, yellow kerchiefs. One of the leaders had turned in his saddle to bark out a command. Without slowing their pace, the riders pulled carbines from under their legs and put them across their laps at the ready.

The lawman, tall, lanky, and lean in the saddle, also whipped his carbine from under his leg. A gleam on the gun, cast by the dying sun, seemed the direst of warnings.

"They're almost here," Tandy shouted. Half the distance had been cut while the gang's saddles were being tightened. The spent mounts were let loose as the men adjusted stirrups and jumped on the fresh ones.

"Go on," Doolin yelled at Rose. "We'll meet you at the cave."

As Doolin helped Rose change saddles, Arkansas Tom started to kneel and bring up his carbine.

"Save it," Doolin ordered over his shoulder, somehow aware of the things happening as he tightened the girth. "We're ready to go!" With one hand he lifted Rose to the stirrup, then jumped to the side of his horse. "Let's get the hell outta here!"

The others dug in their spurs and, in a dust storm boiling over the ground, spread out, hunched low over their saddles. In the confusion and commotion, Doolin's mount shied and whinnied in fright. As he fought down the animal, alone and exposed, Bill looked behind at the oncoming threat. The man in front, the one identified as Chris Madsen, had raised his rifle up and forward.

Doolin tugged the reins around and prepared to mount. Suddenly, his foot gave way under him and he felt a sharp pain, as if he had stepped on a spike. His legs wobbled and he hung with his hands from the saddle like a straw-filled scarecrow.

Bitter Creek saw his predicament, turned and galloped back. Reaching down, he dug his fingers into Doolin's pants top, lifting him literally up and across the saddle. As Bill's foot swung over, they both noted the red blotch from the torn boot that had been cut in half by Madsen's rifle bullet.

"Let's go!" Bitter Creek hollered and slapped the rump of Doolin's horse. They both lay low over the necks of their animals, all too conscious of the bullets flying near them. When they dared a glance under their arms at their pursuers, they saw them receding and coaxed their fresh mounts still faster, racing into the sheltering darkness.

* * *

"I think we lost 'em." Bitter Creek was the first to speak after the gang had stopped. It was pitch black; clouds obliterated the moon. With their horses huddled close together, they listened for their pursuers. But it was quiet.

"We're safe. No cavalry is going to risk life and limb galloping full speed in the dark," Raidler stated. "But you can rest assured they'll be on our trail at dawn with them Indian scouts of theirs."

"We better split up and meet back at the cave," Doolin said in a tight voice. The others looked at him sharply. He was bent over the saddle hanging on with both hands.

"Geez," Arkansas Tom swore. He was afoot in a flash, jumping to Doolin's side. "He's been hit!"

"It's his foot," Bitter Creek stated, coming to assist Doolin to the ground. It was a signal for all to dismount and gather around their leader.

"Do you need light?" someone asked.

"Naw—and have them army riders come down on us?" Doolin's voice bespoke his pain. "It's just a scratch."

"I can't find an exit hole. I think the bullet's still in ya," Tom answered, his fingers probing the foot. "We got to get this fixed up or you'll be in big trouble."

"Damn it, Doolin," Rose stormed. "This wouldn't've happened if you'd listened to me instead of counting that damn money."

Doolin muttered something only he heard. "How the hell could I know someone like Madsen would guess our backtrail? Jus' blame luck, that's all!"

"It was carelessness, Bill Doolin, and there's no other way of lookin' at it," Rose answered, watching Tom work on him. "You're lucky you come out of it with only a torn boot."

Little Dick West grinned up at her. "We got away with a mite more than a torn boot," he corrected. "But you're right at that. We're all lucky we got out of that one."

Tandy remained mounted. Seeing Bill wasn't seriously hurt, she turned her thoughts to her own feelings. She felt elated, and that surprised her. She knew how close they had all come to being captured, maybe even shot and killed. Yet still, right then, she felt elated. She knew if it hadn't been for her, the cavalry would have been upon them undetected. She felt proud. She was as important to the gang as any of them!

"You want us to carry you to the cave?" Bill Dalton asked.

"No," came Doolin's reply. "We split up like I said. I got friends not too far from here where I can patch up my foot. I'll be back as soon as I can."

"I'll go with you," Arkansas Tom answered eagerly. There was no doubt the boy idolized Doolin.

"You do that," Rose said. "I need to go back to the cave anyhow. Got some thinking to do."

"Don't you go doing nothing foolish now," Bill spoke up, aware of the tone of her voice.

"Foolish?" Rose said haughtily. "There's only room for one fool in this outfit."

"I ain't going to argue with you here," Doolin said. "Maybe we did make a mistake. Ain't saying it's true—jus' maybe. I'll give you credit though." He glanced up seriously at Rose. "You're right—things are changing. Means we gotta change too." He looked around at them all. "You all keep your eyes and ears open. See if you can find out what the law is doing. Then, we'll do 'em one better."

There was a general murmur as the men backed away to allow Doolin to mount his horse. "Y'take care now." He managed a grin at them. "I got to take care of this damn foot. Y'all divide up the loot. Give Rose my share. Meet again in a couple of months."

They watched in sober silence as Tom led Doolin out into the blackness, aware that they all had barely escaped a fate worse than their leader's.

"We better split. The farther we can get away from them scouts, the easier it will be." Bitter Creek went to the saddlebags and threw the money onto the ground. The count was made again, slower this time because of the bad light. They'd heisted almost $13,000 and the men whistled in appreciation.

"I think the women are due their rightful share," Little Bill Raidler spoke up.

There was an uncomfortable silence and embarrassed shufflings as the men looked to one another. Tandy stepped forward. "B.C. has my share," she offered.

"Yeah, but you done a good job. You were the one gave the warning," Bill Dalton admitted. "And Rose helped out plenty. I think you two should get something for yourselves."

Tandy was pleased but shook her head. "If anyone deserves it, Rose does. She took part more—and it was she who said we shouldn't have stayed there." Tandy was hoping she could renew her friendship with the woman.

"I'll just take Doolin's share, plus enough for supplies," Rose answered, her voice still sullen over the events. "I don't need no money."

The men seemed to like both women's answers. "We'll compromise and put in a bit for each of you," Raidler suggested. "I think that's only fair and just."

"Let's divide it and get it done with," Red Buck growled. "I got plenty of living to do in the next couple months and don't want to waste it gabbing on the split."

The riders departed in a jovial mood. Their shares of the big haul had been ample and they were all in fine spirits anticipating their activities for the next two months.

"Stay away from the law!" Bitter Creek yelled after them. He and the two women watched them dissolve into the night. Suddenly it was quiet and lonely.

Tandy said to Bitter Creek, "I hope Bill is going to be all right." She knew Rose had heard but the woman bent over, grabbed the half-empty sack of money wordlessly and went to her horse.

Bitter Creek gripped her hand solidly. "Don't you worry. Ol' Bill's been through worse. He'll be back pronto champing at the bit!"

Tandy heard the words but kept looking at Rose. She was a lonely figure, separated from the rest now by some barrier difficult to comprehend. Tandy felt

Rose was affected by Bill's being wounded more than she let on. She'd obviously been hurt too when Doolin hadn't asked her to stay with him instead of Arkansas Tom. It was complicated. Too complicated. She was thankful all the more for her relationship with Bitter Creek.

"Let's go home," she murmured. They deserved the rest.

16

"It's Bill!" Tandy stood up and clapped her hands with joy. It had been a long two months and the summer heat had already begun. It made life uncomfortable in the cave for the three who had stayed. The strain had been great; it was obvious that in the close confines of their quarters, Rose felt like a third arm. The times B.C. and Tandy wanted to be left alone were usually the times when Rose wanted companionship to break her boredom. Her jealousy over their togetherness prompted remarks from her that cut and dampened any spirit of lovemaking.

Tandy had also known that Bitter Creek, although denying it, was getting itchy pants staying in one place for such a long period. The inactivity seemed to be burning inside him and Tandy's nights had become sleepless worrying over the possibilities of his suddenly leaving one day. Whatever prayers she had been uttering those late nights were answered when Doolin rode through the brush and into the glen.

Doolin kept his grin throughout their attentions, enjoying every minute of it. He had a slight limp, telltale of their last escapade; otherwise, he was in the best of spirits. "Got to show you what I'm saving to give to Madsen," and he dug into his shirt pocket to bring out a small lead bullet. "That's the closest them lawmen'll ever get to me!"

"Not if you're not more careful," Rose prompted. She had been content to keep in the background, solemn-faced. Although the two kept exchanging glances as Tandy and Bitter Creek pampered their leader, Rose was determined not to make the first move.

"Aw shucks, Rose," Bill complained. "You still on that? It's over and done with and well forgotten."

Rose came to stand in front of him, hands on hips. She would not be ignored. "If you know what's good for you, Bill Doolin, you had better never forget it. None of us better forget it." She looked at them all, her face serious and stern. "You almost got yourself and the rest of us killed—and you say forget it!"

Doolin winced and sighed. "I know you're concerned for me—" She let out a short bitter laugh but allowed him to continue. "Okay, so I got a bit careless. I paid for it, didn't I? I mean, it's only a scratch."

Rose glanced down at his foot, her face screwed up to hide whatever emotions she was determined to keep to herself. "It should never have happened in the first place. When you start taking too much for granted, that's when we'll get hurt the most."

"I think Rose is right," Tandy blurted, taking a deep breath and plunging in with her own concerns. "I don't want to see you get like the Daltons, thinking they were invincible and no one could touch them. If the law is getting tougher, then we've got to be more careful."

Doolin shook his head, looked at Bitter Creek and shrugged his shoulders. "What you been feeding them women since I been gone? Barbed wire?"

B.C. cocked an eyebrow. "They're only concerned 'bout you—'bout all of us."

Doolin looked at Rose sheepishly. "It's not like I haven't been thinking about it, y'know. Okay, I don't like to admit it, but maybe I did take too much for granted. And you're right, Rose, right as hell! Looks like the law has been maybe getting a bit smarter. But still, they're not half as smart as us." He looked at them again. "I think one of the troubles is we're all sort of tighter'n a virgin bride. I mean, we all go off on our separate ways doing whatever—then we get together to rob a train or bank. Well, I been doing some thinking these last two months."

Rose, still miffed, said, "That's all anyone's been able to do."

Doolin grinned. "Well, got a different idea this time. I think we should, just for the heck of it, when we all get together, forget about robbing and have us a ball! I mean, why the hell not? We deserve it. If we can make up plans to rob a town or a train, why the hell can't we make plans to have ourselves a fling? Y'know—just relax, unwind, enjoy ourselves?"

"Oh Bill," Tandy shouted grabbing his arm enthusiastically. "Do you think we could?"

"Why not?" Doolin had a mischievous smile on his face. "The way I look at it, we've proven we can go and rob a bank or train anytime we want. Well, let's go out and have some fun this time. Can you imagine them railroad people finding out we had ourselves one hell of a celebration on their money? I mean, to me that would be a worse slap in the face then robbin' 'em."

"And just where are we going to have this little party?" Rose asked sarcastically.

"On the way back here, I stopped off at Ingalls to check around. There's not a lawman around."

"I should have known!" Rose turned her back on him.

"Ingalls is the perfect place," Doolin answered. "Its outta the way, we got all sorts of friends there."

"Yeah—I know who you got there!" Rose said.

There was silence in the cave as Doolin glanced over to Bitter Creek and Tandy with a pained expression. "Aw c'mon, Rose," he said. "I'm doing this partly for you. I thought maybe you and me—well, I thought maybe it'll give us a chance to mend some things."

"In Ingalls?" she asked with a bitter laugh. "Isn't that where that Edith woman lives?"

Doolin winced. "Yeah, she lives near there. But

I won't see her, I promise. This is a time I want to spend with the boys—and with you."

Rose's shoulders relaxed and her arms went about her middle. Grudgingly, she turned and gave Doolin a piercing, penetrating look. "You're not going to want to see her?"

"Naw," Doolin grinned. "I promise. This is going to be a time when I'm with you all the way. I promise!"

Tandy saw a slight tinge of red come into Rose's cheek and she clapped her hands enthusiastically. "Oh Bill," she cried out to break the tension, "Do you really think it will be safe for us?"

"It's a safe town, believe me. Most of the folks there I grew up with, and a lot of them rode with us on Halsell's ranch. And they'll watch out for us, too."

"But what about the law?" Rose asked, now anxious to take part in the conversation.

"That's the best part," Doolin grinned. "The government is about ready to open more of the Cherokee strip. There's going to be a big land rush and practically every lawman is over there getting ready, y'know, keeping the sooners out and everything."

"Tilghman?" Bitter Creek asked sharply.

"Heard he's been appointed the new land officer at Perry. 'Sides, someone told me he's laid up with a bad leg or something."

"What have you heard about Thomas and Madsen? Where are they?"

"I told you—they're all up with the army folks

gettin' ready for the rush. That's why I thought of this idea. It's a perfect time for us to get out of here and enjoy ourselves. Won't be a lawman for hundreds of miles. We'll whoop it up until the money runs out, then come back and make plans again."

"You sure we can trust the people at Ingalls?"

"Are you kidding? As soon as I hinted we'd be coming in with all sorts of money to spend—hell, they was ready to keep out the entire U.S. army if need be."

"Can I buy a new dress?" Tandy asked jubilantly.

"Hell, you can buy the whole store. We can stay at the hotel—know the gal who runs it. We can relax, do what we want, buy what we want. We can fish—hell, we can do anything!"

"Oh my God," Tandy gasped. "I haven't been in a real bed in a real room for years!"

Bitter Creek grabbed her waist and swung her around. "Then I say let's do it!"

Doolin turned to Rose and said quietly, "How 'bout it, kid? What say you and me get reacquainted again?"

Rose gave him a long, silent look, difficult to interpret. Finally, she smiled shyly. "I guess you're right at that. Maybe there's a point to being too cautious." She seemed to have made up her mind. "I mean, what's the use of doing what we do if we can't spend high once in a while?"

"That's my girl," Doolin howled. "Whooeee, are we ever going to set that place on fire!"

* * *

Located between Tulsa and Guthrie, the town of Ingalls served mainly to supply the surrounding ranchers, saving them the long and tedious trip to either city. Every once in a while, it was nurtured by road traffic passing through. But mostly, it remained a tiny place, a collection of unpainted, weather-beaten shacks with an air of rejection and despair. It did, however, boast of a main street. On it were a livery stable, two general stores, a church, post office, blacksmith shop, two saloons, a barbershop, three homes and Mary Pierce's establishment primarily for the entertainment of the local cowboys.

Mary Pierce, a large pasty-faced woman, greeted Doolin with a beaming, professional smile. She seemed to have a professional interest in Tandy and Rose as well, sizing them up with several sidelong glances. A younger version of her, who stood sourly behind her, Mary pulled forward and proudly introduced as her daughter. In an adjoining room, two other girls sat lazily on a sofa, watching and inspecting the newcomers with idle curiosity. Doolin waved to them casually, awkward with his introductions. "Over there, the pretty one is Cattle Annie. The one wearing pants we call Little Britches. This here is Tandy—and this here is Rose."

Tandy smiled politely. These women looked seductive and she knew what they did for a living. A year before she would have felt threatened by their presence. Now, she felt more positive about herself. Only once did she sneak a glance at B.C. to see if he recognized or showed eager interest in them. He did neither.

"Where's the rest of the gang?" Mary Pierce asked as they started for the stairs carrying their things.

"We left a note telling 'em to mosey over here. They'll be around eventually," Doolin answered.

"I got plenty of rooms," Mary boasted, "and lots of entertainment."

Doolin grinned. "Don't you go worrying none, Mary. You'll get your fair share of business same as everyone else. I doubt many of the boys will want to stay in town—they more or less like the feel of outdoors. But you can bet your corset, they'll be coming by to see your girls." He stopped and pulled a twenty-dollar bill from his pocket. "Here, you keep this for a starter. Just let me know of any strangers hereabouts and I'll make sure there's plenty more."

Mary Pierce tucked the bill in her bosom without changing her expression. Then she frowned. "There is a new guy in town," she offered. "Set up a tent over next to Murphy's."

"Oh? What do you know about him?"

Mary shrugged. "Sells fish." Her voice dropped, as if she figured her information was of no value. "Simple poke—fishes most of the day, sells 'em for drink."

"I appreciate it. I'll take a look just to make sure. That's keeping an eye out for us." Doolin winked at her.

Later in the day, with the sun dipping towards

the horizon, and a cooling breeze coming up the four took a walk through the town. There wasn't much to sight-see. They had a look at the sagging gray church on one of Ingalls' four corners, then turned right up the main street, more often thought of as the road to Tulsa. The first building on the left was the livery stable, into which Bitter Creek popped for a moment to see if their horses were being properly taken care of. He came out looking surprised that they were. Next to the livery was the smaller of the two saloons, looking as though one big wind would blow it over, and across the street was the equally ramshackle Phanley's General Store and Hardware. Tandy and Rose went over and looked in its window for a while.

The blacksmith, Wagner, was just closing his doors as the four came up to him. Doolin made the introductions. He'd known Wagner at Halsell's, where Wagner had shod horses for a couple months. The two men traded off-color jokes, substituting words they felt were more acceptable to Tandy and Rose and thereby taking most of the laughs out.

"We can get our food supplies over there," Doolin declared cheerily as they continued on towards Bradley's Grocery Store. "We'll have us a look."

Bitter Creek shook his head; by then, he'd seen enough. "I got a better idea. Let's get a drink," he suggested.

In complete accord, as it turned out, they headed for Murphy's saloon, the last building. The two doors swung on rusty hinges into a room just big enough for three circular tables and a standing bar.

"Howdy Murphy," Doolin called out. Choosing a table, he pulled out a chair for Rose while Bitter Creek helped Tandy be seated.

"How do, Bill," the barkeeper answered and came towards them, hand outstretched. "Heard you was in town again. How's things?"

Doolin once again made the introductions. "Y'seen Joe or Sherm?"

Murphy shook his head. "They's likely closed up early and gone home. It's been a slow day." He chuckled. Almost every day in Ingalls was a slow day.

Doolin confided to the women, "Ol' Joe Ketchem and Sherm Sanders used to ride at Halsell's with us. In fact, I guess most of Ingalls one time or another rode for old man Halsell. That's how come we knows most." He reached over and chucked Rose under the chin. "You see, we're in good hands."

Tandy felt just fine. To her, meeting folks in Ingalls was better than walking down some avenue in New York City or Chicago. She knew by B.C's stiffness that he was doing his best to be a proper and attentive escort and she was proud of him. The dust and dirt on Murphy's floor was a magic carpet as far as she was concerned.

"Anything doing for excitement?" Doolin asked casually as Murphy brought their drinks.

The man smiled. "You must be joking. Only thing worth doing around here is putting a line in the river for a catfish and dream of cooking it. Now, that's what a sensible man would do."

Everyone grinned. Doolin said, "Well, seeing that we're about as sensible as they come, guess we'll take up your suggestion."

"You should see ol' Red Lucas for a good spot on the bank," Murphy suggested. "He's right next door—been catching some humdingers. Sort of wacko in the head but not bad company."

"Might take you up on that, Murph."

They found Lucas the next day along the river, flat on his back, hat over his head, two poles rigged upright with forked branches and rocks keeping them in place.

"Mind if we join you?" Bitter Creek asked as they came up.

The man jumped and pushed back his hat to stare at them with half-closed sleepy lids. Then his face broke into a grin. "Shucks no," he answered. "I don't own this river. It's for everyone."

They had brought with them branches, string and bent pins which would suffice for hooks. Bits of jerky from Murphy's breakfast would tempt the meanest of catfish.

"I understand you been having good luck with the bites."

Red Lucas kept grinning as he inspected each person carefully. "This is as good a spot as any, I guess," he answered.

"You been here long?"

Lucas shrugged. "I travel up and down the river mostly. Camp out when I feel like it, move on when I feel the itch."

Tandy only half listened to the conversation,

knowing Doolin and Bitter Creek were feeling out the newcomer. Soon Bitter Creek came and lay down next to her with a sigh. "Harmless ol' cuss," he said lazily.

Tandy stretched, placed her hands behind her head and stared up into the bright sky. "Isn't this heaven?" she exclaimed. "Couldn't you just lie here forever?"

Bitter Creek snorted. "Maybe close to it, hon," he answered. He closed his eyes to soak up the warmth. "But we sure as hell would become spoiled clear through after a while."

Tandy turned on her side and traced his chin with her finger. "I mean, this kind of life—living in a house, with a real bed, coming out to a river whenever we felt like it, lying side by side—"

He opened one eye at her. "Jus' what do you think we're doing now? I mean, you see anyone else 'sides ol' Lucas there taking up the sun? No. And you know why? Everyone else is working, that's why. We're here 'cause we don't have to set our lives to a schedule." He chuckled to himself. "The only schedule we depend on is a train schedule." He nudged Tandy in the ribs.

"Oh you—" she smiled. "You know what I mean!"

"I know what you mean, Tandy m'girl," he answered soberly. "And maybe one of these here days we'll get us a ranch to hogtie us with. But for now, you got to admit this is pretty close to being the best there is."

There was no denying the fact. She was happier

now than she had been in a long time. The next couple of weeks would be etched in her mind for the rest of her life. Even when the others made their appearance, it was as happy a time for her as a big family get-together. The gang members straggled in one or two at a time, far enough between each other to offer at least a day or two's good story telling. Doolin had been correct; two months had not been long enough for them to spend their shares of the money, and learning that no immediate holdup was in the works kindled their spirits tremendously.

Bill Dalton was tempted to return to his folks' ranch only a few days ride from Ingalls, but they all prevailed upon him to stay. "C'mon Bill," Little Dick West coaxed. "This here is Doolin town—and Doolin time to celebrate. Ain't right two of us being gone." Rumor had it that Tulsa Jack had gotten himself in a jail for some mischief and thus would be late in joining them.

Their days were spent either by the riverbank fishing with Red Lucas or in one of the saloons playing cards. Ingalls had rarely seen so much activity at one time. The townspeople were more than eager to please them. Within days, both general stores were cleared out of suits and shirts as each gang member tried to outdress the other. By the time September arrived, all the men were practically exhausted, not to mention the girls at Mary Pierce's Hotel.

Tandy had to smile at these men. Aside from her and Rose, only Doolin, Bitter Creek and Arkansas

Tom stayed regularly in the hotel. The others, out of habit, stayed out in the brush. But then, Dick West had never slept under a roof as far back as he could remember.

It was a lazy summer day. Tandy, seated with her sewing on her lap, looked out the window of her second-story bedroom and surveyed the backs of the dingy buildings. Every once in a while a loud warwhoop came from one of the saloons, which made her smile. Someone had won a sizable pot in faro. She had caught a glimpse of B.C. leading his horse from the blacksmith's to the livery stable. She was a bit sad, for Doolin had announced they should be thinking about getting back to the cave soon. Several had taken their boots in for patchwork; others in the gang were making last-minute purchases of guns, ammunition, new saddles and blankets.

"Did you see that stove at Phanley's?" Tandy asked, preoccupied with staring out the window.

Rose was seated in the rocker at the window, concentrating on hemming a skirt made from material she had particularly liked and bought on impulse. "Mmmmm," she murmured and took the pins out of her mouth. "Bill didn't think we really needed it though."

Tandy yawned. "Lot he knows—he doesn't have to cook."

Rose looked up and studied her. "We've all had a nice rest, but I for one will be glad to get back home. It's never good to stay in one place for this long a time. We've been very lucky."

"But it's been worth it, don't you think?" Tandy asked. "I mean, everyone has been on the lookout for us—they've all been so nice and everything."

"They'll stay nice as long as we got money to give them," Rose said wryly. "When we run out of money, it's so long to our wonderful friendships."

"Oh Rose," Tandy complained. "Don't you trust anyone?"

"Better than living in a fantasy," Rose answered.

"I suppose you're meaning me?"

"I'm meaning you," Rose said firmly. "You can't accept the fact that we're outlaws. We do things against the law. We get shot at because we do wrong. Those things you refuse to recognize."

"I don't think what we do is so bad," Tandy stated. She wasn't quite sure where the woman was headed. "If it's against the law, then the law isn't good either."

Rose sighed. "You see? What I'm trying to say, child, is that you can't accept the fact that we are the way we are. You got to make a purpose of everything. Why can't you just accept? Be free—live free!"

"Because I don't think what we do is terribly wrong. And I'm not quite sure what it is you want either."

Rose sighed and bent to continue her sewing. "One of your problems is your being so involved with Bitter Creek."

"And what's wrong with that? I love him!"

"And what happens when he's not around?"

Tandy hesitated. "What do you mean?"

"You know what I mean. What happens if he is killed—or just leaves?"

Tandy tried to swallow but couldn't. "I don't know."

"Y'see? That's the problem. You'd fall to pieces, that's what. Your whole world centers around him and nothing else. If anything happened to him, you'd crumple into nothing."

"And I suppose you wouldn't if something happened to Bill?"

Rose's laugh was short. "My life isn't geared to his every movement."

"But I thought you and he were getting on together."

Rose shrugged. "Oh, it's been fun. But I also know these past few weeks will come to an end. Everything comes to an end. Soon as we get back to the cave, Bill will go back to Edith. "I know it, he knows it."

"Then why did you come here with him?"

Rose stopped sewing, her head still bent over the material. She was silent for a moment, then shook herself and went on. "And why not? He's better'n anything else around. At least for the moment. But I'm not putting my whole life on the line expecting to be his woman."

"You haven't answered my question though. What would you do if something happened to Doolin?"

Rose shrugged. "Probably for the moment, I'd

stick with whoever was in the gang, as long as they stuck together."

"You mean—anyone?"

Rose thought it over. "Mmmm, probably."

"Even Red Buck Waightman?"

Rose smiled. "Well, maybe I would draw a line somewhere. The point is, if Doolin wasn't around I'd manage. I've always managed, cause I've never got myself close to anyone."

Tandy stared at her solemnly. "I think that's sad. I really do." She shook her head and tears started to well up at the corners of her eyes. "And I don't think you really mean it, Rose. I don't see how you could mean it."

Rose was silent for a moment. "If you want to survive, you'll believe it," she answered then.

Tandy sighed. "Well, I don't care. As far as I'm concerned, Bitter Creek is my life. I don't even want to think about any what ifs!" She stopped her sewing and glanced out the window where she could see the high false front of Trilby's saloon. He was in there, she knew, and her heart went out to him. She just wouldn't think about it, that's all!

17

"Hey, Bill, there's someone out here wanting to talk to you." Charlie Pierce stuck his head through the swinging doors of Trilby's saloon and peered in at the four men gathered around the middle table.

Doolin looked at the pairs of jacks and kings he held. "Jus'a minute," he said slowly. He watched as Red Buck Waightman, whose bet he had called, spread three tens out on the table. "Jeez—one of these days I'm going to be dealt a half-ass decent hand." Doolin slammed his cards down and leaned back in his chair.

Bitter Creek and Bill Dalton grinned good-naturedly as Red Buck scooped up the pot. He had a sneer on his face that was as close as he could get to a winning smile.

"Who's wanting to see me?" Doolin asked, turning his attention to Pierce.

"Good-looking strap of a kid. Says he's got some info for you."

Doolin cocked an eyebrow and sighed. "Better see what gives."

The boy, a lanky towhead, barefoot with a fishing pole dangling over a shoulder, stood his ground in the middle of the street. Like most of his playmates, he had been told of the outlaws and had watched them from a respectful distance. This was the closest he had come to any of them. He gripped the pole tightly and swallowed as Doolin came to the saloon door and called out to him.

"What's your name, lad?"

"Jimmie," was the nervous reply.

Doolin nodded and said easily, "Okay, Jimmie, I hear you got something to say to me."

Jimmie swallowed again and took a few steps closer. He cleared his throat and was about to speak when the other three men came out to watch.

"It's okay," Bill said in a soft understanding voice. "They's all friends of mine. B.C., this here is my friend Jimmie."

Bitter Creek came forward, squatted on his haunches beside Bill and grinned. "Howdy, friend Jimmie. You got something to tell us?"

The boy nodded, took another nervous look at the men, then stared at Doolin. "I thought you'd want to know. There's a couple of covered wagons parked down by the river." He looked them over again with wide eyes to see whether they were impressed.

"Go on," Doolin said softly.

"Well—" The boy fought with himself over giving

out the information. "Well, ordinarily I wouldn't have given it a second thought, but they's filled with men and they got lots of guns with 'em."

Doolin scowled and glanced at Bitter Creek, whose face had suddenly lost its smile. "Go on," Bitter Creek said.

"That's about it. But I knew you all were in town and I just thought it was kinda strange that there's all these men with all those guns."

"You done right, Jimmie," Doolin answered. "But what were they doing exactly?"

Jimmie shrugged his thin shoulders. "I didn't want to stare at 'em too long in case they got suspicious. But it looked as though they were finishing cleaning all them guns and were putting things back into them wagons."

"Jimmie, you see any stars pinned on 'em? You recognize any of 'em?"

The boy shook his head. "Couldn't see exactly. But they looked mighty mean and serious." He hesitated; then his face beamed as he remembered. "Oh yes—I saw that Red Lucas with 'em."

"Ol' Red? He was there?"

The boy nodded. "Acted like he knew 'em."

"What was he doing?"

"Same as the rest. Cleaning a rifle, I think."

"Why the hell is someone like Lucas cleaning a rifle?" Dalton asked from behind.

Doolin pursed his lips. "I dunno," he answered slowly. "Could be it's just a hunting party. Maybe old friends of his."

"Could be a huntin' party for us too," Waightman growled. "I don't like the sound of it."

Doolin got up and stretched. "You done just fine, boy," he said and dug into his pants for some coins. "You go home now and stay outta trouble, y'hear?" As the boy ran off, Doolin shouted after him, "And keep your eyes open too. Keep us posted, okay?"

"What ya think, Bill?" Bitter Creek asked, eyeing both ends of the street.

"I doubt if it's anything serious," Bill answered, but there was a tightness in his voice. "Just the same, we better not take a chance. Charlie, you go around and tell the others what's happened. Tell 'em to keep their eyes out for anything suspicious. Where is everyone anyway?"

"Raidler and West is getting food, I think. Clifton's still at Murphy's where I left him."

"Where's Tom?"

Charlie grinned. "Hell, he ain't stopped screwing since he's been here. He's over at the hotel with the women."

"Okay, you go warn 'em." He watched as Pierce sauntered down the street to where a couple of horses were tied, took a rifle from a saddlebag, then continued on across the street.

"This might be nothing, but Charlie's got the right idea. We'll get our rifles as soon as we finish up this game. Maybe we'll ride out to them wagons and see what them people's all about."

He pushed them all back into the saloon. However, instead of sitting at the far table, they now took one next to the big front window, so that two players could each have a good view of both ends of the street.

"Okay, you bastards." Doolin grinned and began to shuffle the worn deck of cards. "I'm about to start the biggest robbery of my career. Hang onto your seats."

Within an hour, their spirits had returned, the warning that Jimmie had given them nearly forgotten in their absorption in the game. Doolin, whose luck in cards had improved considerably, had even stopped looking out the window. Finally, while waiting for the bartender to refill their glasses, Waightman stretched and stood up.

"Might as well get them rifles," he murmured.

Bill Dalton snorted. "Like hell. You're the big winner. Stay where you are. Besides, Bill's probably right—some hunting party or something."

As Waightman hesitated, Bitter Creek stood up. "I'll go take a walk and see what I see. Got to see if my horse was shod anyway. Hold my seat."

B.C. was in a good mood. His losses at the card table were of little consequence to him. Most of it had been winnings from the week before. What counted was that he was among good friends; the several weeks here in Ingalls had been good for all of them. Bemused, he walked the short distance to Wagner the blacksmith's place, mostly looking up at the top floor of the hotel for a glimpse of Tandy. A window was open up there, he noted, but it wasn't Tandy's, so he gave up looking for her and moved on. Wagner, he found, needed another hour or so for the shoeing job, whereupon B.C. turned and left. He'd walk another hundred yards or so, he figured.

Suddenly, his eyes caught a movement across the street at the far end of the post office. There was a man there in a long white traveling coat; he had just ducked around the building's corner.

B.C. stopped abruptly, a tingling sensation running up his spine. He did not know who the man was, but he did know he could not afford to take chances. Slowly, he edged to the town well in front of Wagner's and took hold of the pump handle as if to get himself a drink. As he bent over, cupping his hand, his eyes darted about. There it was again! The man in the long coat had peered from around the corner again, had seen B.C. and had ducked back. Bitter Creek went ahead and pumped water into his hands. Then, raising it to his mouth, he took a good look towards the other end of the street. What he saw made his stomach churn. A man with a rifle in each hand was running across the road; as B.C. watched, he darted behind the livery stable. Slowly B.C. straightened, his hand slipping down to his holster. Turning slightly, he watched the post office from the corner of his eye. Sure enough, the flap of a coat edged into view.

B.C. waited until the brim of the hat appeared, then drew his pistol and fired. His shot splintered the corner siding. "Whoweeee," he bellowed and ran pell-mell back to the saloon. There was a crack of a rifle and window glass shattered behind him as he burst through the double doors.

The others dove for cover against the floor. Then, as if the one rifle shot were a signal, the whole street suddenly erupted with gun fire, from one end of it to the other. More glass and wood splinters flew across the floor in slivers.

"Get down," Doolin bellowed. Bitter Creek didn't need to be told. Hands over his head, he dove flat on his stomach as the rapid shots began to tear apart the saloon's walls.

In a short while there was a pause and the men slowly raised their heads. "Jeezus Christ, what the hell is going on?" Bill Dalton growled.

Doolin slid over closer to the window sill. "I do believe ol' Jimmie tried to warn us correct." He took off his hat and raised it slowly upwards. A sudden blast of rifle fire filled the little room with breaking glass again, this time from tumblers knocked off the bar.

"Hey, Trilby," Doolin shouted. "You okay?"

There was a stammering reply from the bar-owner from somewhere behind the bar.

"This is a mite one-sided," Bitter Creek complained. Quickly he got on his knees and fired his pistol at random across the street. The others joined him.

"See 'em?"

"There was one by the corner of the post office. I think a couple must be down the street."

"How many are there?"

"Anyone want to go out and count?"

A rifle spat from the blacksmith's open doors and they instinctively ducked, then returned the fire.

"They're spread out pretty good," Doolin observed. Volleys of shots kept coming, it seemed from all directions. Then still more shots were fired—but not aimed at them. Doolin cried, "For Christ's sake, they're firing at the hotel!"

Bitter Creek crawled over next to him where he could have a better view. A window on the hotel's top floor had been knocked out. The gleam of a rifle could be seen up there, puffs of smoke emitting from it. Suddenly, return fire from the ground blasted the frame into splinters.

"God Almighty," Bitter Creek cried out. "They're going to tear that damn building apart!"

Another rifle from an adjoining window spoke out, and again the side of the hotel was spattered as the attackers shot back.

"We've got to get the hell outta here," B.C. murmured. "I'm going for horses. Cover me!"

Before anyone could object, he was up and out the door, gun blazing at whatever apparition he could spot. He ran in a low crouch, zigzaging his way toward the livery stable, until a shot ran out and he stumbled and spun to the ground.

"Let's go!" Doolin shouted. He went out, crouching low, and sprinted to B.C.'s side. Waightman and Dalton followed suit, one firing to the right, one to the left. Their gunfire became more deliberate as they backed slowly to a watering trough, where Doolin had dragged B.C.

"Cover!" Doolin shouted. He stooped, caught B.C. under both armpits and dragged him backward into the stable as the other two knelt and kept up a steady firing. As soon as Doolin had B.C. inside, they turned and sprinted to safety themselves.

"Cover the back," Doolin ordered as he bent over his friend. He quickly found the red hole at the thigh and unwound his bandana to cover the wound. "Can you shoot?"

Bitter Creek nodded weakly. The pain was bearable, until Bill tried to lift him and lean his back against a stall. Then he cried out and grabbed for Bill's leg. No sooner had he done that when Doolin, hit by a bullet fired through the open front door, suddenly spun and crumpled down upon him.

B.C. tugged at the body and managed to roll Doolin off him and onto his back. The side of Bill's face was smeared with blood from a pulsating wound in his neck. Quickly, B.C. pressed his fingers against the hole. "Somebody help!" he yelled.

Dalton scrambled to his side. "Help's coming," he shouted above the renewed gunfire. He took a look at Doolin and whipped off his kerchief. "Use this. The rest of the boys are coming in. I gotta cover for them!"

Dalton scurried to a vantage point by the door and began firing, aiming at heads when he saw them, at shadows when he did not. His shots kept the attackers low, spoiling their aim. One by one, the gang members came zigzagging into the stable and, as the horses screamed in protest, dove head down for cover behind the stalls.

In a short while, the return fire became sporadic, then ceased. Somebody swore outside. Then things grew quiet.

In relative safety now, the outlaws slowly raised their heads. Bitter Creek looked around. "Everyone here?" he asked. Bill Raidler, across an aisle from him, nodded. "All except Tom and the girls. You okay?"

Bitter Creek grunted that he was, then gazed down at the unconscious Doolin. "Ol' Bill got it bad though. Just don't know how bad. Come on over and take a look."

Raidler crouched low and ran over to B.C.'s side. Both of them bent over Doolin. B.C. had bound the kerchief tightly above the wound and the bleeding had all but stopped. Raidler nodded. "You did good," he said. "He's going to have a hell of a sore neck but I think he'll make it." He tied the kerchief a bit tighter.

A few of the others came over. When they saw that Doolin was well tended to, they took up positions near the door and cautiously peered outside—just as a new gun battle started, this one between the posse and the occupants of the hotel.

"Ol' Tom's givin' 'em hell!" Dick West cried out.

"Anyone see who we're fighting?" Bitter Creek called out.

"Sherm said they were lawmen from Guthrie."

"I saw Lucas with 'em," someone called out.

"Goddamn spy," Waightman growled. "I'll boil his balls in oil if I catch him!"

"Let's try thinking of gettin' outta here first," Dalton answered. He turned to B.C. for advice. "We're running out of bullets. We gotta do something soon."

Bitter Creek looked down at Doolin, wishing he would regain consciousness. "We'll try waiting until Bill wakes up. Try to hang on 'til then."

He crept to the door and peered up at the top floor of the hotel. Even from where he was he could see where countless bullets had splintered the siding near the windows. Tandy was up there—how could she survive all that bombardment?

18

Tandy was terrified. Never had she heard such loud noise, seen such destruction, been so confused. He head rang with the echo of the shooting and she squeezed her eyes tight to keep it all away.

She had a picture in her head that would not be dislodged. It was as if her life had come to a standstill with that picture forever etched there. It was of her Bitter Creek at the livery stable, lying motionless on the ground, laying there—not moving, motionless.

She had seen B.C. shot. Then Rose had dragged her from the window down to the floor, where they had both lain in numb horror, listening to the bullets tear through the hotel's thin siding.

Arkansas Tom scurried into the room from the one he'd been in and found them that way.

"You two better get to the other side of the hotel," Tom cried. "This place is getting hotter than a cow in June." He ran low to the window, swung his carbine onto the ledge and began firing rapidly down at the posse.

Rose reached out and grabbed Tandy's hand. "C'mon," she yelled above the roar of gunfire. She turned on her stomach and crawled out the door, practically pulling Tandy with her. Once in the hall, they got to their feet and ran to a bedroom at the hotel's rear. Huddled against a wall there, hugging each other in mute fear, were Mary Pierce, her daughter, Cattle Annie and Little Britches. They stood like frozen statues, seemingly blind to Rose and Tandy when they came in.

"What'll we do?" Tandy asked vaguely.

"What can we do?" Rose spat out sharply. "The law's finally caught up with us, that's what! I told Bill we stayed here too long!"

Tandy felt that Rose was being foolish in looking to blame someone at this point. They had to get out of their present predicament. But no matter how hard she tried to think clearly, her mind kept going back to her picture of Bitter Creek lying on the ground. The other women in the room were obviously helpless; their fear served only to increase her own.

"I gotta go see!" The voice that came out of her was unnaturally loud, almost a shriek. Before Rose could stop her, she'd turned and bolted down the hallway back to the bedroom she'd left.

"Whatta'ya doing back here?" Tom swore when she came in. He had pulled a tall, mirror-topped dresser close to the window as a shield he could stand behind while shooting. The mirror had already been shattered by bullets.

"I have to know what's going on!" Tandy stormed back. She stood in the doorway and waited for a lull in the shooting. "Can you see anything?"

"I counted seven of 'em so far," Tom muttered. "They came up the Tulsa road in a covered wagon, got off and snuck around behind us. Damn them—but we'll give 'em a good fight if that's what they want!"

"Bitter Creek—can you see him?"

"They're all in the stable, all of 'em."

Tandy's heart pounded. "Is he—is he alive?"

Tom got off a shot before answering. "Missed the bastard," he swore, then frowned. "Hell, Bitter Creek's okay—saw him hobbling around. It's Doolin who got it bad!"

Tandy breathed her relief. Then, "What's going to happen?" she asked anxiously.

Tom shrugged. "I dunno. Them marshals look like they're carrying enough ammo to last 'em a week. Dunno if the boys can hold 'em off. They've slowed down their shooting."

"Maybe some of them are hurt."

Tom shook his head, peering over the dresser to see if he could spot any targets. "More'n likely, they're running outta bullets. Weren't exactly expecting company, y'know."

"But we just bought some yesterday," Tandy said, remembering Doolin's and Bitter Creek's purchases.

"Yeah, but it's all up here in Doolin's room," Tom answered. "I got enough to hold off a small army if need be."

Tandy thought it over. "Can we get some to the stable?"

Tom looked at her sternly. "Are you crazy? No one can walk through this firing."

"But we got to try," Tandy cried. "They need guns and bullets, don't they?" She looked at him beseechingly but the boy turned away and began firing out the window. She stared at the floor angrily. "Well, I'm not going to sit here and watch B.C. get killed!" She didn't spend time considering her next move; it was just something that had to be done.

"I'm going to take the things to them!" she shouted and backed out into the hallway.

Tom made a move to stop her, then thought better of it. "Wait for a minute," he called to her. "I'm going up to the attic. I'll give you cover if I can!"

Tandy nodded, then turned and ran down the hall to Doolin's room. The place was a shambles. In one corner lay the rifles and cartridge belts that had been bought at the general store. She grabbed a couple of Winchesters and slung as many of the gun belts over her shoulders as she could manage. Then she staggered over to the bedroom in which Rose and the other women were waiting.

"What the hell do you think you're doing?" Rose asked as Tandy went to the far window.

"I'm taking these to B.C.," Tandy replied. She

raised the window and peered out. Then she turned to Mary Pierce. "Can you get me some more sheets?" She waited for a reply. Slowly, Mary's face cleared up as she figured out what Tandy was up to. She nodded wordlessly and left.

"You can't go out there," Rose protested.

Tandy stared at her stubbornly. "Don't try to stop me, Rose," she warned.

The older woman looked into Tandy's eyes and saw the determination there. She hesitated, then, finally, nodded. "If you think you can do it, maybe you can," she said softly. "Good luck."

Tandy turned to the two sheets on the bed. Quickly, she knotted two ends together, then went to the pile of guns and belts and tied the free end of one sheet around them.

"Can you help me?" Tandy turned to Cattle Annie. The girl nodded. Together, the two of them lowered the bundle out the window and dropped it a few last feet to the ground, watching the tail ends float lazily. By that time, Mary Pierce had come back with extra sheets. These, with Rose's and Cattle Annie's help, Tandy tied securely around her middle. Then she sat on the window ledge and signaled she was ready. Both women took hold of the sheets as Tandy swung her feet out. Slowly, she turned, grabbed the ledge and lowered her body full length down the side of the hotel.

She jumped the last few feet to the ground and lay there, breathing heavily. Her legs, after the numbness left them, felt all right. Quickly, she freed herself of the sheets, retrieved the guns and belts and, carrying them as best she could, stepped hesitantly to a rear corner of the hotel. There she peered around at the back sides of several buildings.

Across from her was the small home of the town's doctor. Tandy eyed the distance, took a deep breath and dashed for it. As she reached that cover, a fusilade of shots rang out, so close Tandy felt sure she'd be hit. With eyes glued shut, she waited for the stab of pain. Then, when the firing continued, she realized no one was firing at her. The shots were coming from the attic of the hotel. Obviously, Tom had found a good position and was keeping the posse nailed down. Quickly, Tandy edged to the far corner of the house and looked out. No one was in sight. Puffs of smoke emitted from the back of the blacksmith's shop and from Murphy's saloon. There were lawmen there, she figured. She knew there might be more lawmen inside Phanley's, almost directly in front of her, though she could not detect any movements. Taking a deep breath, she picked up the hem of her skirt and dashed for the church.

Behind her she heard the quickened firing from the hotel and knew that Tom must have again spotted her and was offering a cover. Panting heavily, she spread herself against the church wall and again waited for a bullet to strike her. When nothing happened, she nervously opened her eyes and glanced around.

Straight ahead and close by now was Phanley's store. She was almost positive someone was in there firing at Tom. Yet Phanley's back door was temptingly open. If she went through the store she'd come out directly across from the stable; the store itself provided the shortest route. Perhaps there wasn't a lawman inside, Tandy decided; after all, there was no actual sign of one. In any event, she decided to try it. Maybe, even, she could grab more needed supplies before dashing across the street.

She glanced at the store again. Things had gone miraculously in her favor so far. She took a deep breath. Now or never, she told herself. She ran towards the back door. Tom opened up firing again. With a jump, she reached the door and leaped inside.

A big man with a large mustache whirled around from the front window and raised his gun. "What the hell?" he bellowed, then, seeing a woman, hesitated.

Tandy blanched, turned and started to run.

"Wait," the man said softly. "I can plug you easy if you take another step."

Tandy stood still on the doorstep.

"What's a pretty little thing like you doin' with all them guns? Whyn't you turn around so's I can get a good look at you?" the man said.

Tandy, not turning, glanced up at the hotel attic. Tom, she prayed silently.

"I'll just have to come get you, you know," the man said affably. "I 'spect what you're doing is against the law."

"Please don't. Please let me go," Tandy said, her voice quivering.

"Naw, can't do that. Wouldn't be right."

Tandy's blood froze as she heard a grunt and a chair being kicked out of the way. The man was coming towards her. She raised her eyes to the attic again, searching desperately for some sign of Tom. Perhaps he was concentrating on the front of the store; perhaps he didn't see her. But she did not move. The man reached her. She could smell his sweat and beery breath. "C'mon back inside," he growled.

Still, she did not move.

"God damn it, when I talk to ya, I mean for ya to listen!"

The man's hand clamped suddenly down on her shoulder, and it was at that point that Tandy moved. She ducked, squirmed and got away from his grasp long enough to take three quick strides into the clearing. Then she managed to trip over her own feet and fall.

"Ow, oh," she cried. She made as if to move and get up again.

The man came lumbering after her.

Oh now, please, Tom, Tandy prayed.

"Whaddye expect, runnin' with all them guns?" the man said. "I'll just take 'em off of ya an—"

His declaration of intent stopped as Tom's bullet caught him in the throat; Tandy heard the gurgle an instant before she heard the gun's distant report.

Instantly she was on her feet, turning back towards the store. The lawman was on his back, staring with wide-eyed surprise at the sky. He was dead. Tandy jumped over the body and ran. It was as if her heart had stopped beating and her mind had stopped thinking; she was alive only to the need to get to the livery stable and Bitter Creek. She ran through the store and out its front door.

Then she was dashing across the street—and into B.C.'s arms.

"Tandy!"

"Oh, B.C.," she murmured.

She was hysterical, her fear and its relief churning in one enveloping emotion. She thought she'd faint. Quickly the gang handed out the much-needed ammunition and guns she'd brought. She hardly noticed. The one solid feeling she had was of his and her heartbeats, his arms safely about her, his head buried in her hair. He was alive!

Suddenly, he swayed and she felt him weaken. Tandy backed away, sobering, and helped him sit down. "Oh, B.C.," she murmured, looking at the blood-soaked rag tied around his leg. "What are we going to do with you?"

She'd tried to make light of their predicament, and the men grinned their approval. But she was desperately concerned, not only for Bitter Creek but for all of them.

"Get back to your positions," came a hoarse voice. The men parted and Bill Doolin weaved up in front of her.

Tandy let out a gasp. She hardly recognized him. His face was caked with dirt, his neck wadded with bloody cloths, his eyes feverishly glazed.

"Oh Bill," Tandy uttered. She reached up and placed a hand gently against his face.

He blinked, as if trying to place her.

"He's been hit bad," B.C. said.

"Oh, Bill," she murmured again, sorrowfully.

Doolin blinked again, then focused on her. "I'm okay," he said. His voice had an even quality to it; it was his eyes and wavering body that gave his condition away. "We gotta get out of here, that's what," he commented doggedly. "Everyone here?"

"Tom's still in the hotel," someone said. Doolin edged forward with Tandy's help to where he could survey the top of the hotel. They could see Tom's gun stuck out of the attic window and hear its report now and then.

Doolin sighed. "Damn! He's got himself holed up good."

"No way he's going to get out," Bitter Creek said. "Them lawmen got the place surrounded by now."

Doolin thought a moment, then sighed heavily. "Damn! Well, maybe he'll find a way."

"Rose is back there too," Tandy spoke up.

Doolin didn't look at her. "They're on their own," he said softly. Then, hesitantly, he offered an opinion. "There's not too much to worry 'bout Rose. She'll pass herself off as one of Mary Pierce's girls. She'll know what to do, y'can bet on it."

Tandy wondered. "We can't leave them though."

Bitter Creek pressed her arm. "There's nothing we can do, hon," he answered. "There's no sense all of us going down. That posse's probably figuring we're waiting on Tom, which means we got a chance to surprise them if we race for it now. We have got to take that chance."

She knew he was right but it didn't seem fair. Then she thought of how the boy Tom had helped her get to the livery stable, and of Rose, so stubborn and strong-willed. Both seemed adequate to most any emergency. With luck, maybe they would be able to make it.

Quickly, members of the gang saddled the horses, helped Doolin and Bitter Creek mount and got up themselves. They made their surprise dash for freedom then, racing out of the stable and up Ingalls' main street before the posse realized what was happening. Shouts and scattered shots followed them but, with one exception, all made it safely to open country on the town's far side.

It was Bitter Creek who came a cropper. He'd lost more blood from his leg wound than he'd thought and was swaying dizzily in his saddle almost from the moment he left the stable. Fearing he would fall, Tandy grabbed his reins and slowed both their horses so as to steady him. Thus they fell behind. Then, despite Tandy's efforts, Bitter Creek did fall. As far ahead the others disappeared over the crest of a hill, she let out a small distressed cry. Bitter Creek, fainting, had slid from the saddle onto the ground.

Precious time was lost as Tandy spurred after his empty mount. Returning with it, she dismounted quickly and tried, vainly, to lift B.C. up by the shoulders.

"Oh, B.C., please, wake up," she cried. She looked around for help. At that moment a lawman, apparently an outpost guarding the edge of town, walked into view from behind a small barn. Rifle in hand, he hesitated, seeing only an unarmed woman some fifty yards from him. He walked slowly towards them. Then, when he spotted Bitter Creek's sprawled body, his pace quickened.

"B.C.!" Tandy screamed. Casting nervous looks at the fast-approaching lawman, she shook B.C.'s body. There was no response. She pulled B.C.'s head to her lap protectively. She didn't know what else to do until the lawman was a short ten yards from her; then it came to her in a flash. She rolled to her knees and drew Bitter Creek's gun from his holster. Cocking the hammer back with both hands, she lifted it and aimed.

The marshal saw and stopped. Quickly he raised his rifle and pointed it at Tandy's face. Tandy found herself staring into the barrel, petrified, B.C.'s pistol suddenly limp in her fingers.

Suddenly, a shot rang out.

Tandy closed her eyes and waited. When nothing further happened, she opened them again in time to see the lawman slumping to the ground.

She looked wide-eyed past him. There, on top of the crest, Bill Dalton was just lowering his rifle. Behind Dalton, just coming over the rise, were Clifton and Waightman, riding back towards her as fast as they could.

Tandy felt tears of relief welling inside her. Then she burst out into uncontrollable sobs. She was only half-aware of the riders helping her to her mount, of Waightman and Dalton bracing Bitter Creek on his horse between them, of their finally racing off together out of danger.

The cool wind felt good. She clung to her saddle horn with both hands, weaving back and forth, utterly spent. Oh God, she thought, we made it! We made it! We survived!

19

Tandy sat close to a small fire in the Indian tepee. The thin soup in her wooden bowl was bitter, but it warmed her innards and felt good. She knew better than to inquire about its ingredients. The one or two chunks of meat thickening the broth were probably dog, but she figured if the Indians could eat it, so could she.

The heavy, nauseating stench of Indian ointments mixed with wet leaves permeated the dark, enclosed tepee. Every once in a while, Tandy would glance over to the two men lying side by side, heavily wrapped in blankets and fur hides. Doolin had finally fallen asleep after struggling deliriously to free himself of the old Cherokee woman's ministrations and medicines. Tandy had had literally to sit on top of him to keep his arms down. Now, presumably, he was sweating out his fever.

She had nearly passed out from the foul smells herself, even though she'd had enough experience with Indian remedies to put some trust in them. Not everybody agreed with her. As Doolin got worse and worse, the other outlaws decided to fetch a doctor from the nearest town.

Bitter Creek had awakened now and then, long enough to sip some of the broth before falling asleep again. He had lost quite a bit of blood, more than anyone realized. When it had become apparent that neither man would be able to make it back to the cave, Charlie Pierce had suggested this small Indian encampment, an old hideout he had used, as a temporary place of refuge.

Waiting for the doctor, Tandy had time to reflect on the incidents at Ingalls. Her own actions, in retrospect, seemed unbelieveable to her. Had she given rational thought to it, she knew she would never have dared take the risks she had. The mere memory of what she had done still scared her. Yet, she was pleased and proud of herself. There was an inner satisfaction in knowing she'd had it in her to meet a situation and conquer it. And with that feeling came a sense of new strength.

The tepee flap opened and Dalton and Raidler came in, leading a short, blindfolded man who stumbled uncertainly towards her.

"Here's the doc," Dalton announced and untied the blindfold.

The doctor blinked, rubbed his eyes and stared at Tandy. He seemed surprised that such a pretty young girl should be associated with the men who had abducted him. Finally, his eyes wandered to the two men on the ground next to her. "These your friends I'm supposed to look at?" he asked in a shaky voice.

Raidler had with him the large black leather satchel they had taken from the doctor's office. "We'd like you to look at them and do whatever you can," Little Bill explained. "As long as you patch them up, you'll get home unhurt. I don't think we have to warn you what might happen if you try something funny."

The man scowled at Raidler. "I'm a doctor!"

Raidler smiled. "We know. You're a good man—so are these two." He nodded at Doolin and Bitter Creek. "We're trusting you to heal their wounds, just as you're trusting us to take you back home." He gave the doctor a pat of encouragement, handed him the satchel, then sat down by the fire to watch.

Tandy watched too, nervously. She was frightened the doctor would find something drastically wrong with B.C.. Somehow, it never occurred to her that he might do something wrong to him.

The doctor kneeled first at Doolin's side and began pulling apart the ointment-soaked leaves. "You sure your Indian friends won't mind my interfering with their work?" he asked. He glanced up over his spectacles. Getting no answer, he shrugged and took some bottles from his bag. "Sometimes they don't appreciate a white man tampering with their work. Damned if I know how things heal with this mud they plaster you with, but lots of times it works." He shook his head as he examined the wound.

Before long, he grew more expansive in one-sided conversation, possibly because the antiseptic he applied had a comfortable familiar odor that made his personal situation seem safer.

"Still," he continued, "I tend to go with a clean wound. Let it heal itself, I always say." He bent down closer to Doolin. "The bullet is still in his neck," he said to no one in particular. He took out a long metal tool and probed. "Yeah, it's a bullet all right." He looked to Raidler for a reaction. The cowboy merely smiled.

"Can you take it out?" he asked.

The doctor hesitated. He checked Dalton's expression, then Tandy's, then Raidler's again. No one was giving him anything. "If you want my honest opinion," he said firmly, "I'd leave the bullet be. I could operate, but not here. And I presume you don't want him moved to my office." He tried a smile. None was returned. He scratched his head. "It's a risky business. The bullet's not too dangerous where it is—he might get a headache once in a while, maybe get a bit dizzy, but it's nothing he won't be able to handle. 'Specially him. He's got a good body, good strength." The doctor looked up at them again. "I'd leave it be."

Dalton pursed his lips. "How do we know that's best for him?" he wanted to know. He seemed perplexed more than suspicious.

The doctor shrugged, feeling more sure of himself with these people. "I thought we started this on trust." He turned to Tandy. "I'm no lawman. I don't care who you all are or who this is or why he caught a bullet. I'm a doctor. I care for all sorts, including animals. That's my profession. I have no reason to lie to you or to anyone."

Tandy managed a tentative smile and looked to Raidler for a better-educated guess on what to do. "What do you think, Bill?"

The cowboy drew in a deep breath. "Is the bullet lodged in the stomatognathic system? Is it likely to interfere with his mandible?"

The doctor stared at him. "I don't know what the hell you're talking about, young man," he said bluntly. "It's in his neck but he's in no danger. I already told you that."

Raidler studied the man's angry face for a moment, then turned to Tandy. "I didn't really say anything—just testing him. The doc sounds okay to me."

Dalton nodded in agreement. "Okay—what about the other?"

The doctor glared once more at Raidler, then went to Bitter Creek's side. He removed the small covering at the calf and probed. "This one doesn't look too serious either. No bullet. I'll clean him up and give him some iron for the blood he's lost, but what he needs most is rest and food."

Tandy closed her eyes and let out a long, thankful breath. "Thank you, doctor," she murmured.

The doctor studied her face. In fact, he studied all their faces. He knew better than to ask who they were. At least two of them were named Bill and maybe more from stray comments he'd overheard. He was irritated at the Bill who'd roused him in the middle of the night and blindfolded him, and he was just as annoyed at the Bill who'd thrown medical lingo at him that he hadn't happened to have heard of. Still, he seemed to understand why they had done these things. They were genuinely concerned about their injured buddies, the girl as much as the rest of them. Outlaws or not, they didn't seem like such bad people. And suppose they were killers—why in God's name would he lie to them? Why take chances with one's life?

A week passed before Doolin was able to mount his horse. Some of the gang had already gone back to the cave, but Dalton and Raidler had stayed to help Tandy take care of her charges. The morning the second group left, she kept hovering over Bill and Bitter Creek to make sure they were up for the ride. Bitter Creek walked with a stiff leg, but at least he walked. Doolin was still shaky, but, Tandy noted, he was able to cope with it, just as the doctor had predicted. He also wanted to leave now and return to the security of the cave, which made sense to her.

When the five riders broke through the poplars into the glen, Tandy got the surprise of her life.

"Look!" she cried. "It's Rose!"

There, at the mouth of the cave, Rose stood in mock solemnity, her long dark hair flowing over her shoulders and spreading fingers of black webbing over her grey cotton dress. "You all took your sweet time getting back here," she shouted, laughing.

"When did you get back?" Tandy asked as soon as she was able to get to her side.

Rose gave her a quick look, then concentrated on watching Doolin as he slowly made his way up the path to the cave. " 'Bout a day after you left. Brought Cattle Annie and Little Britches." She pointed to the two girls shyly waiting just inside the cave's entrance.

Tandy beamed at them. It was going to be good to have more women to talk to. Rose seemed in a much better mood too. "I'm so happy you got out safely."

Rose sneered. "Yeah, we got out okay." As Doolin came up she took a deep breath and drew herself straight. She eyed him narrowly, waiting for him to speak.

He managed a weak grin. "Glad to see you made it back okay." He grew hesitant, looking into her cold eyes. "You had no trouble, I hope."

She shook her head. "No. Once you all left and they got Tom, they left town."

Doolin winced. "They got Tom?"

"When he saw you all ride away he figured he might as well give up. They're trying to blame him for one of the killings; they might make it stick."

"That's too bad," Doolin shook his head. "Tom was a good ol' boy."

"The girls," Rose nodded towards the two in the cave, "they hid me out 'til everyone left. They wanted to come with me, so I said okay." She waited for any objection.

"Sure." Doolin made his way unsteadily to a bench and sat down. "They're welcome here. Maybe it'll keep some of the boys content to stay around more."

"Were you able to figure out who them lawmen were?" Bitter Creek limped to Tandy's side.

Rose shook her head. "Townfolk said they were from Guthrie—no one we knew."

Bitter Creek grunted. "They're getting organized, Bill. How'd they know we'd be in Ingalls?"

Doolin gave him a hard look. "It was that Lucas fella! They must be planting spies all over the place, waiting for us."

"That's what I've been trying to tell you," Rose said. "Things are changing. You better get that through your head once and for all!"

Doolin placed both hands to his head and began rubbing his temples. "Don't be pestering me 'bout that, Rose," he said tightly.

Rose looked at him suspiciously. "It's for your own good, Bill," she stated. "For all of our good!"

Doolin groaned. "Just stop bugging me 'bout it! Goddamn!"

Rose glanced at Tandy and Bitter Creek questioningly.

"It's his wound," Tandy answered and moved over to Doolin. "He gets these headaches every once in a while."

Rose watched Tandy rubbing Doolin's forehead, then came forward. "Here, let me," she said. She took Doolin's head and pressed it to her middle.

B.C. got anxious. "You okay, Bill?"

All the outlaws had come up silently and were watching. Rose held Doolin's head in her arms, rocking him gently back and forth, and cooing over him. Tandy stepped back and took hold of Bitter Creek's hand. She was moved by Rose's gentleness; never had she seen this side of her.

"The doc said he'd be doing that once in a while," Raidler explained. "He should be coming out of it pretty soon."

"What happens if he conks out like that during a holdup?" Waightman asked loudly.

Rose's head snapped up and her eyes blazed at the big outlaw. "He won't!" she said. "He'll pull himself out of this, you wait and see. He just needs more rest."

The men shuffled about self-consciously. It was obvious that Waightman's question was on all their minds. Finally, Bitter Creek sighed and said, "We better stay low for a while. Give him time to get his strength back."

There were eager nods of agreement. It was Rose who broke the silence. "Yeah, we'll all stay here—but we won't be relaxing that much."

"You think we'll be planning something soon?" Bill Dalton asked.

Rose shook her head. "That's up to Bill. What we've got to worry about most now is letting our guard down. If the law's setting up ways to trap us, they're also out there trying to find this hideout. It's time we sent out some kind of a watch or lookout just to make sure no one's snooping around the area."

"I don't like the idea," Red Buck Waightman spoke up loudly. "And, I don't think Doolin would either. What if we're recognized?"

Rose straightened her back. "Bill will go along with it. So we take some chances. It's still better than all of us being jumped by surprise."

"I don't like it," Waightman persisted, and looked around for support.

"I think Rose is right," Dick West spoke up. "I mean, after Ingalls, who's to tell what the hell's happening?"

"We can send the girls out too," Rose said. "Everyone takes turns." She looked around and was satisfied she had won. "Okay. You all work it out among yourselves when everyone goes out. Me, Tandy and the girls will cook and ride too. We'll work around whatever is set up." She looked around to see whether there was any objection. "Bill, help me with Doolin."

Tandy watched as Rose and Dalton supported the weakened Doolin back into the cave. As they disappeared, she reached out to grab B.C.'s sleeve.

"What's the matter, hon?" he asked, sensing her tension.

Tandy frowned, not sure of what she was feeling. "I don't know. I just don't like Rose giving orders, that's all." She wondered if it was jealousy she was feeling.

Bitter Creek smiled down at her. "It's okay. She's only trying to help out ol' Bill."

"I'm worried about him."

"We all are. But he'll be okay." He sighed.

"Things have a way to changing—we got to change too. It'll take time."

She snuggled against him. "If it's time for a change, why not think of leaving for Texas?" It was a hopeful try.

He hesitated, longer than he had done in the past. "We can't, not just now." He looked down at her, hoping she would understand.

Tandy knew what he meant. She knew if the band broke up voluntarily, that would be one thing—they could leave. But to leave under the present circumstances was unthinkable. It would be like never getting back on a horse after you've been thrown. Unthinkable. She was beginning to understand her man. However, understanding gave her little comfort.

20

Another winter. It didn't seem possible that she was going through her third in the cave, one with the Dalton's—so long, long ago, it seemed—and now, her second with Doolin. Tandy looked about her, at the men playing faro, at Rose, Annie and Little Britches sewing patches in shirts and socks.

The group was larger than in other winters, and she felt warm and close to them all, as if they were her true family. Sometimes she was embarrassed by the closer proximity, particularly when Annie and Little Britches "entertained," as they liked to call it. Often she and B.C. found themselves giggling at the grunts, groans and passionate outbursts echoing through the cave from the nearby curtained shelters. "It reminds me of a sow pen during feeding time," was the way Tandy explained it. But she was in no position to carp, for often her and B.C.'s lovemaking sounds mingled with the rest.

She had no complains really. It was a wonder she hadn't become pregnant with all the sexual activity she and B.C. engaged in. Of course, neither of them really wanted a baby, so maybe that was the reason. "No place to raise a kid," B.C. commented one evening as they lay next to each other. "Certainly I don't want to teach my kid this way of life."

Tandy was often tempted to ask whether they would move to Texas if she became pregnant. But she didn't want to put pressure on him that way; she knew it would create worse problems for both of them.

Tandy sighed and went back to preparing the evening meal. Better not to think about Texas. She glanced over at the three women hoping they would not notice her watching them. Rose had changed since Ingalls; she seemed content to stay close to the two new girls or be by herself. Not that Tandy minded, although at times it hurt that Rose had removed herself from her to a point where their conversations were mostly restricted to polite exchanges.

Tandy knew that one of these days she would have to confront Rose on this matter. She felt that in a sense she was being forced into competing for the older woman's friendship and she didn't like that feeling. There was no reason for it in her mind.

"I think we should go out and do something," Rose said later in the evening. They had finished supper and were all still gathered around the fire, on their second mugs of coffee.

The men blinked at each other. "What are you

talking 'bout, Rose?" Doolin scoffed. "It's still winter."

Rose tucked her feet under her and sat on her knees. "So what?" she asked. "We've hardly had any snow on the ground. No one will be expecting it. I mean, it's a perfect time to do a job." She glanced around at the men to see if there were any favorable responses.

"Look at us," she continued. "We've been sitting on our duffs for a couple of months and we're bored with each other. So I asked myself, why not do something?"

There was a stirring among some. "She might have something there, Bill," Dalton admitted. "We don't have to worry 'bout them trackin' us without there bein' a snowfall. We'd certainly be hittin' 'em before they expect us."

Rose rode the growing excitement. "I think we should do something really big! Let 'em know we're still around. Show them that Ingalls hasn't scared us off." She looked at Doolin to catch his reaction.

He was staring into the fire, hands gripping his coffee mug tightly. "I dunno," he said. "We start working the winters and it'll turn out to be a long year. It'll start them looking out for us twelve months 'stead of a few."

"That's just my point," Rose exclaimed. "We been doing things out of habit. I got to thinking Bill, we gotta keep 'em jumping all the time. Gotta confuse 'em. Hit them now, 'stead of spring. We lay low, then hit 'em again nearer summer. We'll confuse them so much they won't know what to do."

"Sounds pretty good," Dick West spoke up.

Doolin struggled with himself. He didn't like admitting it was a good idea. Grudgingly, he nodded. "Okay, if that's the way you all feel. I guess it's as good a time as any." He looked around at them. "Any of you got a plan?"

Dynamite Dan said tentatively, "Well, with the land rush and all, there should be plenty of money in Perry. What about there?" He received a few enthusiastic nods but Bitter Creek shook his head.

"Tilghman is there," he said. "I don't think we should mess around with him."

"Why not?" Red Buck Waightman grumbled. "I'd like to get him in my sights. Maybe we can get rid of him once and for all."

"The time will come when Tilghman and us'll meet," Doolin answered. "Don't you worry 'bout that. But for now, I agree with B.C. We keep away from him and his two friends."

"He's a skunk—and we should get him out of the way!"

"He's one of the best—maybe *the* best," Doolin snapped back. "And don't you forget it! Don't any of you forget it." He glowered at Red Buck, then said slowly to all, "Our fight isn't against Tilghman—nor Madsen or Thomas or any of their like. They're just doing their job, just as we do ours. And they're good at what they do like we're good at what we do. So don't go calling them fool names—'cause they'll plug you full of holes while you're doing it."

There was an uncomfortable silence. Charlie Pierce cleared his throat. "I heard there's money flowing through Clarkson."

"They ain't got no bank there."

"They got a post office which is the same thing," Pierce persisted. "There's money up there, that's what I heard!"

Doolin shrugged and looked around for more suggestions.

Bill Dalton coughed. "They've got a nice little bank in Pawnee. I looked it over when we was there getting that doc. Looks as if it did a pretty good business."

"That's a mite close to home ground," Bitter Creek pointed out doubtfully.

"And what's wrong with that?" Rose asked. "The further away we go the more likely we'll ride into the law. We haven't hit close to home so they don't figure we will. I say we should."

Doolin smiled at her. "That's a good point, Rose. And it's not that we'd be picking on home folks. Bankers are bankers everywhere."

"Yeah," Dalton answered. "But some of them people in Pawnee are friends."

"Just like them people in Coffeyville were friends of your brothers?" Doolin countered.

Tulsa Jack spoke up. "I was around those folks in Pawnee. They're scared of the law, but they're more scared of us. They won't do nothing 'gainst us."

Doolin contemplated all the suggestions. "I agree with Rose," he said finally. "I think we should do something really spectacular to let them people know they haven't licked us. So here's the thing." He looked around at them, pleased with his own idea. "We ride up to Clarkson, relieve that post office of whatever they have. Then, on our way back, we stop over at Pawnee and collect whatever they have."

"Holy hell!" Dick West cried out in delight. "They'll think there's two gangs about!"

Doolin beamed. "That's the idea. We're already getting blamed for things we didn't do. This will confuse 'em all the more."

"What about us?" Cattle Annie spoke up for the first time. "Do we go along?"

Doolin shook his head. "You two stay here this time. Maybe next time we'll take you."

"But what'll we do while you're gone?"

Doolin shrugged. "Keep watch for us, that's what. Ride around the area and look for suspicious strangers. That way, we won't come back to no surprises."

Neither new girl liked that assignment. It sounded dull. They wanted to go on the robbery for the thrills of it. They turned to Rose for help in getting Doolin to change his mind, and when that attempt failed they turned reluctantly to Tandy.

Tandy turned them down too. "I know how you feel," she said. "In the first place, I couldn't change Bill's mind for him even if I wanted to. And in the second—" She was too embarrassed by their sorrowful looks to go on. All she thought to say, as she turned away, was, "It isn't as much fun as you might think. One of these days you'll find that out."

She felt old when she said that, as old as her mother.

Rose and Tandy rode their horses into Clarkson alone. As they came down the town's narrow dirt street, they carefully avoided looking at several men lounging against railings. It was a cold morning. They had wrapped shawls over their bonnets to keep their ears from ringing and were having trouble enough riding into an icy wind to spend much energy looking at men.

Or so onlookers might have thought. Doolin's plan had been well-arranged. The gang members had gone in before the women, one by one or in pairs, to lounge about and attract as little attention as possible. Only later would they slowly converge on the post office.

Rose and Tandy passed them all by. The road was crusted with ice and the horses clipped along unsteadily, now and then stepping into unseen ruts. Up ahead, a wagon rolled lazily across the town's one intersection and disappeared.

"There it is," Rose said, keeping her voice low. She nodded towards the post office several buildings ahead. "You stop at the saloon just this side of it. As soon as I dismount, count to forty and then come in." She rode on ahead.

Waiting where she was supposed to, Tandy felt conspicuous. She tried to appear casual as she peered about. There they all were—Bitter Creek,

Doolin and the rest, watching and waiting at various surrounding buildings. Way down the street, she could spot Tulsa Jack at a railing where their horses were tied. His responsibility was to bring the horses to the post office.

Tandy began counting to herself. One, two, three —. A man was staring at her through the saloon's frost-coated window. Quickly, she found a kerchief in her satchel and dabbed at her eyes, hoping the man would recognize a need for her stopping there and be satisfied. Thirty seven, thirty eight, thirty nine, forty.

She looked up at the man and smiled, then turned her horse towards the post office.

There were two shirtsleeved men behind its counter, one writing figures in a large red book and the other tending to Rose. Tandy hesitated, then walked up to the figure-writing clerk, who looked up, ready to wait on her. She glanced sideways and watched Rose's man count bills out into her hand.

"Sixty, eighty, one hundred." The man lifted his face and smiled at Rose. "It's not too often we get a hundred dollar bill in here," he said politely.

It was an excellent opportunity for Tandy; she turned to the man and beamed. "Oh, really?" she asked innocently. "My heavens! That's why I came in too. My husband asked me to have this bill changed, if you would." She dug out a hundred dollar bill from her own purse and put it on the counter.

Both clerks raised eyebrows and looked at the women suspiciously.

"Can you imagine that?" Rose said in wonderment. "Isn't that a coincidence? It was my husband who sent me here too." Suddenly she was confiding woman-to-woman with Tandy, ignoring the clerks. "Y'know, ever since we arrived with the land rush, our money has gone dollar after dollar for all those piddling little things you need to get a household started. All we have left are large bills. It's too bad they don't have a bank in this town." She turned to the two men who were now listening attentively to their conversation. "But these kind gentlemen—they are so helpful."

Tandy smiled at the clerks. "Why, I do hope you all can be. My husband's still looking to buy a ranch with what we brought from Virginia. He carries these large bills with him all the time, says his pockets bulge too much from them." She clucked her tongue. "I keep telling him one of these days we'll run into a town that won't be able to cash them, but Bill, he just won't listen."

"My dear," Rose assured her, "I just know you won't have any difficulty here. They have lots of small bills in their safe—see there?" She pointed to a black safe behind the counter. "That's where my change came from."

Tandy turned to the men wide-eyed. "Oh, that's wonderful! I'm so lucky! Does that mean I can get cash here whenever I need it?"

The clerks raced each to speak first. "Oh, yes, ma'am," one said. He went to the safe, opened it, came back with a metal box and opened its lid. "As you can see, we do have plenty, just like this lady said." The other clerk, hovering over him, said, "Ah, perhaps your husband would care to deposit his money to our care while he's here? We do pay regular bank interest and perhaps we might be useful to him in other ways, such as finding him a ranch."

Tandy cocked her head and gave him a wide smile. "Why, that's so kind of you."

"I really must be going," Rose said. "It was so nice to meet you. I'm sure you'll love Oklahoma once you find a place and settle down." She left the post office and went to her horse. Mounting, she nodded. It was the signal. Quickly, the gang converged on the building.

Doolin was the first to enter, then Dalton, Bitter Creek, and Raidler. They came in with guns drawn. Before the clerks could make a move, they and Tandy too had guns pressed against their heads.

"Okay, little lady," Doolin told Tandy. "We don't aim you no harm. You can go!" They waited silently as Tandy, looking terrified, gathered her things and ran. Mounting her horse, she had to restrain herself from spurring it to catch up with Rose, who was already at the edge of town, waiting. Her own slow departure was a signal to Tulsa Jack that the robbery was going well and that he was to bring up the horses.

The gang caught up with the two women a mile out of town, laughing and carrying on. Not a shot had been fired. There had been no resistance, no problems at all.

"How much?" Rose called out as they continued on their way at a leisurely pace.

"Not quite sure," Doolin answered. "Almost took ourselves some junk paper but Raidler said we couldn't use it. We got enough of the good stuff though."

They were all in a good frame of mind, most pleased with themselves on how well the Clarkson robbery had gone.

"We're not going into Pawnee feeling this way," Doolin stated at their first chance for a rest.

"Hell, why not?" Tulsa Jack asked. "We can do the same thing there."

"That's just the problem," Doolin explained. "You all think we can do this blindfolded. No, we do this my way. We'll hole up somewhere close by, then slip in at night to check things over. There's no telling what might be in store for us in Pawnee. Maybe they're waiting for us, maybe not."

His speech sobered them. Tandy felt relieved that someone had made sense. She too had been caught up with the ease of the Clarkson robbery but realized now how easy it was to succumb to overconfidence.

They spent several days in the same Indian village where Doolin and Bitter Creek had recovered from the Ingalls fight. The men took turns wandering into Pawnee, usually in the evenings, to inspect the town and to familiarize themselves with the Farmers and Citizens Bank.

"It's not going to be as easy as Clarkson," Doolin

told them on their final evening. "They got word what we did and everyone's a bit on edge. You girls better keep with the horses this time."

Rose objected. "What's wrong with us casing the bank as we did the post office?"

Doolin shook his head. "It's a bigger town for one thing. For another, they've got a sheriff in Pawnee."

Rose glared at him and Doolin glared back. "I'm in no mood for an argument, Rose. There's apt to be shooting—"

"I'm not afraid of being shot at. And I can fire a gun as good as any man."

"Damned if I'm gonna have you shot at," Doolin said tightly. "Just as I know B.C. ain't going to let Tandy be shot at."

"I'm talking about me!" Rose said. "I deserve it."

"Number one," Doolin answered in a soft, controlled voice, "you do as I tell you. Number two, taking care of them fresh horses is as important to us as an extra gun. And number three, you're the one always saying to take care about things. Well, that's exactly what I'm doing. I'm being careful. So, don't you go arguing with me no more!"

Later on, in their bedrolls, Tandy leaned over and whispered to B.C., "I'm glad Doolin told Rose off. And I don't like the way she's always trying to push me aside."

Bitter Creek squirmed around so that he fit better against her, his arm reaching out to bring her head in close against his chest. "Rose is okay," he sighed. "She just gets restless at times. She don't mean no harm."

Rose still bothered Tandy. Granted they had probably all changed during the years, she in particular seemed to have changed for the worse. It was as if she had to prove something and was driving them all as hard as she was driving herself. Maybe she was trying to take over the gang; Tandy didn't know. She only knew she liked Rose much better when she was freer in spirit. She liked everyone better when they were freer in spirit.

The gang split up early the next morning. The men rode toward Pawnee and Rose and Tandy took a string of horses bought from the Indians to a knoll halfway between Pawnee and the cave. They were familiar with this spot and it was a good place to wait, for it was on the direct-line escape route the men would take after the robbery.

Since two lone women if seen roaming the countryside with a string of horses would certainly draw comment, they stayed off the regular trails. Not that it mattered too much. This was mostly flat open country broken only by occasional bellies or dips. Once in a while they would come upon a more traveled route, looking like some faded ribbon fallen from the sky onto sage and black grass. But they saw no one on these trails. More to fear, maybe, were the people in the distant homes they saw—low-lying mud-packed hovels with pathetic-looking windmills in their sparse yards. The windmills looked something like plucked hens clucking over undernourished offspring. There were hundreds of these hovels with their windmills.

"There are too many." Rose shook her head. "Pretty soon, there will be barbed-wire fences 'cause people will start arguing over whose land is whose. Once the fences come, no one will be able to ride across the territory. We'll all be boxed in with nowhere to go."

"I don't think so," Tandy gazed about her. "There's a lot of land here. You watch, people will spread out after a while. The Indians may be scaring them now, but you'll see, there'll come a time when they'll stop crowding."

Rose shook her head. "I seen it around Dodge City. You have no idea what it's like. But then, you like the crowds. I don't. I like my freedom—and I like the openness."

"I do too," Tandy stated. "I just think there's room out here for all of us."

"You're not being realistic!"

"You're the one who's not realistic," Tandy objected. "You're always saying things are changing. Well, so is the land."

Rose said sadly, "Yes, the land's changing, all right. The railroads are trying to bring in more and more people. If we and people like us don't fight 'em, they'll divide up this country into tiny quarter-acre plots. You won't be able to turn around."

Tandy was silent for a while with her own thoughts. "I dunno," she finally sighed. "I just don't know."

Rose glanced over at her. "I'd rather run off and

live in a cave for the rest of my life—away from it all!"

Tandy wrinkled her nose. "That's what we've all done, isn't it? But that doesn't make it right. It's just our choice."

"Not yours, though, is it? I mean, you'd rather hightail it to Texas and ranch it, wouldn't you?"

"I've chosen to do whatever B.C. wants. That's my choice."

"You should be with us 'cause you want to, not because you have to."

Tandy studied the woman. Though Rose had raised this same issue before, she now sensed her deepening hostility. She was becoming more bitter every day. She drew in a long quivering breath. "Just because I'd rather me and B.C. live in Texas doesn't mean I don't support Doolin." It bothered her that she had to defend her actions. "I think I've done my part and I don't mind saying I think I've done a good job of it." Damned if she was going to let the woman get the best of her!

"It still don't make it right," Rose answered. "You're in with us only because of B.C.. There's a difference."

"What about you and Bill? Don't that count?"

Rose snorted, still staring straight ahead. "Me and Bill? There's nothing there, honey—'cept convenience or whatever you want to call it."

Tandy watched her. It didn't make sense. She couldn't conceive of a woman not wanting to share one's life with a partner. Of course, Rose had Calamity Jane's blood in her, which probably accounted for some of her actions. Maybe it was in Rose to live the life of an outlaw, man or no man at her side.

The knoll was easily identifiable. For some strange reason, nature had decided to crown this egg-shaped mound with a ten-foot-high tree, which stood out as an easily recognizable landmark for anyone traveling the territory.

The two women dismounted and tethered the string of horses to the tree on a long rope. Then Tandy tucked herself on the ground against the trunk, stretched out her legs and prepared for a long, peaceful wait.

She didn't have to wait long, however, for the Pawnee holdup was a rousing success.

21

The men were joyous. They were camped far from the knoll, having picked up the girls and fresh horses almost as an afterthought. The animals had not been needed. There had been no pursuit. They had fired few shots, and those more in warning than anything else. They kidded among themselves as they divided their shares in front of the campfire. The two robberies had been more successful than they'd dared imagine and they pounded Doolin on the back for his brilliant planning.

"We better not take any chances," Bill said at last. "This time we split up for a while. Meet in a couple of months. But you all take care. Your names are getting more known and the rewards for us are going to get bigger. Wherever you go, keep your ears open for what the law is doing or isn't doing. We'll talk about what we do next when you all get back."

They split up once again, and the separation once

more created a feeling of emptiness in the four who headed back to the cave.

Bill, Rose, Tandy and Bitter Creek came into the narrow entry to the glen so absorbed in their own thoughts that they at first failed to notice something was wrong. The air was still crisp with yet another month of frost promised for the mornings. Their steps, when they dismounted, were slow and stiff. Doolin was the first to sense trouble. As they approached the cave, he raised a hand and drew out his carbine. They stopped and held their breaths. Things were quiet. Too quiet. Suspiciously, they checked for signs. The cave was silent. The three horses in the small corral whinnied their welcome and stomped the ground impatiently.

"They ain't been fed in some time," Bitter Creek noted. His eyes darted from one place to the next. "No sign of Annie nor Britches neither."

"You girls stay back," Doolin said. He held his carbine ready.

Rose and Tandy edged back towards the tree line. Rose had taken a small hand gun from her purse.

"It's so awfully quiet," Tandy whispered.

Rose didn't answer.

The two watched as Doolin and Bitter Creek prowled the area, then, learning nothing from that, warily went into the cave. A few minutes later, Bitter Creek came out and beckoned the two women over. "No one in there," he shrugged. "Place is deserted. You might as well come in now. We can check around some more."

The cave was dank and musty; it smelled of desertion. Doolin was bent over the stove kindling a fire when the women entered. He looked at Rose and said, "Their things are here, but 'pears they been gone for a spell. You know them best. What do you make of it?"

Rose said tentatively, "Doesn't sound right. I was sure we could count on them girls."

"I thought so too," Doolin answered. "Maybe something's happened to 'em."

Tandy had come from the girls' curtained-off quarters shaking her head. "All their clothes are still there," she stated. "Maybe they just went off to Guthrie or Ingalls for a couple days."

By the time Bitter Creek had finished feeding the horses, they had discussed many possibilities without coming to a conclusion. "I just don't like the feeling I have," Bill said. "Could be they went out and got themselves caught by the law. If that's so, maybe they told 'em we'd be back here soon."

"They wouldn't do that," Rose said. "They'd do most anything, but not that."

"You want us to go out and find 'em?" Bitter Creek asked.

Doolin nodded. "Most likely, if they were caught, they'd be taken to Guthrie. I'll mosey over there and ask some of my friends."

Rose objected. "I don't think you should go. You're too well known around Guthrie and the law's sure to be on the lookout for you after what we just did. Send B.C."

"Bitter Creek's as well known as Bill," Tandy protested.

Bitter Creek reached out and grabbed her hand. "Rose has got a point, hon. Not too many folks in Guthrie know me." He turned to Doolin with a grin. "I ain't got the reputation ol' Bill has."

"You ain't got nothing to be reputable 'bout," Doolin shot back. "You oughta be thankful you ain't got the talents I got."

They all laughed. Bill's remark seemed to break the tension in the cave. Tandy laughed the loudest, doing her best to cover up her fears about B.C.'s safety.

The three of them spent a restless two nights after B.C.'s departure. Doolin grew moody and irritable. He was worried about his friend and continued to suspect the worst with regard to the two girls' disappearance.

"Maybe it's time we found another place," Rose offered. "We've been here too long. It's a wonder we haven't been found out before this."

"This is a damn good place. It's perfect. We'd never be able to find anything like it again. Besides, all our friends know how to get to us."

"That's what I'm afraid of," Rose argued. "I don't think the girls spilled the beans, but just how long do you think it's going to be before them marshals find the right person for the right price? You can bet your boots they're doing everything they can to turn people against us."

Doolin looked at her sullenly. "We'll move if we have to," he said finally. "We'll wait to hear what B.C. finds out."

Rose looked at him in exasperation. "You'll probably do nothing," she commented.

"I'll do what I think has to be done," he said in a tight voice. "I haven't got any of us caught yet."

"Well, if I were you—"

"You ain't me," Doolin interrupted sternly. "I do the telling around here!" They stared at each other in cold silence. Then Doolin tried to smile. "Aw, c'mon Rose. C'mon over here." He patted the empty place next to him on the bench.

"No, I don't feel like it," she said and turned her back to him.

Doolin chewed the corner of his lip. He took a glance at Tandy, shrugged, got up and went out into the night.

Tandy watched him go, then stared unhappily at Rose. It was their battle, not hers. But it saddened her to see the separation between them widening with each week. It put a strain on everyone in the tight confines of the cave. She sighed. Nothing she could do or say would change things. Discouraged, she trailed back to her curtained cubicle, sank onto the blankets and hugged her knees. She was lonely. Oh danm, B.C.! Where the hell are you when I need you?

He returned the next day. Even as they watched him unsaddle and go to the outside rain barrel to wash up, they could tell from his expression that the news was not good. But it couldn't be terribly serious or he would have rushed up to them with it. His slow deliberation suggested more that he was reluctant to share what he had learned.

"Tilghman caught 'em," he said flatly when he finally came up to them. He dropped himself in front of the fire and reached for the cup of coffee Tandy handed him. "As far as I could find out, a posse spotted them riding around about ten miles from here. Rather than be followed back here, they hightailed it for Indian country. Tilghman and some deputies went after 'em and brought 'em back."

"Did you get a chance to see them?" Tandy asked anxiously.

B.C. shook his head. "The story is they clammed up about us and were sent back east to some women's prison on trumped-up charges of prostitution."

"Poor Annie and Britches," Tandy sighed after a moment of silence to digest the information. Arkansas Tom, now them. It seemed as if a noose was beginning to tighten around the gang.

"That Tilghman!" Rose spat.

"No use blaming Tilghman," Doolin stated. "He's doing his job, that's all."

"How can you say that?" Rose asked. "It's getting so a person can't go out for a pee without someone clamping a handcuff on him. Now they're picking on girls!"

Doolin shrugged. "It's not like ol' Tilghman's done something dastardly. We know what he's out there for. If there's a shootout, I sure ain't taking sides with him. But I don't bear no grudge against anyone who's fair and straight. And that's the way I see Tilghman. It's the chance we all take."

Rose paced the floor in tight steps. "I don't see how you can take all of this so calmly." She looked at the three of them. "I think we should do something that will set 'em on their ears, let 'em know they can't go around capturing poor innocent girls. Just like we showed them after Ingalls."

Doolin grinned. "Now look who's not talking sense. We got away with Clarkson and Pawnee 'cause they didn't figure we'd do such a thing. But now they know better. And don't you think they're waiting for us right now? Waiting for us to get even about Annie and Britches?" He let it sink in, then nodded. "We'll get even, you can mark my words on that. We're not going to jump into things, but we'll make it." He jabbed Bitter Creek in the ribs and grinned. "Ain't that right, pard?"

Bitter Creek smiled. "Yep. We've always been one jump ahead of Tilghman and we'll stay that way. No way is he going to get us, not if we stick together like we've been doing."

Doolin nodded and said, "That's right. We all stick together."

Later that night, under the warmth of their blankets, Tandy giggled and whispered to B.C., "We gotta do what Bill said."

"Hummmm," B.C. murmured. "What was that?"

She nibbled his ear and pressed against him, drawing one knee up and over his thigh. "Stick together." She giggled again, then darted quick kisses at his neck.

Bitter Creek smiled in the darkness and rolled over onto his side. "Hmmm, you're in a good mood."

"Well, I should say," she answered. "You've been gone a couple of nights. I got lonely." She quit kissing him and lay dreamily next to him, feeling his warmth and the strength of his arms.

"Well," B.C. laughed softly, "I got to admit you're a sight better than camping out with only a saddle and blanket on a hard ground."

"I had better be!"

"Course, being alone out there allows a man to catch up on his sleep!" He chuckled.

"Oh you!" she chided. "You don't have any romance in you at all."

He shrugged. "I haven't got the gift of words if that's what you mean. I admit that. But that's not saying I don't feel for you in my heart."

She was satisfied with that. On their first meeting she'd recognized that Bitter Creek was not one to waste words. But she felt she knew him so well that words were not necessary. "Oh B.C.," she murmured and snuggled even closer. "At times I wish—" She stopped. Dangerous territory!

"You wish what?" he asked drowsily.

"Oh, nothing," she stammered. But then she could not hold it all inside herself. "There are times I can't have enough of you. I keep thinking of Annie and Britches—and Tom and the Daltons. Slowly, one by one, we're losing everyone. And I think that perhaps one of these days it'll happen to you—and to me—and then, it'll be all over. Never again."

"Shhhh," he murmured and put his arms about her. "Don't you go thinking 'bout that sort of thing."

"Well, I can't help it," she whimpered. "It would be all over. I'd have nothing left then."

"There's memories," he answered. "No one can take those away from us, can they?"

She shook her head. "I know, but—but I need more than that. I need—" She didn't know what she needed. She stopped and swallowed hard. She tried again, and then what she needed came to her in a flood of realization that almost took her breath away. The answer seemed so clear, so simple, that she was surprised she hadn't thought of it before. She knew what she had to have!

She leaned over and kissed him, a long tender tear-soaked kiss. She lifted her face slowly and peered down at him, barely seeing him in the darkness but knowing his face so well that she didn't have to. She thought again. A baby! A baby! It felt good, positive—she would have him forever!

Suddenly, she sat up, drew the nightgown over her arms and tossed it to the ground beside her.

"Hey, what are you doing?" B.C. murmured.

"What does it look like, Bitter Creek Newcomb?" she asked throatily. "I told you, you been away. I missed you, missed you a lot!" She knew the tone in her voice betrayed her desires. She began to unbutton the top of his longjohns but he was ahead of her. Bracing himself, he slid out of them and crept back under the covers.

They embraced, tasting the delicious feeling of

their own moist skins against each other. Bitter Creek bent his head, kissing her neck, first one side, then the other, then in the deep hollow under her chin. Slowly, his head lowered, hands clasping her rib cage, he eased himself down until he reached the valley between her breasts. His hands came up to cup each one, then his lips came down on her hardening nipples, tasting them gently, first one, then the other, gently nibbling the hard round tips, running his tongue over their hardness, gently sucking.

Tandy held his head between her hands, her long fingers digging into his coarse hair. She drew herself up, tight with desire, then bent down and kissed his shoulder. Everything felt so good; she felt good, he felt good. She knew it would be different this time. She was ripe, as she never had been before. She didn't know whether it had been luck, good timing, or what, that she hadn't become pregnant before now. But now it was different, because she wanted that baby—his baby, her baby, their baby. She wanted part of him. She wanted them to create something that was a testimony to their love, their being together.

Her hands pulled on him as she slowly rolled onto her back and helped him over on top of her. She spread her legs apart and felt him slide up against her wetness. He was breathing heavily against her shoulders as he lifted himself. Her hands reached down and found him, eager, throbbing. For a moment she just held him, stroking gently, wanting to rush, yet wanting to hold the moment as long as she could.

Slowly, she guided him to her. She was wet, warm, open and eager to accept him. It was a delicious feeling! She met his thrusts with spasms, half-wanting him to stop, yet begging for more. Soon, she was matching his ferocity, clutching at him, clenching her teeth to keep from crying out in abandonment. Oh God, she thought, it is magnificent!

22

It had been Rose's idea really. As spring came on, Bill's headaches began to act up again. There were times, late in the evenings, when they would hear him pacing around the cave unable to sleep from the pain.

By then, they were used to the sudden changes in his disposition. Though early on, his spells lasted only a few minutes, by mid-May they had increased in frequency and duration. For a while they did little but watch and suffer with him.

"We'll take him to the hot springs," Rose had finally declared. "A few days there might do him good."

So they had gone to Arkansas. It had been a long trip, though not over unfamiliar territory, since Arkansas was an old stomping ground of the James and Youngers. Most of the gang members had journeyed there at one time or another to partake of the soothing baths.

The hot water and sulfurous smells brought back

old memories to Tandy as she and Rose soaked in the area reserved for women only. Long before meeting B.C., she and her Indian maid had sloshed in similar springs, which were considered big medicine by the tribes. They were good memories. She was glad that Rose had suggested they come to this place.

The rest of the gang had joined them in the cave and had readily agreed to accompany them. Doolin, Rose, Bitter Creek and Tandy were staying in a hotel, while the others, as was their custom, camped out on the small town's outskirts. The camp, as usual, was referred to as "Little Dick's camp," since it was he who invariably led the way in pitching his bedroll under the stars.

"When are we going to get to work?" the little gunman asked one evening as they all gathered together for a meal.

Doolin, feeling much better as a result of his treatments, shrugged. "I'm game for anything you boys have in mind."

"There's some good money right in this town," Charlie Pierce volunteered.

Doolin shook his head. "Naw," he said. "I want to stay outta trouble in Arkansas. We might be needing a place to settle down in some day."

"We could swing up to ol' Mizzoo," Dynamite Dan offered. Most of the Kansas boys had no love for the neighboring state of Missouri, out of bitter memories dating back to the Jayhawker abolitionist wars.

"I remember my brothers speaking of Southwest

City as a likely place," Bill Dalton spoke up. "Let's go there and sort of do a job for them."

It was agreed. Doolin laid out his plans and ideas. This time they would be without extra horses but if there was a chase, they could ride back to Arkansas and get lost in the wild woodlands if need be.

A few questions were asked and answered. Then Doolin looked closely at Dalton. "What's the matter, Bill? You look like there's something heavy on your mind."

Bill Halton fidgeted. "Bill, I been doing some thinking while I was gone," he said hesitantly. "I was going to wait until after the job to tell you—but this will be my last ride with you."

Doolin frowned. "What do you mean this is your last ride? Where you going?"

"I only came back 'cause I felt I owed you," Dalton answered. "But I met a girl. We're going to be married—try to settle down somewhere and be forgotten."

"Hell, Bill," Doolin said. "You can't be leaving us. You're too good a man to lose." The others joined him in that sentiment.

"Believe me, I've given it considerable thought. It hasn't been an easy decision. I mean, I came to you in the first place because I thought there was nothing else I could do. And I appreciate your having me ride with you. But it's time I got out while I can. Things ain't the way they used to be and—well, it's just something I got to do and want to do."

The camp was silent. It was the first time anyone had entertained the notion of breaking up, leastways aloud. Tandy looked around and was sure the idea had entered several of their minds. There were embarrassed glances swapped among some. Oh dear God, she thought. Here it was—the beginning of the end of things. She hung onto B.C.'s arm. Maybe the thought would spread to him. And when he finds out about the baby—she closed her eyes and dreamed some more.

Southwest City, Missouri was larger than they had expected. Dividing into small groups, they entered the town from various avenues of approach, keeping their eyes peeled for the law. They felt quite sure that they would not be recognized as long as they did not collect together in any large number.

There were two banks, the smaller only two buildings down from the sheriff's office. This one they passed by quickly, concentrating on the larger one, a corner edifice at a vee in the road. The riders dismounted at various distances from the bank and leaned against buildings as they leisurely rolled smokes.

Waightman and Pierce were on a hardware store's porch. "Whyn't we take both banks?" Waightman growled to Charlie.

"And get caught like the Daltons?" Pierce answered calmly.

"We can buzz them off like flies," Red Buck answered sourly, keeping his eyes on Doolin and Rose just entering their line of sight.

"Doolin don't want gunfire," came the answer.

"Hell, they's only Mizzoos!"

Charlie sighed. He was tired of arguing with the surly man. Red Buck was a bloodthirsty lout in Charlie's mind and he didn't trust him. Still, if there was going to be a fight, it would be good to have someone like Red Buck handy. The man, give him his due, was fearless.

"I don't see why we can't go into the bank this time," Red Buck was saying.

"We're to make sure no one sets off an alarm," Pierce answered. He watched Doolin and Rose dismount in front of the bank. Tandy and Bitter Creek had just entered moments before. Across the street, Little Bill and Little Dick were unhitching their horses and walking across the street to the railing in front of the bank. Tulsa Jack and Dynamite Dan approached from the far end of the street with Bill Dalton. They all clustered around the railing, then disappeared through the bank's doors.

"Okay, here we go," Charlie murmured. He leaned against the porch railing, eyes darting about.

"Did you see them fellows?" a voice spoke out from the doorway behind them. The store's proprietor had popped his head out and was staring at the bank. "They looked mighty suspicious, didn't they?"

Charlie glanced at Red Buck, whose hand was slowly lowering to the butt of his holstered gun.

He turned to the man and shrugged. "Looked like regular cowpokes to me," he replied with a smile. "In fact, I think I recognized one of 'em. We used to ride together for ol' man Halsell over in the territory. I was just saying to my pard here, that one with the whiskers sure looked like ol' Abilene Jack, didn't I say that?"

Red Buck slowly nodded, his eyes boring into the store owner, "Yeah," he growled.

The man frowned and stepped forward to stand next to Pierce, still eyeing the bank. "I dunno. I just happened to glance out my window and saw 'em bunching together right outside there. I tell you, it didn't look good to me."

Charlie looked nervously at Red Buck, then tried a weak smile. "Sure goes to show you how the imagination can play tricks, don't it?"

The man mumbled something neither outlaw understood, then darted back into his store. The two had no sooner returned to their stations when he returned, this time pulling the hammers back on a double-barrelled 12-gauge.

"Jesus Christ!" Red Buck's big arm came down across the man's arm. The gun discharged and put a hole the size of a man's head into the boardwalk. Charlie leaped around, drawing his gun. The man, opened-mouthed, stared first at Red Buck, then at Pierce, just before Waightman lowered the butt of his six-gun on top of his head with a loud, sickening thud.

"Let's get outta here!" Pierce shouted and jumped down to his horse. By this time, other merchants were crowding to their doors. There were shouts as the two men mounted. Waightman, snarling, pointed his gun at a store and fired, blowing the window into a shattering mess. There were screams and people started to yell at the two riders who were not quite sure what to do.

Rose and Tandy emerged from the bank and ran straight to their horses. The others piled out after them, with guns drawn, sacks in their hands. Doolin looked around to see what the commotion was.

"Get a hop on," Charlie shouted over to them and fired his gun at no one in particular, as a warning to keep away from them.

The men mounted as Rose and Tandy galloped down the street. They seemed in no particular hurry, but their guns remained in their hands. "Let's go!" They all shouted and turned to follow the women.

As they galloped past the buildings, bystanders scattered out of their way. A shot rang out as three men piled out of a saloon with guns high. Little Bill and Dick West, closest to them, fired simultaneously. Two men fell as they passed. There were other shots now and the outlaws fired back in the air. As long as no shots were being directed at them, they were content to let things be. Dynamite Dan Clifton let out a war whoop of nervous energy.

They were nearly out of town, passing the last few buildings, when a few more shots sent them hugging their saddles. Doolin weaved but steadied himself as they disappeared past the last building and away from town.

They rode hard for the next few miles until they were assured no one was chasing after them. Doolin raised his hand and they slowed to a stop to gather around him.

"Everyone okay?" he asked, then tore at his shirt.

"You been hit!" Rose said as she edged her horse closer to him.

"Hell," he grinned as he untied his kerchief. "I'm always getting shot at lately!"

"That's what leaders are for," Bitter Creek exclaimed, looking closely at the red furrow along Doolin's ribs. "Better you than us, I always say." He looked up at his friend and grinned. "You got a bit decorated, that's all."

It wasn't until later in the evening when they camped around a low fire that Bill allowed them to wash out the wound and dress it properly. "Damn," he grimaced, his face white as Rose dabbed at the dry blood around the cut. "I don't know why they's always picking on me. Getting damned tired of it!"

"Well," Rose stated flatly without stopping her work, "that's what you get for leaving only two outside." She glanced meaningfully at Pierce and Waightman.

"It was a big bank. We needed most everyone to carry out the money," Doolin answered. "C'mon Rose honey, it's just a scratch."

"Scratch? You're damn lucky that's all it is. You better get it through that thick head of yours, Bill

Doolin," Rose said, "towns are beginning to fight back. You can't expect them people to sit back all their lives and do nothing."

"Geez," Bill winced. "One moment you want us to go rob something. Next thing you tell me we gotta be careful. I don't get you, Rose. What do you want us to do?"

"I—" Rose glared at him, then hesitated. "I just don't want you shot up, that's all!"

Doolin relaxed and grinned. "Hell, Rose, we're all careful. As long as I'm the one getting shot up, what does it matter?"

"Bill Doolin!" Rose exclaimed. "You're a jackass!"

"Goddamn it, Rose," Doolin said. "I don't take you to calling me names, no matter in fun or whatever!"

"I'm not funning," Rose answered. "And you are a jackass whether you admit it or not. You're pigheaded too, for that matter!"

"If you don't like the way I run things," Doolin roared, "why the hell don't you get out?"

" 'Cause you need me. You need all of us," she stated. "And with Bill Dalton leaving, we need each other more than ever."

They were all quiet, sobered by her words. Finally, Doolin spat into the fire. "Hell," he said tightly, "I dunno. Maybe it's best we all break up and just call it quits." Again there was silence as the thought was digested.

"It's not going to be that easy," Raidler said. "There's a reward on our heads already. The law isn't going to live and let live, if you know what I mean. We'd have to go somewhere far away to be safe."

"I'm not leaving the territory. This is my home. I was raised here and I'll die here," Doolin said stubbornly.

"Well, what'll we going to do?" Tulsa Jack asked no one in particular.

Doolin shrugged, still staring into the bright embers. "I dunno—have to think about it." He sighed. "Right now, we break up. I'll send word when we get together again. Keep in contact though."

"Maybe that's the best idea," Raidler continued. "I mean, lying low for a while. Let things sort of calm down."

Little Dick rose and stretched his small frame. "Most of us'll be at the HX riding line, I imagine. You can get word to us over there." It was clear that the final word had been spoken. Silently, the outlaws separated to unroll their blankets and make ready for the night.

Bundled against the dampness of the night, Tandy stared up into the star-studded sky. Her thoughts had mellowed after Doolin had spoken of breaking up. The break-up was getting closer with each day, she felt. If only it would come about before something disastrous happened.

She knew she was carrying B.C.'s baby. She gently rubbed her stomach. It was tempting to tell B.C. now. Perhaps he would follow Dalton into Texas, taking her and the baby to her brother's as he had promised to do a long, long time ago. Maybe this was the time.

"B.C.?" she turned and whispered his name.

He rolled lazily onto his side, eyes still closed. "Hmmm?"

"I got your baby, B.C.," she said quietly. "I'm carrying your baby." She waited and watched his face. Slowly, his eyes opened and blinked at her.

"What?" he whispered sleepily.

She smiled hesitantly, a bit afraid to go on with her news. "I got your baby inside me." She smiled more openly.

He raised his head and studied her. "You sure? I mean, are you really sure?" When she nodded, he slowly shook his head. "How in hell did that happen?"

She grinned and knew the worst was over. She snuggled as close to him as their bedrolls would permit. "I'm mighty proud, B.C.," she whispered. "I'm proud to be your woman and to be carrying your child." She hesitated with a new thought. "Would you mind if I called myself Mrs. Bitter Creek Newcomb?"

"George!"

"George?"

"Yeah. You'd be Mrs. George Newcomb, not Bitter Creek."

Tandy smiled. He had apparently accepted the idea, although he was still on his elbows studying her. "I'm glad," she sighed. "I like that very much." She didn't know how long he studied her, for she fell asleep.

Preparing to leave in the early morning mist, the group was unusually silent. The money had been divided and each man made an overdue inspection of his gear. Self-consciously, Bill Dalton made his way to each one to shake hands and say goodbye.

"Ride tall," Bitter Creek said. "And take care, y'hear?" They gripped hands strongly, nodding and smiling.

"You two are lucky to have each other," Dalton said as he glanced from B.C. to Tandy. "I only hope me and my woman do as well."

"I'm sure you will, Bill," Tandy said, extending her hand. "I know you're doing the right thing."

He smiled at her. "I guess you're about the only one who thinks so."

"Oh, they're just sad that you're leaving us, that's all."

"I suppose I can't talk you out of it," Doolin said as the other Bill came up to him.

The last of the Daltons shook his head. "I only wish there was a way we all could sort of ride off together. I suppose that can't happen." He looked up, as if hoping it could.

Doolin shook his head and managed a smile. "Maybe one of these days our trails will cross again. But not now. I'll give it some thought though, believe me."

They stood around awkwardly, not sure what to do. Then Dalton shrugged, turned and mounted his horse. "Be seeing ya," he murmured and rode away.

The others waved half-heartedly. Then, one by one, they also mounted and moved out, leaving the two women, Doolin and Bitter Creek to themselves.

Tandy felt a kind of emptiness, much like she had felt whenever her mother had ridden off on one of her jaunts. It was as if a part of her had left her body, leaving a vacuum that would take a long time to fill.

Doolin finally turned around to face them. "Well, any ideas where we should go?"

Bitter Creek shrugged. "I dunno. I was thinking me and Tandy maybe should go back to Halsells—find a line shack and rest."

"Hell, you can rest in the cave," Doolin persisted.

B.C. fumbled with a stick he had picked up. "Well, you see, it's Tandy. She's carrying a baby."

"Oh my God," Rose said aloud and came closer to inspect Tandy's middle.

"That a fact?" Doolin said. He stared from one to the other. "Geez, that takes some thinking, don't it?"

"Well, it's not like I'm completely helpless at the moment," Tandy said at last, with a smile. "I got some months you know." She pressed her stomach in to show them.

Bitter Creek said. "Yeah—but it's different now. I mean, you can't be riding all over the countryside."

"Why not?" Tandy asked indignantly. "Indian women do. They give birth on horseback, I hear."

"Well, you're not going to," Bitter Creek answered quickly.

"I'd like to know what the hell you got pregnant for?" Rose asked curiously.

"And why not?" Tandy said. "Why shouldn't I get pregnant?"

"Because you can't be doing what you've been doing and be carrying a baby at the same time," Doolin answered for her. "And what happens after you've had the kid? You going to leave it in the cave while we ride out?"

Tandy shrugged her shoulders. "I don't know. Maybe I'll stay in the cave and wait. I dunno." Tears were starting to well up in her eyes.

Doolin waved a hand dejectedly. "Geez, everyone is running off getting married or having babies. Maybe it *is* time we broke up."

"We can get along without Tandy," Rose stated. "I can do them things easily."

"It's just not the same," Doolin answered.

"Why don't we wait and see?" Tandy suggested.

" 'Cause we should think about it now," Doolin answered hotly.

"C'mon Bill." Bitter Creek turned to his friend and said soothingly, "We can work things out."

"Things aren't that bad," Rose spoke up. The two came up to Doolin with anxious smiles.

"I dunno," Bill answered solemnly. "I don't know what I want to do right now."

"We'll all go back to the cave, rest a while. Then maybe our heads will be cleared enough to think straight." Rose glanced to B.C. for his support but he refused to meet her eyes. "What's the matter with all of you?" she cried out. "Given up? Is that it? You didn't act this way when Charlie Bryant got killed—or Bill Powers or the Daltons—or when Arkansas Tom got captured. C'mon, it's not the end of the world!"

Doolin sighed and stared moodily at the ground. "I just need time to think, that's all."

"Think?" Rose asked. "Think about what? Are you telling me you're a quitter?"

He glared at her. "I'm no quitter," he said vehemently. "It's just everyone's going off getting married or getting pregnant—" He left it dangling.

Rose looked at him scornfully. "What's the matter? Don't tell me you want to get married—or get some woman pregnant?" She studied Doolin and saw she had hit a sensitive spot. "Jesus Christ," she asked in a softer voice. "Is that it?" When he didn't move, she became flustered and backed away. "Maybe—maybe it would be best if we did try something else."

Doolin looked at her, then pressed his hands to his head. "Maybe I'm tired, I don't know. I just want to stop a while, that's all. I've got to have time to think about things."

There was a long moment of silence, then Doolin shifted uncomfortably on his haunches. "What will you be doing?" he asked Rose.

She cocked her head and stared at the horizon. "Don't worry. I'll find something. I might go to Chicago, maybe even to New York. Who knows?"

Doolin watched her for some time, then shook himself out of his trance and turned to B.C. "You?"

Bitter Creek stretched and glanced at Tandy. "I guess we'll wander over to the HX, like I said—see if I can find a job there." There was silence again. "What about you?" B.C. asked.

Doolin shrugged and looked nervously at Rose. "Guess I'll mosey over to Ingalls."

Tandy saw Rose's back stiffen. She wondered whether Rose really loved Doolin and if the possibility of his marrying Edith from Ingalls was hurting her.

"You want to come with us, Rose?" Tandy asked softly.

Rose shook her head. "Naw, why should I do that?"

Tandy was hurt but not surprised at the answer. "I just thought we could be together."

Rose gave a short laugh. "I got things to do, honey. Never could stand being domestic. Don't you worry though. I'll meet you all later on."

"It's only for a while," Bitter Creek added, trying to break the cold spell that had settled down on them. "We'll meet again soon, won't we, Bill?"

"Yeah. Sure! Probably first part of the year. I'll send word out."

And so they parted, Rose and Doolin riding in different directions, never once turning to wave goodbye or take a last look at each other. Tandy and Bitter Creek watched until the two riders were out of sight, then turned to each other.

"Well, young lady," Bitter Creek managed a smile. "I guess we got us some things to think about, don't we?"

"What do you mean?"

"I mean, that stomach of yours. I gotta make sure you take care of my son proper like, don't I?" He grinned.

"Oh, B.C.," Tandy murmured. "We'll manage. You wait and see. We'll manage fine!"

23

They had stopped at the cave for a few days to collect and pack their things. During that time, Bitter Creek traveled over to the Halsell and Turkey Track ranches seeking a job and place to stay, but to no avail.

"The law is putting pressure on Halsell," B.C. explained to Tandy. "Some of the gang are riding the line way out. There's no way of Tilghman or the others finding 'em. But Halsell is worried that with too many of us around, he'd get into trouble."

"It's me, isn't it?" Tandy asked. "You'd be able to work for him but not with me around."

"You hush now," B.C. answered and circled his arms around her. "We're a twosome, remember? Or, I guess I should say we're a threesome now. Don't you worry. We'll find us a place."

The next day he returned jubilantly. "I got us a place," he said excitedly. "There's two brothers run a ranch near Pawnee, Bee and Will Dunn.

They said we could hol' up there—in fact, Will Dunn said we could use his dugout."

Tandy was suspicious. "How come they aren't afraid of the law?"

Bitter Creek smiled. "Them boys aren't too particularly fond of the law either. In fact, the story is they dip into the pot once in a while themselves. Mostly rustling."

"Can they be trusted?"

"Them?" B.C. grinned. "They's more crooked than any of us. If anything, we can turn them in!"

Despite B.C.'s reassurances, something about the two Dunns made Tandy most uncomfortable. Both full-bearded, they had large eyes that seemed to pop out of their heads, giving them the look of wild, frightened stallions. She had to force herself to be polite. It wasn't that she wasn't grateful for a place to live and a job for B.C.; it was just that the men scared her.

Unfortunately for her, both men took a particular liking to her, especially when they realized she was pregnant.

"Neither one of us ever got married, y'know," Bee Dunn said one evening after she had invited both for dinner in the dugout. "Always wanted a daughter. Strange, ain't it? Most men hanker for a son, but me, always wanted a daughter. Big ugly hunk like me with a daughter!" He sniffed and chuckled. "Ol' Will's the same as me!"

The Dunns went out of their way to bring Tandy things she could use to fix up her makeshift home while preparing for the baby. Will had removed most of his personal belongings to his brother's house a few miles away but kept making excuses to return and pick up something he had forgotten. In one way, their actions amused Tandy. They helped her pass the time away while B.C. was working.

As the months dragged on and Tandy's stomach began to bulge noticeably, the two older men began doting over like a couple of prospective grandfathers. There were times Tandy felt guilty over her own feelings about them.

"They don't have no one to call their own," Bitter Creek explained. "They don't mean no harm."

"But now they're beginning to call me daughter," Tandy objected. "I don't want to be their daughter. I don't want to be anyone's daughter."

B.C. grinned. "If it makes 'em happy, play along with 'em. It's really for our safety, y'know. No way are they going to let the law get anywhere close to us with their feelings 'bout you so strong."

"But Bee's talking about us moving into his house with winter coming on," she complained. "We'd never have any privacy."

"No difference from when we were in the cave," he said flatly.

"But there is a difference. I just don't trust them two—no matter how nice they are to me or us. There's just something about them I don't like."

"Okay," B.C. finally said. "I'll tell them you want to stay here. Only thinking of the baby, that's all."

She patted her swollen middle. "He's getting big, don't you think? Maybe when the time's closer, I'll go. Tell them that. I'll come after the beginning of the year. That way, the baby will be born in a nice home."

The first snow came late. Bitter Creek stayed close to the dugout, making sure Tandy didn't have to wade through drifts for water or wood. A few weeks later, a rider made his way to the shed, dismounted and trudged to their door.

"Bill!" Tandy shrieked and threw her arms around the outlaw leader. His face was covered with a beard but the sparkle in his eyes was still there.

"I got married!" Doolin said with a grin. They both pounded his back and brought him close to the fireplace.

"You ol' son-of-a-gun," Bitter Creek beamed. "You just had to go out and do it, didn't you?"

Doolin grinned and leaned back on the bench to look at his two friends. "She's a preacher's daughter—Edith. I guess you know I been courtin' her for some time. When I went back there this summer I done asked her. We got hitched by her ol' man."

"Oh, Bill," Tandy exclaimed. "I'm so happy for you!"

"Well, I got to thinking. All my friends were getting hitched, so why not me?"

"You look none the worse for it," Bitter Creek said. " 'cept for maybe them whiskers."

Doolin stroked his chin and smiled. "I thought it would make things easier for me. Sort of a permanent disguise, y'know what I mean?"

"The law getting to you?"

Doolin shrugged. "Had a few close calls—y'know

—had to sneak out the back way a couple of times. The law knows about me getting married so they're keeping a close eye on her house." He sobered as he talked. "T'ain't easy getting through their lines. But I tell you, it was worth it." They all laughed.

"So, what are you doing now?"

Doolin took a deep breath. "Getting itchy hands. Thought I'd round up the gang and start making plans."

"Can't you find a job?" Tandy asked.

"Aw, y'know me, Tandy," Bill explained. "I been punching and splitting rails, but y'know I can't stay in one place for too long. Besides, the law won't give me a chance to settle down." There was a thoughtful silence. Then he looked from one to the other. "What about you two?"

"We're doing fine," Bitter Creek answered. "And you know we still ride with you." He glanced at Tandy. "But I would appreciate waiting 'til after the baby comes."

"When will that be?"

Tandy said, "I hope not until the snow melts. Then I'll need a couple of months to nurse it—"

Doolin nodded. "Okay. We'll plan to do something in the spring, how's that? But that don't mean we can't get the boys together and hear what's happening. It's a bad time for me to do much traveling myself."

"Why not meet here?" Bitter Creek offered. "We got plenty of bunks." He motioned towards the line of curtained spare bunks lining the wall.

* * *

They came the first month of the new year, 1895. Doolin greeted each like a long-lost brother, and even Red Buck reluctantly allowed him to hug him and pat him on the back. Everybody showed up except Rose.

"Where is she?" Doolin asked around. "Anyone hear where she went?"

"I heard she was raising hell in Dodge," Dan Clifton announced.

"I heard she was kicked out of Dodge," someone else laughed.

"Last I heard, she was headed back for the cave," Tulsa Jack stated. "Must be there by now."

It was Doolin himself who went out the next day to fetch her. He brought her back too. "Look at this hellcat. She didn't want to come, almost had to tie her down," Doolin grinned as Rose was being greeted by the group. "Now, I got my gang back!"

"In toto," Raidler commented.

"Toto—yeah, what I said, all of us," Doolin laughed.

"If I knew you was at the cave," Tandy told Rose later when they were frying up some steaks, "I would've had B.C. fetch you over here."

Rose managed to busy herself peeling a spud. "I wouldn't've come."

"Why not?"

"Wouldn't have felt like it," came the short answer.

"But it couldn't have been no good being in the cave all alone."

Rose straightened and turned to Tandy with a hard gaze. "What are you trying to do? Are you one of them so called Christian people who's got to be together all the time? Did it ever occur to you there's some who like to be left alone? I don't need no one. And I certainly don't need you butting into my life."

Tandy was shocked into silence. She said then, "I was only trying to help—"

Rose laughed bitterly. "I suppose you helped Bill into getting married? I suppose you're helping the gang having that kid of yours?"

"You're angry at me for having a baby, aren't you? You have been ever since I told you."

Rose stopped her peeling and turned to her. Glancing briefly at the men playing cards in the dugout's far corner, she lowered her voice and said, "I'll tell you why I'm mad. I'm mad 'cause I thought you had better sense than getting yourself knocked up. I thought I told you why having a kid in this kind of business is all wrong!"

"But it's different," Tandy cried out, trying to keep her voice from carrying. "It *is* different—and it will be, you'll see!"

Rose snorted her disbelief. "Do you know what having a kid around will do to us? You'll have to stay and we'll have to get special things for it. Or you or B.C. will have to hurry right back. I tell you, it's no good for us."

"Well, I'm not going to give my baby away, like you did," Tandy exclaimed fiercely.

"Then I'll make it so damn difficult for you, you'll beg to get out," Rose said with savage emphasis.

Instinctively, Tandy placed her hands against her stomach. "There's nothing you can do that will change my mind," she said defiantly. "I don't want anything to happen to any of us—but my baby will come first."

"You see?" Rose said triumphantly. "Already, the brat is more important! Remember I told you once that as soon as someone stops caring for the gang something will go wrong? Well, honey, you're starting it. I'm not going to sit by and watch you break us apart or let us get caught. I'm going to fight you."

"And I'll fight you," Tandy answered back just as strongly. "I'll fight you with everything I know—'cause I don't think I've done anything wrong!"

They stared at each other like baleful enemies, their concentration broken only by a knock on the wood-plank door. The men stopped talking and looked at each other nervously. Bitter Creek turned and nodded to Tandy, who hesitantly stepped to the door.

"Howdy, Tandy girl." Will Dunn shook the snow from his hat and stepped inside. He blinked around at the silent group of men, then nodded toward Doolin. "Howdy Bill!" He lifted a hand. "Sort of figured them was your horses out there."

"How do, Will." Doolin relaxed and smiled.

"What can we do for you this time of night?"

The younger Dunn took a deep breath. "I come to tell Bitter Creek and Tandy here that Tilghman is snooping around nearby. He's supposed to be coming over tonight to talk to Bee and me."

Doolin thought for a moment. He turned to Little Dick West, nearest to him. "Better take a look outside." When West had tossed on a coat and left, Doolin turned back to Will. "What's Tilghman up to?"

The man shrugged and sat down on a chair. "I dunno exactly. Wouldn't say. He's been putting pressure on us 'bout some missing livestock." He grinned innocently.

The door shot open and they all jumped to their feet as West quickly closed it behind him. "Two riders coming up the trail. Think one of 'em's Tilghman!"

"Good!" Red Buck grabbed for his rifle. "This is as good a time as any to get rid of that bastard!"

Doolin reached out and grabbed his arm. "There won't be no killing if we can help it!"

"Why the hell not?" Waightman protested. "He's been on our backs too long!"

"I won't have him cut down like some animal," Doolin stated. "He deserves better'n that. And we're not that kind!"

"There's someone coming!" Charlie Pierce called from the window. They all scrambled for their guns.

"Wait!" Doolin cried. "Get into the bunks and cover up. We'll see what the man wants first." He turned to Tandy. "You see what he's looking for."

Bitter Creek came up to them. "Tilghman knows her. He's met us and will remember."

Doolin thought it over. "Okay. Will, you do it. This is your place anyhow. We'll all be behind the bunk curtains." He motioned for them all to take their places. "Handle it right and nothing will happen." Doolin said to the men, rustling in the bunks, "Okay, in there, keep it quiet." Then he said to Will, "What about your horse?"

"I tied it back in the shed with the others," the man answered nervously.

Doolin nodded. "Good. Let's hope he don't go back there."

"I don't like this," Will murmured anxiously.

"You'll do okay." Bill grinned and patted him on the shoulder. "We'll be watching careful." He slid behind the nearest bunk and got quiet.

Tandy had scrambled to B.C.'s side and they had chosen a far bunk together. He lay to the outside of her, gun in hand, the other hand holding together the burlap covering with just enough slit to let him see the door.

There was a muffled knock. Will, still seated in the center of the room, called out nervously, "Yeah?"

The door opened and Tilghman's tall bulk filled it with a flurry of snow. Quickly, the marshal entered and closed the door. He brushed the snow from his great coat, his eyes darting about in the darkness. "Howdy," he said in a booming mellow voice.

If Will Dunn answered, neither Tandy nor B.C. heard him. Tilghman took another look around, then slowly walked over to the fire, stretching his hands before him. Then he faced Will again and placed both hands behind him. "Mighty good to have a fire on a night like this," he said casually.

B.C. shrunk back for he was certain Tilghman was looking directly at him. Soon, the lawman shifted his gaze to another bunk. He cleared his throat. "Y'know how much further it is to Bee Dunn's ranch?"

Will answered roughly, "Find out for yourself."

Tilghman gave Will a quick glance, meanwhile rubbing his hands together for warmth. Bitter Creek could see his lip protrude beneath his dark mustache; otherwise, the lawman appeared calm and in no hurry. Tandy moved slightly and B.C. placed a hand on her arm to quiet her. Quickly he looked through the slit. Tilghman was glancing his way again. For a moment B.C. was sure the lawman had detected the movement. Either that, or the man was half-blind. He gripped his gun tightly, waiting.

Tilghman straightened his big frame. "Well, I reckon I had better be going."

Will didn't move. "I reckon you better," he answered.

Again, Tilghman studied the man. "I thank you for the use of the heat. I'm obliged." He waited a moment for Will to say something, then shrugged and put on his gloves.

B.C. watched the marshal slowly walk the length of the room. He had to admire Tilghman. He was certain the lawman realized something was amiss, that he probably knew people were hidden in the bunks from the moment he had stepped inside. However, he had braved them, deliberately. Now he was leaving, slowly, defiantly, his hands a good distance from the bulge beneath his coat on his right hip. In a moment, he was gone.

There was silence in the dugout. Slowly, the curtains parted and the men piled out. Red Buck drew back the hammer of his carbine and started for the window. "I'm going to blast that bastard outta his saddle!"

Both Doolin and B.C. made a grab for the big man and stopped him.

"What the hell you two doing?" Red Buck complained. "It's him or us! You're damn cowards if you let him get away!" He struggled for a moment between the two, then settled down, flinging Doolin from him. "Shitheads! Goddamn cowards!"

"You kill him," Doolin panted, "and you'll have every damn law officer in the territory here quicker you can spit."

"At least we'd have one less," Red Buck shot back.

"Bill Tilghman is too good a man to be shot in the back." Doolin pointed a finger at Waightman and his voice shook. "Too damn good for someone like you to cut down!" The two stared at each other for a long moment. The others shuffled uncomfortably across the room and found places to sit. It was obvious they didn't want to take sides with either man.

Rose came forward. "What are we going to do now, Bill? Tilghman knew we were here; he'll go for help."

Doolin sighed bitterly. "Yeah, he knew all right. Waightman had the barrel of his gun out so the whole world could see it."

"I—I don't think he knew it was you boys," Will Dunn finally said.

"Maybe not. But he sure as hell knew something was wrong." Doolin frowned. "Rose is right. He'll be back pronto. We'd better vamoose. We all meet back at the cave as soon as the snow melts!"

There were scurried movements as belongings were rolled up and coats flung on.

"What are we going to do?" Tandy turned to Bitter Creek as they packed their things.

"Whyn't you all go up to Bee's place?" Will volunteered. "You can stay there safely until the baby is born. I'll stay here 'til Tilghman returns."

"You sure you can handle him?" Bitter Creek asked.

Will shrugged. "I'll say you all was holding guns on me too. He'll take it 'cause there's nothing else he can do. I'll tell him you all scattered as soon as he left. That way, you and Tandy will be safe up at the ranch house."

Tandy reached out and touched Will's arm in gratitude. "How can we ever thank you?"

Will Dunn looked up at her with a sheepish grin. "Just you being with us is thanks enough, Tandy," he answered. "And don't you worry none. Bee and me—we'll take care of you."

24

"You got yourself a fine boy," Bee Dunn called out from the ranch rouse as Bitter Creek rode up. "Born a couple of hours ago."

Winter was on the wane; there were patches of green on the ground.

Bitter Creek nearly exploded from his horse. "Doggone," he cried. "I'll be doggone—she done it!"

Tandy was nursing the baby when he brushed aside the curtain to the little cubicle at one end of the house. She smiled weakly and pushed the edge of the blanket aside so that B.C. could see.

"Well, I'll be doggone," he grinned. "He's no bigger than a puppy!"

"Isn't he precious?" she whispered.

Bitter Creek's eyes darted over her figure under the blanket. "You okay? I mean, you sure you're okay?"

"Of course I am, silly," she answered. "I did everything Mrs. Whipple said. It wasn't bad, really."

"I can get her if you want," Bitter Creek said,

concerned. The midwife, a neighbor, was but a short ride away.

"She said she'd show up sometime in the morning," Tandy explained. "There's nothing to worry about. Our son is just fine! Just like his daddy."

Bitter Creek stared at the silent form. "Isn't that something! I mean, you and me doin' something like that?" He glanced at Tandy seriously. "I can see you creating something like that, but me—" He shook his head. "It makes a man think, y'know?"

"About what?"

B.C. shrugged. "Maybe we *can* go to Texas. Just this one year more—if we save up enough money, then we could go down to your brother's spread just like you want." He thought it over in his mind. "We'll buy us our own spread and raise him the way he should be raised, him and all his brothers and sisters."

"Oh, B.C., don't joke about a thing like that," Tandy said anxiously.

"I'm not joking. I think it's a good idea. This is going to be our last year. I want to raise my son right. Next winter you'll be in Texas and we'll have a home."

"I'm so happy, B.C.." Tandy grabbed for his hand. "You'll never know how happy I am hearing that." Then she frowned. "But now, you gotta be extra careful, y'hear? Y'can't be letting anything happen to you."

"Don't you fret none about that," he promised. "We're all going to be careful. As soon as you and the babe can, we'll pack up and get us back to the cave. Then, it'll be two or three jobs—easy ones just so we can get enough money to set us up right. Then we'll leave. That'll also give Bill time enough to get used to the idea. I promise!"

It was the latter part of April when all the gang members converged on the cave. As usual, a couple of days were spent on greetings and the swapping of stories. Most of the conversation was focused on Doolin's marriage and Edith's expecting a baby, however, and the men also did considerable doting over Tandy's son, William.

Rose was quiet. From the first, she made it plain that she was not interested in the baby. When the attention paid to it disturbed her, which was often, she would storm behind the curtains and stay there for the rest of the evenings.

Tandy, at first hurt by Rose's behavior, grew almost glad that the woman stayed away. It meant that fewer and fewer hostile words were exchanged between them.

"I decided we stay away from banks for a while," Doolin announced one evening. "For one thing, towns are getting too big and too dangerous for us. More and more strangers are coming in who'd rather shoot us than not. Also, rewards are getting too high so more people want to chase us down. From now on, we take the trains."

"Do we all participate?" Rose asked. She looked meaningfully at Tandy.

"I'll go, if you want me," Tandy said stubbornly.

"I can watch the horses and keep the baby on a sling next to me."

Doolin smiled patiently but shook his head. "We won't be needing you," he answered. "That's another reason we take the trains. There's no chase involved so we don't need an extra string of horses." He turned sternly to Rose. "I've taken thought of everything."

"If you take on a train, you need everyone you can get," Rose persisted.

"We can get along without Tandy this first time," Doolin stated. "Maybe next time we'll take her. Another thing—we stay outta the flatlands if we can help it. We find holdup territory we can get lost in."

"That's going to limit us, isn't it?" Dick West inquired. "Or, do you know of a place?"

"Yeah, I found a spot. It's on the other side of Guthrie, place just north of Kingfisher. There's hills and timber near the tracks. The Rock Island comes into Guthrie from the west and should be carrying some big money. It's a long ride and if there's guards, they should be about tired by then and a bit loose on the lookout."

"Sounds pretty good to me," Charlie Pierce answered for most of them.

"That's pretty damn close to Guthrie," Rose stated. "We could all stop in and chat with your friend Tilghman and his friends."

"Tilghman's over at Perry," Doolin answered, aggravated by Rose's snide remark. "By the time the train gets into Guthrie, we'll have circled around and headed back here."

Tandy tried to hold back her fears as the group readied for the departure. "You take care of yourself," was all she whispered as she pressed into B.C. "Little William wants to see his daddy when he gets big."

Bitter Creek reached down and patted her cheek. "Don't you worry your pretty head. Bill's got me doing something easy and safe."

"Take care," Tandy warned, and was suddenly alone in the glen.

Bitter Creek waited in the timber as the train came to a grinding halt in front of the fallen tree. There was a loud hissing from the engine, as if in final relief. Suddenly, it was quiet.

The outlaws came from both sides, firing their guns in the air as a warning for all to keep their heads inside the coaches. There were three passenger cars and one express. Tulsa Jack took the end car, bursting open the door with a gun in each hand and yelling for everyone to be quiet. Little Dick West scrambled up between the next two cars, glancing behind him to make sure Tulsa Jack had things in hand.

In the front passenger car, Red Buck swung his carbine in an arc to keep the few passengers frozen to their seats. "You all just sit nice and quiet-like and no one will get hurt," he growled.

Bitter Creek had climbed onto the engine platform, asking the two engineers to step down and lie on the ground. It was all done with such calm efficiency that no shots had been returned.

Doolin, Clifton, and Raidler rode their horses up to the express car and ordered those inside to open the door. Behind them, off to one side with rifle in hand, Rose watched for any suspicious move. Doolin emptied two shots into the side of the car and barked out his warning again. Slowly, the door slid open and two men quickly jumped out, hands upraised. Bitter Creek yelled for them to join the two engineers lying alongside the track.

It took not quite ten minutes for Raidler to sift through the sacks and boxes, casting aside the useless papers and tossing the money to Doolin, who stuffed it into mail sacks he had emptied.

"Let's see if we can get any contributions," Clifton suggested and started back to the passenger cars.

"I thought we were to lay off passengers," Rose commented. That stopped Clifton. He turned and waited for Doolin.

"We might as well get all we can get," he then suggested again, glancing from Doolin to Rose. "Most of 'em are strangers. They won't start nothing."

"We start that sort of thing and they'll start taking shots at us just like the townspeople did," Rose answered.

Doolin looked around for other opinions. "Hell, Maybe less people will want to ride the trains. That'll sting them high-pocketed railroad people where it hurts."

"You'll be hurting yourself too when they start fighting back at us."

"No one's going to shoot at us with rifles trained on 'em." Doolin added with a smile, " 'Sides, you wait and see—they'll fuss to them railroad officials, not us!" He motioned to Clifton to go ahead.

"You're making a mistake," Rose shouted after them as the rest followed Doolin to the rear of the train.

"C'mon Rose," Bitter Creek had climbed down from the cab and joined her. "You know you can't change Bill's mind once he sets it."

"He didn't use to be like that. He's changing, I can tell." Rose stared at where Doolin had vanished into the coaches. "He's no longer out to get the banks or railroads. Now it's only the money he wants. Soon you'll forget what it's all about."

"Aw, c'mon Rose," B.C. grinned. "You got it all wrong."

"He shouldn't be picking on them little people," she muttered, nodding her head towards the train.

Bitter Creek opened his mouth to answer but no words came to mind. He frowned. Maybe Rose had something there. He'd think about it. But not now, later.

"We better be going." He nudged Rose towards the horses, which had been brought close to the tracks, as the gang jumped down from the platforms.

The men were in high spirits as they swerved out of the timber and raced for the low-lying hills. It had been a long time since they had participated in as much excitement. They galloped along, yelling and shouting to one another, holding aloft the sacks of loot they had pillaged from the passengers, in general releasing the energy they'd controlled so well during the holdup.

"Hey Bill!" Charlie Pierce yelled out. "Let's stop and see what we got!"

There were cheers of agreement and finally Doolin nodded and slowed down. They searched for a hollow to camp in, finally finding a small glen nestled at the base of a hill. Off a ways, a small stand of timber gave them some cover from the east.

"Did you see that drummer when I dumped his suitcase?" Red Buck chortled. "He nearly shit in his pants."

"Yeah," Little Dick answered without glancing up from his counting. "And you nearly got your head blowed off too."

"Aw, that ol' man was loco," Red Buck growled.

"You manhandle their women like that and I'll blow your head off," Little Dick said, his voice soft and dangerous.

The big outlaw glared at West, but in no way was he going to buck Little Dick's fast gun. "I was only trying to get a little feel."

"You're disgusting," Rose piped in.

"Hell," Red Buck grinned. "Most women like that sort of thing."

Rose glared at him.

Suddenly, one of the horses behind them screamed in pain. They all whirled around as the animal fell to its side. They heard the echo of a rifle at about the same time.

"Jesus Christ!" Waightman pointed to the hill behind them. Stark against the red disk of the setting sun, horsemen sat atop a rise. They came down on them then, at least seven or eight riders, firing their rifles and handguns.

"Get the money," Doolin shouted. He ran for the horses and started to undo the tie line.

Bitter Creek dove to the ground and scooped money up into the sacks. Behind him, Raidler and West knelt and returned the fire. Rose ran to aid Doolin with the frightened animals.

"They got my horse," Tulsa Jack cried out.

"Run for the timber," Doolin shouted. "We'll cover you."

The thin outlaw grabbed a rifle and ran for the distant crop of trees. Red Buck grabbed for the reins of his black horse, which was dancing frantically. Just as the outlaw stepped into the stirrup, the horse let out a sigh and toppled over. "Jesus!" Red Buck cried. He stood for a moment, lost.

"Run for it!" someone shouted, and he turned and took off after Tulsa Jack.

"Mount up!" Doolin cried. He helped Rose onto her horse, then handed reins out to the cowboys who scrambled towards him. By now the pursuers were almost upon them.

"Ride!"

The group dashed out of the glen and up the small slope, headed for the trees. As they approached the fleeing two outlaws, Tulsa Jack raised his hands, staggered and fell. Red Buck stopped and turned the body over. He stared at the approaching riders, then got up and ran. The gang rode past him and finally reached the safety of the timber, where they quickly scrambled off their horses and took up positions to fire at the posse.

At the first returning shots, the pursuers reined up, quickly spread apart and dashed for a slight rise. There they dismounted and began shooting back.

Red Buck, lumbering into the crossfire, screeched in terror; he was winded and could not move faster. Bitter Creek, the last to ride into the woods, saw the trouble he was in. He turned his horse around and headed back. Leaning low over his saddle, he grabbed hold of Red Buck by the pants. In one swift motion, the outlaw swung up behind B.C. and they both headed back into the trees.

"It's that goddamn Madsen," Red Buck howled. "I recognized that bastard shooting at me. I'm going to get him if it's the last thing I do!"

There was a brief spell of quiet as both sides contemplated their next move. Doolin didn't bother to answer Waightman, and Charlie Pierce had his eyes fixed elsewhere.

"Ol' Jack's dead," Pierce stated, staring out at the still form not too far away from them. They all stared at the body in silence.

"What're we going to do now?" Rose asked. Cradling her rifle, she stared at the distant hilltop where the posse waited.

"They're not about to charge us in here," Doolin answered. "We wait 'til dark. Then we'll find a way out."

They took turns keeping an eye on the lawmen while the rest lay back, quietly contemplating their predicament. "How the hell did they get to us that quick?" Little Dick asked aloud.

For some reason they all turned to Raidler. The cowboy shrugged and gave them a weak smile. "Probably by telegraph. Maybe Madsen was fairly close and hopped on a special train back here. At least it's a logical guess."

"Christ!" Red Buck growled. "Now we got the goddamn telegraph to worry 'bout."

"I told you we should have brought fresh mounts," Rose complained.

"And what the hell good would that've done?" Doolin asked. "No one would have guessed they'd be after us so soon."

"No use getting worked up about it," Bitter Creek spoke up calmly. "We're lucky we got out of it with only one down. They could've rode right over us."

"I'll tell you one thing," Red Buck spoke up. "I ain't showing no mercy on any lawman from now on!"

"Just means we gotta be smarter next time," Doolin offered.

"We gotta be more careful," Rose corrected.

"We was careful!"

"You call it careful leaving Tandy in the cave when we need her? You call it careful not bringing fresh horses? You call it being careful taking on a train so close to home just so you and B.C. can get back to your little homes sooner?"

"You don't know what you're talking about," Doolin shot back.

Bitter Creek rolled over so he could face Rose. "You blaming me for what happened here?"

"I'm—" Rose looked at B.C. and decided it would be better to leave that issue alone. She shrugged and half-turned from them. "I'm just saying things have changed and I don't like it."

The group exchanged glances; then Doolin forced a grin. "Aw hell," he said. "We got out of it, didn't we? So it was ol' Jack's turn, that's all. It'll be all of ours one of these days. No need of trying to figure out what we coulda done or shoulda done."

There was silence again as the twilight deepened. "Well," Raidler sighed. "It does show one thing. It appears the law is getting more and more organized. They're probably waiting for reinforcements."

Doolin nodded and rose. "We better get outta here 'fore they come in after us. We'll walk our way to the other side of the timber. Can't be more'n ten miles or so."

They made slow progress in the dark, trying to make as little noise as possible. They had no way of knowing whether they were being followed and stopped frequently to listen.

"They're not about to come in after us," Bitter Creek finally concluded.

"They had their chance and blew it."

"But they got one of us," Rose reminded Doolin bitingly.

"And my black," Red Buck added with a curse. "Goddamn, I just got him too!"

"You can mount up behind me," B.C. volunteered. "Maybe we can find you a mount along the way."

They spent the entire night moving through the timber, emerging from it as the sky began to turn pink with its morning glow. "We'll make a wide circle and head back home," Doolin said in an exhausted voice.

"What about a mount for me?" Red Buck spoke up from behind Bitter Creek.

They had heard throughout the long night of Red Buck's being left horseless. The big man was as sour under the circumstances as any cowboy would be. However, in Waightman's case, being without a horse had taken away most of his bravado and set him to whining.

They made a wide arc, finally settling on a course towards the rising sun. They traveled slow, so as to preserve the horses in case of another pursuit.

They had gone quite a distance when they came upon a small fenced plot of ground, ahead of it a makeshift corral adjoining a shack.

"Turn in here," Red Buck commanded, spotting a horse behind the corral railings. As they came to the fence, he slid off Bitter Creek's mount and headed toward the bay he'd been studying, stopping off to take a looped lariat from a fence post. They all watched as the big man circled the rope around the horse's head. When he'd gotten what he wanted, a stolen horse, they all moved on to the shack to rest up for a while.

As Waightman helped himself to a blanket and

saddle he'd found hanging from a crossbeam, the door of the shack burst open and a tall spindly man in coveralls came limping in.

"Howdy, brethren," he called in a surprisingly loud and resonant voice. "God be with all of you." He raised a hand in a peaceful welcome.

The group eyed the old man nervously. Then Red Buck spat on the dirt floor and continued his saddling of the bay.

"Glory be, brother," the man called out as he took a step towards Red Buck. "The fine animal you took belongs to my son." He sounded as if he was half-explaining and half-apologizing.

"Not no more," Red Buck growled.

"But brother," the man insisted, "that horse belongs to my son. To take another's horse is a dreadful sin."

"I ain't your goddamn brother," Red Buck answered.

"I must protest!" The man reached out to stop Red Buck from saddling but the outlaw kicked his arm away. Before anyone realized his intention, the outlaw drew his gun, snarled and fired. The old man staggered back from the impact, clutching his chest, his mouth open. Slowly, he sank to the ground.

"Geez!" someone breathed.

"Let's get outta here!" Doolin suddenly shouted. They all left the shack, hurriedly mounted and galloped off into open country. It was a fast and furious pace that Doolin led and the others followed it without question. They had gone about three miles when they came to a small cluster of trees. Doolin raised his hand and pulled them to a stop. Wordlessly, he dismounted, untied the bags from the robbery and threw them onto the ground.

Not a word was said. The others looked around, shrugging, then followed Doolin. Soon they were all crouched in a circle, counting the money out into even piles.

When they had finished and pocketed their shares, Doolin rose to his feet. His eyes were hard as he stared at Red Buck. "Okay, you got your share. Now leave."

Waightman looked up, then glanced at the others in disbelief. "What the hell you trying to do?"

Doolin squared off to him. "I'm telling you to get your ass out of sight!"

Red Buck slowly raised himself to his full height, squinting at Doolin. "What the hell you getting off telling me what to do?"

"I've had it with you, Waightman," Doolin answered. "You're too god-damn low to be riding with us!'

"With you?" Red Buck snarled. "Since when are you all coming off being so perfect?"

"Compared to you, we're angels. I'm not going to have you dirtying us up!"

Red Buck drew in a deep breath. He studied Doolin, then slowly looked around at the others to see where they stood. Little Dick was crouched on his haunches looking up at him, his hand hung loosely at his side, close to his gun butt. Raidler and Bitter Creek had sidled away; they'd switched their money sacks to their left hands and were also watching him. Pierce and Clifton were behind him, likewise motionless and waiting.

Slowly Waightman turned to Doolin, having had little success in his attempts to stare the men down. "Shit on you," he murmured and walked over to the bay. Without a backward glance, he mounted and rode off.

Doolin watched until Red Buck had disappeared, then swung to the group, his face still hard and stern. "That goes for the rest of you too. It's one thing to fire back when someone's shooting at you. But I'm not going to have no one gunning down anyone unarmed—or in the back." He glanced at each of them.

"You done right," Bitter Creek spoke up. "I don't want none of that either."

"I don't think any one of us wants senseless killing," Raidler added. The others nodded their heads in agreement.

Rose came forward, head bowed in thought.

"What's the matter with you?" Doolin asked defensively.

She shook her head, hesitating to speak. "We're down one more," she finally said. "When is it going to end?"

Doolin stared at her sullenly. "I dunno," he grumbled. "When there's no one left, I guess."

25

Bitter Creek recounted the entire adventure to Tandy as he played with little William just outside the cave. The mood of the group on their return had been a barometer that something had gone wrong but Tandy had wisely waited with her questions until the two had a chance to be alone.

"Poor Tulsa Jack," she exclaimed sadly. "I'm only grateful that it wasn't you."

"Me too," he smiled. "I tell you, I thought for sure we were all done for." He sighed and leaned back against a rock outcrop. "I dunno. Maybe it's time we stop now, before it's too late."

"Oh, B.C., do you think so?" Tandy said softly. She didn't dare press him beyond that for she had heard him speak in a similar manner many times before. But it was in her nature to be hopeful; she couldn't help that, she would always be. "Maybe things are becoming too dangerous. I don't know which would be worse, you being captured and put in jail or—or you being shot."

"I'm not going to be stuck in no jail," B.C. answered. "It just wouldn't do being locked up like some animal."

"Then maybe we should leave," she suggested.

He nodded. "Maybe it's time I talk to Bill and see what he thinks." He looked at her pensively. "You know I can't run out on him if he needs me. I couldn't desert him like that."

Tandy sighed, then brightened. "But maybe he'll want to change too. I mean, he's got his Edith now. And he'll have a baby soon too. Maybe he'll want to go to Texas with us."

Bitter Creek shrugged. "I dunno. He's got an even freer spirit than me. I don't know whether he'll cotton to settling down."

That first evening they were all sensitively aware of the two cave spaces vacated by Tulsa Jack and Red Buck. The empty chairs at dinner sobered them all. Even the baby sensed the coldness and he cried out in distress.

As the crying persisted, Rose arose angrily and proceeded to slam the dishes on the table as she cleared them. But no sooner would Tandy quiet William, then he would scream again. Finally, Rose turned and faced the group, hands on hips. "One of these days that kid is going to make enough noise to lead the law right into this camp!"

"Aw, give us a break," Doolin spoke up. "We've all had a rough day, even the baby. Leave him alone."

"I'll take him in back," Tandy murmured. She

started to rise with William but Doolin reached out and stopped her.

"Naw, that's okay. You stay put." He chucked the baby under the chin, which temporarily quieted it.

Tandy smiled thankfully. "I think he senses how grouchy everyone is tonight."

Bitter Creek shrugged and gently admonished her. "You got to admit it's not exactly a time to celebrate."

The others cast embarrassed glances around the fire. It was tough to break the mood. Raidler leaned back. "Ah, the sense of death is like an umbrella shadowing darkness on all beneath it."

"Geez, teacher," Dick West grinned, "them words certainly perk us up."

Raidler grinned back. "I was only trying to help."

Again, there was silence. Rose could not stand the idleness. She came forward to stand beside Doolin. "I want to know whether we're going to take time off or do we do another job?"

Doolin took his time in answering. With a heavy sigh, he got up and walked around the cave, leaving the others to exchange glances and then slowly resume their card playing. Hands on hips, Rose followed him. He finally wound up in front of Tandy and reached down to touch the tiny baby she held in her arms. He stared at little William quite a long time, then took a deep breath and turned to Rose.

"I dunno what we're gonna do. All I know now is, I got to go over to Ingalls."

Rose drew herself up rigid at his remark. She

stared coldly at him, then whipped around and walked away.

"Anyone want to come?" Doolin asked sheepishly. Dan Clifton and Dick West stood up at the invitation and gathered their things.

"How long will you be gone?" Bitter Creek asked.

Doolin shrugged. "Dunno. No more'n a couple of weeks. You all stay here. We'll think of something to do soon as I get back."

There was a stillness when the three left. Tandy went in back to put the baby to bed. Rose reluctantly made her way back to the fireside and sat down on the bench to stare into the embers.

"Ol' Bill's taking it hard," Charlie Pierce observed.

Bitter Creek sighed. "He don't like losing any of us. It took something out of him."

Rose looked at them. "Well, I think it's up to us to get him out of that mood."

"How we going to do that?"

"The only way Bill's going to snap back is if we prod him into doing something." She gazed at them one by one with a curious smile playing on her lips. "What say we plan a job ourselves so when he comes back, we can go do it."

Bitter Creek stared at her. It was Raidler who leaned forward with interest. "What do we know about planning a holdup?" he asked curiously.

"Maybe not the details," Rose conceded. "But we can sure get all the information we need to start a big one."

"How?"

Rose bent forward as the men began paying attention. "It's an idea I've had for some time. Little Bill, you can read train schedules, can't you?" When Raidler nodded, she continued. "I thought we could go to some station, say a place like Woodard. We hold it up, get whatever we can, like we always do. But we also get as many train schedules as we can. I think by reading them schedules and whatever shipping information we find, we should be able to select which trains carry the most money and find out where and when we could con them." She looked around for signs of approval. "If the law can get fancy with their telegraphs, I say we can get fancy too. We'd be doing what we've already done—just taking it one step further."

Raidler and B.C. exchanged glances. Little Bill shrugged casually. "It could work."

"We going to wait until Bill gets back?" Tandy inquired, having quietly returned to listen in.

"Why?" Rose asked indignantly. "We're doing this to make it easy for Bill when he does get back."

"But there's only five of us," Tandy objected.

"Woodard's a small station," Bitter Creek stated. "We could do it in the evening with no trouble."

"I think it's better that Tandy stays here," Rose said flatly.

"You'll need me," Tandy shot back.

"If the kid cries, he'll warn everyone," Rose said. "You can't be running around the territory in the dark with a baby strapped to you."

Before Tandy could reply, B.C. reached over

with a comforting hand. "She's right. It'll be no place for you nor the babe. 'sides it's a small job—we can handle it."

"We'll need someone to keep the coffee hot." Raidler tried to help by giving her a wide assuring grin.

Tandy's stomach knotted. She knew they were right but it peeved her that she had to stay. She was troubled about the plan, possibly because Bill hadn't thought of it or maybe even because Rose had. She didn't know why she had such a feeling. Regardless, she felt ill at ease at the thought of B.C. leaving again.

"Do you have to do this?" she asked tentatively.

Bitter Creek turned to her in surprise. "No, guess we don't," he answered simply.

"Sure," Rose spoke up with a bite. "We can all sit here in the cave for the rest of our lives. We can do all sorts of things. I was just thinking of helping Bill out of his miseries, that's all."

"Aw Rose—" B.C. started but she raised a hand and shook him off.

"No, that's all right. I mean, if you all want to stay that's your right. I can understand once you get a wife and a baby you want to stay close." She hesitated. "I just hate seeing the Doolin gang lie down and call it quits. I take pride I'm a member—we really set them people on their butts. But time's flashing by us and I want us to set a mark no one will ever forget. I want us to be in the history books. I know Bill gets discouraged and down and

I can't stand seeing him that way. What he needs is some confidence, that's all, and I just thought we could help him."

Tandy could hardly believe her ears. She knew it was all over for her. She could tell by the quick exchange of glances between the men that Rose had hit their egos dead center. Her butting in at this juncture would fall on deaf ears. Furiously, she turned and stalked to the curtained crib.

She was still sulking the next morning as she cleaned up the cave. Little William was asleep after his feeding. The others had left before daybreak. She had refused to come out to say goodbye.

Only when she was sure they were long gone—would not change their minds and come back—did she go out and sit in the sun.

Whether Bitter Creek had known how great her anger was or had chosen to ignore it she was unable to tell. She was furious that he hadn't at least inquired about how she felt. It only led her to believe that he did know and had decided not to participate in a further discussion. This only infuriated her the more.

Oh Damn! she thought. Things had changed. The excitement was gone; gone also were their ideals and style of life they'd chosen. Or had they ever chosen it? It was even difficult to think back to why they had started living this way in the first place. There was no longer a satisfying answer.

She told herself that she was happy, that, after all, it had been a good life, even with the aches and pains of growing up. She had a good man she was deeply in love with. And they had a baby—a beautiful baby! So then, what was wrong? Why was it so important to her now to get away?

She was still day-dreaming on the bench, soaking up the warm morning air, when she became aware of a rider approaching the glen. Her heart skipped a beat. She got up, ran to the carbine she'd left leaning on the cave and held it waist high, waiting.

Bill Doolin, head bent down to miss the branches, rode into the clearing. He took one look around, spotted Tandy and rode up to her, his face serious.

"Where's the others?" he asked anxiously.

"They all went to Woodard. Why? What's wrong?"

Doolin cursed and looked around helplessly. "What the hell they go there for?"

Tandy started to open her mouth to answer but he held up his hand. "Never mind, can't wait." He looked down at her with such intensity that Tandy was frightened. "When do you expect them back?"

Tandy shrugged. "Late—tonight."

Doolin did some mental calculating, then nodded. "Okay. I think it'll be okay." He turned intently to her again. "Now listen carefully. I just found out that Mary Pierce has told Tilghman where this cave is." As Tandy glanced nervously about, he reached out and shook her shoulder. "It's all right. It's going to take Tilghman time to get up a posse, and he's not going to find this place at night. So I figure you have until daylight tomorrow."

He licked his lips nervously. "I'm going back and stay with Edith. As soon as B.C. gets back, you all get the hell out of here. We'll meet in Ingalls to-morrow." Without waiting for an answer, he turned his horse. Tandy followed him a few steps, unable to think clearly in the sudden turn of events.

Doolin, as his horse reared looked down at her, concerned. "If they aren't back before daybreak, you get out by yourself, y'hear?" He was gone.

Alone in the cave, with much work to do before nightfall, Tandy clasped herself and took a moment to look about. She was chilled with fear, and yet sad too. It sounded wrong to her that strangers would be trespassing on a place she'd known as home for so long a time. She did not worry about Bitter Creek coming back. She knew he would. She worried about having things packed and ready for him.

She took mental note of what the gang might have to leave behind. There were four horses in the corral; three would be able to carry packs. Methodically, she tore down the sections of canvas that had been used as partitions and spread them on the cave floor to wrap things in. She started to lay in the extra rifles, guns and ammunition, then realized the men would surely want to carry their weapons in the event of pursuit. As confused as her feelings were, it was hard for her to plan properly. She took her time collecting Rose's dresses, then decided to pack them in the large straw valise she found in her cubicle rather than crush them in with pots and pans and the like. She folded Doolin's extra suit and shirts neatly. The gear in the other men's cubicles she was less careful with. Thank goodness they always took their bedrolls!

Late in the afternoon, she had all the packing done, including hers and Bitter Creek's. She surveyed her work. Cupboards stood bare. There were no curtains up. The place looked desolate and she found herself hating it. Canvas bundles, smaller sacks and valises were lined up in the middle of the cave. She would try to drag the things outside but loading the horses would have to wait until Bitter Creek and the others came back.

They *would* come back! She had taken time out to make bisquits for them. The coffee pot was warm. She had used the stove for the last time; it would have to be left behind.

Evening came slowly. Tandy bridled all four horses, saddling her own. She eyed the animals as they lazily stared ahead, waiting just as she was waiting. She had dragged the sacks down close to them. Now, all that remained in the cave was the warm stove, near which William lay bundled. After a while, she became aware of the cold damp night air. She went inside and gathered her baby in her arms. There was nothing to do but wait.

She greeted them with rifle at the ready, not sure who was stomping into the gloomily empty cavern.

"What's going on?" Bitter Creek asked, quickly coming towards her.

Tandy held him quietly, absorbing his nearness. She was shaking inside. When he gently pushed her away, she took a deep breath and looked up into his face. "Bill came and said we had to get out."

"Get out?" Rose had come up. "Get out of here?"

Tandy nodded and explained. "I've packed everything. We have to leave by dawn."

"I don't believe this," Rose said angrily.

Bitter Creek pulled Tandy around by her shoulders and frowned into her face. "You sure Bill said we was to get out? I mean, we didn't see no one when we come in."

"There was no one out there," Rose confirmed.

"Tilghman may have wanted you to come in first," Tandy answered. "Most likely, he's not out there yet."

"Is this your way of getting B.C. to leave?" Rose asked sharply.

"No," Tandy answered, her anger rising at the question. "Bill's the one who gave the warning."

Rose attempted a laugh. "Where is Bill? Why didn't he stay to help if that's true?"

"He said he had to get back to Ingalls. That's where he's supposed to meet us."

"Bill wouldn't have left you like this," Rose said disbelievingly.

Tandy glanced at her, then turned to B.C. "It's true. Why should I lie to you?"

" 'Cause you want to break us up, that's why," Rose said. "I been telling them just how much you want to."

Tandy looked at Bitter Creek, bewildered. "Has she been talking to you about me?"

Bitter Creek shifted uncomfortably. "C'mon honey," he said. "I wasn't paying her no heed. I believe you."

Tandy studied him suspiciously for a moment. Finally, realizing that time was running short, she nodded. "I've got everything ready except for loading the horses."

Bitter Creek drew in a breath, then turned to Little Bill and Pierce. "Better load 'em."

Rose placed her hands on her hips and stepped back. "Don't tell me you're going to do what she says?"

Bitter Creek turned to the woman calmly. "And why not? Tandy's never lied to me."

"But she's trying to break us up," Rose insisted. "You don't believe her story about Bill coming here, do you? If we leave this place, we'll never get back together again. She knows that and I know it!"

Bitter Creek said quietly, "Rose, it's better to be safe. We'll load up and leave. If nothing happens, if Tilghman doesn't come, we'll come back."

"We won't, we won't!" Rose stormed.

Raidler finally spoke up. "Rose, take a look at all the packing Tandy's done. That's hard work. She's not crazy—and she'd have to be to do it without an urgent need for it. I believe her too."

"God damn it," Rose shouted vehemently. "You're all siding with her now. Well, I won't stand for it. We're staying here until Bill gets back!"

"Bill won't be back," Tandy answered.

"He wouldn't desert us."

"He's not deserting us," Bitter Creek argued. "No

reason for him to stay here tonight, and I can see him wanting to get back to Ingalls."

"To be with his darling little wife, I suppose?" Rose said savagely.

"And what's wrong with that?" B.C.'s voice was getting tight.

"What's wrong with that?" Rose snorted. "Ever since Bill got married, he's been more concerned about that broad than about any of us!"

"Rose, you got things all twisted and you know it!"

Rose swore. She drew the carbine from her boot and swung it up at them. "We're all going to stay here," she snarled. "Raidler. Pierce—move!" She motioned with the barrel for the two to get closer to B.C. and Tandy.

"What the hell you trying to do, Rose?" Bitter Creek asked tightly.

"I'm trying to hold us together," she answered. "And I'll do it anyway I can."

"We can't stay here, Rose," Tandy spoke up, frightened. "Let us go. Tilghman's coming in at the first light."

"Sure," Rose laughed. "So is Custer and President Cleveland!"

"And if I'm right?"

Rose answered, "Then we fight it out. We can hold off anyone."

"Don't go loco, Rose." Bitter Creek eyed the rifle warily. "If the law comes, they can starve us out."

"Then let 'em," Rose answered dangerously.

Raidler took a half-step forward, a lazy, reassuring smile on his lips. "If one of us went out and scouted the area—what would you say to that?"

"We all wait here 'til Bill comes for us," Rose said evenly. "That means *all* of us."

Tandy stepped in front of B.C. and put her arms around his waist, she was trembling as she said over her shoulder, "You're not going to stop us, Rose. I'm taking William and B.C. and we're leaving whether you like it or not." She backed off from B.C. and headed defiantly towards the rear of the cave.

"No!"

Tandy halted at Rose's sharp command. She hesitated, then slowly turned. In her hand was the pistol she had taken from B.C.'s holster. She lifted it and pointed it at Rose.

"I mean it, Rose," she said, her voice shaking. She held the gun with both hands. "If I have to, I'll shoot!"

"You wouldn't dare!" Rose sneered. "You haven't got the guts to pull that trigger!"

"When it comes to those I care about, I'll do anything," Tandy answered. "B.C. and the rest wouldn't stop you, Rose, but I will!"

Rose measured the girl in the gloom. She spoke harshly, "It's a standoff then."

"No, it isn't," Tandy said. "We are leaving." Eyes fixed on Rose, she called out to Bitter Creek, "Go get the baby."

As Bitter Creek started to move, Rose quickly pointed the rifle at him. "You stay right there!"

Tandy said, "I'm warning you, Rose. Don't try to stop us!" Then to B.C., "Go ahead."

"Bitter Creek—I'm warning *you!*" Rose's voice almost was a screech.

Bitter Creek hesitated, took a sorrowful look at Rose, then turned and walked towards the baby.

Rose aimed the rifle at his back.

Tandy shot by reflex. The gun exploded and kicked high in her hand. She blinked, her head swimming from the echoing noise and her bewilderment over what she had done. Slowly, she lowered the gun and stared at Rose.

The older woman was swaying, her mouth open in astonishment. The rifle was low at her side, as if it had fallen from its own weight, and a red blotch had appeared in the middle of her chest. She looked down at it, fascinated. The rifle dropped from her hand and her fingers absently went up to touch the red circle. She weaved, then sank to her knees.

"Oh my God, Rose!" Tandy shouted and ran to her. She fell onto her knees and cradled the woman. "Rose! I'm sorry, Rose, I'm sorry!"

The men, moving swiftly, gently eased Rose onto her back, her head on Tandy's lap. The woman gasped, a trickle of blood running down from the corner of her lips. Slowly, the men stood up. They had seen gun wounds. They knew there was little they could do.

"Rose," Tandy murmured and hugged the woman, swaying back and forth. "Oh, Rose, I'm sorry, so sorry." She looked around at the three men and saw mirrored in their faces her own truth. She hugged Rose to her.

"That shot will be heard for miles," Raidler said grimly.

Bitter Creek nodded. "We better get packing. Go ahead." Raidler and Pierce nodded and ran out of the cave to the horses.

"We'll try to take her to a doctor," Bitter Creek told Tandy to comfort her.

Rose reached up and grabbed Tandy's sleeve, her eyes wide. "Don't break up the Doolin gang," she whispered in gasps. "Please, for me, don't do it."

Sobbing, Tandy said, "I wasn't trying to, Rose. Honestly, I wasn't!"

Rose nodded. "You gotta promise me," she said faintly, "you gotta promise me you'll keep 'em together—for me!" Her glazing eyes searched Tandy's face.

Tandy wiped at the tears rolling down her cheeks. "I promise Rose, I promise!"

"I had a good plan," Rose went on, seemingly not hearing her. "I tol' B.C. and the others." She coughed and was quiet for a moment, her hand still twisting Tandy's sleeve. "Bitter Creek?" she groped towards him. "It was a good plan, wasn't it? It would've worked, wouldn't it?"

"It was a good plan," Bitter Creek answered softly, taking her hand in his. "Better'n any we ever had." He looked at Tandy and slowly shook his head.

It pleased Rose for she smiled. "Do it—for me? Will you? Will you do my plan—so I know I did something worthwhile?"

"Oh Rose," Tandy cried. "You're a good part of us. You *are* worthwhile."

"I just want to know I did something—something as good as Doolin," Rose murmured. "Promise me?" She was getting weaker but her fingers dug into both their hands.

"Sure Rose, we promise. We'll do it for you," Bitter Creek answered.

"Tandy?"

"We promise, Rose," Tandy assured her.

The woman smiled and her fingers released their hold. "Mnnn, good. I feel good 'bout that. I hope Bill—I hope Bill knows—"

They watched her, not knowing what to do. There was a slight spasm, and then she was dead. They both stared down at the body. Then the realization dawned.

"Ohh, B.C.," Tandy moaned. "What did I do?"

"Shh." He drew her face against his chest. "It wasn't your fault, hon," he muttered.

"Oh God," Tandy cried softly. "How am I going to handle this? What I did?"

"You did what you had to do," Bitter Creek reassured her. "It happens sometimes. We have to do awful things—or what seems awful at the moment. You both were trying to do what you thought best."

"Oh God," Tandy shook her head. "Is this what it's all about. Is this what it all comes down to?"

"Hush babe," he coaxed.

"But who is right?"

B.C. shrugged. "I dunno. I dunno if anyone is ever right—or wrong." He looked down at her. "But I know we gotta get outta here."

"What about her?"

They both stared at the body. "We'll bury her here, where she wanted to stay. No one will ever know."

"Does that mean I have to take her place?"

"In a way, yeah, I guess. No one takes the place of another. But we'll talk about this later. Right now, we gotta get out."

26

The train moved steadily westward, its wheels clicking on the rails with a lulling effect. Tandy rested her head on B.C.'s shoulder, clutching the sleeping baby to her breast, and stared out the window at the flat prairie of central Kansas.

It had been a spectacular two weeks, with one memorable event after another. They had met with Doolin in Ingalls, explained the death of Rose, then jumped into the details of the planned train robbery, more to forget the incident at the cave than anything else.

Afterwards, Bitter Creek and Tandy had traveled to Chicago. This was part of the plan, but they had managed to take a few days off and spent them at the World's Fair. Tandy thought of herself as an Oklahoma prairie girl and the magnificent buildings, displays and lights had been far beyond anything she had ever dreamed of seeing. Now, on their return, she was able to recall every glorious hour of it as she waited and watched.

"Are we on schedule?" Tandy asked, a question she had been repeating all morning.

Bitter Creek grinned patiently. "We're on the right train, right track, right place, right time." They had carefully gone over the train schedules and bills of lading they'd taken during the Woodard robbery, then picked the train from Chicago that would likely contain the most money. Tandy and Bitter Creek had been selected to ride the train. She knew Doolin had asked her to go partly to help her get over her feelings of guilt after the shooting of Rose.

"Have fun," he'd said. "Enjoy yourselves while you can. Just keep your eyes open coming home!"

Though as yet the return trip had been without incident, the train's end car was a source of concern to both of them. It was an ornately decorated private club car which no one was allowed to enter. Tandy, curious, had gotten some information about it from the conductor. An English lord owned it, he'd told her; he was on a hunting expedition with several companions and traveling throughout the west. No, the conductor didn't know how many were in the party; he knew only that a great quantity of food had been put aboard the car in Chicago.

"Do you think they might give us any trouble?" Tandy asked uncertainly.

"I doubt it," Bitter Creek replied. "They'll stay out of it. None of their business, after all."

The agreed rendezvous was the bridge crossing of the Cimarron River. Bitter Creek's job, once the river came in sight, was to climb the ladder to the train's roof, make his way to the engine and force the engineer to stop at the exact site picked.

Tandy clutched little William tightly to her. "You will be careful," she said, for the fifth time.

He grinned. "Aren't I always?"

"Well, I don't want you to go falling off."

"Train always slows down for the bridge. I'll be safe up there, don't you worry none." He recognized the countryside and began to fidget in his seat. "Won't be too long."

Tandy gripped his hand tightly as though never wanting to let go. "You be careful, y'hear?"

He nodded. "You too. Remember—if anything goes wrong, we'll all be meeting at the Dunn ranch."

Tandy nodded and kissed him. "I love you, B.C.," she said simply.

"And I love you—you're my own Rose of Cimarron." He cracked a smile. "See ya!"

The waiting was unbearable. Tandy pressed her face against the window, trying to look ahead for signs of the gang. But her mind went with Bitter Creek. She envisioned him crawling slowly over the tops of the cars, jumping to the tender, finally to the engine. She half expected to see his body tumbling down in front of her window. But nothing happened.

The distant line of low trees and bushes, she knew, marked the winding, shallow river's bank. She looked around to see if anyone in her car seemed suspicious of what was about to happen. Then, as the train began to slow, her heart beat more vigorously. She noticed a few passengers peering out their windows and had pangs of alarm until she realized they were merely curious about the approaching bridge. She looked out her side. She thought she had spotted a horseman in the distance, but wasn't quite sure.

The river suddenly appeared under them and the wheel sounds reverberated as the train slowly started across the low bridge. There was a kind of clapping, hollow echo coming up from the water just six feet below. Ahead, Tandy saw the shadows of the engine and express car spread out on the far bank. Then the train came to a crunching halt, leaving most of the cars still on the bridge, restricting passengers from stepping out.

Shouts and two shots rang out from the far bank. The people in Tandy's coach whispered and pressed excitedly to the windows. One woman uttered a small screech as she spotted the riders gathering at the head of the train.

"It's a robbery!"

There were loud murmurs. Tandy sank back in her seat, hugging William to her, staring at the passengers as they oohed and ahed. She took a quick, nervous look out the window. Horses were prancing near the express car; it was difficult to see the riders on them. Then she spotted Bitter Creek running down the embankment to mount his waiting horse and ride back up.

"Look, there's your daddy," Tandy said softly in William's ear. She pulled the baby up to the window and he looked out blankly. Tandy nervously looked around to make sure no one had heard her.

Suddenly, there were loud explosions to the rear of the train. Tandy twisted around and peered at the bridge. Men standing close to the railing were firing up at the riders with long-barrelled hunting rifles. There were about ten of them and three wore hunting caps. The sun glinted on their varnished gun stocks. Tandy knew instantly they were the men in the English party.

Damn! she thought and looked ahead. There were puffs of smoke as the gang fired back, distracted by this misadventure. The Englishmen, who fired steadily, seemed to be smiling and congratulating each other for their well-aimed shot; they appeared to be enjoying this new kind of sport.

Instinctively, Tandy rose, planning to rush ahead and join the gang, but a man in the seat just ahead tugged her back. "Better duck, lady," he said gallantly. "Ain't a healthy thing to show such a pretty head right now."

Tandy ducked low in the seat over William. The shooting kept up steadily over a span of about ten minutes, then a window shattered nearby and a woman cried out. Cautiously, Tandy rose to peek out the hole that had been left. The English hunters had done an amazing thing. Somehow, they had climbed down the bridge supports and were standing in the shallow river, positioned behind the pilings and firing from that excellent cover. A couple had whisky flasks, which they swigged during lulls.

Tandy got frantic. It was obvious that Doolin and the gang couldn't get to the express car and equally obvious that the Englishmen held them at bay. The outlaws were shooting back but only sporadically, for their targets were mostly unseen. Tandy rose and, hugging William close, started once again down the aisle.

"Hey, lady, get down," someone shouted. A hand reached out but she shook it free.

"I've got to get to the front," she cried obscurely.

Another hand reached out and dragged her down to the seat. "Lady," said a mustached rancher, "I don't know what you're trying to prove, but this ain't no time for heroics."

"But I've got to!" Tandy started struggling in his grasp.

"Crazy woman," someone else muttered. Tandy, held tight, quieted down. Damn, she thought.

Suddenly, the train lurched and the passengers were thrown back into their seats. Another lurch and the train surged forward.

Tandy tore herself from the rancher's loosened grasp and pressed against the window. The Englishmen had scrambled back to their coach. The engine began to gather speed. Ahead, at the end of the bridge, Doolin and the others were struggling to mount their frightened horses. More shots, from the Englishmen's coach now, added to their panic. She saw Dynamite Dan slip from his stirrups and saw Bitter Creek help him up to his saddle. Then the whole gang was galloping away. As they receded towards the horizon, there came a loud hurrah from the last coach—the hunters congratulating themselves on a fine bit of work.

Tandy watched emptily as the riders disappeared.

The train quickly gathered more speed and she slumped in her seat self-consciously. Around her, the passengers began to settle back, straightening their clothes even as they whispered of the excitement.

The rancher who had held Tandy back turned around and studied her forlorn expression. "You okay now?" he asked gently.

Tandy nodded.

"If your husband got trapped in the front coaches," the man continued, "he'll be right back, I'm sure."

Tandy gave him a weak smile and nodded again. She wondered how long it would be before everyone would realize her husband was not coming back. How long would it be before they would connect her with the robbery?

She would never know. Two hours later she was at a Guthrie livery stable, nervously renting a horse and wagon. She had left people at the Guthrie train station still talking of the attempted robbery and news of it was spreading through the town. She gave the stable man the Halsell ranch as her address. "I'll have the wagon sent back as soon as I can," she said, handing out the money. She knew the Halsell name carried weight in Guthrie and hoped that establishing herself as a guest there—as far as the stable man was concerned—would help keep her free from suspicion in the holdup.

It was well into the night when she arrived at Will Dunn's dugout with the baby. Hesitantly, she went to the door and knocked.

"Will, have you seen Bitter Creek?" she asked anxiously as soon as the man opened the door.

Will, enthused at seeing her, ushered her in before answering. He seemed to want to make her comfortable more than anything else. "No, m'girl," he finally said. "Hasn't been a soul hereabouts. They mighta gone up to Bee's place though."

"No, they said they'd come here," Tandy insisted. "Would you mind if I stayed?"

Will smiled sheepishly. "You know better than to ask. Of course you can stay. But wouldn't you feel better at Bee's place? It's lots nicer."

Tandy shook her head and settled the baby in one of the bunks. Then she brought Will up to date on their activities, including Rose's death and the attempted robbery.

"I heard about some lady getting killed. From the description I thought for sure it might be you. Hard telling the two of you apart most times." Will shook his head. "You should get outta that kind of business before it does turn out to be you. Things are getting tight, girl."

Tandy sighed. "You see, Will, we made a promise we'd try Rose's plan. We also promised we'd try to keep the gang together. But—" It was difficult for her to go on. "Well, Bitter Creek and I, we'd already decided we're going to Texas when winter comes. I don't think Rose would mind, do you, Will? I mean, we kept together this long. And if we stay until winter, won't that be long enough?"

Will looked at her, thinking it over. "Maybe you ought to get out sooner."

Tandy's curiosity was aroused. "What do you mean?"

Will shrugged and looked away. "Tilghman and the rest want to catch you all real bad. Them railroad people and politicians are putting the law in the hot seat. They want action."

Tandy watched him, knowing there was more to the story.

Will squirmed in his chair. He had a difficult time meeting her eyes. "They come about—begin to threaten us with all sorts of things. They want us to help 'em."

"What kinds of things they threatening you with?"

"Tilghman says he's got facts showing we got cattle ain't belonging to us. Says he'll slap a warrant on us if we don't cooperate."

Tandy said, "Why, that's awful—using our friends to get to us."

Will sighed. "Well, like I said, them federal people been pushing the law to put a stop to this robbing. I guess they'll do 'bout anything to get to Doolin."

Tandy studied the man, slowly beginning to realize just how uncomfortable he was. "Will?" she asked gently. "Has Tilghman been here recently? Like in the last couple of days or so? Has he been threatening you personally?"

He tried to shrug. "He's been here a couple of times."

"What did he want?"

Will shifted his gaze to his feet. "Wants me to tell 'em when you all will be around."

Tandy let out a sigh. "So that's why you told me I'd be better off at Bee's. You don't want me around. Oh, Will, I'm sorry we've done this to you."

The man shrugged. "I done it to myself, Tandy girl. T'ain't your fault. I got myself into this mess." He looked up at her. "But I wouldn't want nothing to hurt you, you gotta know that."

"I know," she smiled. "But I can't stay here. I don't want you to get into trouble either."

He tried to smile. "I can't go and tell Tilghman anything as long as you're here. You're welcome to stay."

"We'll stay until Bitter Creek comes. Then we'll take off, probably to—" She stopped as he held up a hand.

"Better not tell me."

That night, as she held William in her arms in the bunk bed, Tandy stared up into the ceiling, unable to sleep. She could not sort out the things that were going around and around in her head.

It was ending! She was positive of that. It was as if she were still walking a long passage and it was taking her forever, with curves and blind alleys, pitfalls and climbs. But for the first time, she saw far ahead a faint light, some prospect of escaping from this nightmare. But it was terrifying. She did not know what awaited her in that faint light, but she could discern no trace of Bitter Creek there—not his voice, not his form, nothing.

Tandy wept until sleep came.

27

They arrived an hour after sunrise, a much smaller group of cheerless riders who checked the sheds and bushes with furtive, suspicious glances.

Bitter Creek eased himself from the saddle, sore and weary, a full day's growth of beard darkening his handsome face. He had a difficult time breaking into a smile as Tandy opened the door and rushed out to him.

"Oh, B.C.," she murmured and pressed herself into him, once more feeling secure as his arms slowly encircled her.

"I kept telling myself that you'd be here," he said softly. "I just had to keep telling myself that."

She held him a moment longer, then backed away and studied him. "You look so tired," she commented sadly. Then she glanced at the others. "All of you do. Get down—I'll get some food ready."

They all ate ravenously. Between bites they told of their ride. "We never would've made it to the express car," Charlie Pierce stated. "Them dudes in back had twice more guns than us."

"Then that engineer started the train—no way in hell could we have done anything 'cept vamoose," Dick West added.

Bitter Creek shook his head. "Like I told Bill, I really had 'em pegged wrong. Didn't think they'd try anything against us."

Raidler stopped eating long enough to glance up and add his own thought on the matter. "They're hunters—you could see they had that in their blood. Only this time we were the game."

"It was still my fault," B.C. commented wearily.

Raidler shook his head. "No one's fault. The plan was a good one—Rose had a good idea. It was just one of those unexpected things that happens once in a while."

"Where is Bill?" Tandy finally had a chance to ask.

"He went over to Ingalls to see if Edith and baby are okay. Said he'd meet us back here."

Tandy cast Will Dunn a worried look. "I don't think that's a good idea. We should find some other place."

There was an exchange of curious glances among the men. "Why, hon?" B.C. asked.

Tandy shrugged and averted her eyes. "I dunno. Just a feeling I got."

Dick West cleared his throat. "We could ride over to the—"

Tandy leaned over the table and picked up a plate. "We'll find a place," she said sharply. She looked up at their startled glances. Slowly they looked at Will, then back at Tandy. She didn't waver and they got the message. Amost in unison, they shrugged and went back to eating.

It wasn't until they had ridden out of the ranch that Bitter Creek pulled over to her. "You got anything to say?"

Tandy shifted the baby to her other arm. "Tilghman's putting pressure on Will to inform on us," she answered. "Just like he tried it with us."

He took it in silence, digesting it as they headed for the riverbank and, hopefully, some type of a cave. Suddenly he reined in and called out to the others to stop. "You think Will's telling the truth?"

Tandy nodded. "He was scared. I mean, really scared. From what he said, Tilghman's got him over a barrel about his rustling. It's him or us."

Raidler had sidled up to them to listen. "Knowing Tilghman and the rest, they probably have enough evidence against a lot of people, enough to tie them up good."

"They can't go about threatening people," Bitter Creek answered.

"Think about it. How many people do you know who have helped us out? How many have sold us things or even spoken to us? To the law, that could be construed as abetting criminals. It's enough to frighten most people. Most people don't want to go to jail."

"Jesus Christ Raidler!" Dick West exclaimed. "You don't have to spell that out for us—we're not idjets!"

Raidler shrugged. "It's an effective plan Tilghman's got, all the same. The only reason we've been able to exist up to now is because we could rely on getting help from people around here. Now, especially now since they've chased us out of the cave, they know we got no place to go for that help." He nodded. "It's a good plan, you have to admit that."

Bitter Creek straightened. "Jeez! That means none of us are safe around here. It could mean Bill might be walking into a trap right now."

Raidler pursed his lips. "Maybe. But I think Bill's aware of what's happening. He knows Tilghman's got an eye on Edith, so he's not going to walk in on her in full daylight."

"But he might not know about the other people. He's got to find some place to hold up until nighttime."

"Maybe we better warn him," West suggested.

Bitter Creek nodded. "I think we should." He turned to Tandy. "You go over to Bee's ranch. It's right over that ridge. Stay there until we come to get you."

"But is Bee safe?"

"The Dunns like you so I doubt they'll give you away. But keep your eyes open. We'll come for you when it's dark." He leaned over to kiss her.

"B.C.," she cried out as they turned. "Be careful!" She watched them dip down into a ravine and up again, a much further distance away racing towards the horizon. "I love you," Tandy said weakly at the retreating figure.

* * *

"Of course you can stay here," Bee Dunn boomed happily. "You're always welcome, girl, you should know that."

"We didn't want to intrude," Tandy explained as they settled in the spacious living room. "We saw Will and he told us the law was putting pressure on all of you."

Bee smiled and raised a hand in protest. "They approached us but I told 'em to get the hell off the ranch. They can threaten me all they want but they ain't got the craw to do nothing. Don't you worry none 'bout them. You and the babe can stay in the back bedroom where no one can disturb you."

That night, as they sat in the living room chatting about the past, their conversation was interrupted by the arrival of horsemen at the front of the house.

"Maybe it's them," Tandy said happily, but Bee stopped her from going to the door.

"And maybe not," he warned her. "Let me find out. You come stand by the wall. If it's the law, you can go hide in the back." She went with him, backed against the wall, next to the door and watched as he hesitantly opened it. When he saw who was there, he slipped out onto the porch.

"Howdy Bee," she heard Will Dunn call out. "Y'know Marshal Tilghman and Marshal Heck Thomas."

Tandy froze against the wall. She was afraid her own loud heartbeats would give her away.

"I know 'em," Bee answered sourly. "What's going on?"

Tandy began her retreat to the rear of the house but stopped when she realized the men were not going to enter. Slowly, she edged to the door to listen.

"Sure," Bee was saying. "They come around here once in a while. They come around to most everyone in the area."

"Will here says they might have cause to visit with you," the deep voice of Tilghman stated. "You mind if we come in?"

"You're not welcome here," Bee said flatly.

There was a moment of silence, then Tilghman's voice again. "What's the matter, Bee? You got someone in there?"

"Just my daughter," Bee replied calmly.

There was another pause. "Didn't know you had a daughter, Bee." That voice, Tandy guessed, was lawman Thomas's.

"She's sort of an adopted daughter. Got her baby with her," Bee answered. "They're here on a short visit."

"Then you won't mind introducing us to her," Tilghman said.

Tandy started to retreat again, but there was no movement on the porch. She relaxed.

"I don't want her meeting the likes of you," Bee answered belligerently. "This is my home and I decide who comes in and who don't."

"You're not giving us much choice," the lawman stated. "The time's come when we can't pussyfoot around any more.'

Bee answered tightly. "You go do your dirty work somewhere else, not here."

"You leave us no choice at all," Tilghman said softly. His voice became lower and hard. "We come here to arrest you and your brother Will here."

"What the hell for?" Bee demanded hotly.

"Rustling and harboring known criminals. I got here a warrant to take the two of you in."

There was silence and a rustling of papers as apparently Bee studied the documents. "God damn you!" Bee exclaimed. "We can't leave this here ranch alone."

"That was up to you, Bee."

"God damn your soul," Bee snarled. There was a slight scuffling on the porch.

"Take it easy, Bee," Will yelled out. "No use making it any worse than it is." Again, there was silence.

"Course," Tilghman went on, his voice hardly changing its tone, "we could drop these charges."

"How?"

"By making you two deputies," came the answer. "Can't likely send a deputy to jail now, can we?"

"That's all there is to it?"

"Well, as deputies, we'll expect your cooperation."

"What kind of cooperation?"

"We know from Will here that it's likely the

Doolin gang might be stopping by. We just want to be here when they come."

Silence. A shuffling of footsteps. Suddenly, the voices were dim and far away. Frantically, Tandy groped closer but Bee had taken the group down the steps out into the yard, away from the house.

She leaned against the wall, tears streaming down her face. "Oh no," she moaned, her world collapsing. "Oh no!"

She wanted to go outside and scream at them—at all of them—to get away and leave her and Bitter Creek alone. Get away and leave them all alone! They were going to Texas!

She wanted to scream at them to leave the Dunns alone. Let them do what they wanted. Stop threatening them. Let them be their friends!

She had to get away. She had to leave and warn Bitter Creek and the others not to come here. Tandy grabbed her coat from the wall peg and slipped it on, whimpering and choking deep inside. Silently, she went to the back room where William lay sleeping. She laid out a heavy blanket on her bed, then tenderly gathered the infant up in her hands and wrapped him tightly in its warmth. "Sleep little baby," she crooned. "We're going to get your daddy—and we're going to leave this horrible place forever!"

She slid the window open, then, picking up the baby, crawled over the sill and onto the ground, just as the front door opened and footsteps echoed in the house. Quietly, Tandy slipped back into the shadows near the sheds, where she crouched and looked back.

A dim light went on upstairs. She saw shadows against the windows, then darkness again. Across from her on the ground, three men, one of whom she thought was Bee Dunn, carried rifles and shotguns off to a side yard, where they slid behind a stack of wood piled for the winter. Oh my God! They were waiting! An ambush!!

Quickly, she turned and made her way around the outbuildings, then through a few scattering of trees, until she came out on the road that led to Ingalls. She ran when she could, walked swiftly when the baby's movements hampered her from running. She had gone several hundred yards and was coming around a small bend when she spotted a small cluster of riders just ahead and off to the side of the road. She saw the faint glow of a cigarette. At first, she was fearful they might be a posse but as she peered through the blackness, she was sure she recognized the large white stetson that Doolin wore.

She approached cautiously, hugging William to her. "Bill?" she called hesitantly.

The riders, startled, pulled around, guns drawn. Quickly, they dismounted and walked towards her.

"Tandy?" Doolin said. "That you? What in hell you doing out here?"

"I came to warn you!" She glanced at the band with Doolin. "Where's B.C.?"

Doolin took her arm and stared through the blackness at her. "He and Charlie went in to get you. Didn't you see 'em?"

Tandy started to wail. She clutched at Doolin, then wrenched herself free and started to run back down the road. "I've got to stop him!"

Doolin caught up with her and grabbed hold of her. "What's going on?" he asked firmly.

She fought him, not thinking to answer. All she wanted was to free herself and run to Bitter Creek. "Let me go! Let me go!" Her scream was so loud that Doolin clamped his hand over her mouth. She struggled with him, but he held her close to him. Gradually, she weakened, conscious that the baby was struggling for air between them. Slowly, she sank to her knees and Doolin eased her the rest of the way to the ground.

"Now, what's going on?" he asked earnestly.

"They're there," she moaned. "They're waiting for you.'

"Tilghman?"

She nodded and groped for his arm. "Stop him, Bill—oh please, stop him before it's too late!"

Doolin had only to nod his head to the others who had gathered around. Raidler, West and Clifton ran to their horses and galloped off down the road. They had just slipped around the bend when the gunshots echoed sharply in the night.

Tandy cried out. There was the unmistakeable bang of a shotgun, followed by small pops of handguns. With each shot, Tandy's body jerked as if the bullets had entered her body. With each shot she screamed out her agony and clutched at Doolin.

Then there was silence.

Tandy tightened, waiting for more shots or for some other noise. It was dreadfully silent. She hardly dared to breathe. Her mind, still vibrating from the gunfire, went blank.

"I've got to go!" She started to rise but Doolin pulled her down. "I've got to go, Bill!"

"No," he said firmly. He squatted on his heels beside her, holding her tightly, watching the road for some sign. "Aw, geez!" he moaned. "C'mon, B.C.! C'mon!"

Tandy felt herself melting. Her eyes itched with the tears that were welling inside her. Her breaths were short and it was difficult for her to swallow. They clutched at each other, listening, waiting.

"C'mon, B.C.!" Doolin coaxed between clenched teeth.

Slowly Tandy realized her head was shaking from side to side. "He's not coming back," she heard herself saying in a voice that sounded far away. "He's not coming!"

Doolin hugged her. "Shhhh—he'll come—he'll come, you wait and see."

She shook her head and he reached out with his hands to stop its movement. "No," she said faintly, holding onto the outlaw tightly. "It's over, Bill!"

"No—no—NO! He'll come. He's got to come!" Doolin choked the words out as he stared down the road, waiting.

The horses rounded the curve slowly, almost as

if they didn't want to come back. Doolin counted. There were only three. As the riders approached he tried to distinguish them in the bad light. Little Bill Raidler, Dick West—and Dynamite Dan. The same three he'd sent in.

They came up to Tandy and stopped, looking down at her with tired expressions. Then Raidler cleared his throat. His voice shook. "I'm sorry, Tandy. I'm goddamn truly sorry." He fought for control of his voice. "B.C. and Pierce—they got caught in a crossfire. No way for them to get out. They didn't have a chance!"

"You sure?" Doolin asked huskily.

Raidler nodded, tried to go on, but then backed his horse away from them and went off the side of the road to be by himself.

Little Dick told the rest. "We snuck up as close as we could. Tilghman and Heck Thomas were there. So were both the Dunns and some others."

"Who got B.C.?" Doolin asked. It seemed like a futile question at the moment, but it was important to him.

"Couldn't rightly tell. It must have been the group from the rear. My guess it was either Thomas or maybe even Bee Dunn. B.C. got it first, then Pierce."

Doolin stared up at the two riders, then down at the top of Tandy's head. He reached out and smoothed the dark hair, then reluctantly disengaged himself and rose to his feet. He shook his head, staring down the road, then walked off away from them.

Tandy clutched at her baby, swaying over its small form. She hurt. There were no tears although she knew she would burst fairly soon. She was in no hurry. She knew it was true, that B.C. was dead. Yet she had another feeling—that he wasn't dead. She could feel his arms around her. Or maybe they were Doolin's, she didn't know. The shock of it was over, at least for now. She was numb.

"Is there anything we can do?" Dick West's voice was soft and gentle and concerned.

She heard the words but had to struggle to understand them. Slowly, she shook her head. "You better go—" she heard herself saying and thought how strange it was that she was able to think at all clearly. "Tilghman will be coming down here to look for you all."

There was silence as the two cowboys exchanged glances. "I guess you're right. Maybe we'll meet up again." West and Clifton waited for some kind of an answer but when Tandy didn't respond, they backed away and rode over to Doolin. Their muffled voices drifted back to her. Then the two departed into the blackness.

In a while, she heard someone approaching and Bill Raidler's hand rested on her shoulder. "You all right, Tandy?" he asked.

She nodded and pressed her cheek onto his hand. "Thank you, Bill," she said in a small, calm voice. "I'll be okay. You've been kind to us."

There was a pause and Raidler's voice wavered. "I never spoke much about it, but he was my best friend. I'll never forget him."

Tandy nodded and the tears welled up in her eyes. Oh no, not now, she prayed. Not now, not just yet. She swallowed and nodded again. "Me neither, Bill—me neither."

There was a pause. "Doolin's taking it bad too," Raidler commented, staring at the distant shape.

Tandy nodded and quickly glanced at the outlaw leader, studying the slender silhouette, the night-darkened figure, the white hat.

"What are you going to do, Tandy? You know?"

She shook her head. "I dunno. Maybe go to Texas to my brother's." She sniffled and tried to laugh. "Maybe I'll try and take Rose's place and take care of Doolin. He'll need someone to help him along."

"Yeah," Raidler said gruffly. "He's always needed someone to keep him mellow." He grew restless. "We better get outta here, y'know."

Tandy nodded. "I know. You better get." She looked up at him. "I thank you, Bill, for everything, 'specially your friendship. I—we—appreciated that."

He grinned, bent forward a bit as though to kiss her, then decided against it. Awkwardly, he turned and mounted. He stared down at her with his private thoughts, touched the brim of his hat and pulled away with a savage jerk. He rode over to Doolin and they murmured a short while. Then Raidler was gone.

It was quiet. Now she was beginning to feel the loneliness and it was cold and scary. She looked around in the blackness, her eyes finally settling on the distant Doolin. She gazed at Bill with little thought, giving herself a chance to regain some kind of composure and strength. The baby wiggled and she looked down at it.

"Well, little William," she murmured. "We tried, didn't we? But we're not beaten, not yet. We'll survive—somehow."

Doolin hadn't moved. Slowly Tandy got up, swiped at her dress with her free hand, then looked down the road towards the Dunn ranch. She wondered whether she should go and see B.C. What was there to see? A body? No, she didn't want to see a body. Her memory of Bitter Creek was of him alive, vibrant, loving. She shut her eyes to hold back the tears. No, he wasn't out there lying on the ground. He was here, in her heart, in her soul. That's where she would keep him!

Hesitantly, she turned and carried the baby over to Doolin. "We've got to get outta here, Bill," she said to his back.

He turned, his face drawn out and haggard. He looked at her, then slowly nodded.

"Poor Bill," she said gently.

She had, in two words, said more than Doolin felt he could bear. His face suddenly screwed up. He started to shake his head. Then he reached for Tandy and hugged her close to him, his body wracked with silent sobs.

"I know," she murmured quietly, patting his back. "I know." It was good that someone cried now, she thought. It was good that Doolin released this flood of grief. Her time would come and she would then need his strength. Until then, she would be his strength. It was good that way.

"C'mon, Bill," she said gently and disengaged his arms. "We've got to get out of here."

He nodded, tried to straighten but wobbled. She bent under his arm, placing it over her shoulder. "C'mon, I'll help you."

They got to Doolin's horse. He took the reins and together they walked it out onto the dark prairie.

Life would be different now, Tandy thought. It was bound to be different without Bitter Creek. He was with her, yet he wasn't. And that's the way it was going to be, maybe, from now on. But she was a survivor!

She squeezed the arm of the man stumbling next to her and looked up at him, braving a timid smile. "We might not be large in numbers, Bill Doolin, but we're the best there ever was!"

A two-part television special from Metromedia Productions.

The American west lives again in all its glory as Hugh Cardiff tells his tale—the story of an exuberant young nation and a hero larger than life.

"American history in full color. Garfield sees with near-perfect clarity. His episodes flash vividly."—*New York Times Book Review.*

"A passion that is contagious. Terrific entertainment."—*Los Angeles Herald-Examiner.*

"Vivid. Entertaining and fast-moving."
—*Chicago Tribune.*

A Dell Book $2.50 (19457-1)

At your local bookstore or use this handy coupon for ordering:

Dell

DELL BOOKS Wild Times $2.50 (19457-1)
P.O. BOX 1000, PINEBROOK, N.J. 07058

Please send me the above title. I am enclosing $__________ (please add 75¢ per copy to cover postage and handling). Send check or money order—no cash or C.O.D.'s. Please allow up to 8 weeks for shipment.

Mr/Mrs/Miss ____________________

Address ____________________

City ________________ **State/Zip** __________